THE EMMANUELS

A Story about Faith, Hope and Love

By: Nicole Elise

Averyanya Publishing, LLC

Copyright © 2009

ACKNOWLEDGEMENT

There are so many people who I want to thank. Thank you God for inspiring me to want to write this book and for giving me my life.

Thank you to my husband, Darryl, for his love, support and encouragement; thank you for encouraging me to "just keep at it", thank you to my children, Avery and Anya, they have given me a better understanding of how God must love us humans. Thank you Mommy, for your love and for giving me the love of writing, and thank you for giving me the best example any girl could need to be a "strong woman, and a survivor in this tough world." Thank you Mom Jean – for loving me as if I was your own flesh and blood daughter, you are the inspiration for Jennie/Nana. Thank you to my Aunt Desi for being more like my big sister, my best friend, my therapist, you never laugh at all my crazy ideas or my crazy problems, thank you. A thank you to my two sisters, Candace and Carinne for giving me the idea of the story plot, of the three very different sisters, thank you for your friendship and your love. Thank you Daddy, for choosing to make me your daughter, and for acknowledging the mistakes you made and for the E necklace you gave me. Thank you to my brother Cameron and sister Dawne in California, I'm so happy your'll found me and I love you both.

And a thank you to the rest of my family, those that are here and those that are gone for just being in my life. Thank you Grandma and Grandpa, thank you to my Uncle Bruce and Uncle Howard, my cousins Lonny, Brooke and Sheldon, my sister in law Trina, and my brother in law Tyrone and all of your children and grandchildren.

A thank you to all my girlfriends, who friendships give me inspiration every day. Thank you to my friend and legal mentor Carla, for "ordering" me to finish my book and follow my dreams. Thank you Deidre, Viviene, Crystal, Angela and Michelle and of course my crazy brother Alberto. Also thank you to all the Marines I had the chance to serve with, who inspired me also when writing this book, wherever you all are, may God be with you.

And last but definitely, not least thank you to my family at Face to Face Ministries. Thank you Pastor Melvin and Linda Epps for your patience, teaching and love. Most of all Thank you for teaching me about "God's Love" and His Word and thank you for baptizing me. May God Bless both of you, your family and your ministry.

Prelude
(What does one think of the moment before they die?)

Love, stood on the top of the marble stairs that led up to the entrance of the mansion that she had just spent the past few hours, sharing her body, and her soul with several beautiful strangers. She was so stoned, she felt numb. Her body didn't even feel cold, even though she stood on the top of the stairs half dressed, in the middle of a very chilly, windy night by Los Angelos standards. She had managed to get most of her clothes on except her shoes and her blouse that she was still trying to pull over her bra. She wondered, "how did the best day of my life, the greatest win of my career, end up with me standing out here half naked on some stranger's staircase, waiting outside, in the middle of the night, for either the police or an ambulance to show up and respond to my 911 call". Love was hoping the police didn't show up because there were enough drugs back in that mansion to get a small country high. Being that she was an attorney and considered an Officer of the Court she didn't need to be caught leaving a drug den, half dressed in the middle of the night. Still despite all the craziness of the night she still felt no real fear, except for the few moments that she thought the handsome stranger she had met that night was not going to let her leave. In fact, she thought, surprisingly she felt pretty good, considering everything she had done; she felt no pain, no sadness, not even disgust over what she had just done. She just felt sort of numb emotionally and physically. If it wasn't for that phone call she had just received she would probably still be back in that room upstairs with those beautiful, but sort of sad, extremely sexy strangers. But the call she received a few minutes ago had changed everything. Now the only thing she could think of was fulfilling a fruitless promise she made to the mother of a girl she barely knew, and a girl that she suspected was probably already dead. This she was accustomed to, doing her duty, while feeling nothing inside, and remaining emotionally detached. That was what had always made her so good at what she did. Most times she felt nothing. She felt nothing intentionally. Numbness is what she had strived to feel emotionally most of her life. The only difference was that tonight, after all the drugs, alcohol and sex, she was also feeling physically numb. But some part of her deep down knew something must really be wrong with her to not feel something emotional inside after all that she had been through that day. Now that she thought about it, she had been feeling numb on the inside, and detached from the world around her, ever since, ever since, well ever since…. Nana died, almost twenty years ago. Love's mind was racing with one thought after another, non-stop, while she waited outside on the stairs leading to the mansion behind her, but her very last thought before she died was, "what was the name of the strange man I just spent the last five hours making love to? I didn't even get his name."

Then suddenly she "felt" something pierce through the numbness. She felt a sharp pain run through her entire body. In that moment her whole body felt incredibly alive again. She felt sort of like she had just been electrocuted. The pain she felt intensified, and then it just wouldn't stop. It was then that Love knew, she knew she was going to die. At that moment she also knew it was too late to change all that she had done, too late to finish everything she had left undone, and it was too late to keep the promise she made to the mother of the young lady who was her client. The strangest thing was at that moment she felt as if not being able to keep that one promise was what she was regretting the most. Then the pain that pierced through the numbness continued, and Love felt like her heart couldn't take it anymore, she couldn't think anymore, and finally she felt like she couldn't breathe anymore. Love felt her frantically beating heart that she thought was going to burst out of her chest, suddenly start to slow down. Time was up with no time left for regrets, apologies, or goodbyes, she grabbed her chest as she felt her last heart beat, and she thought to herself, "so that's the kind of stuff one thinks about the moment before they die." Then Love felt herself falling into darkness. Her body hit the ground, but by then she didn't feel the impact, she didn't even feel her body anymore.

The paramedics found Love sprawled out on the ground of the front steps of the mansion, with no blouse and no shoes on. They realized she wasn't breathing and her heart wasn't beating. So they responded immediately with CPR, on the stairs, and then again in the ambulance while they rushed her to the hospital. They were giving her emergency treatment in the ambulance and it appeared that her heart had stopped from a possible drug overdose and excessive alcohol consumption. She had a needle mark in her thigh that was still very fresh and cocaine residue under her fingernails. The paramedics had no idea how long her heart had been stopped before they had arrived and they were working hard to get it beating again.

When Love opened her eyes she realized she was someplace else, she wasn't on the front steps of the mansion anymore, she was in the hospital. She thought she saw someone familiar inside the corner room at the end of the hallway. Then she realized it was Mary Sue, her client. She walked towards Mary Sue's room and stood by her bedside. She wondered when and how did she get there? The last thing she remembered was waiting on the stairs outside for a 911 response to come pick her up. Love began to talk to her client and fulfill the promise she had made to her client's mother. Then Love swore she also heard something else in the room; something even stranger than seeing Mary Sue; yet the sound was so familiar. It was Nana's voice. Now Love was sure. She was positive that she wasn't in a hospital, but that she must be dead, because she heard Nana's voice as clear as a bell. And as real as this scene seemed to her, Love "knew" her Nana was dead. After all, Love was right there standing by Nana's bedside on the day Nana died.....

Chapter 1
Introduction
(Introducing The Emmanuel Women)

Little Faith, Hope and Love Emmanuel[1] stood at their Nana's bed side. In their hearts they knew today would be the last day that they would see their Nana, but what they didn't know was that the three of them were about to embark on three very different and incredible individual journeys that would began, tomorrow.

A year ago, Nana had been diagnosed with breast cancer. The cancer had spread throughout Nana's body. Nana was the type of woman who never liked to go to the doctor. If Nana was sick, she would always say, "God will heal me". Since Nana didn't have any medical insurance, she relied heavily on God's healing. Up until now God always came through for her. When Nana tried to get more life insurance, the insurance company required a complete physical on Nana, because of her age. That is when Nana found out she had breast cancer. Nana couldn't risk leaving her grandbabies behind with no one to take care of them. So she took a mortgage out on the house that she had long ago paid off. The mortgage covered Nana's first surgery that removed both of her cancerous breasts, and paid for the following chemotherapy treatments. She had made it through the chemotherapy treatments, and she thought she had beaten the cancer. But then during a routine follow up appointment the doctor discovered the cancer had spread. It had spread to Nana's liver, lymph nodes, and stomach. The doctors told Nana, the chance of her beating it this time around, was slim. So Nana fought as long as she could, for her grandbabies' sake. Eventually, Nana's organs started failing her, and her body just began to shut down. But Nana's heart, mind and soul, stayed intact; nothing could destroy that. Nana was known as the woman who always cared for everyone else. But, for the first time in Nana's life she needed someone to take care of her. Nana was the neighborhood midwife, counselor, money lender,

---

[1] God is with us

shelter and center of unity. Not being able to care for others was going to be the most difficult thing for Nana to accept.

After six months of practically living in a hospital, Nana made the decision to leave the hospital and live out the remaining days of her life in her home. Nana's best friend, Mary, came to the hospital, to give Nana an update on how her grandbabies were getting along without her. Mary had moved into Nana's home with her and her grandchildren ever since Nana found out she was sick. Nana felt comforted knowing her best friend was taking care of her grandchildren while she was in the hospital. Before Mary walked into Nana's hospital room, she put on her best smile and opened the door. Nana was sitting up in her bed with a suitcase packed, and she was ready and waiting for Mary to take her home.

"Okay Mary I'm ready for my vacation to end." Nana wasn't in the mood for small talk, so she got right to the point of things, and gave Mary the news that she wasn't going to get any better this time, and that she was coming home for good. Nana explained to Mary that she wanted to spend the rest of her days at home; surrounded by the people who love her. The doctors gave Mary instructions for caring for Nana. That same day, Mary brought her long time friend "Jennie Emmanuel", who everyone knew as Nana, back home to her little house on Mathias Ave., in Queens, New York. Nana had so many good memories and a few bad ones in that little house on Mathias. But Nana was the type of person who chose to cherish the good and forget the bad. When Mary helped Nana into her house Nana looked around and immediately felt a sense of peace and joy fill her. All the memories of the life she lived in that little house came rushing back to her. Memories of her happy life with her one true love Lester; memories of raising her baby girl; and memories of being the person to deliver all three of her grandbabies and many, many other children in the neighborhood, right there in that little house. All these memories flooded Nana's mind. All of those wonderful memories happened right there. Nana knew it was in this house that she wanted to live out the rest of her days on this earth until the moment came, that Jesus would take her home.

Now, three months had passed by since Nana had been
home from the hospital. Her physical condition worsened as
each day passed by, but spiritually her faith grew stronger and
stronger. Every day the house was filled with different
neighbors, but instead of coming to Nana for help, they came to
give help to Nana in any way they could. Neighbors dropped off
food. They dropped off get well cards with money they owed
Nana inside of it. The children Nana had cared for over the
years who were not doing well in school would stop by just to
show Nana they got an "A" or a "B" on a test. The local winos
and slackers that Nana always gave a dollar to when she passed
by, stopped in to tell Nana they had finally got a job or decided
to attend AA meetings at the local church. The couples that
Nana had encouraged over the years stopped by to ensure Nana
they were working things out and staying together. Seemed like
everyone wanted to get themselves right, and make Nana proud
of them; before Nana left them for good.

But, Nana's sickness had the opposite effect on her best
friend Mary. Mary fell into a deep depression as each day
passed by, living with the knowledge that her best friend Jennie
would soon be gone. Mary had always felt this deep emptiness
in her that only seemed to subside when being around Jennie.
Mary had started using drugs again, in secret, as soon as she
realized Jennie was not going to get better, and she had been
hiding her drug use from Jennie. Mary was subconsciously
trying her best to self-destruct, before her friend died and she
was left totally alone. Jennie was the closest thing Mary had
ever had to family. Mary's mother gave her up when she was an
infant. Mary ended up spending her whole life in an orphanage,
and in foster homes. She was never adopted. She was born
addicted to heroin. As a baby, she cried constantly. Every
possible adoptive family that would take baby Mary home for a
trial period from the orphanage would inevitably bring her back
within a few days because no one could stand her constant
crying. From the very beginning, Mary was born into a hard life,
born with an addiction, and a childhood filled with nothing but
rejection. Then Mary met Jennie in grade school and they
became best friends, like sisters. Throughout the years Jennie
and Mary had remained friends. No matter how far apart their

two paths traveled the young ladies always found their way back to one another. Mary would disappear for months, sometimes years, once they became adults, but she always found her way back to her friend Jennie.

Now the thought of Jennie not being around anymore made Mary more and more depressed and the only way Mary ever knew how to cope with life was to ease her pain through drugs. Mary had been clean for almost a year since she had come to live with Jennie, but once she found out Jennie was definitely going to die she started using again. She rationalized falling off the wagon, by telling herself, "it's just a little bit, just a little to get me through this rough patch". So Mary continued hiding the fact that she was using again from Jennie and the girls, even though she knew her friend Jennie was relying on her to take over caring for her girls once she was gone. Mary wanted to be there for her friend, but her desire to use drugs grew stronger with each passing day. Lately all Mary could think about was that she would be totally alone in the world without her only friend, Jennie, and then she would feel the need to use drugs to help her cope with those thoughts.

A nurse came by every morning to check on Jennie's condition. When the nurse came this particular morning, Mary informed her that Jennie was having trouble breathing throughout the night. The nurse checked Jennie over and explained to Mary that it didn't look like Jennie had much time left, probably not even a full day. So, Mary kept the girls home from school. Mary believed in being honest with the girls about most everything because that was how Jennie, their Nana had raised them. So she told the girls everything the nurse told her about their Nana's condition. Mary told the girls she wanted them to spend the whole day just telling their Nana everything that was on their hearts, because today would most likely be their last day with her. Nana could barely talk anymore. The pain killers had her physically numbed. However, Nana was still acutely aware of what was happening to her, and that she was dying. Nana's three grandbabies and her best friend, Mary had spent all day in the room with her. They never left her side. They took turns alone with her. They talked to her about everything they held in their hearts. When one of them was finished talking to Nana about their private inner most thoughts, then that person would summon all the rest back into the room with Nana. The girls and Mary took turns making meals and snacks and they ate all the meals in the room with Nana. They moved the TV from the living room into Nana's room, and they watched their favorite TV shows with Nana. They were all trying their best to pretend that what was happening wasn't really happening. So they would laugh and make comments about the shows on TV. They would talk about school and complain about it and having to still go to church on Sunday, even when Nana got to stay home, as if they didn't know that soon everything they did would be without Nana. Although Nana dosed off at times and could not talk much, she always had enough strength to smile when the girls talked to her, and to squeeze Mary's hand when she saw the tears start to well up in her eyes.

Now Mary was the one person who knew everything about her friend Jennie's past, the good and the bad. There were no secrets between the two friends, up until now. Mary couldn't bring herself to tell Jennie she had fell off the wagon again. She knew how much her friend Jennie was counting on her to be strong for her grandbabies. And no matter how sweet everyone thought Jennie was, Mary knew her friend Jennie had a temper. Mary didn't want Jennie to die from popping a vein in her head yelling at her once she told her she was using drugs again. Besides, the girls only knew Jennie as their sweet Nana, and that's the memory Mary wanted them to remember, not their Nana fussing her best friend out on her death bed. Mary knew that to the Emmanuel girls, Nana was the angel who not just always looked after them, but also looked after everyone else in the neighborhood. Although the three girls never mentioned it, they all could not even imagine what life would be like without Nana, and they were afraid to even think of it. The three girls still believed in miracles and they were all waiting for one to happen at any moment despite the fact that their Nana told them it was time for her to go home to be with God.

Nana saw little Faith staring at her, she whispered, "what you thinking about child?", and Faith smiled and said, "I don't know, what you dinkin bout Nana". Faith was missing her two front teeth, and couldn't pronounce words that started with "th". Jennie smiled at little Faith and said, "I'm just reflecting on life baby."

Jennie had plenty of time to reflect on her life while being stuck in bed. There was nothing left to do but reflect on life, she had taken care of everything else, or so she thought she had. She had left instructions in her Last Will and Testament, that she wanted her friend, Mary to become guardian over her three grandbabies, since she had no idea where the girls' mother or father were. Jennie hadn't heard from her daughter in years. Her daughter had chosen a life of drugs over a life with her children. So Jennie had made provisions for her life insurance to go into a Trust for the girls, and for it to be used to pay the second mortgage she took out on the house after she died. She had also pre-paid for her funeral and burial. She thought to herself that her grandbabies would be safe and secure, and live out the rest of their childhood, with her friend Mary, right in the same little house they were born in, until they were old enough to decide to move on.

Jennie started to think about what a full and happy life she had lived. However, there are few people in life that meet the end without some regrets. Her regrets were that she wouldn't be around to see her grandbabies grow up into young, happy women, and she wouldn't be around to see her friend Mary finally accept Jesus Christ as her savior. Finally she was coming to terms that she was getting ready to die without being able to see her daughter one more time, or even know if her daughter was still alive. Since the moment she had found out she was sick and would not be getting better she had contacted everyone she could think of that might know the whereabouts of her daughter, but to no avail. Jennie had no relatives she knew of for the girls to go to, because her siblings had long ago forsaken each other. After Jennie's mother committed suicide her father drowned his grief in alcohol. Eventually all of her siblings tried to get as far away from their father as possible. They were now all scattered across the world, and they had no desire to stay in contact with each other. Nana had no idea how to find any of them. So Mary was the closest thing to a sister that Jennie had. Mary had promised she would do three things for Jennie, take care of her grandbabies, find her daughter, and accept Jesus into her life. Mary promised her she would do those things, and Jennie had no choice but to believe in her. After all, Mary was the only person Jennie had left to count on since her own family was all long gone. Although, Jennie knew Mary was far from responsible in the past, she was now her only option. So Jennie told herself that Mary had really grown during the past year they had lived together and that God will take care of her friend, her grandbabies, and even her daughter. She had faith that God would fulfill her prayers, even after she had passed away and that He would always watch over her loved ones and bring them safely through whatever trials the world would throw at them. Then she let out a sigh of relief from her worries and whispered to herself, "after all my girls names do end with *Emmanuel,* so surely God will always be with them." The faith and trust Nana had in God always gave her peace, when she needed it most in her life. Nana, especially needed it now, now that she was facing the end of her life. So she calmly accepted her fate with peace and with no worries left in her heart. She felt confident that she was straight with God, despite her many failures, and her many regrets over things she had done in her life. She had asked God for forgiveness for her sins and she knew in her heart that He had forgiven her of them. She said one last quiet prayer to God, "Lord, get them through whatever hard times may come for them, even if they don't pray to You themselves, remember my prayers for them Lord." At that moment, Jennie swore she heard a whisper in her head that said, *"my child, worry for nothing, I will answer all your prayers"*. A feeling of total peace and acceptance came over Jennie, and she knew that now it was truly time for her to go home.

Her three grandchildren and Mary were now surrounding her bed. She was staring at the people she would miss most in this world. As much as Jennie longed to see her savior, and to no longer be in physical pain, her heart ached at the thought of leaving her grandchildren and Mary alone in the world. But Jennie knew that voice in her head was from God, she knew He would eventually answer all her prayers, as he promised, and she decided to put her soul into his hands, and to trust that God would watch over the ones that she loved. She could see the distress in the three girls' faces. She felt their sadness, and she wanted to leave them with some last words of comfort. Jennie looked into the girls' eyes, she knew these would be the last breaths she would take, and she wanted to make them count for something. So Jennie looked at the girls, and said, "I love you, and remember…". Then she pointed upwards, towards the words which she had sitting in the three frames above her bed, her three grandbabies namesakes, the frames were placed from the oldest to the youngest grandchild.

"LOVE", love is patient, love is kind. It does not envy, it does not boast, it is not proud. It is not rude, it is not self-seeking, it is not easily angered, it keeps no record of wrongs. Love does not delight in evil but rejoices with the truth. It always protects, always trusts, always hopes, always perseveres. Love never fails. [2]

"HOPE", God the source of hope, will fill you completely with joy and peace because you trust in him. Then you will overflow with confident hope through the power of the Holy Spirit. [3] *and,*

"FAITH" faith is the substance of things hoped for and the evidence of things not seen. … faith is more precious than gold. [4]

The three girls looked upward at the words in the frames. For as long as they could remember those frames hung over their Nana's bed. The girls read the words in the frames silently as their grandmother had instructed them to do. When the girl's finished reading they looked back down at their Nana. In her fragile hands were three silver necklaces that she had hidden beneath her pillow. She had been waiting for the right moment to give the necklaces to her girls. She laid them on her black satin bed spread and motioned for the girls to put them on. The necklaces were beautiful and simple; three identical silver necklaces with an *"E"* charm on each of them. These necklaces would be the girl's first pieces of jewelry. After Love and Hope put their own necklaces on, they helped little Faith put her necklace on. Then Nana motioned for the girl's to come closer

---

[2] 1 Corinthians 13:1
[3] Romans 15:13
[4] Hebrews 11:1, 1 Peter 1:7

to her, and she used her last breath to say, "girls remember your names, "Faith, Hope and Love", those names mean something very special, and let the "*E*" in those necklaces help you to always remember you are the "Emmanuel sisters", no matter what paths your lives may take you, you belong to each other, and to God. And most of all remember, Emmanuel means "God is with you", He is always with you, always." Then Jennie closed her eyes and she quietly passed away. Jennie's last thought was the memory of the joy in Lester's face when their daughter, Esther, was born.

Faith, was the youngest of the girls, she immediately started crying. Faith cried out loud, "Nana, Nana, wake up, Nana", while her sisters held her tight. Hope just kept mumbling and pleading with God, not to let Nana leave them, not to take her away. Hope was a fighter, she was never willing to give up, she had learned CPR volunteering at the hospital and so she got up on Nana's bed and tried to revive her, in vain. Love was the oldest sister, and had always been the one to stay calm under pressure and keep things under control, between the three of them. So Love pulled her younger sister Hope off of Nana, and then she started consoling both her little sisters, as she slowly led them out of Nana's room. Love never even had a chance to shed a tear, she knew it was now her job to care for her sisters.

Mary was in shock and she just stood at the foot of Nana's bed, not knowing what to do. Mary didn't know how to comfort the three girls, so she silently retreated to the outside of the house. It was still midday, and the sun was blaring. Mary stared into the sky, as she sat on the front porch. Love noticed Mary quietly walking out of the room, and she didn't think much of it, she just focused on remaining calm, and comforting her sisters. Love told herself, she had to stay strong for her sisters. So Love just kept whispering to her sisters and to herself, "it's going to be alright, it's going to be alright". Yet inside Love's thoughts were racing, and she couldn't keep from wondering what would happen to her and her sisters, with Nana gone. She knew she was too old to have false hope that her father and mother would magically appear and take care of them. But she also knew she was still too young to take care of her sisters all by herself. The only other adult around was Mary, her Nana's best friend. But Nana never even trusted Mary to babysit the three of them, without another adult, like Ms. Sara, around. Ms. Sara had passed away, herself, several years ago, so she was no longer around to help either. Love thought to herself, "that at fifteen she was already more responsible than Mary was at forty". Love tried to focus on keeping herself and her sisters' calm. She kept telling herself that as long as she was with her sisters, everything would be okay. Love thought to herself that all she needed was for Mary to stick around until she turned 18, just so there would technically be an adult in the house with them.

But Love never imagined that today would be the last day she would be living in her Nana's house or even in the same house as her sisters. Love also would never had dreamed of all the twist and turns the three sisters lives would take, within the next twenty years. At that moment Love couldn't even imagine what tomorrow would be like for her and her sisters. Then Love noticed that Mary was gone from the room for quite awhile now. Love thought Mary must have been calling the ambulance, or the funeral home, to take care of things. Once Love felt like her younger sisters had calmed down a little, she left the girl's in their bedroom, and she quietly closed the door to Nana's room. Then she started looking for Mary. Love called out Mary's name. When there was no answer, Love checked the kitchen, the small backyard, the front porch, but Mary was no where to be found. So Love decided to call 911, herself, not knowing who else to call when someone has died. She just assumed that Mary would show back up.

When the ambulance workers showed up they went straight into Nana's room as Love directed them, and then they came out of her room and announced her, dead on arrival. They explained to the girls that their Nana was unable to be resuscitated. Then they started asking the girls a lot of questions. They noticed the three underage girls were there in the house all alone. They questioned Love, because she was the oldest. Then, Love told them about Mary. Love said, "I'm sure Mary will be right back". She later overheard one of the paramedics call the 911 dispatcher and tell the dispatcher that they needed to send Social Services to the house, because they had three underage girls, with no guardian to care for them. At that moment Love looked down the hallway at her two younger sisters sitting on the bed. Hope was holding Faith, and Faith was holding her favorite doll baby, the two of them looked worn out from crying. Love knew, if Mary didn't come back soon, it didn't look good. She wondered what would happen to her and her sisters if Mary didn't come back home. Love didn't want to think about it, but in the back of her mind, she knew what would happen. She was old enough to know, that the State wasn't going to leave her and her sisters in the house by themselves. She knew they would take them into foster care. Love, remembered times when she was younger, when her mother and father would disappear, and neighbors would call the police, then the police would take them into the station. Love's mother always had her carry her Nana's address in her little girl's wallet. Love would give the police her Nana's address, and after a few hours, Nana would come pick Love, Hope and Faith up. Nana would always mumble, "thank God you had my address, they may have put you girls in foster care's custody." But now Nana was gone, who would come for them now.

At that moment Love finally felt a tear roll down her cheek. It was the first tear she had shed that day. She wasn't sure if she was crying for her Nana, or for herself and her sisters. She quickly wiped the tear from her eye, there was no time to cry, she wondered out loud, "where the heck is Mary?!" Love felt a panic run through her thinking about what would happen if Mary didn't come back soon. Love went and sat down in her Nana's big sofa chair, next to the den table. It smelled like Nana, she closed her eyes and remembered Nana holding her in that chair as she read the family bible to her. Love picked the bible up off of the coffee table next to the chair. She closed her eyes again, thinking she would do what she knew her Nana would do in this moment. So she held the bible tight to her chest and she prayed. She desperately prayed to God, "please, please, please, let Mary walk through the front door. I swear I will die inside if I can't keep us together, please make Mary walk through those doors God, please." And before Love could open her eyes, she heard the front door open. She jumped up, her eyes wide, waiting to see her prayers answered, waiting to see Mary's face when the front door opened. Instead, she saw a Police

Officer, and a young, blonde lady in a drab gray suit. The lady walked up to Love, with a warm smile and explained she was with Social Services. Love felt her heart sink, she felt her hope die, and she began to feel numb inside, then she absentmindedly let the bible slip out of her hands, and it fell to the floor. Love knew if Nana was there, she would say, "*Love don't let the good book stay on the floor, pick it up child.*" But Nana wasn't there, and Love thought to herself angrily, "I can't think of any reason, and I don't even have any desire to pick *that book* up ever again".

Chapter 2
(Introducing Mary)

It had been hours since Mary left her friend's Jennie's house. She couldn't bare to be in it knowing Jennie was dead in her room. So she was desperately trying to score some drugs. And now she had lost all track of time. She couldn't even tell how long she had been gone from the girls, but she thought to herself, "it must not be that long, it's still light outside." Before the ambulance had arrived, Mary had went out to the front porch, just to get some air. Sitting on the stoop alone, made Mary's thoughts start racing in her head. Mary didn't know how to be a guardian for the girls. She didn't know how to handle the death of her only friend. And she felt extremely overwhelmed. She felt like she just needed something to help her get through that day, and that she needed it now. But then she realized, she was out of her stash, and she thought, "I will run to the dealer's house around the corner, and just pick up something to get me through the rest of the day, it will only take me a few minutes, and the girls won't even notice I'm gone. I'll call the funeral home when I get back." So Mary ran around the corner to get her a quick fix. Once she got to the dealer's house she begged him to give her a hit on credit.

"Mary you already owe me a grip of dough, without no money on you, you're gonna have to take care of a few favors for me first before I give you another free hit".

"Let me take care of the favor tomorrow. Jennie just passed away, you know Nana, and I got to get back to her girls."

"Look, I don't care about Jennie or her grandbabies. If you don't have no money then you have to do the work."

Mary hesitated, she wanted to do the right thing, but her skin was itching for a hit, and it was right there for her to have. "Okay then, what do you need me to do?" She told herself she would be really quick about it.

So he gave her the address of a few spots he needed her to make drop offs at, and additionally, he wanted her to offer her special services for his one very rich client as a bonus in retaining his business.

"You know the deal Mary, 10% off the top for you, and it better not be touched until I've heard from each client you arrived and delivered the goods and you return with my money." He had dealt with Mary many times in the past, and he knew she was reliable with bringing his money back, before she took a hit. He also knew her former pimp. Mary's pimp was a very good customer, he never used himself, but it was the best way he knew to keep his employee's loyal. He knew Mary understood the serious consequences of not bringing him his profits back, and that she knew her 10% payment in drugs could not be taken, that it had to be left completely untouched, until she returned what was his to him, and then, and only then, she could take a hit.

"Don't worry I know the deal, I would never cross you." Mary took the knapsack with the dope and then she was on her way.

She had no idea what time it was, or how long she had been gone from the girls, but she started to worry, when she saw the sun starting to go down. After the last stop, Mary couldn't wait to get a hit of what was left over for herself. Usually, she would have never disregarded a dealer's instructions, but today had been so stressful. Her whole body was screaming and itching for a hit, and her mouth was salivating for it. When she got on the train heading back to Queens from Brooklyn, she went to a car on the train that was totally empty. Then she grabbed a corner seat and frantically took a hit. Mary was in such a rush to get the drugs in her system that she was a little careless and she took more than the usual. It didn't take long for her to pass out. When she woke up, her knapsack containing the dealer's money was missing. Mary realized she had passed out, and someone had lifted it off of her. She knew losing the dealers money literally meant she just lost her own life. So Mary knew she had no other choice but to go into hiding. Her survival was the only thing on her mind at the time. She rationalized not returning to the girls because she would put them in danger also, besides her being dead wasn't going to help the girls no how. So she never did make it back to Nana's house that night, and she never made it back to the girls. But she did sneak back to the house a few days later, and tried to find out from some of the neighbors in the middle of the night about what had happened to the girls. The dealer had a price on her head, and one of Nana's neighbors tipped him off that Mary had been spotted around the neighborhood asking questions. He instructed everyone that was part of the game, to bring Mary to him, if they saw her and there would be something extra in it for them. That night they caught up with Mary trying to sneak back on the subway and they brought Mary to the dealer's house. He beat Mary close to death, and then he decided to spare her life. He decided he would keep her in his backroom, for anyone, to do whatever they pleased to her, for however long he chose to keep her, until her total debt was paid off, in his eyes. This wasn't the first time Mary had been beaten and kept as someone's sex slave only this time Mary was sure she deserved it for betraying her promise to Nana, and abandoning the girls. She was his prisoner for months and months, and not one day passed by that she didn't think about Nana and her three granddaughters.

On the day that Nana passed away two Social Service workers had stayed with the girls. They waited with the three girls patiently, until it was very dark and late into the night, but the lady "Mary", the girls had told them about, never did show back up. Finally, the Social Service workers told the girls they would have to pack a few things and that they needed to come with them, at least until, a family member, or this person, Mary, that the girls spoke of, showed up to take responsibility for the three girls.

That night, was the last night the three sisters would spend together. That night the girls slept in an emergency crisis shelter for abused and run-a-way girls. Social Services main goal was to get children out of the crisis shelters and into suitable foster homes as soon as possible. The next day the Social Service Workers showed up, and told the girls that they had found three suitable foster homes for the girls. Both of the women seemed like very kind and caring people. Love noticed the young, blonde lady eyes well up when she watched the three sisters say their goodbyes. The woman looked out of place in New York City with her southern style clothing and her southern drawl. She tried to comfort the girls by telling them the separation would be temporary, only until they could find a foster home that would take all three of the sisters. She ensured them that the goal was to reunite the three sisters, as soon as possible. But then Love overheard the other women whisper to her, "you shouldn't say stuff like that you never really know if we will ever find a home that will take all three of them."

Love, Hope and Faith, said their tear filled goodbyes, on the steps of the shelter home. Faith wouldn't let go, they had to pull her little hands off of her two big sisters' shirts. Love ensured her two little sisters that they would all be back together, real soon. But even when she said the words she wasn't sure she believed them.

The three girls would soon feel as if they were all alone in this world; and now it would be up to each of them, how they would choose to survive in the world, on their own, and without one another to rely on.

(Mary twenty years later)
It had been over twenty years since Jennie had died. Mary had led a very sorrowful life after Jennie's death. She was living with one pimp after another, until she was so old no one wanted her anymore. Then she ended up homeless and living on the streets; that was up until a few years ago. Mary had actually been clean for three years now and currently lived in a small senior citizens home. Mary enjoyed activities at the center, reading books and enjoyed corresponding with the gentlemen she had recently met over the internet. Mary would have never thought it possible to meet a love interest on-line. That was the kind of stuff kids did. But after weeks of sending each other instant messages in the senior citizen chat room, she knew it was all so silly and crazy, but she felt like a teenager in love, for the first time in her life. Now Mary and her new love, emailed each other every single day, sometimes several times a day, he called her on the phone, and had even flown out to visit her the last few weekends, all the way from California. She couldn't believe that after the life she had led, and at her age, she would find the love of her life, and over the internet, of all things.

But today, Mary's thoughts were on her old friend, who had long ago passed away. Mary's thoughts were on Jennie. Today would have been Jennie's birthday if she was still alive.

This day was always particularly hard on Mary. Mary always used to think that between the two of them, she would surely be the first to die. Almost every year on Jennie's birthday, when they were kids, they would go to Coney Island, and spend the whole day there. They started doing this when they were only in Junior High. Jennie's birthday always seemed to fall on a weekday, and Mary and Jennie would cut school and spend the day at Coney Island. The two of them never got caught, and they did it almost every year they were together when Mary's birthday came around. Once Jennie met Lester in High school, he would tag along. Mary didn't particularly like that, but she tolerated it for Jennie's sake, and she started bringing a boy along too. Then when they were older they took Jennie's granddaughters with them to Coney Island to celebrate their Nana's birthday. They always loved Coney Island, the Nathan's hot dogs, the beach and the board walk, and risking their lives riding on that old worn down roller coaster year after year. Those were wonderful memories. Jennie was the only family Mary had ever really had since she never had any family of her own. Mary decided that today, she would start working on fulfilling her promise to Jennie and do research over the internet to try and find Jennie's daughter and grandbabies. Then Mary heard a knock on the door to her room at the senior citizen home. Mary looked up and saw her doctor, Darryl.

"So there's my Doctor, where you been at Darryl and how you been doing lately? I done missed seeing you around. You're a sight for sore eyes."

"Oh I've been just fine Ms. Mary. I've had a pretty easy day. I just finished a round of golf with my Dad at the course around the corner. But you know I couldn't leave the area without stopping by and saying hello to my favorite patient. So how have you been?"

"Oh I was hanging in there, but I'm all good now. I was a little down because here I thought my favorite doctor had gone and forgotten all about me. Cause you know I can't *conversate* with any of these old heads around here. I need a sensitive, intellectual man, like yourself to communicate with."

Darryl started laughing. Mary always seemed to put a smile on his face.

"But seriously Doc I was just thinking about my old friend Jennie. Today would have been her birthday, if she was still alive. I'd ever tell you about the first time the two of us liked the same boy, back in middle school. Oh now that's a story you gotta hear…"

"Your friend, Ms. Jennie sounds like a real sweet lady. Why is it that every time I come visit you, you're telling me some story about her and you growing up, acting all wild and crazy? I would have loved to meet her and I'm sorry she isn't still around for you to have fun with."

"You would have loved her, everyone did." Then Mary continued telling Darryl the story about her and Jennie in middle school. After Darryl finished checking Mary over, he told her how healthy she was, as usual. It was amazing to Darryl that despite the hard life Mary had lived she was as healthy as an ox. Then Darryl asked her what else was going on in her life.

"Well I do have a gentleman friend now, I met him over the internet."

Darryl was more than a little curious, and a little amused. I mean, he could not even imagine Mary knowing how to use the internet. And he had come to think of her in such a motherly way that he couldn't imagine her being interested in a "man". So Darryl sat on the end of Mary's bed with concern in his eyes.

"Lets talk about you and this gentleman friend. Now the rumor is that all the old men are fighting for your affections here at the Senior Home. If that's true what do you need to go meet some stranger on the internet for?"

"I wouldn't say fighting, most of the men here need help eating and bathing. You know I am really too young to be living in a senior citizen home. I wouldn't even be here if you didn't get me the hook up."

Darryl put his finger to his lips. "Now you know Mary that hook up is something you need to keep to yourself."

"I know Doc, but back to what you were asking, I'm not interested in any of the old men here. I've been corresponding with a very, very interesting man, and he is all I'm interested in right now."

"But Ms. Mary the internet?! Ms. Mary if you are lonely, maybe you should really rethink giving one of these old guys here a second look, versus some stranger over the internet. This guy could be a serial killer for all you know."

Mary busted out laughing, she couldn't imagine why a serial killer would want to kill someone in a senior citizens home, where's the challenge in that?

Darryl had been Mary's doctor for over three years now. He first met Mary in the emergency room, on one of the nights he'd volunteer for emergency duty at the hospital. She had suffered a stroke due to a drug overdose while living on the streets and some good Samaritans brought her to the hospital. Darryl had just lost his mother, and he was determined not to lose this poor woman, who seemed to remind him of his own deceased mother. Once Mary had recovered at the hospital, they needed to find somewhere to take her. Darryl presided over the rehab wing in the hospital, and when he met Mary, he felt an instant connection to her. Mary had told him about her life, and how she didn't know if it was possible for her to stay clean, after a whole lifetime of habitual drug use. Darryl thought about his own mother, and how she volunteered so much time at her church, and at the hospital she worked at as a Nurse helping drug addicts, and homeless people; people like Mary. Darryl knew that if his mother was still alive she would want him to help Mary. So Darryl encouraged Mary to voluntarily admit herself into the hospital's rehab facility, and to try and get clean. Darryl would always visit and encourage Mary, when he saw her, and he would say, "it's never too late Mary, it's never too late."

No one had cared about Mary like Darryl did, since her friend Jennie. So Mary took his advice and did just what he said, she was going on three years clean, sober, and for the first time in her life, happy. After the first day Darryl met Mary he looked over her almost every day, like he was her guardian angel. When it was time for Mary to be discharged from the rehab program it was obvious to Darryl that she had no family and no place else to go. Darryl did his research and found a nursing home that had a non-profit pilot program for former addicts, sixty five and older. But Mary was barely sixty at the time. He knew she wouldn't qualify. Plus there was a long list of people waiting to get into the program, and live at the senior home for free. But Darryl pulled a few strings, he promised to give his medical services to the residents and employees at the senior home, free of charge, if they made an exception for Mary and put her name at the top of the list. A few weeks later Mary was a resident at one of the finest senior citizen nursing homes in New York City, all because of her chance meeting with a caring, young Doctor, who had saved her life, in more ways than one.

Darryl was a good person on the inside, but he also was very good looking on the outside. He was a fine looking young man, in his early thirties, with a tall, lean, muscular stature, cocoa complexion and a tiny bit of grayish hair already, in his little well trimmed goatee. He was technically still a bachelor and every senior in the home was always trying to set him up on a blind date with a daughter, a niece, or a granddaughter. But not Mary, she just looked forward to seeing Doctor Darryl, because she knew he would save her visit for last, and just listen to her talk for hours, like he had nothing better to do. Anyway Mary had no children of her own to try to set Darryl up with, but if she did have a daughter she knew she sure would be proud to have Darryl as a son-in-law.

Darryl also enjoyed visiting Mary. He never told Mary his own mother had just passed away right before he had met her, and that she just looked so much like his mother. It comforted him to sit and talk to Mary the way he use to sit and talk with his own mother. Although, the conversations he had with Mary were very different from the conversations he use to have with his own mother. Darryl's mother was born and raised in the church. She had graduated first in her family from high school and college and she became a nurse. She started working as a nurse at one of New York's finest hospitals, and eventually married herself a Doctor. She raised Darryl up to fear God and to care for others. He was with her at the church volunteering or at the hospital constantly. He never complained, he loved being in both places, even as a child. But he was somewhat sheltered by his mother. He was teased growing up, about being a Mama's boy. Regardless, Darryl turned out to be a good, responsible, strong man. He was nobody's mama's boy. He was a confident and capable man in his own right, but he did miss his mother being there, when he needed her to be. Darryl was the type of man any mother would be proud of, strong in mind, body and spirit, and he owed this to how his mother had raised him.

Now Mary, on the other hand, was much different from Darryl's mother. Mary had always chosen to live a hard life; a life without the Lord. Mary had never married, she didn't have any children and she had dropped out of school before she could graduate from high school. With no schooling, and no parents, Mary lived a very worldly life, to say the least. But Darryl didn't care about Mary's past he had grown to love over the years.

"So Ms. Mary, what made you decide to go meet someone over the internet anyway?"

"Well I took one of those library classes on navigating the web a while back and then I got sidetracked in the senior's chat room, then one thing led to another."

"Oh so that's how you met him, but again Ms. Mary all I have to say is you can't trust men you meet over the internet."

"Darryl it's okay I've also met him in person, in fact we spent last weekend together. He says he is gonna come and visit me religiously now, every Friday night, and we will spend the entire weekend together." Mary saw the concern in Darryl's eyes and she was moved seeing that he cared so much about her to be so concerned. "Don't worry about me. Really he is a wonderful, sweet, caring man. I've told him all about my past and he still hasn't went running for the hills. But if it makes you feel better you can meet him next Sunday. We've decided we will be attending that church you are always preaching to me about coming to. I figure I'd finally try going to church, because I gotta say I truly think God sent this man to me. God had to send him, because he is like a gift from heaven, a real angel."

Darryl thought it was nice to see Mary happy, but he was still concerned and wished he could meet this mystery man she talked about. However he was planning a surprise vacation with his girlfriend who had finally gotten some time off from work and he wasn't planning on being back by Sunday. This would be the first time Darryl and his girlfriend actually had vacation time, at the same time. Darryl couldn't wait to get home and surprise her with the trip he had planned. "Look Ms. Mary, I may not be in town on Sunday, but as soon as I get back I want to meet this new gentleman friend of yours so I can find out what his intentions are." Then Darryl gave her a peck on the cheek and headed for the door.

"You sure in a rush Doc. You got a hot date tonight?"

"Yeah, you can say that, I've got a big surprise trip planned for me and my girl."

"Well, you twos have fun, and when you gonna introduce me to your girl, Nene? Ain't that her name?"

"Yep, my Nene. I promise when we get back I'm going to bring her to meet you. Be good while I'm gone."

"I will Doc. You have a safe trip."

Chapter 3
<u>Introducing Love E. King</u>

"Ms. King", paging "Ms. King". Love heard her name being called over the firm's intercom system. Love sighed, "I can't get a minute to myself around here". Love was in the ladies restroom relaxing in one of the reception area chairs and trying to read the Lawyers Weekly while she ate a twinky. The restroom was the only place she could get a little peace at the office. She was figuring out some financial planning in her head regarding how she was going to spend her most recent bonus. She was up for partner at the prestigious law firm of Swanson, Herbert and Schoff. It was one of California's largest, wealthiest and oldest firms. Love was a senior associate attorney with the firm. She had been an associate with the firm for about 10 years now and she was the firm's youngest and "only" black female attorney. She knew that any day now all her hard work was about to pay off.

Love was a perfectionist in every way, especially when it came to work. Love graduated from High school at sixteen and received a full scholarship from Harvard, finished up college at twenty and went straight into Harvard Law School. She did two years as a United States Supreme Court Law Clerk after graduation from Law school, and then started working for Swanson, Herbert and Schoff right after her clerkship. Love had many offers from other firms, but she chose Swanson, because simply, "they showed her the money". And Love's hard work spoke for itself. She was highly respected and sought after in her profession. She was one woman that no one could ever say slept her way to the top.

But that's not to say that she didn't do her share of sleeping around, outside of the office. One thing Love made sure of, she kept her professional and personal life, as separate as possible. Once she had a fling with another student at the firm she interned with the summer after her graduation from law school. He saw her kissing another guy at a club one night, and he took it out on her the remainder of their internship. He barely talked to her again. He went around telling the other interns she was a cold hearted slut. The whole thing was just so embarrassing. It didn't seem to matter to the partners at the law firm because they still gave her an offer upon graduation. After all she was hands down the most qualified graduate, but she chose to clerk with the United States Supreme Court instead. It meant less money, but she knew the experience would be invaluable, and empower her to demand top salary in two short years. One thing she learned from that first law firm internship was to never again sleep with anyone she worked with.

To Love, sex was just an extracurricular activity. It was a way to de-stress herself after a long day surrounded by a bunch of uptight attorneys. And, there was never a day when Love had a problem getting *it*. Any average looking women doesn't usually have a problem getting sex when she wants it, but Love was definitely above average. With her tall, slim stature, long dark hair, dark brown eyes and naturally, soft sun tanned skin, she could have easily passed for one of Hollywood's starlets versus a lawyer. Every man from Rodeo to Compton was infatuated with Love. Regardless of her looks she was still quite interesting. She had studied and could speak fluently in about ten different languages. Even though she was hired to be a Criminal Defense Associate, she also had achieved head of the International Law Department after her first year with the firm, because of her love for languages. She was fluent in all the European languages and the Asian Dialects, where the abundance of the trade negotiations are currently in demand with the U.S. She was the only associate to be heavily relied on by not one, but two departments within the firm. She had made herself irreplaceable to the partners at the firm. She was always using her spare time to learn more in regards to her profession.

Work was definitely Love's first and last priority. If she ever needed to get some more personal needs met, she would go on what she casually referred to as a "date". Most of Love's "dates" always ended up with much more than a good night kiss at the end of the night on the front porch. There probably was not a man from any particular ethnicity that Love had not slept with. Love was definitely and equal opportunity lover. She had never given one day of serious consideration to changing her ways and settling down with one man. Currently, her conquest was a married movie star, whose name shall remain confidential for obvious reasons. Her girlfriends always teased her affectionately by saying, "she was indeed, very appropriately named Love, since she had loved almost every Hollywood heartthrob around town." However, Love always thought the more befitting name for her would have been "Monae", because at this particular time in her life all she cared about was making money, spending money and making more money. Tina Turner sung Love's anthem when it came to men, *What's love got to do with it.*

Love promised herself one thing when she left Queens, New York, that she would never live poor like her Nana lived, and always accepting hand me downs from other folks. Love always rationalized that if they weren't poor maybe her and her sisters would not have been farmed off into the foster care system. Over the years Love became bitter about her Nana's death and her separation from her sisters. She blamed society, her parents, her Nana, Mary, and of course she blamed God. In fact, she blamed God almost as much as she blamed herself for failing her little sisters. Love convinced herself that Nana relied too much on God, and that she would never be like her Nana. So she decided she would rely on herself, and no one else. To Love that meant she would make herself totally independent; emotionally, physically and most importantly financially. Love had been working towards total self independence, ever since the day she emancipated herself at sixteen, and changed her name to Love E. King. That day Love put away her past and she literally took on a different identity. She decided "King" was a good last name to have, because she promised herself that one day she would be living like a King. And she remembered that her mother had told her once that her ancestors had hailed from "the Kings". Nana was always so proud of their last name "Emmanuel", because she said it meant, "God would always be with them". But Love wanted to change her name to also signify that she didn't need to depend on God being with her like her Nana did, she was fine on her own.

After Love emancipated herself, and changed her name, she pretended to be a spoiled rich girl when she went off to college. She became so good at pretending that was what she was, that eventually she became just that. So, Ms. Love E. King swore she would never be poor again, like her Nana was. She definitely, never wore anymore hand me down items. She didn't even like the word, vintage. Even the underwear she wore was always brand new. She had to keep buying new Victoria Secrets, because she was always leaving them behind, after one of her "dates". One guy she had slept with actually called her a slut because she wouldn't stay the whole night with him. But Love never saw herself as being a slut. She thought, "sluts are stupid and I'm anything but stupid". She considered herself, in control, and doing whatever the heck she wanted to do, just like a man would in her position. She would say she knew she didn't want a relationship, so why pretend like she did. Her girlfriends thought she was a sex addict so they tried to form an intervention dinner party for her one night. They told her that any psycho-analyst would have told her she had a problem, if she would just go and see one. But Love didn't feel like she needed therapy. She liked her life, and she told anyone who questioned her lifestyle that she was living her life just the way she wanted to live it. Love merely felt that she was just doing what any man would be doing in her shoes, and no one would be trying to plan an intervention for her if she was a man. Yes, Love enjoyed having sex and having money, and she wasn't about to apologize to anyone for enjoying it. In fact, the fear of becoming poor again, is partly what gave Love her extraordinary drive, and competitive nature. When other people were relaxing on the weekends and sleeping at night, Love was up, thinking of new ways to make more money and increase her profitability, as an associate, and hopefully one day, as a partner. She was a master at time management, and managing others.

So that explains why she was currently hiding out in the restroom, finishing up her reading, finishing up the last bite of her twinky, and finishing up figuring out how much extra cash she would be making once she made partner, so that she could buy her new, dream, beach house. She never wasted time. Every spare moment she filled to forward the completion of her ultimate goal, which was making partner. But, making partner depended on if Love, won all the high profile cases the partners handed off to her. So far in the ten years she had been with the firm, she had yet to lose a case. No doubt that was the reason they were summoning her over the intercom, to assign her another case. Love enjoyed her job, but she sometimes wondered when she would finally be offered partner. She loved the firm she was at, but she was starting to grow impatient. She knew she had not been at the firm as long as others, but she had made the firm a tremendous amount of money, way over any other associate had.

"Love King, paging Love King" Love thought, "there goes that irritating intercom again." The sound of the intercom, rushing Love to finish up in the bathroom, made her remember a time similar to this moment in her childhood with her sisters and her Nana. Love started to think about the time Nana and her sisters were banging on the bathroom door...

"Love, come out of the bad room!" yelled little "no front teeth", Faith. Faith could not pronounce the "th" sound to save her life. Love could hear Hope repeating Faith's pleas, through the bathroom door. Love was about twelve years old and she had locked herself in Nana's bathroom because the neighborhood boys had taunted her for three blocks on the way home from school. The boys taunted Love, saying things like, "yeah, Love stands for loves to eat", said the skinny boy with the two buck teeth. Then the boy who always wore the beanie on his head, like Malcom X, said, "no man, Love stands for only your mama ever gonna love someone as big as you". Childish, corny jokes they were, but for a teenage girl those jokes hurt Love deeply. Yes, you wouldn't believe it to see her now, but Love Emmanuel use to have a serious weight problem and along with that an even more serious self esteem complex back when she was a young girl. Love was always smart, but for a long time she was also very shy, quiet, and lacked even the smallest amount of self esteem. But the new and improved, Love E. King, at least on the outside, was truly a totally different person.

"Tap, tap, tap". "Love, baby what you doing in there?", said Nana.

"She done locked herself in the bad room with a box of twinkys Nana, and she keeps saying I'm fat and ugly, and no one loves me and why they have to go and give me a dumb name like, Love, anyways?"

"Love, I gave you your name, and "Love" is a beautiful name and fits you well". Nana's voice was soft and calming. *"For now you see in a mirror, dimly, but then face to face. Now I know in part, but then I shall know just as I also am known. And now abide faith, hope, love, these three; but the greatest of these is Love".*[5] Then Nana started praising Jesus. "Thank you, Jesus, thank you Jesus". Nana always use to do that.

"What are you talking about Nana?" Love was use to Nana spouting off scriptures all the time, but half the time she had no idea what she was talking about. Sometimes the girls really thought their Nana was a little bit crazy, the way she would just start spouting out scriptures and spontaneously start praising all loud or speaking in tongues. The girls were use to it mostly at home, but it did embarrass them when they were out in public or in church. Nana was the loudest, most dramatic person in the church. The girls always wondered to themselves, "can't Nana tone it down just a little?" And even when Nana got sick, the sickness hadn't seemed to slow her scripture spouting down, not even a little bit.

Although the girls may have been embarrassed, secretly about Nana's passion for God and praising him, they never were disrespectful enough to let her know about their embarrassment. So when Nana spoke the girls were quiet and everyone else was too. As a matter a fact it seemed like the whole universe paused to listen to Nana. I mean she was usually so loud you didn't have a choice, but when she spoke, when she spoke "The Word" it did give all who heard it, a strange sense of a moment of pure peace, and calmness. Even if you had no idea what the heck she was talking about.

So Nana knew exactly how to establish quietness and peace in her household again, and how to get Love's attention from the other side of the bathroom door. "Now Love come on out of that bathroom girl, don't you know *"your body is the temple of the Holy Ghost which is in you, which ye have of God, and ye are not your own"*[6], so God don't want you abusing his temple with a bunch of junk food and sugar, hold up in the bathroom."

---

[5] 1 Corinthians 13:12-13
[6] 1 Corinthians 6:19

Love didn't know why, but at that moment she swore to herself she'd stop overeating and she would never be fat again. It took Love a long time to lose all the extra pounds, but by the time she went away to college she was already tall but she was also as slim as a run-way model. Outside she had transformed into a perfectly posed picture of a model, but her insides were more like an abstract Picasso. Although Love took Nana's advice about not abusing her body by eating too much junk food, she had swore off all that Nana had taught her about God and the bible.

Nana had been dead for over twenty years now but however hard as she tried to forget, Love could not get Nana's words out of her head. Those *Words*, that Nana quoted, always came back to her at the strangest moments. Like now while she sat hiding out in the cushy sofa chair in the ladies restroom at Swanson, Herber and Schoff. She had come a long way from that fat little girl in Queens, New York. Now-a-days Love buried her self-esteem issues way down deep where no one could ever see them. Love worked out, obsessively, counted calories, yet she still treated herself to one delicious, golden sweet twinky, every time she won a case, and she made sure she savored every bite slowly. Twinky's were always her favorite sweets growing up. The sweet twinky she ate reminded her of the past and what a mess she use to be. It reinforced in her mind that now she had control over herself, control over her body, and over her future. Now she was a successful attorney, beautiful, and most importantly, rich. No one in her current world knew of the old, Love Emmanuel, and by this world's standards, putting aside how her friends were concerned about her promiscuity, anyone who knew the new and improved, Love E. King, would say one thing about her, "that sista has got it going on!", and it would take an act of God for Love to admit she thought anything different than just that about herself.

Chapter 4
Introducing Hope Emmanuel

The sunlight was shining through the hole in the interior stone wall. It was the only way Hope could keep track of how many months she had been imprisoned. She had counted the sun shining, and then ceasing to shine every time. But Hope was beginning to question whether she was only there for a few months or much longer. It seemed much longer. A few times she had blacked out, and she wasn't sure how long she had been out. She was starting to question everything. At times she swore she heard someone calling her name. She even felt as if there was a presence in the cell with her, but she knew no one had come in or out of her cell since she had been captured. During Special Ops training they were drilled several times on how to survive in enemy captivity. Hope had been privy to go to a special survivor training course that most military officers were not given the opportunity to go to. All perks of being an Intelligence Officer with a top secret clearance. After passing that with unusually high standards, and being highly successful on every mission, Hope became entitled to even more top secret information and organizations within the military. She graduated at the top of every military school she ever attended. In fact, Hope was so successful at being a soldier and at being an Intelligence Officer, that eventually she was recruited into an elite sector of the military. Half military, half CIA agents, the sector was a secret special-forces group. Once you became a member your name was officially and legally changed, and you were given a totally new identity. You became like a ghost, so that your true identity would be impossible to be tracked, compromised, and used against you or your Country. Hope had to agree to become a ghost, to leave behind her past life and never look back. Once she did that she was officially listed as a missing person, lost in action. This was another reason this special sector of the military, and CIA, was considered elite, and incredibly small. The other agents became your family. The terms of one's admittance into the group was just too much for most officers to swallow. If they turned down the position, they were strongly counseled on the severe consequences to their career, and their personal lives if they were ever to divulge the existence of this special-forces group to anyone they knew. Even if they suspected that a person, such as a co-worker, who may have already heard about this elite force themselves, already knew about it, they were still counseled not to talk or write about this special sector of the military. However, for someone like Hope, she felt as if everyone she loved was already dead to her. In her mind, there was no reason to turn down this position. A position that guaranteed better retirement benefits than most Presidents receive upon leaving the White House.

Therefore, the officers and enlisted persons in this sector were highly qualified, highly trusted, and highly trained. They were also trained to use all means possible to not disclose their missions, and their true identities. Those means included "self-termination", if necessary. She was trained well, and she thought she was prepared for anything, even the possibility of having to use self-termination as a last resort. However, after several months of confinement, and with all of Hope's training she still found it hard to hold on to her sanity and, to hold fast to her directives. If it came down to self-termination, she didn't think she could do it. At her core she was a fighter and a survivor, she knew in her heart that she would have to die fighting. She didn't think she could ever take her own life, even though she had swore she would be able to do it if she needed to during her training.

But this wasn't a training scenario; this was her first real life captivity behind enemy lines. She was now in a cell, with no windows, one slot in the door, and one crack in the wall where light shined through. They utilized the slot in the door in serving her something that resembled food, and one cup of dirty water once a day. The only thing that kept her focused was that tiny hole in the stone wall. Seeing the sun shine through it every day, gave her hope that she would one day be in the sun again. At night Hope was too afraid to sleep. The floor was nothing but dirt, and every creepy, crawling thing in this God Forsaken place found its' way into her cell at night. The third night she dosed off on her straw pilot on the floor and found herself covered from head to toe with what she thought may have been some type of biting ants. Since then she couldn't sleep for more than a few moments without waking back up. She thought she had been there possibly seven months but it felt more like seventy years now. She wondered if she would ever get out of this place. She wondered why no one had tried to interrogate her yet. She wondered if anyone else involved in the mission with her had survived, and if they were being held also. She thought to herself how lucky she was to still be alive, and how fortunate she was to not have been physically tortured or raped by the enemy yet. But because those things had not happened to her, she feared what was to come.

Hope heard footsteps coming towards her. Her heart stopped with fear. Then the slot in the door was opened and a tray of food was set out for her. She felt a wave of relief fall over her, it was just her food, but she was sure they had fed her already earlier that day. She was always starving, and she always felt an aching emptiness in her stomach. She grabbed the tray frantically. She started eating the soupy substance. It smelled horrible, and she had no idea what it contained, and she didn't care. The first day she had arrived there she gagged and vomited from the food. The second day she just tried to drink it down as fast as possible, and then she sucked down the cup of dirty water to kill the taste of it. But after several months the awful taste and smell of the food no longer phased her. She ate it like it was a T-bone steak and shrimp dinner. As the days passed into weeks and then months, Hope would come to look forward to her grub.

She imagined she heard just barely a whisper of a voice. The voice was so soft she could not discern whether it was male or female. It came from the slot in the door. No one had attempted to talk to her since they had placed her in this darkest of holes in this godforsaken place. The voice said, "Tonight they come for you, prepare yourself with prayer and supplication". Then the slot was shut back up that quickly, it was less than a second that had went by but to Hope that moment of fear felt like an eternity.

For the next, what seemed like a full hour, Hope just stared at the door with the bowl still fixed in her hands. She was in shock, paralyzed with fear, and doubted whether she heard what she did, or just imagined it. It all happened so fast she couldn't even recall whether it was said in English or another language. She thought to herself, if she did hear what she thought she heard, was it a mind game, the enemy was now playing with her. For months she heard, and saw nothing. Why would they bother to warn her they were coming for her now? She thought, that maybe they were trying to fill her with so much fear that she would immediately tell them everything she knew. Well if that was their plan she felt like it might possibly work. So far Hope had been able to keep her composure, her sanity, and her optimism. But now she sat trembling with fear. Hope had been on many missions in the past. Only this time the mission went wrong. A bad mission was bound to happen to her sooner or later. She was the officer in charge and she felt responsible for anyone who got captured. She hated herself for possibly jeopardizing the lives of those she considered to be her friends, her Major, and their loyal, young troops. Hope never considered herself a hero, but she promised herself then, that she would prepare for death, rather than betray those she considered to be her friends, and her family; those young Marines that had put their lives into her hands. She thought to herself that she would not get out of this alive, so she wouldn't tell secrets to live just a few moments more. For the first time since being taken hostage, Hope cried. She buried her face in her hands and in the dirt, to silence her sobs. She didn't want to give any satisfaction to the enemy outside by letting them hear her cry like a scared little child. She didn't want them to realize they had accomplished what they obviously had set out to do; break her down by filling her with fear.

After she was finished sobbing into the dirt, she got a hold of herself and she told herself, "Hope, you have to freaking snap out of it." Then she spontaneously screamed out loud in anger. "The first person who steps foot in here I will send you straight to hell, where you belong!" She no longer thought she possessed any compassion, any forgiveness, or any mercy for these people who had killed so many innocent civilian, without just cause. She hated them, and she felt no conflict about the hate she had for them in her heart. Her renewed anger and hatred made her feel alert. She realized that finally breaking her silence, with a threat, was thrilling, it filled her with adrenaline. She felt pumped with instant energy. Her body was still cold, and she was shivering and itching all over. Her skin was bleeding from scratching all the bug bites on her, and she felt like her body had become weak. But as her anger and hatred increased, the fear that had moments ago almost paralyzed her was decreasing. She felt angry and disgusted in herself for being so weak and for crying. Then she let her anger and hatred envelope her and she let it take over until it pushed the fear way down into a place where she could pretend it no longer existed. She started chanting to herself first softly and slowly until her chanting escalated and became louder. She decided she would be as loud for as long as possible, hoping her Major and her troops would hear her if they were still alive.

"I am trained to kill, and prepared to die. I shall have no fear as long as I'm alive." She repeated that to herself, out loud, over and over again. She reminded herself she had conquered all kinds of obstacles, come against all types of hurdles, and survived them on her own. She told herself she would survive this also. She started screaming and yelling and cursing at whoever may have been outside her cell door. "You want me, come on in, and get me, come on in. I'm prepared to die, are you? I promise you this, I will not go down, without taking some of you with me." She stood up and got into a fighting stance and she began to shadow fight. She let her anger and her hatred fill her up as she cursed her enemies out loud. And for the next few days her focus was on killing and preparing herself for a fight. She pictured herself strangling the rebels with her bare hands. She pictured grabbing their guns and shooting them in the head. She played these horrendous acts out in her mind and with her body over and over again. She felt as if she was losing a part of herself, the more human part and becoming part animal inside. When she wasn't fighting the air, she did pushups and crunches to strengthen her body. She decided to keep her strength up by providing herself with extra nourishment. So instead of flicking the biting bugs off of her she started eating them. She didn't know why she didn't think of it before bugs were an excellent source of protein. The bugs became her between meal snacks, to supplement the one bowl of grub she consistently received once a day from the rebels. The sound of the rodents that had plagued her sleep was also resolved. She hunted them in her spare time just to have something to kill. She thought to herself when the time came she would kill her enemies as if they were the rats, with no hesitation, and no regret.

As the days passed by whenever Hope felt her energy dwindling or her anger residing and the fear trying to take over again, she would think of her past, her painful past, and all the people in her life that had harmed her and used her. She recalled those predators from her past and filled herself with her hatred of them to keep her anger, and the fighting spirit fueled inside of her. She told herself that her current captors would pay for every sin that was ever committed against her in the past. She would make them feel her full wrath before she died. Hope swore to herself she would kill as many of them as she could. She thought to herself she had no one but herself to count on all her life, and it only made sense that now at the end she would also die alone. She felt that her anger and hatred was the only thing keeping her alive and she could not let go of it, lest she would surely die. Although she was keeping her body strong by embracing her hatred and anger; she didn't realize it, but her mind and her spirit were becoming weak.

One night she sat in her cell and thought to herself that for the first time since she had been taken hostage that finally she felt she was at a point where she felt totally indestructible and fearless. And it was then that it happened.

Hope heard another person's voice coming from the corner of her cell. She knew no one was in the cell with her and there was no one at the slot in her door, trying to leave her food, but she was positive she heard a voice. She began to check every nook and cranny of her cell and she found nothing. Then she considered that maybe her mind was just playing tricks on her and there was no voice and no one was coming for her. But that wasn't true, because her greatest enemy *had* come for her after all, and it wasn't the rebel soldiers she was expecting. Hope looked up and it was *him*, the one man from her past who instilled fear in Hope like nothing else could, her foster father, Mr. Smith. He was the one man that still haunted her in her nightmares. The one man that caused her to practically become addicted to Tylenol PM, and two glasses of wine, before bed every night, just to get a good night's sleep. He was the reason Hope had never had a healthy, romantic relationship with anyone her entire adulthood.

After Nana died and Hope was taken away from her sisters, she was put into, what New York City Department of Social Services considered one of the most reputable foster homes in the town, Mr. and Mrs. Smith's home, and that was when and where Hope lost her innocence. Since the day Hope left that foster home she had intentionally did her very best to keep herself from thinking about that time of her life. She would block out those dark thoughts whenever they entered her mind, except for the occasional exception of when they entered her dreams. For keeping the nightmares away she had become accustomed to using sleep aids, and wine to help her not dream, or at least to help her to not remember her dreams when she awoke. This was the first time Hope had allowed herself to think about Mr. Smith while she was awake, but this was more than mere thoughts of him, because although Hope did not want to believe her own eyes, he was standing there, right in front of her, and her first thought was, "I've gone crazy!"

Hope stared at the man that appeared before her frozen with fear. "You are dead. You can't be real, I'm …I'm hallucinating".

"In here I'm as real as you are. You think you're invincible don't you? But to me you will always be that weak, little, thirteen year old girl, that will always belong to me."

Hope closed her eyes, and started whispering to herself, "he isn't real, he isn't real." Then she heard Mr. Smith's voice again.

He had no intentions of leaving her alone. He was laughing at her and then he started talking and taunting her. "Get on your knees, just like old times and cry and beg, just like you use to. Beg me to leave you alone, but you know I won't, not until you tell me what I want to hear, tell me you belong to me body, mind and soul. You know how I use to love to hear you play hard to get, how you use to pretend that you really didn't want me at first, and how much it turned me on to hear you eventually say how much you loved me. Oh how I have missed you Hope, but now we can be together forever, just you and me in this cell, there's no one to come and break us up this time. No this time, no one can take you away from me ever again. This time you will forever be mines, my little Hope."

Then quietness fell upon the cell once more, for how long Hope didn't know, but his voice, his horrible voice, had gone away. Hope thought that maybe she had just experienced a rare moment of temporary insanity. After she took in a deep breath and exhaled she found the courage to open her eyes. But when her eyes were wide open, Hope looked around and realized she was no longer in her dark, dirt and stone wall cell. It didn't take her but a moment to realize where she was at. She was somewhere much worse than any jail cell could ever be, she was back in that basement, standing there naked and cold and scared, just like it was twenty years ago, all over again. She was back in Mr. Smith's basement, back in Queens, New York, and she was thirteen again. She thought, "this can't be, it can't be, I'm thirty three years old and I'm a Colonel in the United States Marine Corps", so she closed her eyes once more and kept repeating that to herself over and over again. She was trying her best to regain her sanity, and make her mind remember who she was *now*, and not who she use to be. For the first time since she had been taken hostage Hope wished with all her might that she was back in the one place she had been wanting to escape from for the last few months; back in her jail cell. But every time she closed her eyes and reopened them she was still there in that basement, and standing in front of her was Mr. Smith. She hated him with every fiber of her being; he was the only father figure she'd ever really had, the only man she'd ever had sex with, and the only person she feared more than anything or anyone else she could think of in her entire life. But she had long ago pushed her fear for him deep down and put it away, because her rationale mind knew he was dead. He had died twenty years ago. But if he was dead, and she knew for a fact that he was dead, why was he now standing there in front of her? Then he started to speak again and his voice made her skin crawl.

"Hope, like I said I'm not going anywhere and neither are you. So why don't we take this time to catch up and get reacquainted with one another."

Hope was over being shocked now. She was over being paralyzed with fear. All she knew was no matter how irrational it seemed he was there and no matter how many times she closed her eyes he was not going away.

Hope thought to herself, "now, after all of my preparation it's come to this... I was prepared for a battle, and I actually had filled myself with so much hate for the enemy that I desired nothing more than to fight, and to kill, one of them. Yes, I was waiting and longing and wishing for an ultimate battle with my enemies to the death, better that, than being a pitiful victim, dying as a weak, pathetic prisoner that didn't fight back. But I never expected this battle that I've been preparing for would be with *him*, I thought, I assumed it would be with strangers who are enemies to my country." A part of her wanted to give in to her insanity, because she wanted a fight, and her psyche had brought one to her, so in a strange way she welcomed it. Why not fight, with the one person she hated more than anyone else. She told herself she was ready, ready to finally finish off whatever hold Mr. Smith still had over her mind. She no longer needed someone to come and save her from him, she could save herself.

Even in that moment of accepting her insanity and embracing the need to confront her fears, Hope still did not realize that this was not just a fight against the demons in her mind, but this would also be a spiritual battle for the ownership of her soul.

Hope looked at Mr. Smith, with hatred in her eyes and she stood up and said to him, "in twenty years no man has seen me cry, no man has heard me beg for mercy, and no man has touched me in any place I did not want to feel his touch. I'm not thirteen anymore and I don't fear you anymore. In fact, for the past twenty years I have not feared any man. I've been trained so well that men now fear me." At that moment there was truly no trace of fear left in Hope's eyes or in her voice, she was so ready to finally end whatever hold Mr. Smith still had on her mind.

He stood in front of her not seeming deterred or moved by her little speech, but that didn't scare Hope. Her body was once again the body of a soldier ready for a fight, tall and strong. She was no longer that weak thirteen year old girl, she would never be her again. She waited for him to respond; for him to make the first move. Then he calmly responded.

"My little Hope, confused child of this world, with so much knowledge but such little understanding. I am no mere man. I am so much more. I could never fear you, not you *alone*. And that is exactly why, you should fear me."

Chapter 5
Introducing Faith Emmanuel

Faith was the youngest of the Emmanuel sisters. It had been so long since she had seen her sisters and she was so young when they separated that they seemed like a dream to her at times. Faith could barely remember what they looked like. She held on to an old photograph her sister Love had given her of the three of them in Church, it was a poor picture, too dark to see the girl's faces in it clearly, but it helped Faith to not forget. However much time had passed by, Faith always felt that one day she would find her sisters again, but there were times when she did feel like she held on to her wishes in vain.

There was a fire long ago at the foster care agency in Queens that held the three girls' records. The fire happened before the city offices had decided to switch over to a computer records system. As a result of the fire there were no records of where the sisters had been placed, and no way to find out what happened to them after they reached adulthood. Faith was the youngest of the girls, her sisters were already young teenagers when Nana died, and Faith was only six years old at the time. Shortly after the girls were placed into foster care it became obvious to the agency that the girls had no next of kin to care for them. The three girls were then placed into foster care and sent to separate homes, but Faith was the only one of the sisters who got adopted.

Faith's adopted parents were a couple who couldn't have children of their own. They were also an interracial couple. In those days being interracial made it more difficult for them to convince an adoption agency to give them a baby. So they decided to become foster parents. Faith was the first and last foster child her adopted parents had cared for. They fell in love with Faith at first sight. As soon as they were told she was qualified to be put up for adoption, they petitioned to have Faith become their adopted child. Faith's adopted parents lived in the suburbs of Long Island, New York, but they also traveled frequently out of the country, and they took Faith with them on all their travels after they adopted her.

Since Faith's adopted parents were also her original foster care parents after Nana died, Faith never spent any time with another foster family, unlike her older sisters. Faith's biological parents had abandoned their children several times and each time their Nana would care for them. After Faith was born they left the girls with their grandmother permanently, leaving her to raise the girls without any interruption for six consecutive years before she died. Faith couldn't even recall what her biological parents looked like anymore. Strangely she was never even curious about finding her biological parents, but she was very concerned about finding her sisters. She didn't know if her sisters were dead or alive, but her heart told her they were alive and out there waiting for her to find them, somewhere.

Faith adopted parents had always encouraged her to keep looking for her sisters and her biological parents. They were very loving and encouraging parents to Faith. They were also very unconventional. Unlike Nana, they were not Christians. In fact, her parents were not religious at all. They believed in many different things, but they would tell Faith that most of all they believed in the power of love. They taught Faith to love all her sisters and brothers in the world, regardless of their race or religion. They were good people with good hearts, and they were even spiritual people. However some religious people may say they were also spiritually confused.

Faith's parents were always open with her and anyone else who asked about Faith being adopted. They even allowed Faith to keep her last name Emmanuel and hyphenate it with their last name. After they returned back home from their first extended two year stay in Africa with their newly adopted daughter, they encouraged Faith's desire to try and find her sisters. They helped Faith write letters to her two sisters while they were in Africa but the letters would come back unopened and no addressee. So her parents contacted the agency to inquire on the whereabouts of Faith's older sisters and that was when they were informed about the fire. The agency explained to them that they had lost the girls records due to the fire and had had no contact with the two sisters since the fire. They also said that there was evidence that Hope Emmanuel may have been a victim of the fire. Faith was seven years old by the time she got the news, and even then she realized it would take a miracle to find her sisters, but she never believed they were dead. So they placed ads in the newspapers back in the States, and when they returned to the U.S. they placed the one picture of the girls Faith had up all around the city, but to no avail.

Through it all, Faith's parents gave her plenty of love and emotional support. She had experienced so much loss, and at such a young age. Despite this, she always felt the void of her sisters not being in her life, and it was exasperated by the fact that she was now an only child in her new family. Even though Faith was adopted at a relatively young age, her unstable past made her extra shy and she had a very difficult time making new friends in Long Island, New York. Her parents interracial marriage was always a topic of gossip, her mother was African and her father was German. Her parents were also eccentric, and the small community in the suburbs of Long Island didn't seem to be very welcoming to them. Both of her parents had spent many years serving in the peace-corps before deciding to settle down. They both had deep accents from their native countries, and their house was definitely the most creative house in the neighborhood. They did not belong to any particular church group, and they believed that institutional religion was a major factor in societal strife. Instead they took a little from each religion, and they practiced what they liked and ignored what they didn't like. And Faith's extended adopted family were also a very un-conservative bunch. For instance, Faith's aunt was a lesbian and her and her lover were raising their sons to have a gender neutral view of life. Faith's aunt and cousins lived in the city and came over every other weekend to visit. Faith's other aunt on her mother's side had left Africa with them and came to live in the states. She had since married and lived in Brooklyn with her husband. She was considered a voodoo high priestess and her husband was a famous Haitian fortune teller. The two of them owned and operated a very well known herbal healing and psychic center in Harlem. Faith's mother got her fortune read by her sister before she made any decision she considered important.

So, Faith grew up with a very open-minded view to most everything under the sun. This type of worldview did not make it easy for Faith to blend in at her Conservative Catholic school. But it was the school Faith's parents insisted on her attending because it was the best academically in the city. Although Faith was a straight A student she always found a way to push her teachers patience and limits. At one time Faith considered herself a Budhist and she insisted that during the school's morning-prayer and pledge of allegiance she needed to meditate while chanting a mantra. But she had little patience for the daily meditations other than for shock value and that didn't last for long. She decided to keep the concepts she learned and blend them into her life for really stressful days. At one time Faith said she was Muslim and she insisted on writing her name on every assignment as Aslam Mohammed, her new Muslim name. She also used being Muslim as a reason to leave out of class because she had to go to face Mecca for prayer. But then she realized she loved ham and bacon too much to give it up, and she definitely could not see herself continuing to wear the traditional Muslim women wardrobe when summer came around. So before end of winter she gave up Islam. Faith dabbled in many religions and occults. Her parents always supported her. When the school's Principal called them up to school to discuss Faith's eccentric behavior they told him they didn't find anything wrong with their daughter's behavior. They felt she was on her own path of self-discovery. Faith could barely remember anything of what Nana had taught her and her sisters about the bible.

Faith remembered how Nana had her and her sisters pray every night before bedtime. Nana had her girls praying from the time they were babies. So even now the prayer they all said at night was still stuck in Faith's head.

Faith also had the opportunity to be exposed to Christianity through other sources. Her most significant exposure to the Christian faith was through her friend and next door neighbor, Darryl and his family.

For a few years, every Sunday morning, Faith would spend the mornings with Darryl and his parents at their church. Faith's parents strongly encouraged her to go. They would use those Sunday mornings without their precocious, energetic child around to sleep in and make love all morning. Sunday's were their "days without Faith in the house". Her parents were still as much in love as the first day they had met back in Africa. Sunday mornings worked out wonderfully for both Faith and her parents. Faith got to spend time with her favorite friend, Darryl, who she idolized and adored. He was like the older brother she never had. Faith's parents got a little "couple" time in, while feeling like their daughter was learning things that would benefit her, because they felt as if religion most times divided human beings, they had nothing specifically against the Christian religion. In fact they told Faith many times they really thought Christian beliefs were very good beliefs to live by, especially the, "no fornication before marriage belief". But no matter how many times little Faith asked them her parents refused to come to church with her. So as the years passed by, eventually Faith followed the path of her parents, the people she most admired, even more so than her friend Darryl. Once Faith was old enough to venture out unsupervised she decided church wasn't for her, just like it wasn't for her parents. It was then that she started spending her Sunday mornings doing things she felt were more productive, like seeing a matinee by herself, or going to the book stores and thrift shops in the Village, or hanging out with the few girlfriends she had in the neighborhood.

When people asked Faith, she would say she considered herself to be Agnostic; believing in a higher being, but not in any particular religion, or even that this higher being was anything more to people than just their *creator*. Faith believed that all men and women were truly captains of their own destinies, and that everyone had the choice to do either good or evil in the world. Faith decided to make the choice early on in life that she would be a person who did good in the world, and made changes, just like her parents. Thus and activist was born.

Faith was always involved in some humanitarian cause. She was involved in the homeless movement, green movement, Aids movement, and any other cause she could find because she had a real passion for helping others. So it was no surprise when Faith's first job after college graduation was going to work for a non-profit organization. Being an adopted child was partly the reason why Faith had dedicated her adult life to SACAA (Save

A Child And Adopt). The other part was due to the great losses Faith had experienced throughout her life, and how she wanted to somehow make up for those losses. She wanted to somehow save other people, especially children. She also wanted to always be in control of her own destiny.

Faith did a internship with SACAA when she was still in college and after that she was hooked. She became hands down SACAA's most dedicated International Social Worker. Her job entailed working with Social Services, and adoption agencies to help place orphaned children all around the world into permanent, safe, loving homes. She was assigned to the SACAA main office located in New York. Faith traveled extensively, but she always came back to SACAA's home base in New York. Her job involved going to various continents and countries where civil unrest, war and other atrocities had occurred. Once she arrived at her assigned country her duties were to locate all children who had become displaced and orphaned and facilitate their rescue, get them to a SACAA safe house and then initiate the process to attempt to place them in safe, loving homes internationally. She follow the leads she received from various sources that helped them find children who lives were in jeopardy, and who parents had abandoned them or had died. Once the children were found she had to get them to one of SACAA's safe houses until the international laws were complied with or dealt with in the most expeditious way. Faith would sometimes need to stay in the host country for months at a time before returning back to New York. Her unofficial job description sometimes included the making of bribes, the falsifying of paperwork and the collection of friends in good and bad places. Not until these various tasks were completed, then last but not least, the final task of finding adoptive homes was finally initiated for the children by Faith. In the process of doing her job, she had most likely broken many different laws in many different countries. It was something she wasn't proud of, but something she also considered a necessary evil in saving the children she considered to be her sole responsibility. But no one at SACAA really wanted to know how Faith got her job done. All anyone really cared about was that she *did* always get the job done. And Faith was well known in the organization to get the job done well and quick. SACAA never once questioned her actions, they only applauded her results. Faith loved her job it was her passion and she had always felt compelled to do something with her life where she was saving or helping orphaned children, orphans like she and her missing sisters were.

Faith often had reoccurring dreams that she was running from something while carrying small children in her arms. In her dreams one little child sat on her back and held on to her neck while she ran with him, and there were even more children following behind her and in front of her. She was always surrounded by more children than it seemed capable of her helping. In the dream she was the only one; the only one who could save all these children. She always felt like she was smothering, failing and drowning, and that she and the children were not going to survive without some help. No matter how much she screamed for help to come in her dreams, no one came to help her and the children. Then the children would suddenly start to just die, one by one. The reoccurring nightmare seemed so real while she was dreaming it. Over and over she would wake up in a cold sweat. After the dream was all over she could never remember, what it was that her and the children in her dreams were running from or towards.

Faith always woke up, before she smothered to death from all the little arms around her neck choking her, and hanging on to her for help so tightly. The dreams had started when she was still a child, after her first trip to Africa. Her parents had sent her to a therapist growing up to help her to understand why she always had these nightmares. All the therapist did was ask her more and more questions. Eventually the therapist diagnosed Faith with having post-traumatic stress disorder, separation anxiety, etc., etc." The therapist told her parents that Faith's nightmares were probably due to the fact that Faith lost her sisters, and then lost the friends she had made while in Africa.

Now that Faith was an adult, even after all the therapy sessions she had as a child she still never stopped having the reoccurring nightmares. Tonight was no different from most nights. Faith, awoken from her familiar dream drenched in sweat. For a second she had to regain her bearings because she forgot where she was at. It only took her a few seconds to realize she was back home, in her apartment in New York. Her once childhood friend and now boyfriend, Darryl was sleeping next to her, snoring, and oblivious to her nightmare. She thought to herself, "Darryl has been snoring ever since I can remember, back when we were kids and had backyard camp outs. I should really get him some breathing strips." Then she got out of the bed quietly to get a glass of water and she was very careful not to wake Darryl up. If he knew she had just had another nightmare, he would be up the rest of the night just staring at her; as if him staying awake would keep her from having bad dreams. Darryl was like that, so protective. He had been protective of her long before they had ever started dating each other, and that was only one of the many reasons she loved him. Faith wished she could fall back to sleep peacefully next to Darryl, but she knew she wasn't going to be able to go back to sleep. So she might as well go ahead and start quietly packing for the trip she had volunteered at the last minute to leave for the following day, for SACAA. Her extensive travels made it hard to be in a relationship with any man, but Darryl was not just any man.

The two of them had been best friends since they were kids. He never pressured her about anything, not even the lack of time she sometimes had to spend with him although once in a while he did complain. The only slight pressure he placed on her was the repeated reminders of wanting to marry her one day. Faith was scared to death about marriage. Although she couldn't really explain what it was about marriage that scared her so much, she was definitely afraid of tying the knot. Lately, she secretly dreaded Darryl was going to officially pop the question, instead of informally hinting around about it. So every time she saw him reaching into his pocket or kneeling down to pick something up, she panicked. She thought, "oh God this is it, what do I say". It wasn't that she didn't love Darryl; she just didn't love the idea of marriage.

Faith remembered the first day she met Darryl. She had just been brought home by her new parents and it had only been two days after Nana's death. All Faith could think of was that her Nana was dead and she was separated from her sisters. To Faith her whole world had been destroyed. Faith was walking up to her new home feeling so alone. Then suddenly a ball hit her upside her head. It was a soft beach ball, and the hit didn't hurt Faith's head at all, but she still started crying. But she wasn't crying about the hit to her head, she was crying because she missed her sisters and her Nana so much that it was unbearable. Then a skinny boy came running up to her. He was very concerned. He said he was sorry, and he pleaded with her to stop crying. While he was asking her to stop crying, he asked her what her name was, but Faith was not paying him any attention at all. She was only thinking about her Nana. Through her sobs she whispered out in her baby voice "Nana, Nana".

Darryl found it hard to understand her and he thought Faith was answering his question and telling him her name was "Nene". Darryl was an only child and he had always wished he had a younger sibling. He instantly felt protective over little Nene and he wanted to take care of her like a little sister. Faith's parents assured Darryl not to worry that it was only an accident and that she wasn't hurt. Then they carried her inside, and Darryl ran after them saying, "I hope you feel better little "Nene". When you do you can come over and play with me."

As Darryl got to know Faith better he looked upon her as the little sister he never had, he would have preferred a brother, but he never told Faith that. He taught Faith how to play soccer, baseball, basketball, football, and even how to skate and play hockey.

He enjoyed sharing his four additional years of worldly wisdom about life with little Nene. Faith looked up to him the way younger sisters do with their big brothers. The two kids also shared a unique and almost eerie bond, because they were both, adopted. Darryl had been adopted as a baby, and he had never known his biological parents. His adopted family was the only family he had ever known, unlike Faith who at six years old still remembered her Nana and sisters and that always left a gaping hole in her heart.

Although Darryl was popular in school he still had compassion for everything Faith faced as the new girl that everyone knew was adopted. Darryl would tell the kids not to mess with his little sister and he referred to Faith with another name that he said no one else at school was allowed to call her, Nene. Darryl's nickname for Faith had never changed from what he thought she was saying her name was on the first day he met her. Eventually their parents became very close with one another, despite their religious differences. It was Darryl's parents that encouraged Faith's parents to consider adopting when they had experienced their fourth miscarriage. After Faith was adopted the two families shared something in common. So despite their vast differences in lifestyles and religious beliefs, they still became very close friends, so much so that Faith's parents asked Darryl's parents to become Faith's godparents. It was almost like the two of them were really sister and brother, until something unexpected happened one night.

They say the only thing you can expect out of life is the unexpected. One day Darryl was home from his senior year in college. He was planning on taking a long relaxing summer break from school work before starting his first semester of Medical School in September. He hadn't been home long enough to go say hello to his old friends, or to even unpack his bags, when his mother yelled for him to come downstairs.

Faith was getting ready for her senior prom. She was never the most popular girl in school. She had always been the strange, outcast girl. So she felt grateful to have found a date for the prom. It wasn't that she wasn't pretty, but boys rarely talked to her, and she rarely talked to them. So she was surprised when a very handsome boy from her biology class had asked her to the prom. They were lab partners, but they had never even had a conversation outside of class. She was so relieved to not have to break it to her mother that she didn't have a date for prom, and she was actually very happy to have gotten a date because she really did want to go to her prom.

On prom night she was waiting at the house for her date to show up and she was looking perfect and pretty in pink, just like a magazine ad in *Seventeen*. Then at the last minute her date had called and cancelled over the phone. He didn't even have the guts to do it personally. Her mother had picked the phone up and he just told her to tell Faith he had come down with the flu. Faith had seen him earlier that day at school and he had looked fine. So she didn't believe he was sick for one second. She tried to hide her disappointment from her mother, because she knew her mother would be even more hurt than she was if she saw her crying, but still she couldn't stop the tears from welling up in her eyes. So she just went running up the stairs to her room. She yelled behind her that she didn't want to talk about it, with anyone, "that it wasn't a big deal".

Her mother didn't know what to do, but she knew she had to do something. She ran over to the phone, and she called up the first person she thought could help, Darryl's mother. She told her how Faith had just been stood up on her senior prom night. Darryl's mother wasn't about to let her goddaughter miss her prom.

"Darryl!!!! Don't you hear me calling you? Get down here boy."

Darryl came rushing down the stairs thinking something was terribly wrong with his mother. When he reached the bottom of the stairs his mother explained the situation to him like it was the end of the world and she demanded he get himself fixed up, and go right next door to take Faith to her prom.

Darryl didn't even try to object to his mother's demands, he knew by the tone of her voice she wasn't taking "no" for an answer. Plus he could think of a thousand worse things to be doing on a Friday night than spending it with the little girl next door, who he always considered his little sister. At school he was usually studying most Friday nights anyways. He could hardly wait to start teasing Faith about how she was practically going to her prom with her brother. Yeah, this was going to be fun. When he thought about it he couldn't remember ever seeing little Nene ever wear a real dress before. While he headed back up the stairs to get ready, he said, "fine, I'll take her, but let me remind you Mother, I'm not a boy anymore I'm a grown man."

That night Darryl felt speechless when he watched Faith walk down the steps in her prom dress. It was like he was looking at a totally different person from the girl he had watched grow up next door to him all those years. He knew from that moment on he would never see Nene as his little sister anymore. His little Nene from next door, had grown into a beautiful, sexy young woman that he was definitely attracted to. For the first time he felt nervous in her presence, and drawn to her in a way he was never before. He realized he couldn't take his eyes off of her and that was when he started to feel a little self conscious.

He hoped that neither of her parents noticed how he was looking at their daughter. He thought to himself, "I'm acting crazy, after all this is Nene." So he resigned himself to keep what he was feeling in check. Nene was barely eighteen years old. He decided he would keep his new found feelings for her to himself, at least until it seemed like it was the right moment to tell her how he felt.

So when Faith got to the bottom of the stairs Darryl had composed himself and he simply said, "you clean up pretty good Nene."

"So do you, and by the way thanks for not teasing me about your Mom forcing you to take me to my prom at the last minute like this."

"Who says I wasn't going to tease you? You didn't give me a chance to get any in yet."

"That's why I'm thanking you in advance, for not teasing me, *get it*? I'm *really* not in the mood for any jokes about me getting stood up tonight."

"Got it, you can tell me in the limousine how you got stood up. Now let's get going, my mother says my pay doesn't start until I get you out the front door and you know I need all the money I can get, medical school is expensive."

Faith rolled her eyes and then gave Darryl a look that could kill.

"Okay I'm sorry. I couldn't resist. But I promise that's my first and last joke about you getting stood up and me getting paid to take you out on a date, okay."

Faith giggled and said, "well I have to admit it is sort of funny."

Then the two of them headed out to the limousine that Faith's father had rented for his little girl's special night and Faith's mother made them pause first to pose for pictures.

At the prom Darryl and Faith were enjoying themselves, almost as if it was a real date. Darryl was telling Faith all about what college life was like, and Faith loved it, she couldn't wait to leave High School behind and go off to college.

As each moment went by Darryl had to constantly remind himself that he was with, little Nene. But it was very difficult to convince his self of that when she was obviously all grown up. Every move she made was sensual without her even knowing it, from the way her lips moved when she spoke to the scent that came off of her every time she tossed her long hair back with her soft hands. He reminded himself constantly that he had to keep his hands from touching her soft skin or brushing her beautiful hair, or caressing the small of her perfectly smooth back that was bare in her backless gown. Then she asked him to dance with her because there was a fast song on that she liked. Darryl told her he wasn't a good dancer, and didn't really like to do it. But the truth was Darryl was nervous about being so close to her, the dance floor was really crowded and it was taking all his will power to keep his hands off of her as it was already. He really didn't need to add the temptation of a crowded dance floor to the equation. But Faith insisted she was going to dance at least one time at her prom. So she grabbed Darryl's hand and led him into the middle of the crowded dance floor. Darryl thought at least the song is a fast song.

They were having fun dancing until Faith saw the guy that cancelled on her walk into the auditorium with another girl. At first she panicked, she felt embarrassed. She was thinking she didn't want this guy to see her, but then she realized looking over at Darryl, how handsome Darryl was, and he was obviously older than the other high school boys there. So Faith waited for the young man who had stood her up that night to see her. As soon as she saw she had caught his attention she suddenly grabbed Darryl close to her, and kissed him on the lips. The way Faith looked that night, and the way she had planted that kiss on Darryl had definitely gotten the guy's attention. It got Darryl's attention too.

At first Darryl was in shock by Faith's sudden kiss. He kept his eyes open, as Faith kissed him right on the lips in the middle of the dance floor. But then Faith pulled her lips away and whispered, "please play along he's here, the guy who stood me up." And Darryl understood, the kiss was just for show. The song had changed and now it was a slow couples' only song. Darryl, saw his opportunity and he decided to take it.

"Well if you really want me to, I'll play along. Let us make this a really good show for him." Darryl held Faith's body closer to him, he placed his hands firmly on the small of her back, and he kissed her again on the lips, but this time he closed his eyes, and he allowed himself to let go when they kissed.

Faith felt something she really wasn't expecting. She had never felt like this before when she had kissed other boys. This time she felt passion. She had forgotten where the two of them were, and that they were in the middle of a dance floor surrounded by people. She vaguely overheard herself let out a low, soft moan. She felt like their bodies were about to burn up with the feel of the heat between them. She had kissed other boys before, but when she kissed Darryl she felt something she had never felt before, something she never even dreamed existed. She felt her heart feel like it was getting ready to burst, and when he kissed her she felt the rest of the world disappear. In a few moments she understood fully, all the romantic Shakespearian tragedies they made her read in English class.

After that kiss was over the two looked into each other's eyes, and Faith suddenly felt a little terrified. Faith was terrified about what she was feeling, and what these feelings would do to her longtime friendship with Darryl, and terrified that for the first time in her post puberty life she understood why girls wanted to have sex with their boyfriends all the time. Most of all she felt terrified because Darryl was staring into her eyes, and for the first time since the first day she had met him, she didn't know what to say.

Darryl, knowing Faith so well could already tell she was scared about what would happen next. He instinctively grabbed her and pulled her close to him and whispered in her ears. "Nene, no I mean, Faith, I guess you are not a little girl anymore, are you?"

"No I'm not."

"Did you feel that, I mean did you feel it too, because I felt something, something…"

"Yeah, I felt it too."

The two of them were whispering and short of breath from their passionate kiss. Darryl couldn't help himself from rubbing his lips across Faith's earlobes as he whispered into her ear. Faith felt chills going up and down her spine. She knew she never wanted him to stop holding her, just like he was holding her right now.

"… I don't know how to explain it Faith, but I want you probably more than you want me right now I'm sure, but I'm willing to wait for as long as you want me to wait. We've known each other forever. We will always be friends; that will never change. So don't worry, no rush, no pressure, cause I'll always be here for you, I'm not going anywhere." Then Darryl felt Faith exhale, and he felt her body totally relax in his arms, and he kissed her again. This time, this kiss was mutual and initiated all for them, and not to make another boy jealous.

It seemed like that kiss lasted forever, and like they were the only two people in the room. And it actually must have lasted a pretty long time, because eventually, Ms. Fargo, the guidance counselor, tapped Darryl and Faith on the shoulder and said, "I think the two of you need to cool it off and maybe go get a drink of punch, or go run some cold water on your faces."

They looked at each other and started laughing. They had not only attracted the attention of the guy who stood Faith up, but they had attracted the attention of the whole dance floor. As they walked off the floor someone chuckled, "go get a room guys, what the heck it is prom night." They spent most of the rest of the night kissing each other, holding each other, and trying their best not to imagine making love to each other when they slow danced on the dance floor.

When the prom was over most of the kids went to after parties at the various hotels. Faith's parents trusted Faith completely and they did not expect her home until the wee morning hours. They knew their daughter had a good head on her shoulders, that she didn't drink or do drugs, and they also knew that Faith was not even barely interested in having sex with anyone. They were even less worried about Faith that night considering she ended up going out with the boy next door who they trusted as if he was their own son. However, they never counted on their daughter discovering she was in love that night, and in love with the same boy who had been her best friend next door for most of her childhood.

Darryl would have never betrayed Faith's parents trust in him. However, unlike Darryl, who had already decided he would take things slow, Faith had decided to do things quite differently. Faith had always been impulsive, spontaneous and a person of action and passion. This moment was no different for her, and something Faith had very little of was patience. She had her own plans. So she whispered to the limo driver something that Darryl didn't hear before she got into the car. Darryl really wasn't expecting much more out of the night, except for maybe a promise of a date the next night. He knew Faith was four years younger than he was, and he would have never tried to take advantage of her.

When the limousine came to a stop Darryl reluctantly pulled away from Faith. He thought they were in front of Faith's house and he didn't want her parents to see them kissing. After he caught his breath he began to say his goodbyes to Faith for the night. "Well this was some night, we better get ourselves together in case your folks are waiting up for you." Darryl started fixing his tie and shirt. Then when he looked out the window of the limousine he realized they were not parked in front of Faith's house, but the limo sat in front of the Marriot Hotel. Darryl looked at Faith a little confused. "Oh, you didn't say you planned on going to one of the after parties at the hotel."

Faith grinned at Darryl. "I'm planning on attending more of a private party, care to join me?"

Darryl thought to himself, "wow this is a whole other side I've never seen in Nene." He'd never pictured her being like this, fast. In fact he kind of thought she was still a virgin. He realized by the look on her face that he had been quiet a little too long. She'd looked a little like she was hurt that he had not agreed yet. He didn't want to hesitate a moment longer and he followed her into the hotel. She led him to the front desk where she checked in.

Once the two of them were in the hotel room, Faith said she wanted to just freshen up a little and she went into the bathroom. As Darryl was waiting for her he started feeling guilty about the age difference between him and Faith; and about betraying Faith's parents' trust in him.

Faith was also in the bathroom having second thoughts, not from guilt but just uncertainty about losing her virginity. She remembered how much she had wanted her first time to be on her wedding night, and all the talks her and her mother had about it. Her mother always told her that her virginity was a precious thing a gift to be given only to her true love. Darryl was the first boy Faith had ever found herself so attracted to, to want to give up her virginity. However, Faith always imagined saving herself for her husband, and she wasn't sure if she wanted to give up that dream yet. She couldn't see that far into her future, she couldn't say definitely if Darryl would indeed be, "her husband", one day. She just didn't know. She thought to herself, "but how do I come out of this bathroom after dragging him to a hotel room by surprise, and then tell him, well, I've changed my mind. What do I say, sorry for being such a tease. Still friends?" Then Faith heard Darryl knocking on the bathroom door.

"Nene, before you come out I have to tell you something."

"What's that?" She was hoping he would say he didn't have any condoms on him, but she thought he's a college student he probably never goes anywhere without one on him.

"Well Nene, I want you to know that I want to make love to you so bad tonight. But, I feel sort of guilty about it and I don't want you to think I don't want you, because I do. Also I sort of thought you were a virgin, and if you are I just want to make sure your first time is exactly the way you imagined it, and if you aren't a virgin well I would still want to make sure the first time that *we* made love it was perfect, and not something you may regret later on. Like I said to you back at the dance, I'm willing to wait as long as you want to wait, no rush. After all, what's happened between us is all so sudden and new."

Faith didn't answer Darryl she was too busy feeling relieved. He was scared too, for different reasons, but still he sounded as scared as she did, about the prospect of them having sex. She couldn't believe how wonderful Darryl was, and how she wasn't able to see how much she really loved him before this night. She knew any other boy would not have taken the time to think about how she really felt about having sex.

"Nene is everything okay in there? You haven't said anything. You haven't passed out in there or something, have you?"

Faith couldn't help but laugh at that, and she finally came out of the bathroom. "I'm fine. I was having second thoughts about it too. I just didn't know how to tell you."

The two of them started laughing together. And then Faith blurted out, "you know Darryl I think I love you. I mean I've always loved you, but I think I'm in love with you, do you think I'm crazy?"

"Nene you've always been a little crazy but I'm crazy too because I know I'm in love with you. I knew it the moment I saw you come down those stairs tonight in that dress. I guess we've always loved each other, we just didn't realize that love could turn into something, well into this, but I swear to God I feel like I'm in love with you, like I was meant to spend the rest of my life with you." Then he grabbed her and kissed her once again.

She felt and aching and longing in places she had never felt before. But she was still scared and she caught her breath and pulled away from him. "Darryl, by the way, I am a virgin, and I've always imagined saving my virginity as a present for my future husband. Until now I tonight I never realized how hard that promise would be to keep."

"Do you want me to take you home?"

"No."

"OK then, I promise you where you are weak I'll be strong. I will make sure you leave here with your virginity."

Faith laughed at him, because he said it with such conviction and it was so overly dramatic

The two of them spent the rest of the night and many nights after that kissing and holding and loving each other, without letting their love for each other turn into sex. It was a wonderful, carefree, romantic summer of first love.

However, when it was time for Faith to go off to college and for Darryl to go to medical school the two eventually drifted apart after the middle of their first semesters. They both knew the distance that had grown between them emotionally was because of Faith. Faith could not imagine the two of them being in a long distance relationship with each other. Darryl tried to reassure her that he could wait, and that he wanted no one else, she couldn't believe him. So she started to distance herself from him. She stopped returning his phone calls and she made up excuses to avoid seeing him whenever he said he wanted to drive up and visit her at her college.

Darryl was heart-broken. He poured all his hurt into his school work. Medical school kept him busy enough with all its' demands. Also, deep down, Darryl knew Faith was really just afraid of how close they were getting. He had known Nene practically her entire life, and she couldn't fool him no matter how hard she tried. Whenever he saw her or spoke to her he could tell she was still in love with him. So he told himself he would be patient, it was just a matter of time. After all she was much younger than he was. He knew in his heart that one day they would end up together. They stayed friends as they had always promised each other they would and they continued to keep in contact with each other over the years. They saw each other every holiday as the years went by, whenever they both would visit their parents. Both had other people they had dated over the years, but neither of them ever fell in love with anyone else.

Once Faith graduated from college she got a job working with the SACAA organization and an apartment in the city. Darryl had conveniently rented an apartment very close to Faith's. They were practically neighbors, and Darryl took advantage of this opportunity by stopping by Faith's place unannounced to take her out for coffee, dinner, or just to take a walk around the city. They exchanged keys in case of emergencies, and Darryl always checked on Faith's place when she was out of town. It was all quite innocent at first being that they had always remained friends. So the close proximity made it easier to stay in touch with each other when Faith was in town. When Faith wasn't in town, and was across the world with her job at SACAA, they kept in touch by text messages, emails and phone calls. Eventually Faith's defenses broke down and she admitted to Darryl and to herself that she was in fact, still in love with him. The two of them embarked once again on a romantic relationship. Darryl wasn't surprised when Faith told him she was still after all those years, a virgin. He knew in his heart that Faith never stopped loving him. But he made sure he kept the promise he had made to Faith on her prom night. He continued to be patient, and he still didn't put any pressure on her about them having sex. He told himself he was fine with abstaining, because he still believed that one day Faith, his "Nene", would be his bride, despite her avoidance when he brought up the subject of marriage.

Faith made it clear that she wasn't in any rush to change things with marriage. It was the perfect relationship for someone like her. It was not so perfect for someone like Darryl, but Darryl loved Faith so much he was willing to accept whatever she gave him, versus not having her at all. Besides, being a doctor kept him distracted plenty. And with the death of his mother he had become obsessed with finding out who his biological mother was; something he had never cared about knowing in the past. Darryl's father refused to discuss the matter with him. Darryl did not press the issue with his father because he assumed it was his father's grief that was making him act so irrational whenever he brought up the subject of finding his biological mother. Darryl understood his father's grief, because he also felt like no one could ever replace his mother, so he had not pushed the subject with his father in years.

Faith had finally finished packing and now she just stared at Darryl while he slept. She thought about crawling back into the bed with him and trying to fall back to sleep. But he had such an annoying snore she didn't know how he slept so peacefully through it, and then she wondered how she would deal with that snoring for the rest of her life. She giggled at the thought, and felt a sudden overwhelming love for him. She always felt like that when it was time to leave him again. She questioned why she was crazy enough to leave this fine man behind, without a ring on his finger. She didn't know why she didn't just marry him already. She loved everything about him and she had loved his parents too.

His mother's death had hit her almost as hard as it had hit him. Faith remembered what Darryl's mother told her before she died, she said, "you are destined to be my son's wife." Then she gave her, her wedding ring and she told Faith to, "always believe in her son's love for her." That was Faith's last memory of Darryl's mother, her beloved Godmother. Faith had never told Darryl about the ring his mother had gave her, it was all too much pressure she felt, on herself. So she decided she would hold on to it until the right time came around to give it to Darryl.

Darryl was everything she could ever want. He was so patient with her, understanding, kind and loving.

In fact, just that night he tried to surprise her with a vacation he was planning for the two of them in Hawaii. Faith had told him a while back that she would be off all week, because the agency was making her use some of her accumulated vacation time. But then she took on a last minute assignment, when her co-worker came down sick and couldn't go. She was so selfish she never thought twice about letting Darryl know about it. She didn't realize how much he planned his own life around her. She felt like a real jerk when she had to tell him she couldn't go to Hawaii with him. She could see how disappointed he was, although he tried to hide it. She wanted to make him happy and marry him, in her hearts of hearts, but something just kept holding her back. She didn't think it would be fair to marry him and still do what she did with SACAA, and be gone all the time. Sure she could take a job or make a lateral transfer within SACAA where she stayed based in New York and did not travel, but she felt compelled to keep doing what she did. She was afraid to tell Darryl the threatening positions she put herself in sometimes on her many assignments, because she did not want him to worry. She wondered sometimes how he put up with her, she knew she was self-absorbed, compulsive, obsessive about her job, and very anxious about everything, so much so, that she found it impossible most times to just do nothing and relax.

Darryl on the other hand was so laid back, especially considering he was a doctor. He always slept like a log, without interruption, and never seemed to worry much about anything. Sometimes she wondered how they could be so different but so much alike at the same time.

For instance she was never a good sleeper. She routinely went months with maybe four hours a sleep a night. When most women were peacefully cuddling up with their partners at night, Faith was sitting up watching Darryl sleep, while her mind raced with thoughts about what she had to do tomorrow or the next week.

It was very early in the morning when Darryl finally opened his eyes. Faith kissed him and said, "good morning sunshine." Faith was already showered, packed and dressed.

She had a habit of being meticulously early to everything. "I'm sorry I gotta go Darryl. You do know how much I love you and I'm so sorry about Hawaii, I'm really going to miss you. I promise you I will make it up to you. I promise."

"Don't worry Faith you don't need to make it up to me." Darryl's tone was short and sarcastic, especially when he said her given name, Faith. He usually called her Nene. Faith felt a deep sting in her heart. She thought, "I've finally pushed him too far."

Darryl saw the hurt look in her eyes he realized he shouldn't have pretended to be upset and that she had taken him seriously. "Yeah, what I mean is you don't have to make it up to me because I've decided I'm going with you. Just give me a minute to shower. I'm already packed anyway for Hawaii. I've got a passport in my wallet, plenty of credit and cash and I've already taken a week off for vacation, why not just go with you? I guess you are going to have company on this work assignment and I guess Hawaii will have to wait for another time. Good thing I thought ahead to get myself a passport when you first took this job with SACAA. I figured it would come in handy one day. So I guess this also means I'll finally find out what the heck it is you do for a living Nene?"

Faith thought to herself, "This man is truly amazing. I would be crazy to let him get away." "Well you better get moving, you know how crazy the airport customs are now a days, and I hate rushing and being late. Oh that's right you don't know how crazy it is, you've never flown before! Oh my God this is going to be your first time on an airplane. Who knows if you will even be able to get a ticket on the same plane as me last minute like this, there is so much to do..." Faith was so happy that Darryl was coming with her and so anxious thinking about all the details that needed to be attended to, but Darryl just felt happy and relaxed. He wasn't worried he knew everything would work out fine. Plus he figured he'd save his worrying for the plane ride because he never was a fan of flying. He had mentally prepared himself for his first flight to Hawaii, flying to Africa he was not prepared for, but he would go to the ends of the Earth for his Nene.

Chapter 6
Love's New Assignment

Love had just finished reading her magazine when John walked into the ladies restroom.

"Love there you are, what are you doing? You weren't even using the bathroom, were you? Don't you hear the partners summoning you for the last twenty minutes to the board room?"

Love and John had formed a bond because they were the only black attorneys at the firm, they started at relatively the same time, and they were also around the same age. They were very competitive with each other, but also they both knew when it came right down to it they had each other's back. They had many late night sessions together at the office, and it was clear there was definitely a strong attraction between them. However, Love never dared act on her feelings towards John. Love didn't have a problem with sleeping around, but she did have a problem with sleeping around at work. She never wanted to do anything to tarnish her professional reputation at the firm. So herself and John just enjoyed playful office flirtation, and gradually they became close platonic friends.

Love gave John a "you're really annoying me stare", and she said, "of course I heard the intercom, can't a girl use the restroom around here without being stalked. Oh you are aware you are in the women's restroom aren't you?" Then Love got up and followed John to the board room where the partners were waiting.

"You're not even going to wash your hands are you? Don't try to hand me any food at this reception, Love."

"Shut up John, I didn't even go to the bathroom in there, you know I was only hiding out."

When the two of them got to the boardroom Love saw on the boardroom table there was a big spread of cake and other treats. First thing Love thought was she wished she didn't use up all her calories on that twinky, now she was going to have to work out an extra hour tonight if she ate anymore sweets. Love eyed the sweets trying to decide which one was the best. Then she caught Mr. Swanson the senior partner smiling at her affectionately.

Mr. Swanson had always thought Love was just the sweetest, smartest, and most delightful young lady lawyer he had ever met. He praised her accomplishments at the firm as if she was his own daughter, and in fact he looked at her like the daughter he had never had.

What Love adored about Mr. Swanson the most was how he obviously thought of her, and it made her work even harder to never let him down. Love was usually very open and unashamed about her liberal attitude towards sex, except around Mr. Swanson. He was sort of a father figure to her and she only wanted him to see her as a perfect young lady.

Mr. Swanson walked over to Love and gave her a gentle pat on the back. He was grinning from ear to ear, but Love didn't think anything of that, he was always in an exceptionally good mood.

"So John you finally found our young associate Ms. Love King, or shall I say our Junior Partner, Ms. King?"

When Love heard the words partner come out of Mr. Swanson's mouth, it made her totally forget about that cake on the board room table. She thought they were throwing another one of their "let's all celebrate, eat and get drunk because Love just won that case that earned our firm another million dollars." But this celebration was different, this was her, you have arrived celebration. She was finally, a partner, well technically "junior partner", but that was okay with her. All she wanted to do was contact her realtor about purchasing that beach house, and call her girlfriends up so she could treat them to a drinking and partying celebration that night. She was already trying to figure which man in her little black book would be most appropriate to end the night with; it had to be someone really spectacular.

All the attorneys and paralegals and legal assistants were there and they all hugged and congratulated Love and she could truly not think of a time when she felt more accepted and adored by her peers. As everyone settled down and started chit chatting and eating and drinking Love sat and daydreamed about the first time she could remember feeling like everyone admired and accepted her, it had to be when she first started college. Before college she didn't have many friends. Love had always been the nerd all throughout school. College is where Love started changing into the confident woman she was today. College is also when Love first started writing in journals. The journal was originally an assignment her creative writing teacher gave her in freshmen year, but Love continued it pass the freshman class and still wrote in her journals every day. Love had thought about becoming a writer, but she didn't think she would make money doing it. She obtained her undergraduate degree in English and International Studies, but instead of pursuing a writing career she opted to attend Harvard law school. At the time she couldn't think of anything better to do. She scored high on her LSAT's and she received a full scholarship to attend. Several of her friends from college were also accepted into the same law school. Although Love was very popular she never allowed herself to get but too close to anyone in college. She trusted no one completely. Her current friends in California didn't really know the true Love, where she was from, or about her past. Her true identity was contained only in her memories, and the pages of her journals. Her journals almost became her best friend. It was the only place she felt comfortable enough to disclose her inner most thoughts, secrets and fears. Her journals had become her confidant and her therapy. Unlike most of her Hollywood friends, Love didn't believe in psychologist. Her friends all thought she was a little crazy and really needed to see a shrink. But she didn't think so, although she did admire how much money psychiatrist made doing what they did; she just wasn't ever going to give any of them her hard earned money. Besides her journal writing was the only time she felt like she was actually doing something she loved. Deep down she didn't really love practicing law, but what she did love was the winning cases, the respect and recognition she received from all her wins, and most of all she loved the money she was paid for doing something that came so easy to her. On the other hand, Love enjoyed writing so much she sometimes would do appeal briefs for other associates and partners just to past the time, if she didn't have a jury trial going on. She just loved writing, researching and reading.

Love thought to herself, "I sure have some good stuff to put in my journals tonight." Making partner was a big theme contained in many, many pages of her journals. It had been her most important goal for so many years now. She could hardly believe she had finally achieved it. Things had been going so well for Love lately in her career that the recent pages of her journal were filled with one legal success story after another. However, there were some journal entries that were not filled with happy entries of successes and dreams come true. Actually most of her past journal entries were just so painful that if she didn't journal it down her sub-conscience would have surely blocked them out forever.

Then Love's thoughts were interrupted by Mr. Swanson. Mr. Swanson walked over and sat next to Love. He started to tell her about her next assignment which was extremely important. He told her to follow him to his office so they could discuss it in private. Mr. Swanson must have been one of the only men Love could recall since college that had not ever made a pass at her or even a flirtatious comment to her. Mr. Swanson was also old enough to be Love's grandfather; but that had never stopped other men of his age from pursuing her. Love felt totally comfortable with Mr. Swanson, and she also felt the need to constantly please him, as if he really was her father. This fatherly fondness she had for him caused her to volunteer for the cases no one else wanted. She took them on partly to please him, but also partly because she wanted to make partner. When it came right down to it Love was still searching for that elusive father figure she never had and still trying to replace the emptiness in her life with her accomplishments. She was smart enough to realize this much on her own without any help from counseling. Love figured everyone in this world is messed up in some way, and she was no exception. She had the feeling that this meeting with Mr. Swanson, was going to include him asking her to take on one of those difficult cases, and she knew she would accept it. Love was sure Mr. Swanson's speech would start something like this, "Love you know you are our firm's most valuable asset, and because of that there are certain very sensitive cases and clients that I only trust in your hands." She had heard his speech many times before. Then she knew he would offer her one of his rare Cuban cigars. Then he would asked her to come sit on the balcony with him while he grabbed one of the many bottles of expensive brandy he kept in his office, and then he would offer her one of the two 14K gold and diamond engraved shot glasses he kept on his desk. It would be as he was pouring the brandy into their glasses that he would began going into the details of the case he wanted her to handle. It was like the dancers' warm up before a ballet. The warm up was going just as Love expected, now she was preparing herself for him to get to the main event. The two of them were enjoying the smoggy LA view of the beach from the balcony. Love had taken her first sip of the brandy in her glass. Then Mr. Swanson surprised her, and changed his routine, and he said "Love I was wondering, are you happy?"

Now this really caught Love off guard. She wondered, "is he dying." Mr. Swanson never asked her questions about her personal life. So she thought to herself, "oh he must be wondering if I am happy here at the firm, that's all." Love thought, "maybe he thinks I am looking at making a move and that's why he has made me partner." So she replied, "Am I happy? Why of course I'm happy Mr. Swanson. I love this firm, I love my job, and you have just made my dreams come true by making me the youngest partner in this firm's history. Seriously, who in my shoes wouldn't be happy?" Love hoped her answer would extinguish any doubt he may have had about her loyalty to the firm. Truthfully Love had no desires to go anywhere else. Love really did think that she was happy at the firm and her answer was a sincere and honest one.

But Mr. Swanson never doubted Love's devotion to the firm when he asked her if she was happy. For the first time he felt an interest in Love's personal happiness. So he responded to Love's obvious declaration of devotion to the firm by explaining the meaning behind his question. "Love I meant, are you really happy with your life. When you leave here and you go home tonight, will you still be happy? It's just that I'm concerned about you Love."

"Concerned about me, why?"

"I have heard a few rumors about your lifestyle."

Love wondered out loud, "rumors, what rumors?"

"Love, I'm going to just be frank with you but I've heard you really have a reputation shall I say as being a bit of a playboy, or in your case I guess the better term would be a playgirl. I know this is probably none of my business, but I'm sure you are very prudent in the area of protection, but I wonder about you being lonely or being alone. You see I've learned the hard way that no matter how much money you make and accumulate over the years it doesn't bring you happiness if there is no one around to spend it on, or better yet to spend it with. Love you know I have no children, no wife, the firm is my family. That's my fault. See I had a reputation for being a bit of a playboy in my days too, and every woman who ever fell in love with me I ended up breaking her heart. Also I'm actually incapable of having any children, have been all my life. However out of the 5 wives I had all of them wanted to adopt, but I wouldn't agree to it. I was too selfish. My view was my wife was there to devote her life to me and my desires, not to anyone else's needs, not even a child's needs. So sooner or later each wife left me because I was emotionally or physically unavailable."

Love tried to show she was listening intently, but inside she felt partly ashamed that Mr. Swanson had found out about her reputation. At the same time she felt an overwhelming, childlike love for him because no one had ever expressed such concern for her since her grandmother was alive. It had been so long since anyone asked Love if she was really happy. Love didn't say anything until after she thought Mr. Swanson was finished with his fatherly lecture, and advice.

"Mr. Swanson I hope that what you heard about me won't affect your personal or professional opinion of me, because your opinion means the world to me. But really you needn't be concerned. I am just not at a point in my life where I want to settle down with anyone. I love my job, and I'm not lonely, not at all."

"Okay then, Love if what you're saying is true let us talk about me. I guess I've become more sensitive because you see, I've met someone. I've met a wonderful woman, over the internet believe it or not. She lives in New York, in a small senior citizen community home, and the best thing about her is she has no idea that I'm so rich and even after seeing me in person she's still crazy about me. I've been visiting her and she is stunning for her age, and funny, and smart, but she has had a hard life. I've come to love her so much, and now all I want to do is take care of her for the duration of my life. I've been visiting her every weekend for the past two months. She thinks I'm a divorcee, which I am, but she also thinks that I live off of a nice little pension and savings, which isn't quite the truth. She doesn't even know my real last name. So I know she loves me for me and not my money."

Love thought to herself, that his behavior was totally unlike anything she had experienced from him before. He was always an open book. Although it was sort of second nature for most attorneys to be skilled at deception; Mr. Swanson always seemed to be so honest an open, someone with no personal secrets, and no hidden agendas. Love couldn't believe he was telling this lady he had met such lies.

"I know, what you must be thinking Love. It is very deceptive of me to not tell her the truth about myself. It started out innocently, she just assumed I was a senior citizen, someone of average income, living out their retirement years, and I never corrected her. At this stage of my life I'm looking for a true companion. I'm not looking for a beauty queen or a trophy wife. I'm looking for someone I can live the rest of my days with, and be assured that they love me just for me and not for my money. Anyway, this weekend she doesn't know it, but I'm going to propose to her and if she says yes then I will tell her the truth about my finances and of course my real last name, occupation, all my previous marriages, and all the other details I've left out about my life. But other than all those things, everything I feel about her is the truth, and that's what really matters, right?"

Love couldn't help but look at him with disbelief, was he really so romantically naïve.

"Oh jimity crickets she is not going to marry me when she finds out I've kept so much from her, is she?"

Love started laughing she had never seen Mr. Swanson look so vulnerable before. For the first time since Love had come to know him, he appeared to lack confidence about getting something he wanted. Mr. Swanson was a man accustomed to always getting what he wanted. And now it appeared to Love like he had just worked himself into a sudden panic in realizing that his new girlfriend just might not say yes to his upcoming marriage proposal. Love wanted to reassure him. "Mr. Swanson any woman who says no to you would have to be out of her mind. Don't worry of course she will say yes."

"You're right Love. But just to be on the safe side I have a plan and well Love this is where you come in and the assignment I am about to ask you to do for me isn't exactly firm business, but it is very important to me."

Love felt even more confused. She thought, "what could she possibly do to help him with this romantic crisis he was having?"

"You see, my girlfriend has a very hurtful past, which includes the fact that she gave up her only child for adoption when he was first born. This is her biggest regret. So one of her dreams is to find her son and ask him for forgiveness and to raise a child that no one wants, and then to give it all the things, and all the love that she never had. You see, I know all these things about her because one day we just played a game, *what would you do if you were a millionaire*, and she said she would use the money to take care of as many unwanted children as she could and then she told me about the child she had given up."

"That must have not been much of a challenging game for you, since you are already a billionaire?" teased Love.

Mr. Swanson smiled and went on with his story. "Well she also told me if she had a million dollars she would spare no expense and search the ends of the earth to find her son and some other loved ones she had lost over the years. She said she would tell her son how sorry she was she gave him up, and how she has thought about him every day. Then she would explain to him that she knew he would be better off with the people who adopted him, because at the time she was addicted to drugs and homeless. Love, when she said these were the only two things she would do if she was a millionaire, well it touched me on levels I didn't even know existed in me. So my plan is that after I ask her to marry me I want to be able to tell her I made her two biggest dreams come true, finding her son for her and adopting an unwanted child for us to raise together as husband and wife."

"Mr. Swanson that is such a wonderful thing for you to want to do for her, but what if she says no to your proposal, what will you do then with a child?"

"Love I've already decided that I love her so much it doesn't matter if she says no I will still bring her son to her so that she can meet him, and I am ready to be a father so I want to adopt a child not just for her, but for myself. You see just getting to know her and love her, has made me realize I am ready to open my heart and finally give all I have to someone else unselfishly. And I've also realized I am ready to retire from the firm."

Nothing else Mr. Swanson had said to Love today had shocked her more than that last statement. People like Mr. Swanson and Love, did not retire, they just died doing what they did as attorneys. Mr. Swanson was not a partner who just advised others; he was still in court litigating every day, and from what Love observed he loved doing it.

All Love could say was, "Wow".

"I know, Wow. I never thought I would want to retire one day. I always thought I would die doing what I do. But my priorities have changed Love. So you are probably wondering what it is I need you to do for me, right? You know you are one of our firms most valuable assets, and because of that there are certain very sensitive cases and clients that I only trust in your hands…..and this is why I'm sharing all of this personal information about my life with you, because I have a special assignment that I only trust you to take care of for me."

"Oh, and what is this assignment, coordinating your wedding plans, or your retirement party? Seriously Mr. Swanson, the suspense is killing me, and you already know your every wish is my command, but I really can't imagine what you would need me to do for you."

Mr. Swanson gave Love a warm smile, because he knew the words she had just spoke were sincere.

"Love I want you to handle finding my girlfriend's son, and finding a child I can adopt for us, all by this time next week. Well you actually have a little more than a week, eight days to be exact. You see I'm proposing to her next Sunday. We have a date for me to take her to church. She says it will be the first time she has step foot into a church in over thirty years. Anyway my plan is right after church service is done I want to get down on one knee and pop the question. I figure with a crowd around I'll have more success of getting a "yes". People are always more agreeable when under pressure by spectators."

Love smiled and thought, "now there is the Mr. Swanson I know and love, always thinking like a lawyer, and planning out his best strategy for success."

"After I pop the question, I would like you to be waiting in the wings with her son, and also our new bundle of joy. So what do you think about my plans, and what do you say about helping me carry them out?"

"Well I'm confused. This sounds like work for a detective and an adoption agency Mr. Swanson. Plus the time constraints also make it sound a little impossible. You want someone to find her long, lost son, and find a baby that some adoption agency will let you two adopt within the next nine days, impossible?"

"Actually that would be in the next seven days that I want "you" to do all this because I'm planning on proposing to her in exactly eight days from today."

Love looked at Mr. Swanson in amazement. "Okay, and then somehow I am suppose to get them to you, all tied up in a big ribbon for them to be there on the day you pop the question? It just all sounds, with all due respect, well just a little bit crazy, Mr. Swanson."

"I know, I know. It may sound crazy, but when you get to be my age, you don't try to waste any time when you have a dream that pops up in your head. If you have the means, you make that dream a reality as soon as possible, because you know that there is just no telling, life on this Earth is very, very short and you realize you've got to make the most of what you have left. Love I have a dream to marry this woman, and to make her dreams come true, and I am going to make it happen. Besides one thing I have learned over the years is that whatever I truly desire and go after I will get it, if I believe. Also Love, there is something else this old, crazy, geezer has, and that is lots and lots of money, connections, and people who owe me favors, and now I am ready to collect on those favors. Collecting on those

IOU's will now be at your disposal in completing this task I have given you. See there are some countries that I know of where I can actually adopt a child in less than a week if I desire to, and believe me I have connections as far as satellites can reach. But I can't do the leg work myself, I have promised her that I will be spending my vacation, all of next week with her. And I admit this idea of proposing next week and the very special gifts I plan on giving her were, sort of a spontaneous, actually I decided on it yesterday. But I had a dream, or a vision of the two of us married and surrounded by children the other night. I'm sorry that I have given you such an impossible deadline, with no offer to assist you with it myself. But she thinks I have spent my entire life fortune on a penthouse suite in Manhattan for us to vacation in this week. I can't disappoint her. But I know you Love and I know if anyone can get this done for me, it is you. I can't trust a detective or some adoption agency to work with the urgency and motivation I know that you will have, for me. You are also the only attorney, well the only person in my life right now that I trust enough to hand over full power of attorney for a whole week, for the purposes of getting this done for me. I have full confidence that you will never take advantage of the power I place in your hands, or that you would ever betray my trust. So I will be giving you full access to all my accounts cash and credit, my private jet and anything else you need to accomplish this for me. I know you are already are fully knowledgeable of International Law, and I'm sure you will get up to speed on Adoption Law in no time. Of course this is confidential business between me and you, but I am sending with you someone to assist, someone I know you trust, that would be John. He knows everything about this assignment also."

"John, why John?"

"I will feel more comfortable with John going with you. The two of you seem to work very well together. You ever notice he also seems to work out a lot. I heard he paid his way through college and law school doing the amateur boxing and fighting tours. He is also a black belt, very athletic. So besides his legal expertise, I also would feel better about him working with you concerning your safety in the different places you may have to travel in order to take care of this assignment for me. Of course after you have completed this assignment, there will be a sizeable bonus waiting for you and for John too. And I will be putting in my personal recommendation that you be given senior status as partner as soon as possible, despite the fact that there are others who have been here longer, eagerly waiting for senior status to be bestowed upon them, and John will be slated as next up when another junior partner slot becomes open. So what do you say to all of this, will you do this for me? But before you answer, this goes without saying that my request is a personal one, and if you decline I would never hold it against you."

Love was touched by the confidence and trust he had in her. She had no idea of this hidden romantic side of him and that touched her too. His fiancée was indeed a lucky woman. But most of all she was in awe that someone his age could still feel such passion for another person. For a moment, she secretly wished she could find a man who felt that same passion for her, and someone she could return those feelings to. Then Love briefly thought about Mr. Swanson's questions about her happiness and wondered if him sending John on this assignment with her was his way of trying to secretly be a little matchmaker himself. She quickly put that thought aside, because she wasn't trying to get tied down to anyone now that she was a partner, and maybe even looking at receiving senior status all in the same week. She thought to herself this day had truly turned out to be an incredible day. Then finally she got out of her own head and decided to stop over thinking everything, and just simply answer her mentor's question.

"Okay Mr. Swanson, I accept this impossible assignment. But of course you knew I would. I could never say no to you. Now I think…….., I'll need a list of all your connections and the countries that you know of that will allow a quick adoption to a crazy, old, unmarried man like you. If possible the name of your girlfriend, her long lost son and the adoption agency she went through. The power of attorney I'll need that ASAP, of course and anything else I need I can get your personal secretary to handle. Oh, don't worry I won't mention the personal nature of this assignment to her, if you don't want me to."

Mr. Swanson said approvingly, "now that's the spirit, but there is just one little thing I forgot to mention to you which may make this assignment a little tricky."

"Oh something you forgot to mention. Somehow that doesn't surprise me. What is it?"

Mr. Swanson took a swig of his brandy. "Well knowing the name of my girlfriend will not really help you. You see the adoption, her giving her baby away, was not done by legal means. My girlfriend... Let me explain, at the time she was pregnant she was actually going by a street name then, and she also sort of sold her son on the black market; I guess that's what you would call it anyway. So there was actually no adoption agency involved, or Social Services. You see she was addicted to drugs and she was also a prostitute at the time she gave birth to her son." Mr. Swanson noticed how Love's eyes grew ten times wider as he talked. "Please don't think badly of her Love. She is not the same person she was back then. She says she was essentially being held hostage at the time by her dealer/pimp. Now she does recalls the name of the dealer who set up the "adoption", for lack of finding a better word for it. She recalls where he was located and some minor details about the people they sold her baby to. She says the couple paid for her freedom and her baby's freedom from the dealer. She told me they were a nice couple who couldn't have children of their own."

"They couldn't have been that nice. How did they end up getting involved with a drug dealer and a pimp in the first place Mr. Swanson?"

"Well from what she tells me they were at a local restaurant eating at the time she went into labor. One of the other prostitutes went running out and went into the restaurant yelling that she needed a doctor. The girl got the couple to follow her. The husband told her that he was a doctor, and his wife was a nurse. They delivered the baby and promised to come back and check on her and the baby, which they did. She knew she couldn't raise the baby and asked them if they would raise him. She says they asked her several times if she was sure about giving him up. She told them over and over again she didn't want the baby. They told her they would raise her baby up to know that his real mother loved him and that was why she gave him away. She never received any money from all this, but the couple paid her dealer a considerable amount of money to let her leave with her baby. She refused to take any money from the couple because she didn't want them thinking she gave away her baby for money. But the couple was kind; they paid for her to stay in a clean room at a hotel for a month and brought her new clothes. She says she always thought about her son she gave away, but she just wasn't in a position to care for the child and she knew he would be better off without her."

"Mr. Swanson, did she ever get her son's adopted parents names?"

"No she didn't. Not their last names anyway. She said they were African American and that they told her they lived in the suburbs, in a place called, Roosevelt, Long Island. Actually she said she thought they had let that slip out on mistake, because they seemed to be very scared being that they were doing something illegal. So, that's it Love, that's everything I know and now you know it. Oh and my girlfriend's street name I guess is more important for you to know since that is the only name she gave them, she called herself "Princess". That's the name she gave the couple the name they would have known her by. She said she never picked out a name for her son, because she didn't want to feel attached to him in anyway. I also have a DNA sample in the safe belonging to her, and don't ask me how I got that without her knowing about it. But you can have a doctor test her DNA along with the young man's DNA once you find him, to confirm he is her son. We don't want to drag the wrong person into all of this because that would only cause more pain. You have to understand Love that she grew up all her life with people raping her emotionally, and physically. She never had anyone show her love, except for one old friend who eventually inspired her to get off drugs and straighten her life out. But by the time she had gotten off drugs, her son was long gone. When she had the child she was a homeless, drug addicted prostitute, with no money and an abusive pimp controlling her, and she had nowhere to go, and no means to raise the child. So giving him away was the best thing to do in her mind, and the money made on the deal was not something she asked for, but all of it went to her pimp. Coming into contact with this couple saved not only her baby's life, but her life too. It would take many, many years before she finally got her life straight and got off of drugs for good. She is very lucky she is still alive today, and I'm lucky she lived through her past life, so that now I have a chance to give her a fresh, new future filled with happiness and my unconditional love."

"Mr. Swanson I can't believe what a romantic you are. You're a good man to be able to not judge her and still love her. Not most men could be like that. I promise I will do everything I can to make this happen for you, I promise." Love gave Mr. Swanson, a warm and generous hug and left his office thinking, she just had to come through for him. For a moment the financial benefits to her didn't even come to mind, she just wanted to succeed in this assignment just to make Mr. Swanson happy.

Chapter 7
Hope Battles Her Greatest Enemy

Back in a small jail cell in the middle of nowhere, Hope tried her best to hold on to her sanity. She stood there staring at her hallucination and ready to fight *him,* her foster father. But instead of responding to her, he just sat down and laughed at her and said he wasn't there to fight her, that he wanted to talk. She told herself to turn around and ignore the hallucination in front of her, because her rational mind knew it could not exist. The man that stood before her was simply a figment of her imagination. The sum of all her childhood fears, brought forth by her exhaustion, isolation and confinement. "I'm not going to believe what I am seeing, he's not real and I'm not going to continue to have a conversation with someone that doesn't exist. This is not real, this is not real, this is not real! I will not respond anymore to something that is not real. He does not exist. He is a figment of my imagination!"

"But I do exist, and I told you I'm not going anywhere. Why should I? You know you really want me here. In fact, you practically yelled out my name with all your cursing and hatred. Admit it, you want me here. If you didn't really want me here, how could I be here? You wanted me to come to you. You want to fight, to hate, to kill and I know all about those things. See we are made for each other. We are one and the same. No one understands you like I do, and no one ever will, Hope. Look Hope, maybe we got off on the wrong foot. Hey, maybe you are right, maybe I'm not real. Maybe I am just a part of you that you've summoned forth to help you get out of this situation you've found yourself in. Maybe that's why your old foster daddy is here after all. After all, every girl needs her daddy in rough times like this." He gave her an evil smirk and a sickening laugh fell off his lips. "So what are you thinking, little one?"

Hope looked up at him and as much as she told herself he didn't exist she couldn't help responding to what was before her, be it real or imagined. "You want to help me? How could you help me; why would you help me? You never did anything to help me before, only to hurt me." Then she quickly shut herself up. Hope told herself, "stop talking to him. Do not respond to something that you know is not there! Even if I'm hallucinating, along as I'm aware it's a hallucination, I'm not crazy and I'm still sane."

"Well, I know you hate me Hope, but whether you believe me or not, I loved you. I just wanted you to be all mine. The only way I thought I could ensure you would always just belong to me was to spoil you for all other men that may have come along after me. See, I knew if I did this that every time another man would come close to you, you would remember me. And it worked didn't it?" He waited for Hope to respond, but she didn't say a word. "Now I wish you could return my love Hope, but at least you still remember me, remember the hatred you felt for me. I'd rather you hate me than forget me. So, I know even after I was long gone that I would still have power over you, and that your memory of me would keep you from all others and eventually bring you closer to me. And my plan was perfect. That is evident by the fact that I am here talking to you at this very moment. You still belong to me; mind, body and soul. By the way, do you know if the rebels do come for you, how they torture female soldiers? Your trainers have trained you for the possibility of gang rape, haven't they? Well don't fret at least I've prepared you in some ways for it. I know that must be your greatest fear, being raped again, but see that is my greatest fear too. I don't want to have any other man touch you, feel you the way that I did. I was your first and I want to be your last. I intend to be your last. Therefore, I have come to you with a solution. They will come to you in force most likely. Despite all the training you have been practicing and preparing for, you know deep down you will not be able to physically overtake more than one or two of them by yourself. You must know they will torture you, they will rape you and they won't kill you until you have told them everything they need to know. So, I propose the only solution is, to take control of the situation, take matters into your own hands. Don't wait for them to come and torture and kill you, take your life into your own hands. Just like Jesus use to say, no man can take my life, "I lay it down." I think it is what Jesus would want you to do in this situation. You can also do that; you can lay your own life down, before they come to take it. Hope, do it now, before they come for you, before you no longer have control over your fate. Besides, being dead isn't that bad. After all I'm dead and I'm still right here talking to you, ain't I?"

Hope couldn't take the sound of his voice anymore and she started yelling. "Shut up, shut up, you hypocrite, shut up!" That was one of the many things that made Hope hate him so much. It wasn't just for the horrible things he made her do, it wasn't just that he raped her, sodomized her, demeaned her, and played crazy, sadistic head games with her that had haunted her all her life. She hated him most of all because he was a hypocrite.

In the beginning she believed in him. She believed he was a good man, and he had everyone else believing he was a good man too, even his own wife. She couldn't help but think back about all the horrible things he did to her and how he smiled that disgusting smile all while doing it. So many things he did, so evil, and so senseless. Like when he would bring the animals home from the pet shop that he owned to torture her with. He would wait until she fell asleep at night and sneak into her room and put a tarantula or a snake into the bed with her. Then when she would discover it, he would be the first one to rush into her room and he would tell everyone she was just having another nightmare. He would bring home one of the grown attack dogs that he bred at the shop, and have it lay on top of her in the basement. He allowed her to suffer through the animal drooling on her face and growling at her. Every time she would close her eyes he would say, "open your eyes and remember all I have to do is say one word and the dog will attack you." He had a boa constrictor he kept in the cage in the basement and he would force her to feed it the little bunny rabbits he would bring home for it to eat. He would force her to sit and watch while the snake slither slowly around the bunny and then suddenly wrap itself around it and squeeze the life out of the poor creature. He would taunt her in front of others without their knowledge, by giving her the nickname, bunny boo. He would remind her if she didn't behave, that one day, when the snake grew big enough he would put her in the cage with it when it was hungry. He would go into detail about how the snake's venom wasn't poisonous, but it's bite would still hurt, and how it may not be capable of swallowing her but it would try and suffocate her to death while trying. He would always laugh when he said and did these sadistic deeds, as if it all was just a big joke, a big game to him. Despite all that he did to her, still what she hated most about him was he was such a hypocrite, such a liar, and he had everyone but her fooled about what he really was. On Sundays he was the assistant pastor at their local church, but Monday thru Saturday he was the devil to her. Everyone at church loved and respected him. He would bring all the cute little puppy's and baby bunny rabbits to Sunday school for the little children to play with. Then they come home Sunday night, and he would make her feed the rabbits to his snake. He sold the puppies to the drug dealers and dog fighters across town. But he would tell his wife that he was giving the puppies away or selling them to good families that would take good care of them. He would take Hope with him on those cross town trips, and tell his wife how he was going to drop the puppies off to the different families that had adopted them. He would say how he wanted to expose Hope to seeing all the good homes and good people that were in the world.

His wife always believed whatever he told her. She was allergic to most animals and therefore couldn't keep them in the house, so that was another excuse for her husband to keep his pets in the basement, and for him to constantly take showers before he got close to her. His wife's allergies were also the excuse he used to have a reason for spending extra time with Hope. He would say Hope was his assistant in caring for the animals since his wife couldn't help him. So his wife was never concerned about what Hope and her husband were doing in the basement. Why would she be? She trusted him. She was also a very beautiful woman, with nothing to be jealous about, and Hope was a mere child who hadn't even blossomed into puberty yet. She never knew what was going on right under her nose.

On the weekends when her husband told her that he was taking Hope with him to deliver the puppies to good families, he was actually taking Hope with him to drug houses where he would get cash in exchange for the pups along with some drugs. Then the rest of the day he would force Hope to do drugs with him, and subject her to spending entire Saturdays in a drug house. Lucky for Hope he was too territorial to share her with another man, and she was usually so high she couldn't remember much of what happened by the time they were back at the foster home.

Unfortunately, Hope could not forget what he did to her in the basement of his house, because those times her head was clear and sober.

Another thing Hope hated about him was that he could also quote the bible all the time, just like Nana use to do. He would smile and laugh and hug a person in a way that made him seem like he was some kind of angel for God. He made Hope hate everything about church and God eventually. He was such a hypocrite and he made a farce of it all, and she had no more faith in the church, in people, or in God, by the time he was finished with her. So when Hope finally left his foster home she never again stepped foot inside a church. She never read the bible again, or even said another single prayer. She couldn't even bring herself to bless her food anymore. God was a farce to her. He just wasn't real. And as far as she was concerned all Christians were either weak, good hearted, naïve creatures like her Nana and her foster mother; or they were hypocrites that secretly had an evil heart that they hid behind religion, like her foster father.

So Hope decided when she ran away from New York that she would never again be weak or religious. She promised herself that she would become a strong, independent, fearless woman, who was the same person in public as she was in private; no pretenses, no secret intentions to hurt others, she would just be a good person who did good deeds, and she didn't feel like she needed religion or God to do good or to be strong in this world.

Up until this very moment in her jail cell, Hope had felt like she had at least accomplished that much within her lifetime. She was an overall good person, in her opinion. Yes she had killed before, but only in self defense and in defense of the innocent, but she had also saved many, many lives while in the military. She had sacrificed her own personal life to join this elite agency and dedicate herself to rescuing people who couldn't rescue themselves. She didn't do it for the money. She did it because it was the only thing she ever wanted to do. She had rescued, young girls being mutilated and held by drug lords and rebel forces all across the world. She rescued people suffering from ethnic cleansing by ruthless rebel groups. She had rescued hostages. She had stopped terrorist groups from killing thousands and hundreds of thousands throughout the years. She felt proud about her life. Time after time Hope volunteered for the assignments that had humanitarian aspects to them, and this was why she volunteered for this assignment. This is why her troops, the men and women, who depended on her respected her so much. They knew she would do anything for any of them, and they had confidence that when she gave them an order, she would never lead them to do something which was wrong. Thinking about her troops made her think of what was to come.

She had to admit, her hallucination, well *he* did have a point. The enemy was coming for her and it was just a matter of time. She swore to herself she wouldn't allow them to touch her like he had, she'd rather die. He had put her through enough torture for a lifetime. But how could she avoid being tortured, being raped once they came for her. There was no way for her to kill herself in this cell. There was no rope to hang herself with, nothing sharp to cut herself with, no poison to take, no water to drown herself in, there was nothing....., unless, she just banged her head against the wall, over and over again, but she would probably just knock herself out for a little while and eventually wake back up with a terrible headache. For a moment she couldn't believe that she was actually entertaining the thought of killing herself. But even if she decided to kill herself she evaluated the situation and she realized there was no way to do it in there. So her only option was to fight and hopefully disarm one of her captives and use their own weapons against them. They would surely shoot back at her and kill her, and if they didn't she could save one bullet to shoot herself with. She rather die fast and fighting than surrender to her fate and face a slow torturous death. But she feared what would happen if she couldn't disarm one of them, or if they were smart enough to come in and get her without any weapons on them. Hope had been trained on what to do in these situations, but actually being held captive and imagining her fate was vastly different than just training for it. Just then she heard his disgusting voice in her head again. She looked up and he was still there, he refused to disappear.

"I know what you are thinking little Hope. Like I said, no one understands you the way I do. You are thinking, how? How could I take my life? After all there is nothing in this cell except you and me, and even my existence is questionable. You are probably weighing out your options. Don't worry you know I am smart, I'm crafty, I'm clever, and I always have the answers. Now, notice the chipped rocks on the ground. I'm sure you could find a nice sized one and scrape it against the wall long enough to sharpen the edges. You could do that. It may take a few hours, but eventually you could make the edges as sharp as a knife, if you were persistent. Then you could slit your wrist or make it quicker and go for the jugular. You're a military woman, that part I'll leave up to you to figure out. After all you were trained in the quickest and most efficient ways to kill people. And you've killed plenty of people during your military career haven't you? But hey we are talking about taking your own life now, you have every right to take your own life, it is your body. It is your right to do to it what you want, isn't it? That body doesn't belong to me anymore, from what you say your body belongs only to you, right?"

Hope did believe that to be the truth. Her body, her mind, her soul, only belonged to her now. Not him, not God, not anyone else. In fact she felt no man should tell any woman what to do with her own body. She hated to admit it, but he was really starting to make sense to her now. Then she reminded herself he was only a figment of her imagination. So she didn't respond to him. So Hope started spending her time feeling around the dirt floor of her dark cell almost absentmindedly at first. She did this for hours on hours, digging and sifting through the dirt, until she found the perfect size rock. It was already a little sharp. It already was shaped sort of like a shank. She thought to herself this is just an option. An option I am just considering for now.

For the next two days that went by Hope spent them awake. She sharpened her rock against other rocks and the wall, as quietly as possible. She would practice fighting when she got tired and the adrenal rush would propel her on. And repeatedly, he would reappear. She hated him, but he kept reappearing it seemed at the times when she was just ready to give in, relax and fall asleep. He would distract and agitate her and get her all worked up again and when she just couldn't ignore him anymore, she would scream at him to leave her alone. Then she would return to her busy work. For days straight she spent almost every single moment that she was not talking to "him", fighting the air and the walls, and sharpening that rock. Her hands were bleeding from all the scraping and punching the walls. Then one day she realized she had finally scraped herself a perfect killing weapon. Now the only decision left to make was whether she would use this weapon against her enemies or perhaps as "he" had suggested to her, use it on herself. Whatever she did, it would be her choice, not another's. She felt a sense of satisfaction that she had taken control over her life and death again. She so desperately needed that sense of control again. She was no longer just a victim sitting and waiting for someone else to decide her destiny.

Hope had stayed awake from the fear with the help of the demon in her head and in her cell for three days straight. She suddenly realized that she had not slept in three days. She kept track of the days passing by, by the little stream of sunlight that was her only hope that there was a world outside her cell. That sunlight, her slightest hope fought its way to shine through the tiny hole in the brick mortar of her cell everyday like it was doing it just for her. She felt sick from the food they were feeding her. She felt cold from the lack of clothes she wore and the chill was felt down to her bones. She was exhausted from the constant exercise and from her worries about fighting the guards when they came for her. And "he" also had kept her awake with his constant reappearances to taunt her in her mind. She was afraid to go asleep. She thought, "who knows maybe another devil from my past will appear to mentally torture me in my dreams. Like someone I've killed." Hope was very aware that she was losing her mind and that made her more afraid to sleep. At any moment her cell door would fly open, and there would stand there men who hated everything she stood for, freedom and justice. They would be ready to rape her, ready to torture her, and ready to kill her. She looked at the stone she had crafted into a knife and she picked it up and just admired it and stared at her handy work. She thought to herself, "despite all of "his" faults and how much I hate him, he is a very smart man and some of what he said makes perfect sense to me right now."

It was then that he reappeared, as if he could hear Hope admiring him for just that moment in her head. "Hope, you look so tired. I know you've been thinking about my suggestion. I see you've finished. Looks like you did a good job. It looks very sharp. You know it's the best thing to do. It's the only way to save yourself from what is waiting for you outside that door. No matter how strong you have become, you cannot beat them all."

Hope thought he almost seemed like he was truly concerned about her. She felt within that moment that he was all that she had in that cell, all that was with her, and that he wasn't the same man who had tortured and raped her all those years ago. Maybe he did love her in his own sick way. She brought the shank closer to her wrist. She thought to herself she would cut her wrists swiftly and deeply. Then she would cut her jugular vein too to be sure. But she knew she had to do it quick, before she lost her nerve. So she took a deep breath, and prepared herself. Before she exhaled she slit her left wrist, the blood oozed out like water from a faucet, and she stared at it in disbelief. She thought, "did I really just do that to myself?" She felt so low and ashamed at how desperate she had become. And she started to weep.

It was then that a blinding bright light shined into Hope's eyes. She realized it was the first morning sun shining through that tiny hole in the wall. She happened to be crouching in the exact spot where the stream of light fell when the sun rose every morning. And the sunlight brought with it, a ray of hope, that maybe tomorrow she would be delivered from her captivity. And as if it just had dawned upon her, she remembered how much she really did love life. She remembered how much she loved her life and how she chose to live for others. Despite all the terrible things that had happen to her in her past, one thing she had never lost was hope of a better future, if not for herself then a better future for the one's she would rescue and save through her missions. She remembered how her Nana would always tell her that, "she was a born fighter, she was a warrior, and a conqueror." She was the middle sister, but she fought not just the children that bullied little Faith, but also the bigger kids that teased her older sister Love. She was their conqueror, the strong sister out of the three, the brave one with enough courage for them all. Love was the smart one, the calm and responsible older sister that took care of them, and Faith was the innocent, little dreamer, and she was so compassionate, she was always taking in the strays in the neighborhood, trying to care for all of them. Hope thought about her Nana, her sisters, her troops, and she didn't want to give up and die she wanted to hold on to the slightest bit of hope that the sunlight brought to her that morning. Then she threw the shank against the wall, and she tore off her shirt sleeve and wrapped it tightly around her wrist. She hadn't cut deep enough to kill herself, but she was already losing a lot of blood. While she was bandaging herself to stop the bleeding, she heard his voice in her head again, he was screaming in anger, trying to confuse her again. She looked up and he was standing in front of her screaming.

"You coward, you stupid, stupid woman! You are pathetic. Now what are you going to do? You weak, simple minded slut! Well I'll tell you what if you don't have the nerve to do it; I'll do it for you."

Hope looked in his eyes and saw nothing but hate in them. She couldn't believe for that even one second she thought he might have actually loved her in his own sick way. Hope closed her eyes tight. "Go away, you're not real, so you can't do anything to me. You are just an hallucination, that's all." She kept her eyes closed, and repeated to herself, "he doesn't exist, he doesn't exist, get him out of your mind, because he doesn't exist."

When it was quiet she opened her eyes up, to see if her hallucination had finally disappeared. She looked around and he was gone. But then she heard a low growling coming from the corner of the cell. It leaped forward, and to her amazement and horror she saw a fierce Lion standing in front of her, ready to devour her, and it appeared so real she could feel it's hot breath on her face like the heat off of a furnace, and the smell coming out of its massive mouth was more putrid than any smell in this world. She jumped up in shock and the Lion leaped towards her. Then she fell backwards and hit the back of her head against the stone wall. She was lying on her back, when the Lion pounced on her, she was frozen with fear, it all seemed so real, but she knew it couldn't be. She blinked her eyes and when she opened them back up the lion had transformed itself into a dog, a jet black Rottweiler. Its teeth were glaring at her, and it's hot stinking drool dripping on her face. She kept closing her eyes, and telling herself, "it's not real, it's not possible". She felt the pressure on her chest disappear. She tried to sit up, but she couldn't, she felt paralyzed, she looked down, and she saw the dirt moving around her. She realized it wasn't the dirt moving. Then she saw its shiny head. It was a boa constrictor, at least 15 feet long and thick, and twice the size of the one "he" had kept in the basement, in his cage at the foster home. She couldn't move, the fear had her paralyzed, she couldn't even scream, not that screaming would have saved her anyway. The snake wrapped around her. She could feel it squeezing the life out of her, suffocating her to death. It was happening just like he said it would happen all those years ago. And she couldn't move, she felt like her eyes and her heart would burst from the pressure the snake was squeezing into her. This was her worst nightmare coming true, and finally she didn't scream out in pain, but she cried out in surrender, and her last bit of sanity had left her.

Now, to her all of it was totally real, as real as the prison which held her captive at the moment. Everything at that moment was as real as anything else in her life had ever been. Then just as suddenly as she had surrendered to the insanity, the snake was gone and "he" reappeared. He threw his body on top of her, and she felt him kissing her and groping her breast and penetrating her, she wanted to die now, she wanted to find that knife she had made and finish the job that she had started. She had lost her will to fight, and to scream, what was the point anymore; she couldn't save herself from this insanity. When it was over she had already decided she would find the knife and complete what she had started. She heard him whisper in her ear, the same things that he use to whisper to her as a child.

"Little Hope, just tell me your mines, that you love and worship me and I will stop, I promise. I will stop this and I will take all the pain away."

Hope just shook her head saying "whatever you want, just stop, please stop", and the tears stung her cheeks like acid as she felt them fall from her eyes.

"No, I won't stop yet. I can't stop, until you say the words. I need you to declare it, say it out loud Hope. Say I love only you, I belong to only you, I worship only you, say it!"

Hope was about to yell out all that he demanded from her, in that moment of complete insanity, fear and weakness, but some unseen force bound up her voice, and kept it from her. She couldn't speak but her mind took her to a memory. A memory of her Nana....

She was little and back in church with Nana. Nana, was at the altar, like usual. Nana was praising louder than everyone else in church. Nana use to embarrass Hope and her sisters. She was so loud. Hope remembered Nana crying and yelling like she was an insane woman in front of everyone in the church, it was so embarrassing. Nana was yelling, "Jesus, Jesus, Lord help me, save me Jesus!", and then, Hope's voice suddenly returned to her and in one breath she yelled out as loud as she could, "JESUS! HELP ME, SAVE ME JESUS!"

All of sudden Hope felt him fly off of her body, as if a strong wind had snatched him up and thrown him off of her. She heard him land in a loud thump against the wall. She kept her eyes shut tightly, too full of fear to open them, and then she heard not his voice anymore, but she heard another familiar voice in her dark cell.

"Hope, open your eyes Hope, open your eyes."

Hope opened her eyes as the voice commanded her, because she knew by the sound of the voice exactly who it belonged to, it was her Nana. Nana was standing in front of her tall, beautiful and strong! Nana was stronger and more beautiful than Hope had ever remembered her being. Nana stood before her all in white, and around her neck was that massive cross that hung over her bed all those years. The same cross that she was laid to rest with. Nana's skin was young and glowed so bright that it lighted up the whole cell. This was not the weak and sick

Nana that Hope last memories of her were. Nana had thrown "him" off of her, and now he was on the ground injured in the corner of Hope's cell. Both Hope and him were staring at Nana in complete awe.

Hope looked at Nana in amazement. "Nana is that really you?"

Even injured and defeated he persisted in trying to deceive Hope. "Of course it's not her she is a hallucination just like I am silly girl. Maybe she can fight off the demons you have created in your mind, but she can't get you out of this cell, because she is not real, and neither am I. She also can't keep those guards from coming in here and raping and torturing and killing you, and neither can I because I'm not real. What is real is this prison, you and those guards, those men outside, they are real and only you can stop the guards, by finishing what you started and slitting your other wrist and your throat. Only you can SAVE YOURSELF! If you don't have enough guts to do it, to save yourself from the rape and the torture, than do it for your troops, don't allow them to see their leader demeaned and tortured to death. Remember Hope your Nana's bible also says, "lay down your life for your brethen".

Hope thought about her troops and what he had just said, but she didn't take her eyes off of Nana. She was too stunning not to stare at only her. Her presence was commanding.

Then Nana intervened and she turned to "him", and she yelled in a booming voice with full authority and confidence, "GET THE BEHIND ME SATAN!" And then Nana turned back towards Hope and she spoke softly to her beloved granddaughter. "Hope, remember what I taught you. Hope, "he" is a liar, a deceiver, and he is your enemy, but make no mistakes about it, he is real. Even if he is not flesh and blood, he is real, *"for we wrestle not against flesh and blood, but against principalities, against powers, against the rulers of the darkness of this world, against spiritual wickedness in high places"*[7] But Hope, God is also real, and God is here in me, I too am real, and Hope, God is in you. So remember if you lean on God, you are so much stronger than any evil that comes up against you. If you depend on God to fight for you, with you, you are the warrior,

---

[7] Ephesians 6:12

the conqueror, the survivor, I always told you, you are. God is the sunlight that has shined into your dark prison every day. God is the love and faith and hope, all in one that has managed to stay in your heart all these years. God is all those things and more. God loves you Hope. Remember when I told you I gave you your name, "Hope", a most beautiful of names. God told me to name you that. Remember all I've taught you about God. But now I want you to remember, that your life, your name, and all that I have taught you in the bible, came from God, not from me. I didn't make it up Hope. I am only God's helper, his messenger sent to you and your sisters in the beginning of your lives. That was my purpose."

And then the light surrounding Nana became so bright that it blinded Hope and she heard another voice that she recognized right away, although she had never heard it before, except only in her spirit, in her dreams. This voice instantaneously calmed Hope and filled her with peace. It was a soft whisper, like a sweet smelling wind, the voice filled all her senses, her mind, her heart, her soul and the entire cell with its sweet aroma.

"Hope my child, *I knew you when you were formed in your mother's womb and I named you Hope and I loved you even then, and I declared you would be filled with Hope, united with Faith and with Love and have strength through Christ and be a conqueror for those you love. Remember my child Hope, neither death, nor life, nor angels, nor principalities, nor powers, nor things present, nor things to come, nor height, nor depth, nor any other creature, shall be able to separate you from my love, the love of God, which is in Christ Jesus*[8]" then within a blink of an eye, the light was gone, and Nana was gone, but "he", the one who hated her, and tortured her as a child remained.

He still was on the ground, in the corner of the cell and he stared at Hope with a hatred and evil in his eyes that was stronger than Hope had ever seen in him before. Yet her strength and her spirit were renewed and she felt not one inkling of fear in her anymore. He now appeared to her as the weak one, and she was now the strong one, stronger than she had ever been before. He started to lift himself to his feet and he propped

---

[8] See Jeremiah 1:5 and Romans 8:38

himself up on all fours like a dog. Hope summoned all the strength she had in her to bring herself to her feet to stand against him. She now stood before him on her feet in a fighting stance. He transformed himself into a massive cobra and like lightning leaped towards her. Hope instinctively dodged the attack with one decisive, defensive move, and then in one swift movement raised her leg up and swung it down with a lethal force. Her leg landed right down on the cobra's head. In one blow Hope crushed his head with the heel of her foot. He now laid in front of her no longer the poisonous cobra but transformed back into the pitiful, sick man she had called her foster father. She saw the weapon that he had convinced her to create and to use on herself, and she picked it up, and for once and for all she plunged it into his heart, getting rid of her demon forever. And then it was done. She would never fear him again.

Hope fell to the ground, exhausted, and she just stayed there quietly with her eyes open for hours as she enjoyed what seemed like the sweet smell of roses that fill her cell and the peace of not hearing his taunting voice and his lies in her head anymore. She thought to herself, "I will close my eyes and rest just for a moment", and then finally after three long days, she fell asleep, and she slept deeply and peacefully. She started to dream about her past, her past before Nana's death, before foster care, before the loss of her innocence. She dreamed about when she still had her Nana and her sisters. She dreamed about a time Nana made her feel safe and all was right in the world.

"Nana, Nana…Nana, Nana. Wake up, Nana."

"What's the matter child?", whispered Nana.

Little Hope answered quietly, holding back her sobs "I can't sleep, Nana. I had a bad dream and I can't sleep."

"What was the dream about child?"

"Something was holding me down Nana, and I couldn't move, Nana." Then a voice called out my name it said, "Hope, Hope, open your eyes." And then I woke up."

"Hope, you keep having that same dream child. Did you recognize the voice?"

"No Nana."

"Did you trust the voice?"

"Yes."

"Well then maybe it is God's voice calling you, and you should listen to it child."

"I did Nana. I opened my eyes and then I came in here to you." Little Hope stood at the foot of Nana's bed and wondered when Nana would just tell her to get in the bed with her like she always did, instead of asking her so many questions. It was as if Nana could read her mind, and at that moment, Nana said, "come sleep with me child, everything's okay Nana's here, and then they prayed". Nana's home was the one place Hope felt safe at as a child. Nana's bed was the warmest and safest place in the whole world to Hope. Nana's bed was old, and the mattress was lumpy, but Nana's plump, warm body, filled the bed with warmth. Hope would always put her little, cold feet under Nana's legs, and Nana always said, "brrrrr... you have the coldest feet, you must be half Eskimo." Then Hope would fall asleep peacefully looking up at the moonlight shining off of the cross that hung over Nana's bed.

"Remember Hope whenever you have a scary dream, whenever you are scared, just call out to Jesus, and just pray, wherever you happen to be just get down on your knees child and pray, pray the fear away."

"Okay Nana, I will, but right now I have you, I'm not scared when you are here."

"I know, but on those days when I'm not around, you know maybe like when you are in school, lean on God, you can always lean on God and pray."

"Nana, I'm sleepy."

"Go to sleep child, and have sweet dreams."

When Hope awoke from her dreams and her childhood memory, it was in the middle of the night. She realized she was still in her prison cell. She was not in the safe and warm bed belonging to Nana that she had just dreamed of. Suddenly, her past and her present had all come together. She realized that dreams, visions, prophesies, good and evil all existed in this world, and that every word her Nana spoke to her in her past was instructions and guidance for this very moment in her life. She was truly awoke now, and aware for the first time in her life. She knew Nana and God had never forsaken her, she had forsaken them. The only thing left she could think of to do was the one thing she had not done in over twenty years. Hope got down on her hands and knees and she, prayed… Amazingly even after twenty years of never saying a prayer out loud, never thinking of them, she remembered all the prayers Nana had said with her as a child.

Psalms 23
The Lord is my shepherd; I shall not want.
He maketh me to lie down in green pastures;
He leadeth me beside the still waters.
He restoreth my soul;
He leadeth me in the paths of righteousness for his name's sake.
Yea, though I walk through the valley of the shadow of death,
I will fear no evil: for thou art with me;
Thy rod and thy staff they comfort me.
Thou preparest a table before me in the presence of mine enemies:
Thou anoinest my head with oil; my cup runneth over.
Surely goodness and mercy shall follow me all the days of my life:
And I will dwell in the house of the Lord forever.
And Hope declared, "I will no longer fear the things from my past or what lies ahead for me in my future."
And she prayed again….
Matthew 6:9-13
Our Father which art in heaven,
Hallowed Be thy name.
Thy kingdom come.
Thy will be done in earth,
As it is in heaven.
Give us this day our daily bread.
And forgive us our debts,
As we forgive our debtors.
And lead us not into temptation,
But deliver us from evil:
For thine is the kingdom,
And the power, and the glory,
Forever. Amen.

And Hope declared, "I forgive you, you were a sick man, a tortured soul, and I only pity you because you died in your sins. And Forgive me Lord for forsaking you, forgive me Nana for being ashamed at what I thought was your weaknesses. You were stronger than I ever imagined, and I your grandchild have inherited your strength. Forgive me for my sins Lord and help me not to sin again."

And she prayed again...

Psalms 51:1-3; 10

Have mercy upon me, O God, according to thy lovingkindness:

According unto the multitude of thy tender mercies blot out my

Transgressions.

Wash me thoroughly from mine iniquity, and cleanse me from my sin.

For I acknowledge my transgressions: and my sin is ever before me...

Create in me a clean heart, O God; and renew a right spirit within me.

And Hope declared, "I believe you sent your son to me to save me from my sin, believing in Jesus my savior, is the only way my life can be saved for eternity, I know now I can not "save myself", only Jesus can."

And she prayed again...and again and again, and again out loud with all abandon to the Lord, praying in her tongue, and in tongues unknown to her, but known to her God, until she prayed her last prayer out loud for that night...

Psalms 116:1-4

I Love the Lord, because he hath heard my voice and my supplications.

Because he hath inclined his ear unto me, therefore will I call upon him

as long as I live.

The sorrows of death compassed me, and the pains of hell got hold upon me:

I found trouble and sorrow.

Then called I upon the name of the Lord; O Lord, I beseech thee,
Deliver my soul.... And he has delivered me, Amen.

And Hope declared, "Thank you God from saving me from my demons, from myself, from hell, and for saving my soul. My life and my soul are precious things, and I shall never again choose to give up own my life." Then Hope realized she had prayed through the entire night, because she saw the sun shine once again through the hole in the wall. She could not believe that a whole day had went by since she had saw her Nana battle a demon from her past. She could hardly believe that just 24 hours ago she had almost taken her own life. Nana's words were in her head, "God is the sunlight that has shined into your dark prison every day. God is the love and faith and hope, that has managed to stay in your heart. God is all those things and more." Hope was exhausted and as the sun rose it comforted her and she fell back into a peaceful sleep. She slept through the entire day and night and when she awoke... She prayed again, and again, and again, the following day, recalling every prayer she had ever heard in her childhood church, every sermon she had ever sat through, she prayed every prayer her Nana had ever said in her presence, and every prayer she could recall reading from the bible.

And when she was done praying that day, she just started talking, talking to God about her old fears and thanking him for taking all her fears away, and she talked to God about her desires, and her old pains, and her anger, and he comforted her, and she praised and worshipped God and gave him thanksgivings for all he had brought her through. She talked and prayed and praised out loud, she had no reason to care if anyone thought she was crazy, she knew she was very sane, very aware, and very strong in mind, body and spirit. Instead of fighting and preparing for her enemy, she just prayed all day long. She did this all day, until the sun had gone down and the night had come once again. Then in the morning she prayed again. It had been twenty years since Hope had picked up a bible or went to church, but God's words came back to her instinctively, and only one voice spoke in her mind, that of her Almighty Father God.

In the past, Hope had forsaken God in her anger, forsaken him in her pain; but she realized now God had never forsaken her. Hope spoke out loud, "God is our beginning and our end, and he waits for us to come back to him, patiently, because he is time's maker and destroyer. He is the Alpha and Omega, and the author and creator of peace. God has given me peace." Hope knew in her heart that God had forgiven her for forsaking him. Finally she felt complete and prepared for anything that might come and she felt filled with her namesake again. The name God had inspired Nana to give her at her birth, Hope. In the past Hope had prided herself in being self-reliant, self-efficient, independent and most of all physically and mentally strong. But now, she was sure that her body was physically weaker than it had ever been in her adulthood, weak from the lack of food and the terrible conditions she now lived in. But she didn't feel weak inside. For the first time she possessed spiritual strength. That kind of strength she now understood could transcend the physical world. And that kind of strength, well that kind of strength can move mountains....

Chapter 8
The Journies
(Faith and Darryl's journey)

As Faith and Darryl boarded the plane, Faith started reminiscing about the first time she ever flew on a plane. She was just a child when her adopted parents took her on her first family trip to her mother's homeland in Darfur, Africa. However, that trip was not a vacation. They were going back to Africa so that Faith's mother could spend time with her own mother who was terminally ill, before she died. Faith's mother had left her homeland many years ago when she was a teenager because her cousin had gotten her a good paying job in South Africa.

It was in South Africa that Faith's adopted parents met. Her father was a teacher in South Africa at the university back when apartheid still existed and her mother was a nanny and housekeeper for the couple he rented a room from. Although he was white he never agreed with what he saw happening around him in South Africa. He became an underground organizer assisting other White and Black South Africans in their fight against apartheid, and he held secret sessions where he taught the Black South Africans who could not go to the university. His future wife was also one of his students. The family that rented the room to Faith's father was very well to do and always away at social events. This left Faith's parents plenty of time alone in the house to get to know one another, with only the children and no other adults around. At first, their relationship started innocently. Faith's father hated any form of prejudice, and when he met his future bride he wanted to teach her as much as he possibly could. He told her about his travels all around the world, and how different things were in other places compared to South Africa. She was amazed by his stories and flattered by the attention he showed her, but she still never considered his feelings for her were more than a friendly teacher student relationship. But he was immediately attracted to her. He thought that she was the most beautiful woman he had ever seen. He was impressed by her natural intelligence despite her lack of formal education. And he felt especially touched by all the love and kindness she showed the children she cared for, even when she thought no one else was watching her with them. The children she cared for looked to her as their mother because their own mother was rarely at home.

It didn't take long before the teacher student friendship between the two blossomed into something more. They kept their love for each other a secret, and hid it the best they could from everyone. They knew their feelings were too strong to hide for too much longer. So eventually, Faith's father secretly arranged for himself and his secret fiance to leave South Africa. He applied for a job as a professor in France. He had a friend on the university's board of directors. The board was looking to diversify and expand their student exchange program, and he suggested a few of his South African students be accepted. He falsified some documents and his fiance's name was included in the midst of the other students that were approved for Student Visas to attend the University in France. Once they were in France they were married. After being married for a few years and after his wife had received her degree he suggested something to her that he had been contemplating long before meeting his bride. They joined the peace-corps together, and returned to Africa for their first assignment. Eventually they settled in the United States, but they always used their summers to volunteer in third-world countries. It had been a very long time since they had been back to Darfur, and this would be Faith's first time in Africa.

Faith's mother felt an enormous amount of guilt for letting so many years pass by without returning home. She was elated to finally be a mother when she adopted Faith and she couldn't wait to write home and tell her own mother the news. That was when she discovered that her own mother was dying. She decided right then that she could not put a return visit back home off any longer. She had to see her mother one more time, and she wanted her mother to see her beautiful daughter Faith and bestow blessings upon her.

So the newly formed family prepared to leave for Africa. This family trip would mark the start of Faith's special interest and love for her African brothers and sisters.

Faith and her parents stayed in Africa for close to two years, before returning back home to the states. They had decided to stay on another year after Faith's grandmother died. They tried to help improve the lives of the other people in the village. Faith's mother and father started up a school for the children in the village and they assisted in obtaining clean water, agricultural necessities and medical supplies for the villagers. Living conditions in the village had improved greatly since the family had arrived. Faith attended school with the other children in the village and assisted her father and mother in all things. She also had plenty of time to play with her new friends. Besides missing her sisters, Faith was very happy in the village, and she felt loved and accepted by her new family and friends. Life seemed simple in the village. The other children adored Faith and were curious about her American look, her American accent, and the places in New York she had been. When the family had to abruptly leave Darfur it was very difficult for Faith. Faith's Aunt was the only living family member that her mother had left. So when they left Darfur they took her with them. Faith's mother made it clear to her husband that she was not going to leave without her unmarried, younger sister because the political climate in Darfur was growing increasingly unstable.

Faith maintained a vivid memory of the day they left Darfur. She recalled the four of them waving goodbye to the friends that escorted them to the small plane. All of her little friends were waving and smiling and yelling her name and how they loved her as she boarded the plane. Faith knew she would return to Africa one day to see all her friends. She thought maybe she would come back on summer vacations with her parents, and when she grew up that she would even join the Peace Corps like her parents did and work in Africa. She never dreamed all her friends in Darfur would be gone by the time she would eventually return.

After Faith and her family were back in New York for some time, Faith would repeatedly ask her mother and father when they were going to go back to Darfur to visit? Her parents always found ways to put off the conversation. Faith and her friends initially kept in touch by mail with short notes and pictures they would send to each other. Until one day the letters just stopped coming.

When Faith was ten years old she overheard her mother crying in the kitchen, she came in and asked her parents, "what was the matter?" Her mother and father looked at her like someone had just died. Faith thought something had happened to Auntie. Then her mother said, "Faith the village, my village, has been destroyed in Darfur, all the people there were killed." Faith had known how bad things were getting there because even at her young age she followed the current events very closely despite the fact that her parents tried to shelter her from it, and Faith said, "everyone, mama, everyone was killed?!".

Faith turned around in silence and went into her bedroom. She couldn't believe what her mother had just said. It was just earlier that month she had received a letter from Asla, one of her friends in Africa. The letter talked about how bad things had gotten, how they were not allowed to leave the village at anytime and how they slept in fear every night. But at the end of the letter Asla was hopeful, she signed it, "I think I will come to college one day in America and we can be roommates. Soon when all of this is over we will see each other again. Your friend Asla." And now Faith thought, "was Asla, was all her other friends gone forever?" Faith couldn't believe it. She wouldn't believe it, until she saw evidence of it for herself. So the next day Faith skipped school and spent the day at the library. She looked up all the articles on Darfur, all the magazine articles, newspaper prints she could find, and she saw the headlines and the pictures. She didn't break to eat lunch or to rest her eyes. Then she came across one Associated Press article. There was no mistaking one picture she saw, it was her mother's village. The young people's mutilated bodies were on the ground in the picture. The bodies covering the ground were unidentifiable. The huts were all burned down. She felt like she could almost smell the stench of death off of the newspaper pages. Her head and her heart told her, her friends were gone, gone forever.

Once again, Faith had lost people dear to her. At that young age it seemed to her that anything she loved would inevitably be ripped away from her. She couldn't understand why? Why was it that God allowed horrible things like this to happen to people all around the world? Why didn't a nation as great as America do more to help these people? She didn't understand why they didn't even mention in class what was happening in that part of the world? This was when Faith's life took on a new meaning for her. From that day on Faith became an activist, the youngest one definitely in her community. Her passion was for any cause that had to do with saving people, and children around the world, especially in Africa.

Her parents continued to go on trips every summer to different countries and to Africa with a non-profit organization. They always brought Faith on the trips. But even before they found out about the destruction of her mother's village they never went back to Darfur. One of the reasons they had left so suddenly was because it was becoming unsafe to stay there, and they didn't want to put Faith's in danger. They continued to spend their summers helping make villages livable and start schools up for the children in safe rural areas. When Faith asked why they had not returned to visit Darfur they would explain to her that their first priority was to her and her safety, so they could not return to Darfur. Every summer Faith would travel somewhere different around the world. She saw firsthand how other children in the world desperately needed her help. Once when Faith was nine, her family spent the summer in Ethiopia during a famine. When she was ten, they went to Liberia. When she was eleven they went to Sudan, and at twelve they returned to where her parents had first met, South Africa. But they never returned to Darfur, even after things had stabilized there. Faith's parents thought the memories of all the people they had lost there, were just too painful.

Once Faith graduated from high school and went to college she majored in International Studies with a minor in African studies. She became fluent in several different African dialects. She could tell you at any time the current events going on in every country around the world and especially on the African continent. Although Faith had been to Africa many, many times this trip was still special to her because this would be Faith's first trip to Africa with Darryl.

It was also Darryl's first time in Africa, and his first time on a plane. He was most excited about spending a whole week alone with Faith. Spending an extended period of time together more than a night was something they had not been able to do in a long time. He also couldn't wait to see Faith in action. He often wondered about what Faith's life at work was like.

Before Darryl knew it the plane was taking off. Darryl immediately started to tense up and his eyes grew wide. Faith laughed out loud. She loved teasing Darryl. "What's wrong babe?"

"Oh, nothing I'm just taking in the sights."

"You know there is no reason to be scared of flying. It is as safe as driving in a car."

"Faith, if God wanted me to fly he would have given me wings."

Faith held on to Darryl's hand. She knew this would be one of the very rare times that she would be the calm one, and Darryl would be the nervous wreck inside. Still, she had a good feeling about this trip and about going on it with Darryl.

(Love and John's journey)

It was four in the morning, and John was exhausted. Love had been running him non-stop since yesterday afternoon when she summoned him into her office. She gave him a list of things he needed to do before their jet left for New York. He had no idea why he was chosen for this assignment because he had no expertise in adoption law, but he hoped it was because he was handpicked by Love. He had to admit he would jump at the chance to be working closely with her even if it involved digging trenches. But Love was all business so far and acting like a task master this entire trip. She had barely cracked a smile since they had departed the airport in LA. Her attitude so far made him wonder what it was about her that he found so attractive in the first place. She truly was not an affectionate, warm and fuzzy type of woman. It was almost an oxymoron that her name was Love, but still there was something about her that had always drawn him to her, and it wasn't just her incredibly good looks.

But despite his attraction for her throughout the many years they had never crossed the lines of being just friends, and they had become very good friends. As the years passed by he was able to catch glimpses of her softer side. He knew she took on pro bono cases for beaten and abused women and children and that she didn't even tell the firm or log in the hours to receive credit. He knew she told everyone she was up early working every Sunday. But when he tried to call her on her cell one Sunday, thinking she'd be at the office, someone answered her cell and told him she was busy serving breakfast at the shelter and they could give her a message. He later spied on her and found out Love had been going down to the shelter for years handing out money, clothes and food to the homeless early nearly every Sunday morning, before she went into work. Then there was the look of pain and longing in her eyes whenever she saw a baby. It was obvious she wanted to be a mother one day. After seeing there was much more to Love than just ambition and good looks, it was almost impossible for him not to fall for her. He tried hard to convince himself that he wasn't in love with her, but eventually he gave up trying. It was just too hard to deny it, at least to himself.

Of course he never let her know how he felt. She already had plenty of other men fighting for her attention, and she made it well known that she was in no way open to any office romances that might damage her reputation with the partners. She also made it very clear that she was not at all interested in settling down with one man at this time in her life. John respected that about her even if he did not agree with her lifestyle. He liked her straightforwardness and unapologetic way of living her life the way she wanted to. John also knew that even Love couldn't deny that from the moment they first met there was some kind of unexplainable, crazy electricity between the two of them. But he knew her well enough to know she would never admit she felt anything for him other than friendship.

The attraction John felt towards Love he felt the very first day he saw her at the firm. But the playful flirting and the friendship between them all started one late night at work. The two of them were working on one of the many assignments they were given together as the two new associates at the firm. Love had only been at the firm for two weeks, just a one week less than John. They both had something to prove because everyone assumed they were the firm's affirmative action poster children, being that they were the first black attorneys the firm had ever hired. That night Love had taken off her shoes. She was taller than most other women but without the high heels she always wore on she seemed very short to him. But that night when she stood across from him and took her shoes off, he had looked over at her and she seemed very tiny and vulnerable to him. It didn't make matters any better that she had pulled her long hair back into two ponytails and borrowed his extra large Dallas Cowboys sweat shirt he kept in his office to put on because the air conditioning in the building was freezing. The sweat shirt swallowed up her small frame. Suddenly she looked like a child to him and he just busted out laughing. In his defense he was a little loopy from working so late. Love demanded to know, over and over again, "what was so funny?", and she had this pouty, stubborn, headstrong look on her face just like a child would have, and that just made him laugh more. Finally he told her how he was just laughing because she looked like a little school girl.

Love had a knee jerk reaction to John's teasing and she took the shoe that she was still holding in her hand and threw it at him. Her shoe knocked him square in his head, even though she wasn't aiming for it. She felt awful and she ran over to him, thinking she had really hurt him. As she leaned in to inspect his bruised head, their eyes met. In that moment they almost kissed, but an interruption stopped them. The night maintenance worker opened the conference door and asked if they had any trash. Then the two of them looked at each other and they both busted out laughing.

They agreed they had both worked enough for that night and that they needed to take a break. They went out and got an early breakfast that Friday night from an all night diner and they walked along the beach and talked for hours afterwards about nothing really, but about everything, but work. From then on the ice was broken between them. After that there were no more uncomfortable silent moments between them, no cut throat competiveness, and the two of them instantly became best buds at work, and over the phone. Although the physical attraction they shared for each other often made the atmosphere tense if they had to be alone.

Ten years had passed since that night. John could hardly believe they had known each other for so long. He thought, the two of them were so young, back then. But since that night their lives had gone down two very different paths. Love was now partner, and he had over the years deepened his spiritual relationship with God and was actually contemplating leaving the practice of law one day and pursuing his call to God as a full time minister. John had not told Love or anyone else about what he was contemplating yet. Love and him were still friends, but they had not had a chance to sit down and have a long talk together in a very long time.

In the past John and Love had talked about their personal lives, their career goals, and the people they were dating. John clearly did more listening than talking in regards to the dating he did. He realized that Love acted like a man, when it came to dating men. He was amazed at how easy it was for her to behave like she did, *just like a man.* He wondered how she was able to date so many different men and never appear to become attached. Eventually John thought to himself his chances with Love had clearly sailed away a long time ago, back when she first started telling him about her various boyfriends. After a few years had went by John figured Love looked at him as if he was one of her girlfriends. But little did he know that Love was secretly very fond of him still in a very non-platonic way.

John was a very attractive man, and Love was generally appreciative of all handsome men, but John was also unique and special to Love in so many ways. She oftentimes had dreams about him at night, and going into work and seeing him was really the best thing about working at the firm. But Love did everything she could to make it clear to John and to herself that what was between the two of them was just friendship. So to diminish the physical attraction and affection she felt towards John, she forced herself to tell him all the details of her love life. These details she gave to him to make it clear they were friends and would never be nothing more. Love understood that a woman should never share so much about her love life with a man she ever had real intentions in being with. So she treated

John like a girlfriend to put a stop to any possibility she may have of going down a path of starting a romantic relationship with him. John was also the type of man Love was afraid of falling in love with because he was so unique to her, it was clear he was a very "good man". A part of Love felt like she didn't deserve someone as good as John. She thought she would eventually just break his heart by doing something to mess things up.

John was a co-pastor of his church, and he always asked Love to come visit the church on Sundays. John had been practicing abstinence for years now. He didn't drink alcoholic beverages, and he didn't swear. He hadn't always been like that when they had first met, almost ten years ago, but over the years his faith and devotion to living as a Christian grew stronger. Although Love sometimes suspected that every so often John back-slided, because sometimes for no apparent reason he seemed really down with himself. She knew his disappointment in himself couldn't be because of work, because besides herself, John was one of the most respected and retained attorneys at the firm.

Outside of work their views were quite different. John believed that love and sex were meant to coincide together, unlike Love. Love believed love and sex worked out best when separated. So Love continued to feel that anything more than friendship would never work out between them, because they were so different. Even being friends was somewhat of a struggle lately, because of their differing beliefs and strong opinions about their beliefs. The two of them had many late nights filled with philosophical conversations over the phone. Those conversations always ended in frustration for both of them, but they would always agree that they just disagreed on certain things but of course would always remain friends. Despite their differences they enjoyed each other's company and the strange, complicated friendship they had formed.

But lately their relationship had been strained. Ever since John started being a co-pastor at his church, his work focus was decreasing. John's focus was no longer on the firm, but on God and his church. He started passing the good assignments over to other associates. All the other associates were happy to have the opportunity to prove themselves so they were very happy with John. But Love was disappointed in him. She took his decrease in his work and lack of work dedication personally, because they were the only two African American attorneys at the firm after all. In a way John was always a reflection on her and vice versa. Also she sort of felt like he had abandoned her in some strange way. John told her he needed to decrease his workload so that he could spend more weekends and weekday evenings at the church. John was alternating giving sermons every other weekend with his pastor who was mentoring him, and he was leading the new member bible study classes at night.

In contrast to John, Love still gladly took each new assignment. Love's schedule and priorities had not changed from when the two of them had first met. Work was her priority, she released the stress every Friday and Saturday night, partying and drinking and having sex, and early Sunday morning she got up at 5 am went for a run, 7am she went to the homeless shelter, (that part no one knew of), and by 11am she was at work until 6 in the evening and then home in time to unwind and get a good night sleep for the upcoming work week. It was clear that John's and Love's goals in life had drastically moved in opposite directions. The further their goals and beliefs strayed from one another, the harder it was to keep their friendship afloat. It seemed to Love that all John had to talk about lately had to do with something about God or the Bible or his church. Love really wasn't trying to hear all that stuff about God and the church; that kind of talk irritated her and even made her angry at times. She knew it was irrational to have that sort of reaction, but she couldn't help it.

None of this changed John's fondness for Love, despite her obvious change in attitude toward him. He was happy to be assigned an out of town case with her. He was also looking forward to spending time alone with her and hoping they could use this chance to reconnect with one another. However, Love seemed to be making their time together as difficult as possible. It seemed to John that she was trying her best to drive an even wider wedge between them, and he couldn't understand why. The firm's jet had finally landed in New York. This was John's first time in New York, but he knew this wasn't a joy trip, it was business. He would have to vacation in New York another time. John knew Love had mentioned she was from New York, although she spoke very little about her own childhood. John wondered how Love felt about being back in her hometown.

Love looked out her window. She was back home for the first time in years, but there was no warm and fuzzy feeling that came over her. There was nothing left in New York for Love and nothing about the city that gave her any joy in being back there. Love had not been back to New York in almost twenty years, and of all the hotels for Mr. Swanson's secretary to book them in she had picked the same hotel Love stayed in before flying off to college. It was like a very bad *dejavu* trip for Love. She told herself to focus on the job at hand and to keep all the bad memories that kept creeping into her mind away while she walked into the hotel lobby.

John smiled at Love when he saw the hotel they were going to be staying in. "Now I like these accommodations, but I guess I shouldn't expect less traveling with one of the firm's Partners."

Love didn't return his smile.

"Well let's check in, get a good night's sleep and I'll meet you first thing in the lobby tomorrow morning, at five."

"You sure you don't want to at least get some dinner together before you turn in Love?"

"No thanks John, I'm not really hungry and I'm sort of tired. I'll see you in the morning."

The next morning John walked down to the lobby fifteen minutes late and Love was already waiting for him outside in the limousine the firm had rented for them. John said, "good morning" to Love and their driver. Love just got straight to business as usual.

"You're running a little late John. Did you get enough rest? You sure you're ready for today?"

John usually had a cheerful disposition and that morning was no different. He had a big, warm smile on his face. "You know I was born ready. I just had to get some cash from the ATM and run back up to the room to leave a tip for the maid. Sorry I'm a little late." (John noticed Love didn't even crack a smile at him, and she didn't say good morning to him either.)

"By the way you know you could start out with a, "good morning John", that would be nice."

"Your right, I apologize I'm not a morning person. Maybe after my first cup of coffee, I'll be in a better mood for you."

John thought even though Love was saying she apologized, her tone was still sarcastic. Then John wondered if maybe the fact that she was appointed partner just two days ago already had blown up her already big head, but something told him it was more than that. It was as if she was personally mad at him about something, but what he had no idea? John wondered if she no longer wanted to work with him, because he had been slacking off lately at work. Love had complained that she thought he was letting his competitive edge at work slide ever since he had become co-pastor at his church. He wondered had he been so slack that she no longer had confidence in his legal abilities? He knew as a new partner, despite their friendship, she would want the best lawyer at the firm assisting her. One question was answered for him by her mood. She definitely did not request him being assigned with her to this case. One of the other partners must have assigned him to work with her.

The driver put John's two bags in the trunk and then John got into the limousine. As soon as John sat down, Love immediately started going over the plans of what they needed to accomplish to complete their assignment.

"Lets' see, so the private investigator we hired located where the first black doctor in Roosevelt, Long Island lived. Hopefully he still lives in the same residence. You would think for the money we gave him, the investigator could have given us more information than just an address and name. Even if we did give him less than 15 hours notice. So we should be at the good doctor's house in about 50 minutes. We need to find out today who his son is and where he is at, and then try to speak to him today if possible. We're on a tight schedule. I hope this doctor is the same one we're looking for John."

"He will be, don't worry about it Love. The investigator said at that time there was only one African American doctor living in Long Island, New York. It's got to be him."

"Hopefully you're right. We also need to be on the plane no later than the end of tonight to get an international adoption accomplished before this impossible seven day deadline Mr. Swanson has given us. And about the other portion of our assignment, finding a child for an expedited adoption.., so John, what did you find out when you checked your research on adoption laws and the different countries Mr. Swanson has connections with?" Before John could answer Love's first question she was already asking him another question. "And which country is most likely to allow us to take a child out of their country for adoption within the next few days, and be swayed to skip a few steps because of their ties to Mr. Swanson?"

"Well of course an adoption here in the states is ruled out. Our country has very strict home study and background investigation requirements."

"I'm well aware of that."

"So according to my research I've narrowed it down to about five different countries, four of them being in Africa, and also China, however, Mr. Swanson's connections in China are dated, going back over thirty years. He does have a very influential associate now working in the Ethiopian government. By the way Love you do know Adoption and International Adoptions are not my expertise, ..., and I was wondering why I was even assigned this case with you?"

Love abruptly answered. "Mr. Swanson wanted you on it, but I have no idea why. He just respects you I suppose. But you know this area of practice is not my specialty either, but he wanted people on it that he trusted. But just let me know if you're not up for this and I will call back to the firm and see if I can get a last minute replacement. I know since we will be away for a while it will mean you missing bible study classes and Sunday service back at the church."

"No that's not what I was trying to say. I was just wondering. Sorry if it sounded like I was making excuses or complaints. Really I'm happy to be picked for this. I'm happy to just be here with you, Love. You know I miss working on a case with you."

Love felt awkward. She knew this was John's sincere attempt to get close to her again. For so many reasons she wanted to keep her distance. So she tried to just brush his last comment off. "Well that's good to hear. But getting back to business at hand, you mentioned Mr. Swanson's has a very influential associate in Ethiopia, who is that?"

"The President."

"Well that settles it, I guess we're going to Ethiopia tonight then."

"Surprisingly, it even appears that Mr. Swanson owns a lot of stock in Starbucks and he also has coffee bean farm land in Ethiopia he owns and sells coffee beans to Starbucks Corporation. I was sort of surprised about that."

"I don't know why that would surprise you. I mean we are talking about Mr. Swanson he has his hand into almost everything, and he didn't get to be one of the richest men in the country just by practicing law."

"Well I was sort of surprise because Mr. Swanson hates coffee. Now if he had stock in a distillery that wouldn't surprise me." Then John gave Love another quick grin. Anyway, I think we can call in some favors very easily there, because their adoption laws are not very strict anyway, and they have plenty of orphans there. It seems like the president is actually a friend of Mr. Swanson's. His secretary told me to let her know if she should call ahead if that was where we were planning on going."

Love looked off absentmindedly she was thinking about how she could really use a good cup of coffee right now. Starbucks coffee sounded really good right about now. It would get her going. Then she said in a very sweet voice to the limousine driver, "excuse me, can you please stop at the nearest Starbucks, before you head to our destination?"

"No problem Ma'am."

Love hated it when people called her Ma'am; it made her feel old. She used a very more detached, serious voice when she spoke to John next. "John why don't you make the call to Mr. Swanson's secretary and tell her to call ahead to the Ethiopian President and explain to them who we are and what we need, and that we need meetings set up with all the appropriate officials first thing Monday morning if possible."

"Okay, I'm on it." John thought to himself, she is even more polite to our driver than she is to me. He told himself not to take it personally. She is probably under a lot of stress now because she is trying to prove herself by being successful with her first assignment as partner. The driver pulled up to Starbucks, and he asked Love and John if they would like him to go get their drinks. John replied, "that's alright I will run in". Then John asked Love and the driver what they wanted. Love, said "a Grande, Ethiopian Blend, no cream or sugar", the driver said "I don't usually drink coffee, but I have always been curious about Starbucks coffee, so I will just get the same thing she just said, but I would like a little cream and sugar, and thanks."

"No problem." When John got back into the car he handed everyone their drinks.

Love took a few sips and just the taste seemed to instantaneously calm her. Logically Love knew coffee should make her jittery but it seemed to have the opposite effect on her. Then Love said, "thank you John, this is just what I needed", and she flashed her first genuine smile at him that morning. No matter how badly Love behaved just one smile from her made up for her poor behavior with John. John felt the same undeniable affection for Love as he had always felt. John attempted to start up a conversation with Love once again now that it seemed she was in a better mood from her coffee fix.

"Isn't it a coincidence that you are going to get to visit the country where your favorite Starbucks coffee is grown?"

"Yeah that should be interesting. Maybe I can get some beans "to go" while I'm there. I mean our boss does own some coffee bean farms, right." Then she flashed him that smile he loved so much once again.

"But it is sad how the Ethiopian farmers are really very poor..."

This type of talk started to dampen Love's mood, but John didn't seem to notice.

"I wish there was something I could do to help the farmers, you know. Did I tell you, some people from my church are forming a missionary group to go to Africa. Oh and Love did you know that some people say that the Ark of the Covenant is secretly housed in a temple in Ethiopia, and how Ethiopia has a whole group of Ethiopian Jews and Christians? They say when Queen Sheba came to visit King Solomon, you know that's in the bible, well many historians feel she was from Ethiopia and that she in turn brought back the Jewish religion to her homeland. Wouldn't it be amazing if we could actually see the Ark of the Covenant, if it was actually in Ethiopia?"

Love was staring at John with a blank expression on her face. John assumed she was wondering what the heck he was talking about. "I'm sorry Love, I just assumed you knew what the Ark of the Covenant was, but a lot of people don't if they are not religious. I've been spending so much time in the church and bible study classes that sometimes I forget a lot of very intellectual people don't know much about what is in the bible."

Love was still staring at John, but now her smile had vanished. "John, even if I knew what the Ark of the Covenant was, how would seeing it be amazing to me. You know I don't believe in any of that stuff. Furthermore, in regards to the whole sad social status of the Ethiopian farmers, John, did you really have to tell me all of that and ruin the first pleasure this morning, my coffee, by trying to make me feel guilty about drinking it?" After she felt like she had said her peace, she went back to staring out the window. The only thing Love hated more than losing money, was talking about God, religion or the bible. Love had decided she didn't believe in God after Nana died, after being shuffled around to the fourth foster home in less than a year, after the fire that killed Hope, and after deciding that Faith be better off without her. Love was sure now that if God existed he wasn't concerned her. Her goal in life was about doing one thing, pleasing herself. Love had convinced herself that happiness equaled money, and power and freedom. Money brought freedom to be and to do whatever she wanted to in life. While Love quietly contemplated all the reasons she did not believe in God. John was thinking about how Love's bad attitude was really starting to get on his last nerve. Then he decided to finally say something about it.

"Love, you know how much I care for you. I know you try to put up this hard exterior, but deep down I know you really do have a big heart. I just don't understand why you try to always pretend like you don't care about anything else, but making money, and spending it. I know there is much more to you than that. I'm going to be honest with you, I've known for years that you volunteer at the homeless shelter every Sunday morning, and I know you must be working on all those pro bono cases for the neglected and abused on your own free time too."

Love didn't like this, she wondered how John knew about her personal affairs, had he'd been checking up on her? "John this is why I really didn't want you on this assignment with me. You need to figure out how to not blur the line between friendship and business. We don't have time for you to psychoanalyze me on this trip. Really, I didn't ask you to become my psychologist, last time I checked. I mean just because you have gone all Christian doesn't give you the right to do, I don't know whatever you are trying to do. You use to be just like me when I first met you, remember. Now this is my first assignment as partner. Frankly all I care about is completing this assignment swiftly and successfully. The only reason I go to the shelter and do pro bono, is it looks great on a resume. So please let us stay focused on the assignment, okay."

"Okay then, I understand you want to make a good impression and complete this assignment. Hey, you know I've got your back. I will do everything I can to help you be a success. I just figured that we could talk about other things besides work. I mean we are still friends right, and we really haven't connected with each other in a while. Look, maybe you didn't ask me to psychoanalyze you, but we are friends. I'm just trying to talk to you as a friend. Someone needs to; I mean you have to admit, you've got issues."

John didn't realize it but he had really pushed a button in Love with his last comment. Love was beyond just being irritated with John. Now she also was feeling pissed off, and offended. Love thought to herself, "who does he think he is, what makes him think I need talking to like I'm some kind of child? Just because he done got all spiritual, now all of a sudden I've got issues, and he thinks he can fix my issues."

"John, you and I are co-workers. I have plenty of girlfriends. If I want advice I will ask one of them for some. I don't want advice from a man I barely spend any time with, outside of work. You ever think maybe you are the one who has got the issues. You ever think that maybe the reason you started getting all into the church, and discovered there is more to life than money is because you couldn't keep up with the competition at work. Maybe church is your out for not being able to cut it at the job. Look at the evidence, me and you started at the firm at the same time. You could have been the one who was made partner the other day."

"Look Love I know my advice and maybe even my friendship may not be what you want, but it is *what you need*, and even if you don't consider me a friend, I will always consider you one. One more thing Love you can count on me, no matter what, I will always tell you the truth, even if you don't want to hear it."

Love knew she had gone too far, telling John he was just a co-worker to her, she didn't mean that. But her pride kept her from apologizing, and from letting him know that she did need his friendship. Love knew John was the only person in her life that spoke the truth to her, even when she didn't want to hear it. But Love couldn't bring herself to apologize. So, instead she just stared out of the window.

They arrived at their destination in Long Island. Love thought to herself that it would be a miracle if this doctor was actually home. John, ranged the doorbell, and they waited for a while before someone answered. Then a somewhat short, dark complexioned, white haired, older gentleman, opened the door. With a warm and genuine smile, the elderly doctor said, "may I help you?"

"Sir, we are looking for Doctor Carlson."

"Well that's me son, unless you are looking for my son. He's also a doctor. I'm retired and now I just teach at the university. How can I help you two?"

Love smiled. "Sir, my name is Love, do you mind if we come in and talk to you? It's sort of a long, complicated, story."

The Doctor was very trusting, especially for a New Yorker and he invited them right into his house. Besides a lovely lady riding up to his house in a limousine didn't really seem like much of a threat to him.

Love started explaining the whole story; about how her and John were looking to find his adopted son, to introduce him to his possible birth mother. The Doctor listened attentively, while he offered them some coffee. After about thirty minutes of fully explaining things, Love was quiet, and she waited for the Doctor to respond.

The Doctor walked away from them quietly. Then he explained how his wife had recently passed away, and then he started to confess how they came to adopt his son. He confessed to Love and John that they were correct, his son was never actually legally adopted by them. He said his wife and him knew it was wrong, but they never regretted what they did, but they did regret the lies they had to keep telling to cover it all up. "But my wife is gone now, and I'm too old to care about what's going to happen to me anymore. I just don't want to carry the secret about how I actually got my son anymore. We told him we didn't know who his adopted parents were. We told him that it was a closed adoption and the information was sealed. We never have told him that his birth mother was in such a bad state, so far gone on drugs and she was also a prostitute. I doubted she was even alive anymore. But now that you say she is alive, I know my son will want to meet her. He had asked about her a few months after his mother had passed away. But right now my son is out of the country, but if you leave me your information when he gets back I will explain everything to him and give him your numbers."

"I'm sorry Sir, but is there any way you can tell us how to get in touch with him? You see we are on some pretty tight time restraints."

"Is his biological mother sick? He will never forgive me if she dies before he has a chance to meet her."

Love didn't correct the Doctor about his presumption, and she motioned to John to keep his mouth shut.

"Well Sir all I can say is time is of the essence. Do you think that maybe you can give us the location of your son? I can give you all my identification to ensure you I am legitimately trying to locate him to get him in touch with his biological mother."

The Doctor looked at Love and he couldn't help but trust her, she looked as innocent as an angel. He explained to Love that his son was traveling to Ethiopia with his girlfriend and he

gave her the name and phone number to the hotel he was staying
in. Then he asked Love to give his son a note he wrote down
that explained everything to his son about his true adoption and
asked his son for his forgiveness for lying to him.

Love felt compassion for the Doctor. She knew exactly
what it was like to live with secrets all your life. A part of her
sometimes wanted to confess all her secrets to someone just to
get the burden of them off of her chest. But Love knew she
wasn't the confessing type. She trusted no one enough in life to
tell them all her secrets. Love hugged the Doctor before leaving
his house. "Sir, don't worry, I'm sure your son will forgive you
of everything. Also we aren't going to report this illegal
adoption to the authorities either. We are only interested in
trying to reunite your son with his birth mother. You can rest
assure that what we have discussed here today is confidential."

"Thank you Miss."

"Are you positive that the lady who gave you your son
called herself Princess?"

"I'm 100% positive that is what she said her name was.
I mean that is definitely a name that a person wouldn't forget,
even after all these years."

Love and the Doctor exchanged agreeing smiles before
she left his home. Once they were back in the limousine John
said, "wow, that was surprisingly easy." Then John called Mr.
Swanson's secretary and gave her instructions to schedule flight
plans with the firm's jet company and hotel accommodations for
them in Ethiopia.

Love was thinking, "what are the odds that his son
would be vacationing in the same place we can set up a quick
adoption for Mr. Swanson." Although she would never admit it
to John if she did believe in miracles she would have to say this
coincidence seemed to be one. She called Mr. Swanson up while
John was on his cell phone making arrangements.

Mr. Swanson answered on the first ring, "Hello Love,
tell me something good."

"Well Mr. Swanson I can hardly believe it myself but
everything is going smoother than I would had ever imagined.
We might actually have this assignment completed before the
seven day deadline if things keep going this smoothly."

"Love I think that's because it's destined for me to marry her, and I also think it has something to do with the fact that I picked the perfect person to get the job done for me. Love, I knew you wouldn't let me down. Just keep me updated. You caught me here at the jewelers picking out engagement rings. Let me get off the phone now I have to haggle this jeweler down. I don't care how rich I get, I never pay full price for anything, that's just bad business. Take care and don't give John too hard of a time. He's a good man you know."

"I know. And I also think you might be trying to do some match making of your own by sending him out here with me, but just so you know John and I are strictly professional associates Mr. Swanson, and that is the way it's going to stay. Okay?"

"Okay Love, if you say so. I have to go now, keep up the good work."

Forty-five minutes later, Love and John were boarding the company jet out of airport and heading to Ethiopia.

Chapter 9
Hope Springs Eternal

For the first time in several days Hope decided to have something to eat. Funny thing was she knew she should be famished but she didn't feel so. When the rebel guard dropped off the tray through the slot in the door this time Hope didn't ignore it as she had been doing the past few days. Today she felt famished and she retrieved her tray of food and even whispered just barely, "thank you". She had never said thank you to any of the rebel guards before that day. It would have seemed ridiculous, even traitorous to do so just a few short days ago. But now she felt thankful for everything, for just being alive. Hope walked over to the other side of the cell and sat down against the wall, and started to eat. It must have been at least three or four minutes later when the person behind the door said very quietly, "you're welcome."

Hope was stunned for a moment by the short and simple response. She realized how much she missed human contact, and she immediately had the urge to say something as quick as possible to the person on the other side of the door to keep the conversation from ending. The only thing that came to her mind was, "so what is your name?"

There was another pause and then the person behind the door finally responded.

"My name is Amir Ishmael Abdul."

"Well that is a mouthful, but it is a beautiful name, did you know Amir means, Prince?"

"Yes I do, but I assure you that was only my mother's wishful thinking. I'm no Prince. So what is your name?"

Hope thought to herself that this rebel soldier Amir sounded like he was so young, just a boy. His voice was so youthful no matter how much he tried to deepen it. Hope could tell he was trying to sound rigid and hard. She could also tell that Amir seemed eager to want to talk to her, maybe as much as she wanted to talk to him. Hope noticed that Amir spoke English very well. Of course she had her suspicions that maybe he was only communicating with her to eventually try to get some vital information out of her. But at the moment her desire for human contact won out and she was not concerned about his motives. Hope knew that there was no way she would hand over any information that was vital. So she decided she would continue her conversation with this young man. She thought to herself, "for all I know this rebel may be the last person I ever speak to on this Earth." So Hope finally answered him, "you mean you don't already know my name young Prince Amir?"

"No I don't, none of the others have talked or told anything to us, about you. They are all very loyal to each other and to you. But it is obvious that you must be their leader, as strange as that seems. Is that much true?"

Hope ignored Amir's questions. "So the others are all still alive and well, like myself?"

"Yes they are being treated as well as you are, per orders from our leader. All of you are considered very valuable commodities, for now. Our leader feels that all of you can be used as bargaining tools, at least he feels that way for now."

"Your English is very good, Amir."

"My mother was educated briefly in America. She dreamed that one day I would go abroad and attend a university. So at an early age she taught me English. However, my mother's dreams of me going to a university died when she died. Shortly after my mother's death my father returned to my village, and took me out of school and brought me to come live here with him and to join his rebel forces. Ever since then I have been living with my father's rebel army and fighting for them."

"So you're telling me that your father is the leader?"

"Yes, my father is the leader of this camp. There are other forces in allegiance with him, but he is the leader of this particular platoon. He is training me to eventually become his second in command. For now my father feels I am still too young to command. My opinion does not matter to him though. I must only obey him and wait until he says I am ready. So I must do these menial duties such as serve our prisoners their meals, and of course whatever else he commands, until he decides I am ready to lead at his side." Amir was very talkative and curious about Hope. He continued talking and asking Hope questions about herself. He asked Hope if she knew that she was

the only female prisoner there at the camp right now. He asked
her if she knew all the rebel men in the camp were offended, and
repulsed by her supposed role as leader over the other captured
men. Then Amir went on to tell Hope that the men feel they will
be cursed by Allah and will forever have a woman rule over
them if they were to even look upon her lustfully, and definitely
if they were to lay with her.

Hope was wondering where he was going with all this
unsolicited information. Then Amir interrupted her thoughts by
talking again. Hope thought, "he's a little chatter box, just like a
lonely child."

Amir continued talking. "So you see you have nothing
to fear. No one here would dare violate you. They don't even
want to touch you less they be cursed by Allah. They will only
do what they are required to do by my father in watching over
you, and then kill you if he eventually commands it."

Then Hope realized that Amir was trying his best to
comfort her in his own way. But she found it sort of funny how
he went about doing this, and she could not help laughing a little.
It was the first time Hope had laughed or even smiled since she
was captured.

Amir was confused. He didn't want anyone to hear her
laughing while he was with her. He quickly demanded she be
quiet. As soon as she was silent he asked her why she was
laughing.

"Well, what you just said was probably the funniest
thing I've heard in a really long time, or either being confined
for so long has just given me a very strange sense of humor."

"I agree with you about you having a strange sense of
humor. You're definitely the strangest woman I've ever met."

"So Amir, why aren't you offended or repulsed by me?
Aren't you afraid you will be cursed by Allah, and forever be
ruled over by a woman for talking to me also? Or did your
father tell you to strike up a conversation with me and get
information out of me?"

"No, my father wouldn't want me talking to you either.
Plus he is away right now patrolling. He left me here in the
camp. My mother would not have disapproved of me talking to
you. She had spent a few years in America, when she was very

young on a student Visa. Then she decided to return home, because she was betrothed to my father. At that time the village had high hopes for my father that he would become a very influential force in our government. So I heard my mother's parents pressured her into carrying out the duties they expected from her. She told me that if she had not returned home she would have shamed her father and her whole family. Since my father was gone all the time fighting, my mother and I spent all our time together, just the two of us. I was her only child. She told me many stories about America; and about her life before she was married to my father. She told me how women were treated very different in America. But that's not the only reason I'm talking to you, none of the men left behind here with me really want to spend time around me. They all think I'm a spy left behind by my father to tell him about any of their indiscretions. See my father is a very strict leader. He is hard on his men, even cruel to them. So they think that I will report back to him about anyone I overhear complaining about his harsh treatment, or report anyone I hear questioning his orders. So I guess I do miss having someone to talk to, and I especially miss talking to my mother. I guess talking to you, another woman, reminds me of talking to my own mother. My father does not talk to me. He only gives me orders. I miss my mother, and I also miss my friends back at my mother's village."

Hope could hear the pain in Amir's voice. He sounded so childlike and she felt sad for him. "How long ago did your mother die Amir?"

"It has been almost three months now since her death. She died the night of my thirteenth birthday party."

Hope couldn't help but think that was around the age when she first went into foster care. For the first time she felt sadness for someone she was suppose to hate someone she considered to be the enemy. She also felt compassion for someone who she knew she was suppose to have no mercy for, at least according to her mission orders. Hope thought to herself, "I could be this boy's mother. My God, he is only fourteen."

Then Amir said he had to go, but before he left he asked Hope again what her name was.

"I guess you can call me whatever the other men call me, if you want. It really doesn't matter to me."

"No I don't think I want to call you, "that cursed woman". Amir understood she did not trust him, but he didn't really expect her to. The fact was that he didn't care if she trusted him enough even to tell him her name. He just liked having someone to talk to again. "I'll call you, "strange woman", instead." Then he let out a very short, quiet laugh to himself as he walked away.

Over the next few days Hope and Amir talked much more to each other, but Hope still had not given him her name. Amir's father was gone so Amir had no one keeping tabs on him, and no one who cared about what he was doing with his spare time. Sometimes Amir would talk to Hope for hours when he would take guard watch duty over her prison cell. Hope would tell him all about the different countries she had seen. She would tell him about the different books she had read, the movies she had watched, and the music she had listened to. Amir was like a sponge just soaking it all up. He would imagine and try to live out his dreams of seeing the world through Hope's stories.

Amir talked about his mother and his friends back at the village. He talked about the girl he liked back at his village, but how he never had the courage to tell her before his father took him. He told Hope if he ever made it back to his village the first thing he would do is take that girl into his arms and kiss her. He said, "she would probably smack me right afterwards but it would be worth it. Besides, now that I've killed men I'm no longer fearful of a silly girl's rejection."

Hope teased him. "Really you would just go up to her and kiss her no fear at all?"

"Okay maybe I would try to strike up a conversation with her first."

They spoke of more serious matters also. He told her about all the death and destruction he had witnessed in the few short months he had joined the rebellion. He explained to her how his father was the most ruthless man he had ever known. He told her how his father forced him watch as he kill people, and how some of the boys he killed were even younger than him.

He explained to Hope how he had no doubt that if he ever embarrassed his father by not following his orders that his father would kill him without remorse or any hesitation. Amir explained that if he disobeyed his father's orders it would cause confusion in the camp. His father would have no other choice but to kill him, to ensure order in his camp. Amir was his father's youngest son, but all of Amir's older brothers by his father's other wives had died fighting in the rebellion forces. "My mother was his youngest bride, until her death. She almost died giving birth to me and afterwards she was unable to bear him anymore children. I secretly suspect my father had someone poison her food the evening of my coming of age ceremony, the night that she died."

"Amir your father does sound like a harsh man, but why would he poison her, what could he profit from doing that?"

"My mother suddenly fell ill and then died all in the same night. She was just fine earlier that day. My father served her food to her that night and stated he was serving her in honor of her giving him such a fine son. It would have been disgraceful for her not to eat the food he had served her. You see, just the week prior to that my mother had secretly spoken out to the village leaders against my father's treatment of the village's women and young men. She disagreed with the rebellion, and she disagreed with how he was forcing all the young men to come fight for him even if they did not want to, and with how he was forcing the young women to lay down with the men at their whim, as if they were prostitutes. She wanted the villagers to stand up against him. Then later that night she fell sick and by morning time she was dead."

Hope was touched by how easily Amir had opened up to her, and she in return also told Amir about her own past, but without giving any specific details she told Amir her story. She told him how her father and mother were not there for her and her sisters. She told him how her and her sisters were then separated when her Grandmother died. She told him about the horrible things that happened to her while being in foster care. She also told him that she understood the guilt he must have felt when he had to kill in the past, because she had killed men too. Hope even shared with Amir how all the horrible things she had experienced as a child, and as a soldier had kept her up many a sleepless night. Although Hope opened up to Amir on an emotional level, she still had not told Amir any specific details about herself. She still had suspicion towards him and his unexpected, sudden friendship. But she had shared more about her emotional struggles with him than with anyone else, ever before. She found it amazing how close she felt in such a short period of time to a complete stranger who was nowhere close to her own age. Hope assumed this closeness she felt was because in the back of her mind she thought Amir might be the last person she would have contact with before she died.

And Amir felt very close to Hope also. He admitted to her that he could not sleep at night because of his nightmares. He said the faces of the boys he had killed haunted him in his dreams.

Hope understood exactly what he was feeling. She was haunted by the faces of the men she had killed in wars, at least up until recently. Hope felt like although herself and Amir were generations apart, raised miles apart in different areas of the world, and even polar opposites in their religious views, that still it was as if they were kindred spirits who shared similar life experiences and similar fears.

Then Amir told Hope that he thought if there is a hell he would surely go to it for all the things that he had done, and he asked Hope how it was that she stopped the nightmares she had from coming back.

Hope explained to Amir that she use to think that she would go to hell, because she had killed people during war also. She told Amir that her only comfort was that she would tell herself, "there is no hell, there's only life on this Earth." "But now", Hope went on to explain to Amir, "Now I no longer think I will go to hell. In fact I'm confident when the day comes I'll end up in heaven." Hope continued to tell Amir, that now she was no longer fearful of death, and she told him, because of this she now sleeps peacefully throughout the night.

Amir thought to himself, "how could someone in her predicament, imprisoned, be so calm and so at peace at a time like this?"

Hope could feel Amir's fear, his sadness, his despair about his future, even without seeing his face, she could still feel it. Then Hope said the first thing that came to her mind to help him, "you should pray Amir."

"Pray? Pray for what?"

"Amir, you should pray about your fears or whatever else is on your heart. If you want we can pray together right now. Pray to God and Jesus to save you from this place. Then believe and trust that he will answer your prayers. He has answered my prayers. I know he will answer yours if you believe."

"How has he answered your prayers? You are still imprisoned. I think that maybe you've been praying for the wrong things." Then Amir couldn't help but laugh a little. Hope couldn't help but laugh too. But surprisingly Amir continued asking questions about praying, about Hope's God and her Jesus.

He said, "I've heard of Jesus, "Jesus, the prophet", why should I pray to him, if Allah cannot keep my nightmares from keeping me up all night, if Allah cannot stop this hell I live in everyday of my life, how can Jesus, just a mere prophet, change my life?"

Hope said in a soft, calming voice, "not Jesus, "the prophet", Amir. Pray to "Jesus", our savior, your savior. That's if you want him to be your savior." Then Hope suddenly remembered all the names her Nana use to call Jesus, and how whenever Nana was feeling sad or afraid, she would just start calling on Jesus. Before Hope even finished completing her thoughts, she realized she was calling out Jesus' names, just like Nana use to. Hope overheard herself talking and praising, like she never had before, it was as if some unseen force was actually just talking through her, and she was a bystander watching herself.

Hope was softly reciting all the many names Nana would call Jesus, "*Jesus, the truth, the way, the light, Jesus, my redeemer, my conqueror, my creator, my faithful friend, my hiding place, my quieter of fears, Jesus, King of Kings, Lord of Lords, Jesus, Prince of Peace, Joy Unspeakable, Everlasting Life, Neverending Love, Jesus, the Alpha and Omega, Exalted*

Name Above All, My Only Hope, My Salvation, Son of God, My Lord, My Savior, Jesus, Jesus, Jesus."[9]

      There was a very long silence and pause, after Hope stopped talking. Hope had never witnessed to anyone before. She couldn't help but think to herself in the silence of her cell that Amir must be thinking she has gone crazy and that he probably got up and walked away. Hope was sure she was screaming Jesus praises so loudly that she stirred up the whole prison camp because she felt on fire with passion for God at the time. But actually Hope was speaking so softly, without even knowing it she was being very quiet. When she spoke to Amir, she was as quiet as a whisper, as soft as a summer's wind. She couldn't see Amir through the slot in the door. But if she could have seen his face, she would have seen that Amir was moved to tears by all of Hope's words. He had tears falling from his weary eyes for the first time since his mother had died, tears were streaming down his cheeks. He was kneeled down on the ground, with his face to the floor in total awe. He was in awe that a strange woman's tiny, soft voice could make him cry. Amir had never felt so moved before, as he did at that moment, by the sound and sincerity and love that came from Hope's voice, out of her little cell, as she, *gently whispered*[10], her praises about Jesus to him. Amir thought to himself, it was as if there was a light in her that even the cell walls could not snuff out. He wanted more than anything to have that light. A light bright enough to kill all the darkness inside of him, and surrounding him. Amir thought to himself that whatever it was that she had in her he wanted it, he needed it. He needed to find a way to hold on to his own hope and faith even in the face of evil and death. Then Amir wiped the tears from his face and said, "can you tell me more about "your Jesus?"…..

      "Sure, I can, you were so quiet I thought you had walked away."

---

[9] John 14:6, Colossians 1:16, 1 Corinthians 1:9, Proverbs 1:33, Psalm 32:7, 1 Timothy 6:15, Isaiah 9:6, 1 Corinthians 2:8, 1 Peter 1:8, John 3:16, Jeremiah 31:3, Revelation 1:8, Philippians 2:9, Ephesians 2:12, 1 Corinthians 10:4.
[10] 1 Kings 19:12.

"No, I couldn't even move while you whispered those words to me, it was so powerful. But I do have to go. It will have to wait until tomorrow for you to tell me more. I have to get back now, but tomorrow, we will talk more about Jesus, okay. Oh, and you don't have to whisper, no one is close enough to hear you, besides me. And your Amharic is excellent, much better than my English. You never mentioned you spoke my native language. You sounded as native as my own late mother." Amir said his goodbyes for the day to Hope, and assured her once again he would be back tomorrow.

Hope thought to herself after Amir was gone, "*I was speaking Amharic,* I've never even been trained in that dialect?" Then Hope's thoughts were interrupted when she heard Amir's footsteps running back towards her cell.

"One more thing before I go. You never did tell me, what your "real" name was. I'm growing weary of calling you the "strange woman"."

There was still a part of Hope that felt like she shouldn't fully trust this young man. She was trained to never give the enemy any personal information about herself, no details, even your name. She had already told him too much about her life as far as she was concerned, but at least she had not given him any traceable details. To tell him something as simple, but real, as her birth name would be in her mind to betray everything she took an oath towards in regards to her loyalty to the Corps. She was still not ready to forsake her loyalties in those regards. So she answered Amir with a question, "what does it really matter what my name is?"

"I understand, you don't trust me so you don't want to tell me your name, but I will still be back regardless, to hear about the one named Jesus."

Chapter 10
Faith lands in Africa

"I love coffee, I love tea, I love a colored boy and he loves me….first comes love and then comes marriage, then comes the baby in the baby carriage.",

"Faith, Faith, Nene, wake-up Nene, we're here." Darryl was gently trying to wake Faith. He thought she looked like an angel when she slept. He rarely got the chance to watch her sleeping. He always seemed to fall asleep before she did.

Faith was dreaming. She was dreaming about being a child and watching her older sisters jumping double-dutch. Faith remembered how she felt, sitting on the stoop, watching them jump rope and wishing she knew how to jump double-dutch. At that time Faith only knew how to jump straight rope. Her sisters were still teaching her how to jump dutch, and they rarely gave her a chance to turn the rope, because she was "double handed". Double handed was what the girls who sort of turned the rope, off rhythm were called. She remembered how much she admired and envied her older sisters. How she thought they were so beautiful, funny, smart and so good at everything, and how she wanted to grow up and be just like them. She wondered if she was anything like her older sisters now, and would they be proud of her if they knew her? She was waking up from her dreams and to the sound of Darryl's soft voice and gentle nudges. She thought his voice was so beautiful. Darryl was whispering in her ear, "baby, we're here, we're here…"

Finally, Faith woke up, and she looked out the window. She still was feeling a slight sadness from the dream she had just woken up from, and the ache she always felt from missing her sisters. However, she couldn't help feeling a renewed excitement shortly after realizing she was back in Africa. Africa was like a second home to Faith. Faith had been to Ethiopia several times in the past. The first time Faith was in Ethiopia she was with her parents when she was a little girl. Faith thought to herself how lucky she was to be one of those rare people in the world who actually did something they loved for a living.

Darryl was excited to be in Africa too. This was all very new and adventurous for him. Although he would have been just as happy spending a week in Hawaii with Faith or even at home in New York without any distractions to keep them away from each other. Traveling to foreign countries was never one of Darryl's desires, because of his fear of flying and infectious diseases. But once he was on solid ground he allowed himself to feel more excited. "I can't wait to check into that hotel and take a nice hot shower and a long nap. That was a long flight."

Faith smiled, she knew Darryl was not the outdoorsy type and he was a little obsessive about being clean. She remembered when they were kids he would complain about camping out just in the backyard. Faith would be pretending they were in the woods and that she heard a bear or a wolf, and Darryl would say, "we could go roast these marshmallows right in the den at the fireplace and play scrabble." But even back then he would endure spending the night outside, because Faith wanted to.

"Darryl I usually go straight to the village or community that SACAA has set up in and retrieve the orphans, and I reserve the hotel rooms for when I'm finished at SACAA to bring all the children back. So you should know that the SACAA facilities are usually more like huts and tents, than hotels. I guess I should have warned you about that."

"Oh, well then so we aren't going straight to the hotel? Well I hope the SACAA facilities at least have hot showers, don't they?"

"Sometimes, sometimes not, but how about this, since it is your first time out with me, we can check into the hotel first and freshen up, before we hire a driver to take us to the SACAA facilities."

"Now that sounds like a plan."

The two of them checked into the Hotel, it was a quaint little hotel close to the airport. Their room was clean, with a huge ceiling fan above the bed and it had a shower. A shower was all Darryl needed. Darryl immediately dropped his bags and told Faith he was going to jump in the shower, and then take a quick power nap. Unlike other people Darryl could not sleep on the airplane. He was just too wound up and tense the whole flight. While Darryl was in the bathroom, Faith got on the phone and started making arrangements to obtain a driver as soon as possible to take them to the SACAA's village location. The hotel's concierge explained to her that it would be difficult to get a driver to take her out to the villages. He explained that any driver was going to demand a very high fee to travel out to the villages because of the civil rebellion that was currently going on. Faith explained to the concierge that she was with SACAA, and that she was familiar with similar situations and she was willing to pay whatever was demanded to a competent guide and driver.

"Yes Ma'am then I will make the appropriate calls and ring you back."

Next, Faith called the United States Ethiopian Ambassador's office. The embassy and the Ambassador worked closely with SACAA representatives. She informed them she was in town and was just informed about the recent uprising. She asked if it was possible to get some military escorts to go with her to the SACAA station at the designated village. The representative told her they were going to make some phone calls and call her back, and that they were already advised by SACAA that she was expected to arrive today. The next phone call Faith made was for room service. She ordered one of everything on the menu, it was a short menu. One thing she liked about working for SACAA was that they never questioned her expense account. They had total trust in her and as long as she got the job done, she pretty much purchased whatever she wanted on the corporate credit card. Still she would never abuse the trust SACAA had in her. She used the card only for legitimate travel expenses. But Faith's supervisors knew every time she brought an orphan back to the New York SACAA facility, that she brought them there with a new wardrobe, new toys in their new backpacks, and plenty of junk food in their tummies. Faith ensured that the children would love America before they ever stepped foot on the soil.

With no one left to call and nothing left to do but wait, Faith thought, "I guess, I'll just sit back and relax, and wait for the phone to ring." Then she noticed she was just now hearing the water start to run in the shower. So she decided to surprise Darryl.

Darryl was letting himself relax and just enjoy the warm water running over his head and body. He had his eyes shut tightly. He was focusing on allowing his body to relax from the tension built up in him from flying. He still hated flying, but at least now he was over his fear of doing it. Then Darryl felt the soft touch of Faith's hands on his back.

Faith whispered, "I thought you might need a little help, washing your back, and those other hard to reach places."

"Nene, I didn't even hear you come in." Usually, Darryl would tense up over such a situation like this with Faith. He had still not broken his promise to her that he would keep her a virgin for her honeymoon, it seemed like he had made that promise to her an eternity ago. But today Darryl was so tired from being awake for the last 24 hours traveling that he didn't have much of a fight in him. Plus he knew Faith was a big tease from prior experiences. She would stop herself when she felt as if she was going too far. Actually he was getting irritated with the games Faith played while he tried his hardest to keep his promise to her. Maybe if he displayed less concern about keeping his promise to her, she would be more concerned about accepting his marriage proposals. Faith was now rubbing her soft hands filled with soap suds up and down his back. She was already driving him crazy. "Faith, you are a notorious tease, one of these days...."

She interrupted him by putting her finger on his lips and she whispered in his ear, "shh". Faith knew by now she was safe around Darryl. She knew he understood her commitment to keeping her virginity until marriage. Besides he did say he was a Christian and she knew that was what he was taught was the right thing to do.

Darryl could feel Faith's soft skin now brushing against the small of his back. She was making the hairs stand up on the back of his neck. He thought to himself, "this is something I could not have patience with if I was not a Christian, not positive she is my one true love and that she will eventually marry me. But still she takes things too far sometimes. Sometimes she acts like a crazy woman, because only a crazy woman would get into a shower naked with a man, and fully expect that man not to try to take things any further. After all I'm not made of stone. I am not Superman or Jesus. I'm just a man." But regardless of what Darryl thought about Faith's crazy teasing, he still wasn't going to complain about her games out loud, at least not at this very moment. He was finally relaxed from the warm water and too tired from the long flight to complain or to try and restrain himself this time.

Faith continued to lather up the soap in her hands, when she said in her best baby doll voice, "oops, there is no washcloth in this shower, just soap, so I guess I will have to use my hands to wash everything on you?"

Then Darryl felt Faith's wet, soapy hands, and then her wet naked body rubbing the small of his back, he could almost taste how sweet she was in his imagination. Darryl loved Fatih's body. He thought she had the most perfect shape he had ever seen. In fact there wasn't anything about Faith, inside or out that he didn't love. He felt her lay her head on his back. He felt her long hair get heavy with water and cascade down the sides of his abdomen. He let out a deep sigh realizing then he had been holding his breath in without knowing it.

Faith slowly moved her hands around the small of Darryl's back to the front of his chest, while she pressed her body against his back harder. Faith loved the feel of Darryl's body against hers. She had dated other men while she was away at college. But she had never let herself get close to any of them, emotionally or sexually. Darryl was the only man she ever trusted with her heart. He didn't even attempt to turn around and face Faith in the shower. She had started lathering up his chest with her hands and then working the lather with her hands all the way down his body. She made sure she didn't miss a spot. Faith had every inch of Darryl's body covered with thick white soap suds. She decided she whisper a few things in his ear before she got out of the shower. Another thing Faith liked to do with Darryl, was talk a little nasty every now and then. They were apart so often. Between his job at the hospital, his volunteer work with the senior citizen home, and her travels with SACAA, talking dirty over the phone became sometimes their only source of remaining intimate for weeks on end. So Faith had become very comfortable with talking a little dirty to Darryl; something she could never imagine doing with another man. She whispered, "tell me that it's all mine baby."

Darryl smiled. "You know it is."

"Yeah I know, but I want to hear you say it."

"It's all yours baby, so what you gonna do with it?"

"Bang, bang, bang", the knocking at the door startled Darryl, but Faith was sort of expecting it. She had ordered room service before she got into the shower with Darryl. She also knew the planned interruption would be a backup in case she unexpectedly lost her self control in the shower.

"Room service, … room service."

Faith gave him a kiss on the small of his back, and jumped out of the shower so quick without saying a word.

"So Faith you're not going to answer my question?"

"Baby, we don't want our food to get cold. I'll give you an answer next time."

Darryl smiled to himself and thought, "that's what I figured." Darryl came out of the shower feeling refreshed and he walked over to the table on the balcony to join Faith. She was already eating a muffin and reading the local newspaper.

"Wow what a spread, the two of us will never be able to eat all this food Faith."

"Don't worry compliments of SACAA."

"You see anything good in the paper?"

"Oh, I don't know, I guess just the usual stuff." "Well what's usual in Africa? Remember I'm new to all of this."

Faith reluctantly looked up from her newspaper at Darryl. She knew this was a question she wasn't going to be able to avoid. "It looks like some international peace keeping group has been taken hostage by rebel forces and the rebel forces have been on sort of a killing spree throughout the villages recently. Other than that, there seems to be a good sale on shirts and shoes, and also traditional African garb for us tourist, going on at the local shopping mall tomorrow. But, I think we will be on the way to SACAA facilities by tomorrow."

Darryl thought Faith was just joking about the whole rebellion force, and the killing spree comments she had just made. He knew she had a strange sense of humor. So he just asked her calmly, "so how far is this facility we are going to tomorrow, and why are we waiting until tomorrow to go? I thought you said you wanted to get to the village today, as soon as possible?"

"I did want to go today after we freshened up and napped, but well you know with the whole rebellion thing going on out in the villages, I thought it would be prudent to first see if we can get some military escorts before we venture out there."

"What the......, Faith, you're telling me you were not joking about this rebellion, and hostages, and killing spree stuff?!"

"No babe, I mean it's right here in the paper." Faith turned the paper around and pointed to the front page article for Darryl to see. Faith knew that although she was use to civil turmoil in all the countries she visited, this wasn't Darryl's idea of business as usual. She started to regret bringing Darryl with her. He was going to make her job more difficult, and bringing him with her was definitely going to make their relationship more difficult, here on out. She knew how much he worried about her. Now he would be worried every time she left the country to go on another assignment. "Seriously babe, don't worry. I'm sure it's nothing for us to worry about. This kind of stuff happens all the time when I'm on assignment, and I've always come home to you safe, haven't I?" (Although she didn't mention to Darryl that one time she was shot at by the cocaine Farmers in Nicaragua, and the scar on her shoulder was actually from a grazed bullet not from playing soccer with the Nicaraguan children like she had told him.)

"Now I see why you never really want to talk about your job Faith. Why you are so evasive whenever I ask you about what happened on your assignments. Your job is really dangerous Faith, and you know how I would worry about you if I had known that. I see now you've been pulling the wool over my eyes for years about your job. You have just been patronizing me all this time. You know that you can do good in this world without jeopardizing your own life in the process. I do it every day as a doctor, and I have no desire to put myself in harms way, and inflict any pain on my love one's if they lost me.

You know you can be a social worker right at home, there are plenty of children right at home who need help."

"Really Darryl, it's not that dangerous, whenever I am in a country where there is some civil unrest they always give me military escorts. You are making much to do about nothing, really."

Darryl gave Faith an unconvinced stare. She knew he wasn't buying anything else she said to him, not one bit, so she decided it was probably best to just keep her mouth shut, and come up with something to change the subject.

Darryl thought to himself, that after he married Faith, they were going to seriously discuss her quitting her job, or at least transferring into a safer position within SACAA. Then he thought to himself, that after he knocked her up she probably wouldn't have a problem doing something safer when she had her own kids to care for. While Darryl was in mid-thought planning his strategies against Faith's career in his mind; Faith decided she had remained silent long enough, so she started talking.

"So Darryl, you feel clean enough now?" She had a grin on her face. She was trying her best to change the subject.

"Look, that won't work. I know you are trying to change the subject, but it just so happens I wanted to bring the whole shower thing up to you anyway. Faith, are you just insane or are you trying to drive me insane. I mean I love you. I respect you. I know how you want to save yourself for marriage and all that, and I'm okay with that. I'm a Christian and well that's the way God wanted it anyway, so I can deal with that. But seriously, why do you play me the way you do? Jumping into the shower naked, rubbing your body all over me, come on Faith. What do you think I am, made of stone or superman or something?"

Faith couldn't stop giggling, and she eventually composed herself enough to give Darryl an answer, plus she was elated they had changed the subject. "Baby I know you are not made of stone, although you were as hard as one a few moments ago, (more grins and giggles from Faith). But I do think you're my Superman. I know you are the only man who can handle anything I dish out." Then she got up and wrapped her arms around Darryl's neck and sat on his lap. "Baby forgive me, I'm sorry, I was a naughty girl. I'll be good from now on, I promise."

"Yeah, I've heard that before. But you know you could just do one simple thing to solve this problem, it's called, marriage."

"I know baby, be patient, one day, one day. And you know when we do get married, I guarantee you, I will be worth the wait, and the two of us will just laugh about all the teasing I put you through."

Although they knew each other pretty much all of their lives, it had been only about two years since they had reconnected and gotten close again, and intimate. They had been exclusively dating each other now for almost two years. Darryl knew Faith was worth the wait. She was everything he had ever wanted in a woman and more. The fact that he would be the only man she ever had sex with when they got married was definitely an added bonus, to him. Nowadays, not in a million years, did he ever think he would actually marry a virgin. But the truth was he didn't really care if she was a virgin or not, he just wanted her.

"I know you are worth the wait, Faith. But just how long are you going to make me wait. Also keep in mind that due to all this waiting I can't guarantee you that our first time is going to be worth the long wait for you, maybe the second time around, but the first time, I can't guarantee that."

Faith busted out laughing. "I guess that's fair. And hey, look at the bright side, if the first time is incredibly bad at least I won't know any better. I mean it is not like I will have anything to compare it to."

"Hey, hey, hey, wait a minute now, I'm not saying it is going to be bad now, just maybe a little too fast, that's all I'm saying. In fact, don't even worry about all that, believe me it won't be bad. I have never gotten any complaints about that in the past and I'm not about to start now." While Darryl was letting his ego get the best of him, Faith heard the phone ringing, and quickly retorted, "oh really, no complaints, is that true, so does that mean you are going to present me with some letters of recommendation on our honeymoon or something"....

Then Faith put her slight jealousy on the back burner and picked up the phone. It was the ambassador's office. "Hello, yes I am…" She was very quiet for a long time as she listened to the person on the phone. Darryl was watching her attentively, watching how the expression on her face changed from happiness to worry. Then he heard her say, "well I'm still going. Okay, first thing, 5:00am that sounds good. Thank you for the escorts Sir and you have a good night too." When she hung up the phone she sort of stared into space for a moment.

Darryl could see the look of worry on her face. "Nene, what's wrong?"

"Darryl, I won't sugar coat it for you, but the rebellion is "really" serious. The ambassador just told me that they have several SACAA members, reporters and other officials missing right now. He also said that the UN sent a covert recon force to retrieve the hostages to avoid starting an all out war, but there has been no word from the UN force in months. The government has refused to negotiate with the rebels as they demand, so they have been terrorizing the villagers and refuse to turn over the hostages. They have not had any contact with the villagers or the SACAA facility in days, so they have no idea where all the children are. They have had reports from villagers that have made their way back into town. Those villagers say that there are abandoned children just roaming around unsupervised and hungry. They say many people have been killed already. The ambassador says they can give us some possible locations where persons may be camping in relation to the reports they have received. But they recommend I abandon this assignment and go back home. Although he did say that if we decide to still try and retrieve the children and our other SACAA employees, they will send a small group of military men with us as escorts. They are planning a military operation in three days where they will just go in full force if they do not hear back from the UN group or get further support from the UN on this crisis. The ambassador said that the way the local militia is, anything seen, and not in a uniform will be in danger if they go in full force, because no one can tell whether it be a man, woman or child who is a rebel and who is not."

Darryl was just quiet. He thought to himself, that it all sounded so much like some movie or news report on CNN. He could hardly believe what Faith was telling him was real. Then he said what he thought was the obvious thing to do. "So, I guess this means we're going home. Boy, this was a quick trip."

Faith looked Darryl in his eyes, and said, "You can go home, and I understand if you do, but I can't Darryl. I've never abandoned an assignment before. To me, my job is more than just assignments, leaving would be abandoning the children. Most times, I am their last hope. Looks like this time I am definitely their last hope of survival. There are little children out there, with no one looking out for them. They have no parents and as far as I know every SACAA worker has been taken hostage. I have to try to get those children out of here. That's my job, but it's not just my job, Darryl, I just feel compelled to do it. It's hard to explain and I don't expect you to understand, because sometimes I don't even understand it myself."

Darryl knew then, why Faith kept putting off marrying him. She was practically frantic right now having to explain her feelings about her job to him. It was as if the children out there were her own flesh and blood children. He always thought that Faith was just one of those people afraid of commitment, and that she was a true free spirit who he just needed to have patience with. But now he realized it wasn't that she was afraid to commit, she was already committed to something else. She was committed to these children. She had made her commitment to these faceless, nameless, countless children who she felt responsible for. Darryl thought something that he had never thought before, "I may always be second to these children in her life." She was right about one thing, he didn't understand it.

Faith was staring intensely at Darryl waiting for his response. She knew this one moment would define the rest of their relationship, forever. Knowing this made her eyes well up with tears because she knew this may be the moment he finally bailed on her.

"You're right Faith, I can't understand why you feel the need to continually risk your own life for children you have never even met before." He tried to quickly analyze what she was telling him in his head, before he spoke further. He thought about being a doctor. He could understand her desire to save people she didn't personally know, that was what he did for a living every day. He just couldn't understand her putting her own personal safety at risk to save them. But two things he knew he was sure of, 1. Faith was set on doing this type of work, with or without him, and, 2. He would risk his life any day, without any questions or doubts for Faith, his Nene. He loved her completely. He loved her without any doubts and she was second to nothing in his life, but God. He knew he wanted her whether he was second, third or fourth on her list, it didn't matter. Then he knew what his answer was.

"....but although I may not understand it, if you are determined to put your own life on the line, I'm not going to allow you to do that without me being there to protect you. So I guess we will go get these kids and then get the heck out of here. Just one more thing I need to say."

Faith was wiping away the tears from her eyes. "What's that?"

"After this is over, we're going to Hawaii for our next trip, before we do another SACAA vacation." Then Darryl gave her a smile reassuring her of his love.

Faith felt relieved.

Darryl decided to lighten up things up. "So we're leaving at 5:00am, huh? I think if we're going to be risking our lives tomorrow we should have a little fun today."

"That sounds reasonable to me."

Darryl went and grabbed her and swooped her up into his strong arms like a little child, and then he said, "you know all that stuff I said about the teasing, well just forget about it, for tonight. Let's start by you answering the question I asked you in the shower."

"You will have to force an answer out of me."

Darryl threw Faith on the bed and started tickling her. Then the two of them started play wrestling on the bed, until that turned into hugging and kissing and until they both eventually fell asleep in each other's arms..... and before they knew it, 5:00 am, came much sooner than they expected. They were awoken the next morning by someone knocking at their hotel door. Faith went to the door. "Yes?"

"Ma'am, your escorts are here, they are waiting in the lobby."

"Thank you very much. Please, tell them we will be out in 10 minutes." Faith wasn't use to having to rush. She was usually habitually early for everything.

She woke Darryl up and they were both rushing to get ready. Faith was about ready to leave out, but Darryl was feverishly looking for something out of his suitcases. Faith always had a separate survival backpack prepared in advance, with everything one would need. She packed enough for her and Darryl this trip.

"Babe, don't worry I have everything we will need for emergencies, and we won't be gone for more than a few days tops."

"I'm looking for my doctor's travel kit. You never know if I may have to do an emergency procedure out in the field that demands more than a regular first aid kit, and I need my bible, and.... Here they all are, okay, I'm ready."

Faith had already did her hair, showered, dressed and brushed her teeth in less than 10 minutes. Darryl was still standing there with no socks and shoes on, talking about he was ready. Faith couldn't help but giggle at how unorganized he was. "I know we're going in the bush, but you still might want to put on some shoes, oh, and brush your teeth first. We want our escorts to protect us not run from us because of your morning breath."

"Excuse me. Well at least we'll have a secret weapon in case our escort's protection fails us."

Faith laughed. "That's true your bad breath could ward off the rebels. So are you going to use that as an excuse not to brush your teeth?"

"No, I'm going to brush them as soon as I find my toothbrush. But I wasn't talking about my breath as the secret weapon, I was talking about you taking off those boots you have on if we get in a bind. Those smelly feet would run anyone off." Faith laughed because she knew she couldn't really argue with that one.

Finally, Darryl was ready, ten minutes had turned into 30 minutes by the time they were ready to head out to meet their escorts. Faith noticed that there was a rich looking, young black couple at the reception desk. The woman was so striking, she looked like a model, the man was also tall and handsome. The couple was checking in while Faith and Darryl were walking out of the lobby. Faith wondered what a couple of American looking yuppies were doing way out here. This wasn't exactly the best tourist destination to go to in Africa. Darryl was more concerned about checking out their military escorts. He was concerned about how many and how strong the escorts standing by the jeep looked. Darryl counted five of them and he was impressed by their obvious confidence, firearms and their size. One of them handed Darryl one of his rifles as soon as Darryl greeted him.

"Thanks, but you're going to have to show me how to work this. I've never handled a gun or a rifle before."

The escort had a wide friendly smile on his face and he seemed amused by Darryl. "No problem, I'll show you on the ride how it works, I'm Sidney".

Faith and Darryl hopped in the back of the jeep with Sidney and two other men.

Abdul, one of the other escorts said, "so you're the medicine man from America, huh?"

"Yes I am, how did you know?"

But before Abdul could answer Darryl's question one of the other men with a huge smile on his face interrupted, "my mother named me after a famous actor in America, Denzel. Do you think I look like him?"

Darryl started laughing, before he knew it, Faith answered Denzel. "Definitely, you could be his twin."

Darryl realized he didn't introduce Faith. These were some very handsome men and he wanted to make it clear to them that Faith was his. "Oh, this is my fiancée, Faith."

The Commander was sitting next to the driver. He yelled back to Darryl, "We all know Ms. Faith, she's been here before. Every time she talks all her escorts to death about her American doctor man, about how wonderful he is, blah, blah, blah. I often wondered what brave man could handle listening to her talk non-stop for the rest of his life. I must admit, we were expecting someone much bigger."

Darryl laughed out loud. He thought, "I should have known everyone here would know Faith already." But he was surprise to hear Faith told people about him. Then in less than a minute they were on the road. Sidney was explaining to Darryl the workings of the rifle that he gave Darryl to hold, while Denzel was taking off his boot and sock to show Darryl his foot fungus.

Faith smiled at Darryl and his ability to make friends so easily and to take everything in stride, but her thoughts quickly returned to the children and saving them.

Chapter 11
Love's body is in Africa
But her mind is still in New York

Love and John were both worn out from the long flight. They were standing at the counter checking in, both in a daze. Then Love realized the man checking them in had asked if they wanted a King size or standard bed. Love had to correct him, "Sir we're not a couple, we'll need two rooms please."

The young hotel clerk replied, "Yes Madam, I apologize." Then he gave Love and John two keys and told them to call him at the front desk if they needed anything at all.

Love said to John, "It is so early in the morning, how about the two of us get a little shut eye and meet back here at say 10:00am?"

"That's fine with me I could use a shower and a little shut eye."

When they got to their rooms they found they had been given two rooms right next to each other with a connecting door that did not lock. Normally Love would had went right back downstairs to complain. The walls in the room were paper thin and with no lock on the connecting door they might have well had been in one room after all. But Love was so tired she just wanted to flop down on her bed and fall fast to sleep with all her clothes still on. She told John they could take care of the room situation later. After all it wasn't like she didn't trust John to be in a room next to her with a connecting door that didn't lock. Before Love dosed off into sleep completely, she notice the smell of something irritatingly familiar. It smelled like cotton balls. It was the hotel comforter that was on her bed. The smell reminded Love of something in her past, but what, she couldn't recall. It didn't take long for Love to fall asleep. She had been up for hours straight, traveling and drinking coffee. Now she had finally crashed from the caffeine and adrenaline induced high that had kept her awake. Once she was in a deep sleep she started dreaming, about her past....

"Love, the phone, it's your sister, Hope."

Love was lying on the thin, tough, mattress at the girl's group home. The blankets at the group home always smelled like cotton balls. She hated that smell. She jumped up and ran to the phone in the main office at the group home. It was rare that she ever got a call. It was also rare that she ever got to talk to either of her sisters.

The social worker said that Faith's adoption was a closed adoption, but that her adopted parents promised they would still bring Faith to visit the girls after they felt she was adjusted to her new home. The three of them had a visit together up at the social services building some time after Faith was adopted. After that visit, Faith's adopted parents explained to Love and Hope that they would be leaving the country for a while because of a family emergency, and they were not sure exactly when they would return, but they promised they would bring Faith to see them again as soon as they were back in the country. Although Love could tell that little Faith missed them a lot, Love could also see that Faith was happy and already in love with her new parents. Maybe it was easier for Faith to adjust because she was so much younger than her and Hope were.

Hope also was taken in by a new foster family. The foster family that took Hope in was very strict about her phone privileges and visits. So Love rarely got to speak to Hope either. It had been a very long time since the last time Love had seen her two sisters face to face and lately Love felt totally alone.

But she knew Hope felt that way too. Hope had told her the last time they talked over the phone that she hated her new foster home.

Love was in a group home for girls who had been in criminal trouble or who were repeat runaways from foster homes. She had been caught running away from three foster homes within the past two months. She also had been picked up for shoplifting several times. Each time the stores decided not to press charges because they felt sorry for her when they found out she had no relatives and only a social worker to come and pick her up. Her caseworker, Ms. Armstrong, would have been ready to give up on finding her a new foster home, if not for the potential she saw in Love. Love's grades were excellent. In fact she had already been skipped one grade level, and was set to graduate high school, two years early, at the age of sixteen. Love's social worker was trying to keep her in a traditional public high school versus having her attend school inside one of the secured group homes. Graduation from a traditional high school would help her chances in getting a scholarship and acceptance to the college of her choice. Love had made close to perfect scores on her SAT's, and she was expected to be number one in her graduating class. That is, if only she could stay in school long enough to finish all her classes. She only had a few more weeks before graduation.

Love had already received several conditional offers to attend universities across the country based on merit scholarships. But of course those scholarships and early acceptance letters were contingent on her actually graduating. Ms. Armstrong was able to work out something with Love's school. The school's representative dropped off assignments to the classroom at the group home. Love completed her assignments and had them ready the next morning for pick up. The following week Love would take her finals, and all this was already set up through both schools.

Ms. Armstrong, was a very caring and diligent social worker. She routinely went above and beyond what her job required. She knew the only reason Love ran from her foster homes was to try and contact her sisters. Love did not adjust well to any of the foster homes Ms. Armstrong had placed her in. So now Love had been placed in the girl's group home as a last resort. Ms. Armstrong told her it was just a temporary placement. She told Love she would be there just until she found another family which was willing to take her on, or until she graduated high school, and was eligible to be considered emancipated or go off to college as a ward of the state.

Love didn't mind the group home. Love felt like at least she was learning new useful skills from her various roommates. Also, she didn't have any adults trying to pretend they were her parents and that they really cared.

When Love picked up the phone at the group home she heard Hope say, "Love is that you?" Love yelled excitedly, "Hope, Hope, I've missed you!" Then she heard her little sister Hope break down and start to cry. Hope was making huge sobbing and animal like gasping sounds. Hope's crying went on for what seemed like forever to Love. Love's happiness and excitement to hear from her sister, quickly turned into worry and concern. Once she heard Hope quiet down, she asked Hope what was wrong.

"Love I can't take it anymore. I just want to kill myself. I can't take it. Please, can you come get me? Can we just run away from all of this?"

"I'll come, where are you? What happened Hope?"

"I can't say, not now. My foster parents went to bible study without me. I said I was sick. But he will be back home before you know it. I know he won't leave me here alone for too long. He will make some excuse up, to leave and come home early."

Hope sounded frantic and Love could barely understand her, so she asked her again. "What happened Hope? What is wrong?"

"I'm sorry, Love. I just can't tell you, not yet."

"Okay, just leave then and I will meet you somewhere Hope."

"I can't just leave. He has got the next door neighbor watching me. That mean, old lady is always watching the house to make sure I don't run away, or have anyone come over while they are gone. I tried leaving once before, and she called them up at the church, and they had people picking me up before I was even a block away."

"Well what do we do? Won't your neighbor still call someone when she sees me come there?"

"I've thought about this, and I have a plan. Afterschool, meet me at my bus stop at 3:30pm. I will pack some clothes in my book bag. I've got thirty dollars saved up. The two of us can just hitchhike or catch the train until we get far enough away. One day we can come back for Faith. After we think it's safe to come back, but she is out of the country right now with her adopted parents anyway."

The only times Love had ever run away from the foster homes was to try to see Faith or Hope. The idea of leaving Faith all alone made her sad, but Love knew Faith wasn't really alone, like her and Hope were. Faith was happy and she had been adopted into a good home. So Love told Hope she would be there at the bus stop tomorrow, waiting for her. Then she asked Hope again what had made her so upset. Hope still refused to tell her and she just said, "I love you big sis, more than anything. Thank you for doing this for me, I'll see you tomorrow."

Love was a pro at run-away attempts, but she wasn't so good about not getting caught. However, after three weeks in the girl's group home, she was confident that she gained enough knowledge to make it on the streets, at least for a little while. That night Love found it hard to get to sleep. She kept tossing and turning. She was trying to figure out in her head just how they were going to run away, and where they should head to once they met up with each other. The hardest part would be finding a way out of the group home. She needed to meet Hope at the bus stop at 3:30pm. Love had her first final exam scheduled the next day and she knew after that she was scheduled for independent study in the supervised classroom until 3:00pm. At 3:00pm all the girls were escorted to the living area where they had free time until they were escorted to the dining hall. Love knew the only way she was going to get out of the group home without being noticed was to bribe one of the guards. The question she had was who to bribe and what to bribe them with. She didn't have any money and she rarely spoke to the guards. She had only been in the home a week and a half. So she decided to get out of bed and speak to Jesse.

Jesse was the most experienced and seasoned girl at the group home. Love had made a sort of friendship with Jesse. Love had been doing Jesse's homework every night since she had arrived at the group home and Jesse in return made sure none of the girls at the group home bothered Love. The relationship was working so far. So Love went to Jesse for advice.

"Jesse", Love was whispering Jesse's name and nudging her lightly, hoping not to wake up any of the other girls.

Jesse was groggy and had an attitude about being woken up. "What you waking me up for?"

"Jesse I need your help."

Jesse still had an attitude, but now she was wide awake. "What's up some girl trying to mess with you?"

"No, it's about my little sister, Hope. I spoke to her tonight and she was real upset. She said she can't take it no more and she wants to kill herself. So she wants me to come and get her and for us to get out of town. Can you help me Jesse? How can I get out of here without the guards catching me?"

"Well, if you've got enough money, almost any of the guards will hook you up and look the other way. As long as you don't snitch them out if you get caught. Most of them don't care no ways, because they just doing this job on the side anyways."

"Well I don't have any money Jesse."

"Then I guess you and your *sista* just out of luck. They don't call this place a secure facility for nothing you know."

"But Jesse, Hope really sounded desperate over the phone. Is there any other way I can get around the guards without any of them catching me?"

"Now you know I've lived here going on five years. All the times I've ever ran away I was caught. Believe me if there was a way to get out of here without paying them off, I would have found out about it by now. Look why don't you call your sister up and tell her to wait? Ain't you set to go to some fancy college once you graduate anyways?"

"I am, but you had to hear her on the phone, Jesse. I've never heard Hope cry like that before, even when our Nana died. Something is really wrong and I couldn't say no to her. I couldn't tell her to wait weeks from now or maybe even months from now so I can go to some college."

"Okay I hear you. There is another way to *jump* without getting caught you know. But I don't know if you're gonna be willing to do it."

"What is it? I'll do it, whatever it is."

"There's one guard and he'll hook you up if you give him *some*, and if what you give him is real good he'll even give you a little extra cash on the side."

Love hadn't told Jesse or anyone else she knew, but she was still a virgin. The thought of losing her virginity to some stranger made her feel sick, but if that was what she had to do to get to Hope she would do it. "Jesse can you hook it up for me tomorrow, because I need to be out of here at least by 3:00pm tomorrow to meet up with Hope."

"Are you sure *School Girl*?"

"I'm sure."

"Okay then, but dag, I guess this means I'm gonna have to get one of these other girls to do my homework. You know the rest of them dumb though, I might as well do it myself."

Love smiled. "You don't need me to do your homework, you can already do it yourself if you wasn't so lazy Jes. I know you are book smart even though you pretend you are only street smart."

"Maybe you're right, but don't tell no one."

"Your secrets are safe with me. Hey thanks Jes. I owe you one."

"Don't worry about it girl. I've got sisters and brothers out there myself. I just don't know who any of them are since my mama was a whore, and my daddy wasn't worth one cent."

Love knew, Jesse meant that as a joke, but it was just too true to be funny. Love realized how lucky she was to have had Nana all those years. If it wasn't for Nana she knew her and her sisters would probably have been much worse off by now.

The next day Love was so nervous she had bitten all her fingernails down. It was nearly close to 3:00pm. Jesse hadn't spoken to Love all day. But usually, Jesse and Love did not talk to each other until they were back at sleeping quarters to exchange the homework assignments. Jesse didn't want the teachers to think her and Love were friends. She said if they thought the two of them were cool with each other they might become suspicious that Love was actually the person doing Jesse's homework. Even though Love had not spoken to Jesse she trusted that Jesse would keep her word to her. Like usual the guard escorted the girls to their living area to relax until it was dinner time. It seemed like any other normal afternoon, except the guard whispered, "hang back", to Love when she walked by him to get into line with the other girls.

So Love made sure she was the last girl in the line. Her heart was racing while she walked down the corridor. She looked at the man who had whispered to her; he wasn't ugly, but he wasn't handsome either. Before they turned the corner of the corridor he nudged her towards the employee's restroom.

"Stay here", he said. Less than five minutes later he was back with an extra uniform in his hand.

"Come on, quick, put this on. It should fit. My shift is over and I've already checked out."

After Love had changed into the uniform the guard gave her, they left out of the employee's exit door. Love kept her head down as she passed through the metal detectors, but no one was paying her any attention any way. It was shift change. The employees at the group home were busy coming in and going out. Love followed the guard to his car and they just got in and drove off. It all was so simple and it went so smoothly. Then the guard said to Love, "it's 3:05pm. I hear you've got to be somewhere by 3:30pm. So where you want me to drop you off at?"

Love gave him the location of Hope's school and asked him if he could wait for her and drop her and her sister off at the nearest Greyhound. He replied nonchalantly, "we'll see", and for a split second Love thought maybe he's just helping me, *just to help me*. But then Love noticed that while they were talking he had driven his car behind an abandon building. He got out of the car in a hurry. "Come on, we don't have much time."

Now Love was scared. She suddenly realized he could do anything to her in this building, even kill her, and probably get away with it. But she also knew if she tried to run now he would catch her, and that would just make things take longer. Love didn't want Hope waiting for her for too long. So Love obediently followed him into the building. He pointed to a dirty mattress on the floor. There were old crack pipes lying around, and the smell of urine. Love noticed for the first time how sweaty he was, that he was overweight and his fat finger had a wedding ring on it.

"Um Sir, I've never done this before."

"Oh first time you've done this with a stranger? Well just look at it this way, at least you are not giving something for nothing, like most girl's do. Consider this just *quid pro quo*."

"Well yeah, but also, it's just the first time I've ever done *it*."

He looked at her pleasantly surprised, and you could hear it in his voice. "For real, well this is really my lucky day. I ain't ever did it with a virgin before. You aint' shittin me, are you?" But before Love could answer his question, he abruptly laid Love down on the dirty mattress. Then he said, "don't worry, I'll be real gentle. Just lay there nice and still and it will be over before you know it."

Love did exactly what he said. She kept her eyes closed the whole time and thought about something else, anything else. He smelled like old spice and marijuana. It was painful at first, but as he had promised the whole thing didn't really last that long.

"I'm finished. I guess you weren't telling lies about this being the first time." He looked down and pointed to the blood.

Love looked down in disgust.

He continued talking like what they just did was nothing. "Usually I'd use a condom, seeing that most of you group home girls got something, and I'm married and all. But I figured I'd take the risk this time since you said you never did it before. Besides you even look like a good girl. Don't worry, I ain't got nothing. My wife would kill me if I brought something home to her, and I ain't never known anyone to get knocked up first time around either."

All the time while he was talking, Love was cleaning herself off. She took her white tennis socks off and cleaned herself with them. It was the cleanest thing she could find at the time. "Sir, will you wait for me and my sister and drop us off somewhere?"

"Sorry I can't do that, I've got to pick my kids up from daycare by 4:00pm, and I'm already running behind. But, I can drop you off somewhere, if it's on the way. Here is a little cash too. Maybe you and your sister can catch the city bus or subway with this." He gave Love twenty dollars and dropped her off down the block from her sister's school. It was exactly 3:30pm. Love thought to herself, "at least that would be the last time I ever have to see him again." Then Love ran towards the busses. She looked and she looked, but she didn't see Hope anywhere. She waited and waited, and almost all the kids were gone. Then Love started asking the few kids that were still waiting for their bus, "do you know Hope, have you seen Hope Emmanuel?"

Finally, a girl came up to her and said, "you looking for Hope?"

"Yeah".

"Hope's out sick today. I'm in her homeroom and I also live right down the block from her. I'm suppose to bring her, her homework assignments."

Love felt her heart drop, and she thought to herself, "had all this been for nothing?" Then Love said to the girl, "Well I can take her homework assignments to her. I was supposed to meet her here today. We have a class project we're working on together."

The girl looked at Love a little suspiciously. Love look to old to be in junior high and it didn't help that she had on the navy blue guard pants, a white t-shirt, and penny loathers with no socks. Even in a city like New York her wardrobe seemed strange to the girl. But the girl still gave Love, Hope's homework assignments. She really didn't want to drop them off to Hope, but her mother had volunteered her services because Hope's foster father was their pastor.

So Love got on the school bus. She told the bus driver she had forgotten her school bus-pass, and he let her right on. Love didn't know what she was going to do when she got there, but she figured she couldn't go back to the group home so she might as well go to Hope's home. What Love didn't know was that Hope's classmate who had gotten off the bus three stops before her, had already made it to her house and called Hope up to tell her she gave her assignments to her friend in the funny clothes. However being that Hope was sick her foster father answered the phone. He had been telling everyone who called for Hope that day she was too sick to come to the phone.

Once Love recognized the street that Hope lived on getting closer, she got ready to get off the school bus. Just when Love was getting ready to tell the driver to let her off, she noticed a police car sitting at the far corner of the block that Hope's foster home sat on. So Love sat back down. She wasn't sure why the police were out there but it worried her. Love stayed on the bus until the last stop and then she finally got off. Love tried calling Hope's foster home several times. Each time Hope's foster father answered. The third time Love called she got the courage up to ask to speak to Hope. Hope's foster father said, "sorry she can't talk she is in bed sick." So she decided to catch the train up to Manhattan. Love had already spent five dollars out of the twenty she got from the guard, on pizza, phone calls and a soda. It was around 11:00pm and Love decided to call her caseworker, Ms. Armstrong, because she didn't know what else to do. She knew Ms. Armstrong would be upset at her, but she was really the only person she had to call.

Ms. Armstrong met Love at the pizza parlor. It was obvious Ms. Armstrong was really upset with Love when she walked into the pizza parlor her face was red with anger. Love could tell by the wrinkles in her forehead that she was in for a lecture about running away again. Ms. Armstrong sat down and the first thing she said was, "so what was your reason for doing it this time?"

"It doesn't matter, you wouldn't understand."

"Love, haven't I tried my best to be in your corner from the very start. Don't you want to go to college? Don't you want a better future? Why do you insist on trying to do things to sabotage yourself? All you have to do is complete 3 more finals and then you can choose from several universities to go to, even Harvard. What could be so important for you to risk all of that for?"

Love answered in a soft, little voice, with her head hanging down, "my sister".

Ms. Armstrong's stern expression softened a little and then she said, "Love I know you miss your sisters, but right now there is no way you all can be together. You have to learn how to accept that."

"I know, but Hope called me up at the group home. She hardly ever calls me, and she sounded real, real upset. She was crying, uncontrollably. I think something bad is going on with her over there."

"Hope is in a well respected foster home. The family she is with has had several children in their home over the years before her, and not once have we ever heard any complaints from any of those children. The father's a pastor. In fact Hope, herself has not given her own social worker any complaints during any of the home visits. I would know, because her caseworker's office is right down the hall from my office, and her worker was my mentor."

"I hear what you're saying Ms. Armstrong and I hope you are right. But all I can tell you is that I know my sister, and I have never heard her cry like that before, not even when Nana died."

"Did Hope tell you what was wrong with her?"

"No she wouldn't tell me."

"Look, if it makes you feel better, I will do a surprise visit on Hope's foster home tomorrow morning. Hope's caseworker is out on maternity leave so she won't be able to get to it. I will tell you tomorrow how it went. Don't worry Love I'm sure everything is fine."

Love looked up at Ms. Armstrong and gave her a genuinely sincere smile of gratitude, "thank you Ms. Armstrong. Hope's foster dad said she would be home sick for a few days when I called. So I know she should be home all day tomorrow."

"I'm sure she is just sick and really missing you, little Faith and your Nana being there to take care of her, just like you miss all of them so much."

Love thought to herself, "maybe that was it, maybe Hope just was sick and feeling sad. Hope was always a really big baby whenever she came down sick with anything." Love doubted anyone would take care of them the way Nana use to when they were sick. Love also knew that even she would cry sometimes, late at night, when she got to missing them real bad. Love looked at Ms. Armstrong and said, "maybe you're right."

"Sure I am. Now back to you, how did you get out of the group home anyway?"

Love looked Ms. Armstrong straight in the eyes and lied, "I snuck out in the bottom of the dirty laundry bin and jumped out the truck when they came to a stop." Love thought to herself, "that sounded so good maybe I should have actually tried getting out that way."

Ms. Armstrong didn't know whether to believe Love or not. She looked at Love suspiciously. "It doesn't even matter, because it's not going to happen again, right?"

"Right, I promise."

"You have just three more test to take Love, then graduation day, and after that you can even be emancipated and leave early for the college of your choice, or just remain a ward of the state and go to college. You've got to stay focus. So now we have to figure out how to take you back to the group home without them thinking you ran away. I tell you what let's go back now, and I will tell the night supervisor that I forgot to sign you out and that we were running late for an orientation tour and dinner at NYU for prospective freshmen."

"You mean you are going to lie for me?"

"Hush your mouth, child. I'm not telling a lie, simply a little fib, not really a lie."

Love didn't know many white women. She definitely didn't know any southern white women and Ms. Armstrong seemed to be just like something straight out of *Gone With the Wind*. She was a beautiful, blonde, voluptuous woman with the deepest southern accent Love had ever heard in any movie she had ever seen. But it seemed like everything about Ms. Armstrong was sweet, sincere and honest. Love couldn't help but like her.

Ms. Armstrong, continued talking to herself. "Lord forgive me for telling this little fib, but if I don't tell this fib, they will take this poor child back to juvenile detention and lock her up for sure." After she finished talking to herself out loud she looked over at Love and said, "and if you go to *juvi*, you will miss your last three finals, and ruin your chances of graduating and going to college. Now we don't want that to happen." Then Ms. Armstrong was talking out loud to herself again trying to ease her own conscience about lying. "Remember, Rahab lied and saved the lives of her entire family. So I think, sometimes God will forgive us for the little lies we tell, if we are telling them for a greater good." Then she looked over at Love like she had just remembered she was still sitting there. "But I know you don't know what the heck I'm talking about child."

Love didn't respond but she did know exactly what Ms. Armstrong was talking about and who "Rahab" was in the bible. Love knew Rahab lied about the Israelite spies to her townspeople, how Rahab lies led to the ultimate fall of the walls of Jericho, and the Jewish people claiming the land. Love knew all of this because Nana had put the girls to bed every night with a different bible story. Love had not forgotten any of the stories Nana told her from the bible. No matter how hard she tried to forget, she couldn't. But the one thing that stuck in Love's head when Ms. Armstrong mentioned Rahab, was that Rahab was a prostitute and a liar. Love thought to herself, "in one day I've gone from being a basically honest virgin, to a liar and a prostitute, just like Rahab; but nothing I did saved anyone."

"Now, before I take you back to the group home we are going to have to get you some proper clothes to put on. Love, are you listening to me? We need to at least make it look like you've been to a college orientation and social dinner."

So they stopped by Ms. Armstrong's home and Ms. Armstrong gave Love an old plaid skirt that she had her put on, some socks to wear with the penny loafers Love already had on, and a white button down blouse.

"Love this use to be my old school girl uniform. I saved it for sentimental reasons. You can keep it. Why don't you go and take a quick shower and fix your hair."

Love turned on the shower and scrubbed her body until her skin was red, and she sobbed into her washcloth until she couldn't cry anymore. When she emerged, all dressed and clean, with her long dark hair pulled back nicely in a pony tail, Ms. Armstrong noticed how red her eyes were.

"Come here child." She stood Love in front of her full length mirror. "Love, don't be discouraged. Look at yourself. You are beautiful and you are so smart. You already look like a college girl. You can be anyone you want to be. You can start fresh when you go to college. No one has to know about the juvenile arrests, the group homes, that you were a foster care child. Just remember, you can be anyone you want to be, it's up to you, you just have to keep it together and get through the rest of this week. If you can get through this week, then you are on your way to having a bright fresh future."

They drove back to the group home. On the ride to the group home all Love thought about was Ms. Armstrong's words to her that, "she could be anyone she wanted to be."

It was close to midnight when they arrived at the group home. Ms. Armstrong gave the night supervisor the same story she told Love she was planning on telling them, about the college orientation and social dinner. The night supervisor saw Ms. Armstrong's credentials and never questioned her explanation. As the night guard escorted Love back to the girl's sleeping quarters, Ms. Armstrong whispered to Love, "remember – you can be anyone you want to be."

The next time Love saw Ms. Armstrong was at her high school graduation. Ms. Armstrong had made arrangements for Hope to attend Love's graduation also. The day before her graduation Love had her emancipation hearing at the courthouse. She was now a free woman and considered an adult at sixteen. She had successfully made it through all her finals, receiving A's in all her classes, and she was offered several full tuition scholarships. She had decided to accept Harvard's scholarship offer, but she had not told Ms. Armstrong or Hope the good news yet. She knew how excited they were going to be and she was saving the announcement for the going away dinner that Ms. Armstrong's had planned at her home.

After her emancipation hearing, Love thanked her court appointed lawyer and left the courthouse feeling like a free woman. She was filled with the expectations of a better future. Love had over a thousand dollars in her suitcase, along with a suitcase full of brand new clothes, thanks to the relationship she had continued with the security guard at the group home. Love had threatened to tell the guard's supervisors and his wife about their affair. She knew if she told he would not only lose his marriage but also his job. So, in return for her silence the guard gave her enough money to buy a first class plane ticket and new designer clothes for college, and she still had money left over. She couldn't wait to fly first class. Love had totally found a way to ignore her conscience. She had become a master at rationalizing every little dirty deed she did. She had also become a master at manipulating people. The cheating guard couldn't wait for Love to go off to college. He had went from taking advantage of Love to now being bribed and used by her. He feared that at the last moment Love might contact his wife and tell his supervisors at the group home, just to spite him.

On Love's last day at the group home he slipped her an envelope with all the money she had demanded and more. Then she whispered to him, "it was a pleasure doing business with you. *Quid Pro Quo,* right?" After that day the guard never heard from Love again.

Love checked herself into a very fancy hotel in the city after her emancipation hearing. She went shopping and she brought some gold bracelets for Ms. Armstrong, and Hope as going away presents. Love thought, "everything was looking up." Ms. Armstrong, and Hope had assured her that everything was fine with Hope. All Love could think about was Hope coming to stay with her during holidays at college, and that one day the two of them would share an apartment together.

The next morning at her graduation, Hope told her she was just feeling sad and sick on the day she had called her up crying over the phone. Love never told Hope what she had to do in order to run away that day. That one act changed the way Love looked at life entirely. After the graduation ceremony they all went to eat brunch and agreed to meet back up at Ms. Armstrong's house that night for dinner at 8pm. Ms. Armstrong explained that she had some business to take care of at work, and that she would bring Hope to her house for dinner with Love that night.

Love went back to her hotel room and she was getting a little bored all alone in the room. She decided she had nothing better to do than to try the hotel booze in the wet bar. It didn't take her long to get drunk. That night marked the first time Love had any alcohol, and it was just the beginning of many more drinks to come.

Chapter 12
Hope's Misery

Hope and Ms. Armstrong never told Love about what happened the day after Love ran away from the group home. Hope was trying her best to also "forget about things", and just move on.

Ms. Armstrong had followed through on her promise to Love to check up on Hope. On the morning Ms. Armstrong went to see Hope she ran into Hope's foster mother, Mrs. Smith. She was leaving out of the house to go to work. Mrs. Smith was a little surprised to see Ms. Armstrong until Ms. Armstrong explained to her that she was doing a routine visit because Hope had been out of school.

Mrs. Smith was a plump, warm, and kind woman. She taught at the local school, and she was known for her kindness and her integrity. Long before Mrs. Smith was married she had planned to become a nun, until she had met her husband. The two of them met each other at bible camp when they were teenagers. Mr. Smith was an altar boy, and Mrs. Smith had taught the children's bible class. They fell in love quickly, and soon Mrs. Smith no longer wanted to become a nun. She daydreamed about getting married now and having lots of children to care for. She had always loved children, and had always wanted to be a teacher. She knew she could do as much good working in the church with her husband as she could as a nun. Her husband told her how it would be a terrible waste for a woman who loved children so much not to have some of her own. But, after years of being married and trying to start a family she found out her beloved husband was unable to give her children. A fertility doctor told them Mr. Smith had a rare sperm count deficiency and he would probably never be able to father children. Her dreams of having children were crushed. But all she could think about was comforting her husband, because it wasn't his fault. She told herself, "it was just the will of God." What she didn't know was that her husband knew all along he couldn't have children. When he was eighteen he had an affair and was afraid he had fathered and illegitimate child. He consulted a doctor about getting a vasectomy and then he found out after test were taken that there was no possible way he could have fathered anyone's child, due to his rare condition. Mrs. Smith never knew any of this and she decided to take in foster children. Hope was just one of many, many foster children that she had had taken in over the years. She cared for all the children with unconditional love. So when she saw Ms. Armstrong she was surprised, but not concerned. She was confident she was caring for Hope properly, just like all of her other children she had cared for over the years. Mrs. Armstrong asked her why Hope had not been in school lately, and she explained that Hope had been out of school because she had the flu and that her husband also had it. Since she was running late for work she showed Ms. Armstrong where she kept the extra keys, under the flower pot, and she told her to just let herself in. She said her husband would probably be asleep in the basement because he had been sleeping down there ever since he got sick so that she wouldn't get the flu.

Ms. Armstrong thanked Ms. Smith for her hospitality and she thought to herself, "Love was just worried for no reason at all, because it is so obvious Mrs. Smith is nothing but open and honest." Then she let herself into the house with the extra key.

Ms. Armstrong was familiar with the Smith's house already, because Hope's social worker was her mentor. The first four weeks after she was employed she followed her mentor everywhere. Love Emmanuel was Ms. Armstrong's first assigned case. Her mentor wanted her to feel comfortable on her first independent case so she worked it out where they would split up the sisters' caseload. She received Love's case, and her mentor took Hope and Faith. Faith was adopted in no time, but the other two Emmanuel sisters had been in the foster care system for as long as she had been employed with the Department of Social Services. Since then her case load had increased greatly, but her first case, Love, and her sister, Hope would always be special to her. As soon as she entered the Smith's house she called out Mr. Smith's name.

"Mr. Smith, your wife told me to let myself in." Ms. Armstrong could hear the sound of a drill coming from the downstairs basement. When no one responded to her introduction, she figured, Mr. Smith was working in his basement and she decided not to disturb him, and to just go talk to Hope. After all, Hope was the reason she was there. So she headed upstairs to Hope's bedroom, but Hope wasn't in her bedroom. She checked the one bathroom that was in the house and it was also empty. It was a small house and it only took her five minutes to check the three other bedrooms, and the kitchen and family room.

Then Ms. Armstrong became concerned, she thought Hope may have ran away. She decided she better interrupt Mr. Smith and let him know Hope wasn't in her room and may have even ran away. The sound of the drilling was incredibly loud and Mr. Smith did not answer to her knocking on the basement door. She looked at the keys in her hand and one of them was labeled basement so she used it to let herself in. The sound of the drill got much louder as Ms. Armstrong walked down the steps leading to the Smith's basement. When Ms. Armstrong got to the end of the steps, what she saw put her into a temporary state of shock.

She was raised in a small family, and in the church. Her father was loving and kindhearted to her and her siblings. She was raised to be aware that there was good and evil in the world, but she had only been an eyewitness to the good growing up.

What she was now witnessing was the worse example of evil she could have ever imagined. She had walked in to see a sight her mind could barely register as being real. Mr. Smith, the man her agency had great respect and trust for, was standing with his back to her and with his pants and underwear down at his ankles. He was holding a drill to poor little Hope's head. He was bent over little Hope, with his drill in one hand only inches from her head, and with his other hand he was groping Hope. Ms. Armstrong could not believe what she was seeing. Hope's eyes were shut tight and her arms and legs were tied up.

She stood there on the bottom of the stairs still in shock. She felt like her heart had stopped, and as if she had been standing there forever, paralyzed. But actually she had only been standing at the bottom of the stairs for a few seconds in her disbelief. She had never felt such fear and disgust before. Then she felt hate! That hatred she felt for Mr. Smith in that moment, gave her body the electric shock she needed to regain move. But before she could turn and run, for no apparent reason at all Mr. Smith turned around and looked straight at her. Mr. Smith was also in shock seeing her standing there. He was positive he had locked the basement door.

Ms. Armstrong thought to herself that Mr. Smith looked inhuman, like a devil, or a demon from some nightmare. In her mind she yelled, "Jesus, help me!" She was not a physically strong woman. Her only fighting skills were from a two hour self defense class Social Services sponsored. She was also a very small, almost pixie like framed woman, but she was top-heavy for her small frame, and that only made her less athletic and more clumsy. Her first instincts were to run for help, not to stay and fight. She thought there was no way she could defeat this monster by herself.

Mr. Smith's first instinct was to kill Ms. Armstrong. He would worry about what to do with her body afterwards. This wouldn't be the first time he had to dispose of a body. But in his rush to get to her, before she made it all the way up the stairs, he tripped over the drill cord. It didn't help his coordination any being that his pants were still down at his ankles, but he was still faster and stronger than Ms. Armstrong. He grabbed hold of her foot. He yanked her so hard it caused her to fall face down on the stairs. She banged her head with such blunt force that it caused her to gash open her forehead. The blood from the open wound in her head started gushing out and it was dripping into her eyes. It was a miracle she did not lose consciousness. She struggled to get her foot out of his grip. He dragged her back down to the bottom of the stairs onto the basement floor, but she was able to get her foot loose. Then she moved quicker than he did with his underwear and pants still down. She scurried on all fours on the floor to the sound of the drill she still heard running. She grabbed hold of the drill in just enough time to roll over with it in her hands. She could barely see him because blood was dripping into her eyes from the gash in her head. He was already in the process of pouncing on top of her when he saw the drill in her hand, but he couldn't stop himself from falling on top of her because his body was already in motion. He landed right on top of her, and right on top of the drill. The drill plunged into his heart. His blood splattered all over Ms. Armstrong's fresh ironed white dress, which was already stained with her own blood oozing out of her head. His body laid on top of her and flinched with spasms of pain. She screamed out loud in horror. Then she rolled his revolting bloodied body off of her. She was now covered with his blood. She used her dress to wipe the blood from her eyes.

She said, "Hope, open your eyes, open your eyes Hope, your safe now." Hope kept her eyes closed shut. It was as if Hope was comatose. Ms. Armstrong untied Hope, and scooped her up in her arms. Then she ran up the stairs and out of the basement with Hope and they were outside within seconds. She ran down the street with her Hope still in her arms as if she had superhuman strength. She still had the irrational fear that it was possible that Mr. Smith may not be dead, but he was definitely dead. She just wanted to get as far away from that basement and what she could only describe as Hell on Earth.

Hope was silent and still in shock, but Ms. Armstrong was screaming for help as she ran down the block with Hope in her arms. It didn't take long for neighbors to hear her screams. Several 911 calls were made that day reporting that there was a crazy, screaming blood soaked little white woman, running down the street with a black girl almost the same size as her in her arms.

A police car responded and told her to stop. The police pulled their guns on her at first, not sure if she was also armed and crazy. They ordered her to put the child down. They had to scream it several times, before Ms. Armstrong regained her mental senses and did as they instructed. Once they saw she was not armed, they proceeded to calm her down. Then she slowly told them what had just happened. Hope couldn't talk yet. She was still outside of her body. This wasn't the first time Mr. Smith had abused Hope, and she had learned to adapt to his abuse by almost willing her spirit to be in another place in time while it was happening.

The police put Ms. Armstrong and Hope in the back of the police car. Then they called for some back up. After two other police cars showed up they entered the house. They confirmed everything that Ms. Armstrong had told them was true. When the police came back out of the house, they told Ms. Armstrong and Hope the news. Mr. Smith was dead.

By then Hope had returned to her body. She was still quiet. When she heard the news, that Ms. Armstrong had actually killed Mr. Smith she could hardly believe it. But to Hope the memories of Mr. Smith were always with her, he was still alive in her mind, and in her dreams almost every night after his death.

The Department of Social Services allowed Hope to temporarily stay with Ms. Armstrong until they found her another suitable foster home. Hope had become very attached to Ms. Armstrong. She told Ms. Armstrong that she was not ready to tell Love what had happened. When she asked Ms. Armstrong how Love was doing, Ms. Armstrong told her all the good news about Love, about Love's success in school, and about all of Love's scholarship offers. Ms. Armstrong was hoping that by telling Hope how well her older sister was doing it would give her a reason to keep working towards a better life for herself, despite the abuse she had experienced. Hope asked Ms. Armstrong not to tell Love what happened to her because she wanted to tell her everything herself, when the time was right. Hope didn't want Love to give up on her dreams of going away to college just to stay behind for her in New York. So Ms. Armstrong told Love she had checked on Hope and that Hope was safe and sound. She explained to Love that she would be bringing Hope with her to her graduation ceremony.

On Love's graduation day Hope could still not bring herself to tell Love all the horrible things Mr. Smith had done. She didn't want to spoil Love's day. All Love talked about was how happy she was to be going to college and how she couldn't wait for her little sisters to come visit her on campus. Love said she was saving the news of which college she was going to attend for dinner that night.

Hope had not seen Love look so happy since before Nana had died. Ms. Armstrong did promise she would get permission from the Department for her to go visit Love as much as possible.

After the graduation ceremony, they all made plans to meet up at Ms. Armstrong's place later that night for dinner and they said their goodbyes. They were having such a good time at the graduation that Hope didn't want to leave Love, but Ms. Armstrong had set up a meeting with some possible new foster parents for Hope up at the Social Services building, and she didn't want them to be late.

While Ms. Armstrong and Hope were in the Social Services building for their meeting with Hope's new foster parents a fire broke out. The fire spread throughout the whole building quickly. Hope and Ms. Armstrong were in the interview room with her new foster parents when the alarms went off. There were ten stories in the building. The elevator was not working but they managed with others, to make it down the stairwell. Ms. Armstrong was holding Hope's hand tightly, so she wouldn't lose her through the smoke and crowds of people trying to run down the stairs. Then the ceiling came down above them. Ms. Armstrong lost her grip on Hope's hand. The ceiling caved in causing a barrier between the two of them. People were franticly screaming because they could not pass by the barrier. They were trapped. They couldn't go back up, because the fire had started up top, but they couldn't keep going down the stairs either.

Hope was screaming, "Ms. Armstrong, Ms. Armstrong." Ms. Armstrong was trapped with the others.

"Keep going Hope. I'm going with the others to the staircase on the other side of the building. I will meet you outside".

Hope only had two more flights to go down to get out of the exit door to the outside of the building. Ms. Armstrong pleaded with her to keep going, but Hope wouldn't budge. Then someone grabbed Hope from behind. It was the man that was just introduced to her as possibly her new foster father. Ms. Armstrong had whispered to Hope earlier that she had a good feeling about the couple in the interview room, but Hope didn't trust the husband. Hope started kicking and screaming when he grabbed her from behind. But he dragged her down the stairs anyway, and finally got her outside of the building and to safety. His only intention was to get Hope out of the burning building. This man had raised three of his own girls with his wife and he had never once touched them or any other child inappropriately, but Hope didn't know that. She felt an immediate disgust towards him because he had touched her. In his efforts to fight Hope's attempts to stay in a burning building, he had to grab her body any way possible to get her out of the building and to safety. He didn't realize how effected Hope was from the abuse that had previously happened to her, even though Ms. Armstrong had already explained to him and his wife Hope's history.

Hope was kicking and screaming not just because she didn't want to leave Ms. Armstrong, but also because feeling this man's hands grabbing her reminded her of Mr. Smith. She had sworn to herself she would never let that happen to her again. After they were safely away from the burning building he let go of Hope, and as soon as he released her, she yelled, "don't touch me, don't you ever touch me again". Then Hope turned around in the crowd of people and started yelling out, "Ms. Armstrong, Ms. Armstrong."

When the fire department arrived on the scene they roped the building off, not letting anyone re-enter, and made all the survivors wait across the street for medical care. They waited but Ms. Armstrong never made it out of the building and Hope was devastated.

The lady introduced to Hope that day, as her new foster mother, tried to comfort Hope. She wanted Hope to come home with her and her husband and she told Hope that the next they would make some calls and find out what to do. They didn't know what else to do, none of them were hurt, and the whole scene was so chaotic. No one seemed to be in charge.

Hope also didn't know what else to do, so she got in the car with them, and kept a suspicious eye on her new foster father. She explained to them that herself and Ms. Armstrong were suppose to meet her sister Love, at Ms. Armstrong's apartment that night for dinner. They asked Hope how they could get in touch with her sister. Hope gave them the number to the girl's group home. They called the number after they reached their home, and told Hope, the group home said Love, had been emancipated by the Court's yesterday, and that she hadn't returned to the group home since. The group home explained that they had no further information on Love or any legal authority over her any longer. So the couple promised

Hope they would take her to Ms. Armstrong's house later that night at 8pm to meet up with her sister. Hope knew exactly where Ms. Armstrong lived since she had been staying with her the last few days.

Back in her hotel room, Love saw the news about the fire on television. So she tried calling Ms. Armstrong's home and no one answered. Then she called Hope's foster home, and no one answered there either. In fact the message Love got when she called Hope's foster home said the number had been turned off. Love really started to worry now. It was 7:30pm, and the dinner was planned for 8pm. Ms. Armstrong should have been home if she was preparing a dinner for all of them. So Love decided to take a cab straight to the scene of the fire. The fire had happened so much earlier in the day that now there was only the search and rescue crew from the fire department left at the scene. A fireman had a list of people names that were in the building that day, and Ms. Armstrong's name was on that list. Then he explained that they took all the injured and dead to Queens Hospital and they would let all the family members know then who survived.

Love went to the hospital and waited there half the night. While in the waiting room she tried calling Ms. Armstrong's house hoping she would answer and tell her she and Hope had just stepped out for a moment, but no one ever answered Ms. Armstrong's phone. Finally one of the doctors came out with a list and said these are the people they have determined were in the building earlier that day. These people either did not survive or are still missing. They were reading the names off alphabetically by last name first. Ms. Armstrong's name was first on the list. Love couldn't believe it, but then she realized, "Hope, Hope doesn't know what's going on." She got up to leave the hospital. Since she couldn't reach Hope by phone she would have to go directly to Hope's foster home and let her know what had happened to Ms. Armstrong. Before Love got out of the front door she heard the doctor call out another familiar name, "Emmanuel". She turned around in disbelief once again. She couldn't have heard what she thought she heard. Love turned to the man standing next to her. "Excuse me Sir, did he just say, "Hope Emmanuel?"

"I think that is what he said."

Love walked up to the doctor reading the list. "Excuse me, I thought I heard you say a name?"

The doctor asked, "what was the name Miss?" Then Love said in a whisper, "Hope, Hope Emmanuel?" The doctor looked at his list, even though he knew he did just say that name, it was still fresh in his mind. He couldn't look Love in the eyes again when he said the name again out loud. "Yes I did just say that name, I'm sorry. We will have grief counselors out here shortly to assist the families and friends of the victims."

Love just turned around and left the hospital. She thought, "he had to be wrong", and she headed for Hope's foster home. When Love arrived at the Smith's home she found it boarded up, with red crime tape outside. She banged on the door and no one answered. She went to the next door neighbor's house, and they told her that all they knew was there was some kind of terrible accident, and everyone left the house.

Love thought to herself, "what the heck is going on?" She didn't know what else to do, so she just headed to Ms. Armstrong's home. When she got to Ms. Armstrong's home, it was three hours after the time they had planned to meet for dinner. Hope had already been there, and was waiting on the stoop for two hours with her new foster parents. Then they finally left and Hope wrote a note for Love with the address and telephone number of her new foster parents, and then she wedged it between the screen door and front door for Love to read. Right after they had left, Ms. Armstrong's boyfriend arrived at her apartment. He let himself into the home with the extra key he had, and he did not notice the note Hope had left. When he opened the door he had inadvertently let the note fly away. He was so distraught after they read Ms. Armstrong's name off as a victim in the fire at the hospital that he didn't even notice the note. He left the hospital in a daze right after her name was read off. When he walked into the apartment he didn't even turn on the lights or close the front door behind him. When Love finally showed up at Ms. Armstrong's apartment she found him sitting on the couch, crying his eyes out. She introduced herself to him and explained who she was. He said he already knew all about her, and her sisters. He explained how proud Ms. Armstrong was of her, and how she always talked about her to him. He also knew about the dinner she was planning.

"I actually was looking forward to spending the night hanging out with the guys while the three of you had dinner, but now I wish I could just have one more second with her." Then he looked up at Love and said, "but I'm sorry, I know you have lost your sister too. I'm so sorry."

Love looked at him like he was crazy. "My sister isn't dead. I know they said her name at the hospital but it must have been some mistake. Why would she have been with Ms. Armstrong anyway, instead of with her foster parents today? Our dinner wasn't planned to happen until tonight at 8pm and the fire broke out early this afternoon. The two of them never mentioned they were going to be together today when I saw them at my graduation this morning."

Ms. Armstrong's boyfriend realized then that Love didn't know her sister had been living with Ms. Armstrong, and that she was with Ms. Armstrong when the building caught on fire. "You better sit down. You see I know for a fact that Hope was with Debbie, Ms. Armstrong all day."

Love didn't want to hear any more of what he had to say; she was in denial. "Look, I don't want to sit down. You don't know what you are talking about, you don't even know my sister. I told you, she is not dead!" Then Love ran out of the house. Ms. Armstrong's boyfriend yelled after her, "I'm sorry", but he was still too distraught to summon up the strength to run after her.

Love caught the subway back to her hotel and it wasn't until she got back there, that she sat down on the bed and looked at the picture she always kept with her where ever she went. The picture of herself, her sisters and Nana, and then she cried. She was thinking, "Nana is dead, now Hope is dead too, and Faith is adopted and out of the country." She felt like she had no one left in the world, "even Ms. Armstrong was dead now." She cried herself to sleep while drinking down the entire re-stocked wet bar in her hotel room.

Chapter 13
Back to Love

John had gotten out of the shower. He could have swore he heard Love crying in her room, but then it stopped....

Love was still in a deep sleep, her body was in Africa but her spirit was still in the past, in New York....

The next morning when Love woke up in her uptown Manhattan hotel room, her eyes were puffy and red and she realized she wasn't dreaming that Hope and Ms. Armstrong had died in a fire, they were actually dead. She drunk some more booze and fell back to sleep that following day.

When Monday morning came she got up and took a shower in the hotel room. She looked at herself in the mirror and at sixteen years old she felt more like sixty. She remembered Ms. Armstrong saying to her, "you can be anything you want to be". If nothing else, Love, knew she was a survivor, and she knew that whatever she was going to be in life now, she no longer wanted to be herself anymore. She wanted to put all the painful memories and her past life away forever. Since she was alone in this world she knew she had to look out for herself, because no one else was going to. Before the fire, Love had planned on spending the summer in New York close to her sister Hope, but now she just wanted to get as far away from New York and do it as fast as possible. She called the airlines to see if she could exchange the plane ticket she brought for August for a flight leaving out first thing that day. They told her if she could make it to the airport in time they had a flight leaving within the next two hours. So Love caught a cab to the airport, she boarded her first plane, she sat in first class, and although she should have been filled with excitement about her first flight, she stared out the window, unimpressed and feeling empty inside. She eventually fell asleep and she didn't enjoy one second of the extra amenities she was previously looking forward to getting while sitting in first class.

To the other passengers and the flight attendants, Love looked like a tired, hung over rich kid with her bloodshot red eyes hidden behind sunglasses and her designer clothes. Love told the flight attendant she wasn't in the mood for anything, but maybe a drink. The flight attendant looked at her suspiciously, "honey aren't you a little too young for a drink?"

Love admitted she was too young to drink, and then she slept through the rest of the flight and she started to wake when she felt the plane landing. When the plane landed, she made a promise to herself, to be someone new, to never be or remember the person she was before she boarded that plane. As she stood waiting for her suitcases at baggage a young man in kakis and a blue jacket stood next to her. He had dirty blond hair and a nice smile. He said, "hi, I was sitting on the plane right across from you, I don't know how you managed to sleep through that awful flight. I wanted to kiss the ground when that plane landed and we got off."

"I guess I had a pretty rough night last night."

"Yeah, I know how that is last day of enjoying your very short vacation before getting back to the life of academia. I'm taking classes this summer to make up for the one's I goofed off and dropped last semester. I'm Jonathan, what's your name?"

"My name is Love, and actually I'll be starting my freshman year, at Harvard this semester. I was accepted for early admissions, and at first I decided to wait till the fall, but I figured why not start early, I've got nothing better to do."

"Well that's great, I'm a junior there. Do you have a ride already to the University, because if you don't you can share mine. We can stop at the café and get some java on the way in. Although after that long nap you had on the plane, I guess you are probably wide awake now."

"Thanks, I'll take you up on that ride, and the coffee too. I think I could still use a picker upper." Love had never had coffee before, but today she was starting new. If drinking coffee is what preppies in college did than that was what she was going to drink. Once Love and her new friend, Jonathan had retrieved their baggage, Love followed Jonathan to the front of the airport. There was a limousine driver waiting at the door for Jonathan. The driver looked very professional. "Mr. McDaniel, nice to see you Sir, did you enjoy your brief time off?"

Jonathan replied, "yes, I had a great time Dave. Oh, Dave, this is Love. She's starting her freshmen year at Harvard.

Can you get her bags for her please? She will be driving in with us."

"Of course Sir, and very nice to meet you Ma'am."

Love made sure to act polite but unimpressed, and she simply said "nice to meet you too and thank you" to Dave, when he took her bags. Once they were in the limousine, Jonathan said, "Love", that's a very interesting name."

Love smiled, and said, "I know".

"So what's your last name?"

Love had already put in for a name change when she was emancipated and it was approved. She had long ago decided she didn't want to go by her Nana's name anymore. "King, my name is Love E. King."

"What's the E stand for?"

"Oh nothing important."

When Love checked into admissions she made sure she showed them all the proper court paperwork so that they officially struck any records of the old Love Emmanuel, ward of the state, and replaced it with the name of the newly emancipated and full tuition merit scholarship student, Love King.

From that day on, Jonathan took Love under his wings, and the two of them became instant friends. Most of the other students started to think Love and Jonathan had a thing between them, but their friendship was very platonic. Jonathan was gay. No one at school knew. Eventually Jonathan grew to trust Love so much that he told her. Love promised him she would never tell. She didn't care what he was, she knew all about having secrets you didn't want others to know about.

Jonathan had a boyfriend back home in New York. His boyfriend went to NYU and their relationship had been going on for over three years. Love shared with Jonathan that she was from New York also, but that was about the only thing from Love's past that she told Jonathan, or anyone else about. Everyone Love met in college thought she was a rich girl from somewhere in New York. Jonathan and Love traveled home to New York on the weekends together her first semester. Love spent a lot of time at Jonathan's home on the weekends, but Jonathan never spent any time at Love's home. He didn't know that when Love wasn't with him she was in a hotel somewhere

all by herself drinking and sometimes studying. Love told
Jonathan that her parents' were prejudiced, and that most of all
they definitely did not want their daughter to bring anyone home
who wasn't rich or black, or at least had 1/8 black blood in them.
Jonathan sort of got a kick out of that. He thought it was
hilarious that he was the victim of reverse discrimination. He
would joke Love and say, "finally the rich, white man is the one
being discriminated against." He understood how Love must
have been embarrassed of her parents' beliefs yet afraid to stand
up to them. He could never bring himself to tell his own parents
that he was gay. He knew it would kill them, and that they
would hate him. But funny thing was his parents didn't care
about color at all. Eventually Jonathan's parents saw so much of
Love that they assumed she was Jonathan's new girlfriend. So
Love, Jonathan and his boyfriend Christopher, (who Jonathan's
parents thought was their son's best friend), hung out together
every weekend. Christopher's brother would also hang out with
them on the weekends, so that Love wouldn't feel like a third
wheel.
      Love truly grew to care for Jonathan. Her friendship
with him was the closest relationship she had in her life at the
time. But still, she lied to him. He suspected she didn't tell him
everything, but he never questioned her. Also becoming friends
with Jonathan helped Love keep up her pretend persona as the
rich, black kid from the suburbs. Love was on a full merit
scholarship, she didn't need to worry about money for school,
books or her living expenses, as long as she kept her grades up.
Still she needed money to keep up with the rich kids she had
become acquainted with. She started school with every fashion
label imaginable, benefits of her bribery of the group home
guard. But she couldn't keep up appearances with the same
wardrobe she had started school with for the next four years.
Love needed money to keep up with the other rich kids, if she
was going to continue to pretend she was one of them. She
needed money for the clothes, money to keep up with the
partying, with the weekend ski trips and spring breaks in Fort
Lauderdale, all of that took money to keep up her charade. Luck
so happen that not all the men Jonathan knew were gay. Connor
was Jonathan's boyfriend's brother. Connor was the polar

opposite of his brother Christopher. Christopher was gay but Connor was a well known ladies man. Although Connor was now engaged to be married, he was attracted to Love.

Jonathan brought Love to Connor's wedding as his date. Only Connor knew Jonathan was really his brother's date and not Love's. The wedding was beautiful. Connor's new wife was a debutante socialite. After the honeymoon she was always away and involved in some social event. Therefore Connor was left with a lot of free time on his hands. On the weekends he stayed with his brother Christopher at their family's beach house. Jonathan and Love would come to visit often, and Connor was flirting more and more with Love on each occasion. So it didn't take Love long to disregard the fact that he was married, he certainly didn't act like he was married.

Late one night while on spring break, Jonathan, Christopher, Connor, and Love were all hanging out at the two brothers' beach house in the Hamptons. Jonathan and Christopher had turned in early for night. They left Love and Connor alone out on the beach. They all had been drinking and smoking marijuana all night out by the bonfire on the beach. Love felt very relaxed and very comfortable around Connor. During the past year of spending time together they had become good friends, although the physical attraction between them was undeniable. They had been flirting with each other since the first day they met, but they had never acted on their attraction. Connor was already unhappy in his marriage. It didn't take long for him to realize that his new wife was more interested in her social calendar than spending time with her husband. So that night Connor couldn't think of anything to keep him from leaning over to kiss Love for the first time. Love had wanted Connor to kiss her since the first day she had met him. That first kiss from Connor almost made her forget all about the group home guard. Connor was nothing like him. The only thing the two of them had in common, were that they were both married men. After a while Love and Connor's kisses became really heated. She *wanted* to make love to Connor. She had never felt like that with the security guard; that was just a business arrangement. In that moment, she wanted to make love to Connor more than anything she'd had ever wanted before.

Connor was pulling down Love's bikini, and for a split second she felt guilty and she breathlessly whispered, "wait, you're married, maybe we should...."

Connor had been holding back his feelings for Love for a year now, and he didn't want to hold back any longer. "I don't love her, and I don't even think she loves me. I want to leave her." And after that Love didn't give him anymore objections. Both of them were already high. Love felt as if they were making love while floating. She didn't think sex could feel so good. She wondered if it was the drinks, the marijuana, or was it just him. The two of them woke up the next morning on the beach, wrapped in the beach blanket. Love's head felt a little hazy, but she did remember what had happen between them that night. Now that she was clear headed she regretted what she had done. Connor was married and they were all friends. She said, "Connor, what did we do?" She was making a statement, but Connor thought she literally did not remember what had happened and that she was actually asking him what had happened between the two of them that night.

"We made love. Don't you remember? It was beautiful, and you are beautiful Love. You are the most beautiful woman I've ever known. Oh God, I'm so sorry, I thought you wanted to, but I took advantage of you. I shouldn't have..." And for the first time Connor really took a good look at Love. He thought to himself, "she is so tall, and sexy, but when I really look at her face, in the bright early morning sunlight, with no trace of makeup on it, my God she looks like a child, like a little girl." Then Connor asked Love, "how old are you anyway, nineteen, twenty?" Connor had always assumed Love was at least the same age as his brother, Christopher, who was a senior at NYU, and his brother's boyfriend Jonathan who was also a senior at Harvard, where Love attended. Jonathan and Christopher were twenty one, and Connor was four years older than them. Connor didn't realize that Love was only in her sophomore year, he just assumed she was also a senior.

Love answered him nonchalantly, "I'm seventeen." Love never worried about her age. She was always naturally more mature than her peers, and she was always mistaken for being older, because she was usually the tallest girl in the room.

"You're not serious? You're only seventeen?"

"I graduated early from high school. So I started my first year at Harvard at sixteen, and I'm a sophomore now, and now I'm seventeen. Christopher and Jonathan know how old I am, I just figured you did too."

Connor was just silent at first he felt like a child molester. He couldn't believe she wasn't even eighteen yet. "No Love, neither one of them ever mentioned it. The two of them are always so wrapped up in their own relationship, haven't you noticed. I think they were just relieved that they didn't have either one of us here as a third wheel, and we would give them time alone. It never even dawned on me to ask you how old you were. I just assumed since you are in college and friends with Jonathan, that you were at least the same age as him."

Love didn't think much about age. After all she had been through in life she definitely didn't feel like she was only seventeen. So she just said, "oh."

Then another shocking thought came into Connor's head, and he just blurted it out. "Love, this wasn't your first time was it?" Love was quiet, and she couldn't find the courage to answer him, then tears started falling from her eyes.

Connor immediately thought to himself, "God, this was her first time. I'm a real jerk." What Connor didn't know was that Love was crying because, she had a flash back about her very first time with a man.

She was remembering the sweaty disgusting guard from the group home, the smell of the urine in the abandoned building, the dirty mattress, and how she had to clean herself up afterwards with her own socks. It was all too disgusting to think about, and she was sure Connor would be disgusted with her if she ever told him about her past experience. So she decided she would simply answer him honestly and say "no, that it was not her first time", without all the details. But before she could even answer Connor, he started kissing the tears rolling down her cheeks and he started talking softly to her again.

"Love, please don't cry, I'm so sorry. Your first time should have been special. Instead it was with a married jerk. A married jerk who took advantage of a young girl that had too much weed and too much alcohol. I'm so sorry. Can you ever forgive me?"

Love's was so touched by his reaction. She thought Connor would treat her like slut, and that her relationship with him would be another kind of business arrangement. Love looked at Connor and she could see he was sincere. She wanted to make love to him again. She didn't care that he was married. She wasn't concerned about what he could give her in return. She just was so attracted to him physically and emotionally, and she wanted to be with him more than anything. So she decided then that she would let him continue to believe in his assumptions.

"Connor, don't worry about it, make love to me again while the sun is rising on the horizon, and this time I promise I will remember everything. I can't think of a more beautiful or special moment, like this one. So let's pretend like this time is my first time."

He did exactly what she asked. He thought it felt like their bodies were made for each other. Afterwards, he wanted to spoil her so that day he took Love shopping. He brought her enough clothes to last her the rest of the year, and he brought her, her first diamond necklace. Later Love told her friend Jonathan what had happened between her and Connor. Jonathan had no problems with Love's secret relationship with Connor, just like Love had no problems with his secret relationship with Christopher. The only thing was that Jonathan worried that Love would end up getting hurt.

When Jonathan and Love returned to school that weekend they had formed an even closer bond by the sharing of their mutual secrets. A few days after Love had been back to school from spring break, she received a package from Connor. Inside was a credit card, with her name Love King on it, a cell phone and a round trip ticket to Jamaica to meet him for the upcoming weekend. Love thought to herself, "it doesn't get much better than this." If she had any guilt at all about her relationship with Connor, it was hidden away somewhere deep in her subconscious.

So Connor funded Love's extracurricular activities, and living expenses the rest of the time Love was attending Harvard.

Eventually, Love felt herself starting to have deep feelings for Connor, and that made her feel vulnerable. She started to think about him, and miss him too much. She hated feeling like that, and she wanted to make those feelings go away, but she didn't know how.

About a month after returning to school after spring break Love realized she had missed her period. She knew it was Connor's, and she knew she didn't want it. She did feel like she was falling in love with Connor, but she still did not want a baby. She told Jonathan about it first. Jonathan tried to talk her out of it, but she told him she had made up her mind and she made him promise not to tell anyone. She ensured Jonathan that she was fine with what she was doing, and that she didn't have any doubts or guilt about what she was going to do. She just wanted her friend Jonathan to be there with her in case something went wrong. So Jonathan suggested they tell their friends at Harvard that they were going on a weekend trip to stay in his family beach house in the Hamptons and that once they were there they could take care of it somewhere discreet.

After Love's procedure her and Jonathan were riding back to the beach house in the cab. Love had dosed off in Jonathan's arms. She started dreaming about her own mother, who she barely knew, and her Nana.....

It was Love's birthday. She was turning four. Although she was so young, she still remembered the day clearly in her dream. Love's mother and father were temporarily staying with Nana while they tried to get clean, once again. Love's mother was pregnant with Hope at the time. Nana had just finished baking Love's cake and putting the icing and candles on top. Love ran into the bedroom with excitement to ask her mother if she was coming to watch her blow out the candles and sing happy birthday.

Love's father had just left her mother, stating he didn't want her anymore and she was also going through withdrawals. She was definitely not in her right frame of mind. She had good intentions in trying to get herself clean for herself, her child and the unborn baby she had in her belly. But her body wanted the drugs so badly she felt bitterness towards the child in her belly, who had forced her to stop taking the drugs. She felt bitterness about having any children at all with a man who had just walked out on her, and now her first child, Love, and her first burden, was in front of her, getting on her very last nerve, talking about some damn birthday cake, while she was in excruciating pain. So she unleashed all that bitterness and pain on her first born.

"I don't care about your damn birthday, if it wasn't for you, if I would have gone ahead and got rid of you when I had the chance, maybe my life wouldn't be worth nothing like it is now, maybe I would have had a better life by now."

Love was young, but she still knew exactly what her mother meant when she said, "get rid of you." She had heard Nana turn clients away many times saying she was a midwife that helped bring life into the world, not take it away. Love ran into Nana's room, shut the door behind her and she started sobbing. Nana had overheard what Esther had said and she went to go check on Love. Nana scooped Love up in her arms, and then she said, "Love remember, every child is precious to God, even when you feel like no one else in the world loves you, remember God loves you, for the bible says, *"you, (Almighty God), guided my conception and formed me in the womb.*[11] *And God said, I knew you before I formed you in your mother's womb. Before you were born I set you apart.*[12]" Then Nana said, "I love you, and even if it don't seem like it your mama and daddy love you too. They are just having such a hard time loving themselves right now, and if you don't love yourself it's impossible to really love another person, even if it's your own child. Most of all always remember, God loves you, he loved you first before anyone else, because he knew you first, before you were even born while you were still in your Mama's belly."

The cab came to a stop in front of the beach house. Jonathan woke Love up. "Love we're here. We're at the beach house."

Love looked out at the beach house. The memory of her dream and Nana's words were still fresh in her mind. She thought to herself, "I killed something precious and innocent for my own selfish reasons. No matter how bad off my mother was she still never did that. Maybe I didn't love it, but God did. I

---

[11] Job 10:10.
[12] Jeremiah 1:5.

know God and Nana will never forgive me for this. This is worse than anything else I have ever done." And at that moment Love could not contain her sorrow, shame and pain for the terrible thing she had just done, she broke down sobbing uncontrollably. She hated herself, she knew she had done some bad things, but she had always been able to justify them in the past, but there was no justifying things, not this time. She hated herself most of all because she couldn't honestly say that she was positive she would have done things differently if given a second chance. She still didn't feel ready to have a baby, and the temptation of getting rid of her problem was just the easiest solution for her, even now she couldn't say to herself she wouldn't have done it again. She thought, "what kind of person am I, knowing it is wrong, and still I can't say I would not have done it if I could go back in time and change things?" She felt that she had become this Godless monster, and she didn't know how to go about changing herself now. She decided that as soon as possible she would get her tubes tied, no child deserved to have someone as selfish as her as a mother and she didn't think she would ever want a child.

Jonathan was filled with compassion for Love. He could not even begin to understand what she was going through. He had to carry her out of the cab and up to the beach house because she had fallen to pieces. He tried for hours to console her, but he couldn't, and finally he broke his promise to Love and he called his boyfriend Christopher. He explained to Christopher what was going on with Love. He asked him to call his brother, Connor and explain to him what had happened. Two hours later Connor arrived at the beach house. Jonathan was surprised, he wasn't sure if Connor cared enough about Love to do anything. He was just hoping for him to call and at least talk to her, but he never expected he would actually show up.

Connor thanked Jonathan for breaking his promise to Love. Then he ran up the stairs to her; her eyes were bright red from crying. He quietly took her into his arms and held her for a long time.

Knowing Connor cared enough to come and see her helped. Eventually she stopped crying while laying there in his strong, warm arms. After she stopped sobbing she took a long nap. When she woke up from her nap, Connor asked her why she didn't tell him she was pregnant. She simply said, "because you're married", and she didn't say anything more. But the truth was she didn't want to tell Connor because she was partly afraid he would tell her to keep it and she knew that wasn't what *she* really wanted. Love felt like maybe Connor was already falling in love with her even though he hadn't said it yet. She still suspected he was because of the way he looked at her. She didn't want to be a mother or a wife to anyone. She didn't believe in things like marriage and family, none of that ever lasted in her opinion. But now Connor felt more in love with her and at fault for what he thought he had caused her to do. He was convinced he had taken away her innocence and virginity, and now he was also convinced that he had scarred her for life. He thought, "any other woman would have kept the child even if they didn't really want it, knowing that my family is one of the richest families in the world, but not Love. She assumed that I was married and wouldn't want the baby or her, she didn't care about using being pregnant to trap me, like so many other women would have done, just to get at my money." To Connor, Love was his innocent, child like mistress who he just wanted to take care of, now more than ever."

But the whole ordeal caused the opposite effect in Love. Love felt even more disconnected from God, and as a consequence she also felt even more disconnected from anyone else who tried to show her love. She didn't think she deserved to be loved by anyone now, and she didn't want to get close to anyone. She cared for Connor, and she may have even been in love with him, but not now. Now, she felt that she just couldn't let herself get close like that to him, and that she just wasn't capable of real love. And she felt she wasn't worthy of anyone else's love for her.

When Love returned to school that weekend, she swore she would never talk about what she had done ever again to anyone. But not talking about it couldn't stop her from thinking about it and feeling all those feelings of shame, guilt and self-hate. When she felt like that she found Jonathan and without even talking about it he already knew what was wrong. The two of them would go out, drink and party, until they end up doing something crazy that they regretted the morning after, like streaking through town or the time they went and got tattoos on their rear ends.

If it wasn't for her sophomore creative writing class, she may have been thrown out of school for her behavior problems, but no matter what she did she always managed to maintain straight A's. Still, it was obvious she needed another emotional outlet besides drinking and partying or she was on a short path to self destruction. Then one day her creative writing teacher gave the class a writing assignment to start journaling all their thoughts down every night. The journal was to be for the students' personal use only and was not required to be shared with the teacher or the class. Loved tried the teacher's suggestion and did the journaling assignment, and she realized then that she had a passion for writing. To her writing was therapeutic. Once she placed her feelings down on the paper she was able to somehow survive through another day. She started drinking and partying only on the weekends and she became more focused on school and her goals. She continued her affair with Connor until she graduated from law school, but she also had many encounters along the way with other men that she didn't tell Connor about. She also continued her friendship with Jonathan, but she still kept her guard up even with the person she considered to be her best-friend. Her journal entries every night is the only time she totally let herself go.

Love broke up with Connor shortly after law school, right after he presented her with divorce papers and an engagement ring. She wouldn't accept the ring or his proposal. After seven years of dating him she told him she just didn't love him enough to get married. Connor never spoke to her again. But she remained best of friends with Jonathan. They kept in touch with each other over the years, and Jonathan and Christopher was who she spent most every holiday with, until Jonathan died from contracting Aids. His death came the same year Love started working for Mr. Swanson's firm.

Apparently, Connor wasn't the only brother who was a cheater. Jonathan had always remained faithful to his lover Christopher. But Jonathan didn't know that when they were apart at their separate colleges Christopher was not being faithful to him, until years later after they had finally came out of the closet and moved in together. Jonathan went to the doctors, because he had a cold that was just not going away, and in fact seemed to be getting worse. The doctor asked Jonathan if he had ever been tested for the HIV virus, knowing that Jonathan was gay. Jonathan explained to his doctor that he was in a committed relationship with the same man he had been with since he was a senior in high school. Jonathan thought there was no possible way he could have contracted the virus. After the test came back positive, Christopher admitted to Jonathan that he was unfaithful in the past, back when they attended separate colleges. But Christopher had changed his ways years ago, when him and Jonathan had came out of the closet and started living together. Despite the betrayal Christopher and Jonathan stayed together until the end.

The last time Love saw Jonathan in a hospital. At the time she was working as a clerk at the U.S. Supreme Court. When Christopher called her, she immediately drove from DC to New York, and went straight to the hospital to be with Jonathan. She could hardly recognize the beautiful boy she had been friends with for so many years. He was in the hospital bed looking so weak and sickly. Love immediately felt angry at Christopher for giving her best-friend this horrible disease. Jonathan saw her glaring at Christopher who sat in the chair in the corner of the hospital room.

Jonathan looked at Love and said, "even now, even now that I'm dying; I would not have done anything different. I love him. I always will. And I love you too. If I was not a gay man, you would have been my lover, and Christopher would have been my best-friend, I'm sure of it. In a perfect world that is how it would have been, and I would probably not be laying in this hospital bed now. But Love we don't live in a perfect world, and there is no such thing as perfect love or perfect people. Please forgive Christopher, because I forgive him."

Love promised Jonathan, she would forgive Christopher. She always knew they loved each other, and even now she could just feel the strength of their love.

That night Love lost Jonathan. She lost the one person she considered to be her best friend. Love took vacation time for

Jonathan's funeral, she needed time to grieve, time to get her head straight. She just couldn't return back to work. Losing Jonathan was like losing the only family she had left. Jonathan's funeral was the last time Love took any vacation time off. A few weeks after his funeral Love was offered the job at Mr. Swanson's firm and she accepted. She needed the change of scenery, and moving from the east coast to the west coast seemed like the best way to make a fresh start. Plus the money they were offering was incredible. She had never been on the west coast before and she was ready to live life in the sun.

It was ironic that the first person she met when she got to her new firm in California was a young lawyer named, Jonathan. Everyone at the firm called him John. This lawyer, John looked nothing like her old friend Jonathan, but he did possess the same warm smile and openness that Jonathan had possessed when he was alive. He was also a snoop just like Jonathan and he asked a thousand questions. At first Love felt like he was interrogating her or either sizing up his competition when they first met, but eventually she realized he was just very nosey. As it wasn't long before she realized John was a hard person not to like. John was the perfect replacement friend for Love. He helped her cope with the lost of Jonathan in her life, without even knowing it. They began to have nightly conversations, where she actually opened up and told him all about her friend Jonathan, and how his death had devastated her. But when John would ask her about the rest of her past and her family, she would simply say she was an orphan, and she refused to say anything more. Although she wouldn't totally open up to John, he did get her through that difficult time of getting past losing and grieving the death of the one real friend she had, and this eventually caused them to form a bond.

Love didn't think she would ever have a friend like Jonathan again, but John was definitely a close runner up. The big difference was that unlike Jonathan, John was definitely not gay. Love also felt an instant, extremely strong, physical attraction for John, and she could tell he felt it too. But Love didn't want a real relationship with any man, and she didn't want to get involved sexually with anyone she worked with. So she decided very early on, that John would remain, just a friend, and nothing more.

Chapter 14
Love Awoken

Love was dreaming about the first time she met John when she heard knocking on her door. After a few seconds of being disoriented she realized where she was, that she was in a hotel in Africa with John. She felt like she had just dreamed about her entire life. It seemed no matter how much she tried to escape her painful past it always found a way to haunt her, in her sleep. She had been sleeping so deeply, she wondered just how long she had been asleep. The knocking started up again and it was John at the door. She thought it eerie that he was her last thought in her sleep, and the first voice she heard once awoken.

"Love, are you okay in there? I thought I heard you crying. Is everything okay? Look I've been knocking for a while, I'm coming in, I hope you are dressed."

There was no lock on the enjoining door to Love and John's hotel room. Love had been crying in her sleep, reliving every moment of her past. Love oftentimes cried in her sleep, because she rarely cried when awake. She figured it was her body's way of releasing tension she didn't have time to release in the day time. She hadn't

slept overnight with a man after having sex since she was with Connor. So no one knew she routinely cried in her sleep. John was the first person to overhear Love crying in her sleep, since Connor. John was in the room before she could get her wits about her and get out of bed. When John opened the door Love was sitting up in the bed, her eyes blood shot red with her most recent journal opened up and the other journals laying all over the bed. John assumed the books on the bed had to do with work.

"Look at you Love you're overworking yourself, you're going to work yourself right into a breakdown."

"John, you don't know what you're talking about. I'm fine."

"You're not fine I heard you crying. What is it if it's not work that's got you all stressed out and crying?"

"Oh I just had a bad dream, but really I'm like I said I'm fine now."

"Do you want to talk about it?"

"No I don't, but I do want you to get out of my room, so I can get out of bed and get into the shower. That is unless you came in here for another reason." Love tried flirting with John to get him off the subject of worrying about her, and her flirting with John really wasn't anything out of the ordinary. She flirted with everyone.

"No, I came in here, because I was really concerned, and as much as I'd like to take you up on your semi-offer, I think you mostly are just trying to get me to stop asking you questions about why you've been in here crying, right?"

"Hey you're the one that's always right about everything." Love gave him a little smile. After he left her room, she whispered to herself, "girl you gotta get yourself together." She got out of bed and turned the shower on, but not until she had safely and securely put her journals away. As soon as she was out of the shower she heard John knocking on the door again. She thought to herself, "he is definitely a busy bee this morning."

"Hey Love I heard the shower turn off and I took the liberty of ordering us room service. Are you decent enough for me to come in your room yet with the food?"

Love decided to have a little fun with John, so she said, "oh sure, come on in." John walked in backwards while rolling the room service cart into the room. When he turned around he saw Love standing there in her towel. Her skin was still moist and her hair was still damp. She walked over to him and gently brushed up against him while she sat down at the little table in the hotel room. John couldn't help but notice how short the towel wrapped around her was and how thin and clingy it seemed to be on her damp body. The towel just barely covered her thighs and through it you could see the full imprint of her nipples. He knew that she was toying with him and what she knew to be his Christian convictions, but she had never done anything this outlandish. After a brief momentary lapse of lust, John regained his self control and he looked down at his food and said,

"Love I thought you said you was decent?"

"What are you talking about John, I'm decent, there is nothing hanging out. Everything is covered."

"Very funny Love, go put some clothes on, before you catch a cold."

Love thought, "what a kill-joy he is, in the past he use to at least say a few flirty comments, at least he'd attempt to have a go at it, but now he acts as if we've been married for twenty years, (or at least what I assume marriage would be like after twenty years), boring as hell." So Love got up to go put on her clothes, but then she felt sort of challenged and she decided she wasn't giving up on trying to get a rise out of John that easily. It wasn't in her character to give up, not that easily. So she went over to her suitcase on the dresser and pulled out some undergarments. She gently put her feet through her lace thongs while leaving the towel on, and then she placed her arms through the lace bra, as she simultaneously let her towel fall to the floor.

"Can you come over here and do my bra up John? I just did my nails and I don't want to mess them up."

John couldn't help but look at her out of the corner of his eye. They had known each other for too long now and he knew she was just playing games. He knew she would never really sleep with someone she worked with at the firm, and that made it even easier for him to pretend that was not interested. Plus he knew it would drive her crazy thinking he didn't want her anymore. He smiled to himself when he said,

"what all these years of wearing those things and you can't fasten it up yourself?"

Love never backed down to any challenge, and she felt like John had just made this a test of wills. She knew most women would have felt rejected or at least embarrassed by now, but not her. She was determined to test John's religious convictions, break him down and then of course she would walk away and leave him hanging. So she slowly walked over to him with no towel on, in just her underwear and her unfastened bra. Once she was arms length away from him she stopped.

"John, usually I have no problem fastening my own brazier, but like I said I just did my nails. I really do *need* you in the worst way to lend me a hand right now."

John got tense when Love started walking towards him, so he stood up from his seat. For a second he thought about her crying earlier and he thought maybe she's having a breakdown. Now that she was standing so close to him he could feel the heat off of her body, and she could feel his hot breath on her forehead. Love was tall, but John was much taller and she loved a tall, dark, sexy man. John was every one of those things. She turned around in front of him, and then grabbed his hands from behind. He had his hands clenched tightly to his sides. John couldn't deny how good it felt to have her standing so close to him and to feel the touch of her soft hands. She placed his hands on her waist and then she rested her hands on top of her head as she waited for him to fasten her up. John let his hands softly slide up Love's waist and he took his time fastening her bra. He thought to himself, "she smells like cocoa butter and lavender." Just as he was having that thought, without realizing it he took a deep breath in of her aroma. She was standing so close to him he couldn't help himself, and he absentmindedly brushed his lips gently against the crook of her neck.

Love wasn't expecting that, and she felt a sudden jump in her heart and a chill go down her spine. After he had her fastened up she walked away quickly into the bathroom to put on her sweats and she yelled to John, "thanks".

John thought, "thank God she is just a tease, because a whole year of abstinence almost flew out the window." So now that it appeared Love's games were over; John decided to act as if what had just happened had never occurred and get down to business. "So where do you want me to start first? After we eat do you want me to follow up with the embassy and government officials about the adoption, or do you want me to track down the doctor's son?"

"Why don't we split the duties up between the two of us John? I'm partner now but my arms aren't broken. I can still carry my weight." Suddenly Love felt the need to apologize to John for her somewhat rude behavior during the last few days. "John I guess I owe you an apology for the way I've been acting lately."

"You think so?" John said sarcastically. "Don't worry about it Love, I know you've been under a lot of pressure, and it's true that we haven't really been as close as we use to be lately."

"I have to admit John I think my behavior has been about more than me just being under pressure. I've sort of resented the way you just became distant so quickly after you got back into the church."

"But I've asked you lots of times to come to church with me Love."

"Now you know I wasn't about to go to church with you. Anyway, no matter what the reasons are that we have drifted apart, I want you to know that I still consider you a good friend, and those things I said I didn't mean them at all. It is just going to take some adjusting for me to get use to you acting like a *real* Christian now. You use to be like a carbon copy of me, except male. Work was our first priority and now it's like we are so totally different."

"I'm still your old friend, John. Accepting Christ and God in my life has just made me reevaluate my priorities. God is my first priority now, and He is always going to be first with me for now on, but make no mistake about it, you are still and will always be a top priority to me too. I will always care very much for you."

"I know you do, and I care about you too." Love started to feel a little uncomfortable, so she decided to change the subject. "How about you get on the phone in your room and work on tracking down the doctor's son, and I will get on the phone in here and work on following up with the adoption office, they have already been notified that we were heading out here, so that shouldn't take me long."

Once they finished eating John went back to his room and Love got on the phone in her room. Love found out that the government would allow her to do what they called a pending adoption, which would allow her to take a child out of the country on a temporary Visa until the adoption was finalized with the Ethiopian Courts. The only problem was, all the children at the local orphanage, ran by SACAA were missing, due to the recent political uprising. The adoption official explained to Love that as they spoke they had military forces going out to the orphanage site because there had been no return communication in days. Love asked how long it would be before she would hear anything else. The official had no answer for her, but he said he would definitely contact her as soon as he heard anything.

Love went into John's room to see what he had found out about the doctor's son and to let him know it looked like they were going to have to sit tight and just wait in regards to the adoption. John was in the bathroom. So Love walked over to the desk in the room thinking he would have written down notes on whatever he found out. Instead she saw on the desk John's bible and it was opened up. She couldn't help but notice that his bookmarker was a picture that they had taken on the day of his baptism. Even though Love didn't believe in church, she still went to John's baptism, because she knew that to him, it was important. Seeing that picture of the two of them that was taken over a year ago, made Love realize, how much John really did care for her. She was so touched that he had saved the picture and carried it with him in his bible. Seeing the picture of them also made her realize how strong her own feelings for him really were. Even if, she would never admit it, her feelings for John, were real, realer than anything else in her life right now. She looked up when she heard the bathroom door open.

"Oh hey Love, so what did you find out?"

"Not much, they havn't had any contact with the orphanage in days, and basically they said they will contact us as soon as they hear something. So although we have the go ahead to do a pending adoption, we don't have a child available to adopt."

"I've sort of had the same problem finding the doctor's son. I found out he is traveling with a SACAA representative and that they went out with a military convoy to check out the whereabouts of the orphans. But he is staying in this hotel, and he has to come back here eventually."

"So basically John unless we are willing to risk our own lives and go and find the doctor's son and the orphans ourselves, we are going to have to wait until they return before we can get anything done. This is just wonderful. I knew things just seemed to be going too smoothly. It took us no time to get the paperwork needed together, the clearances, the whereabouts of the doctor's son and fly all the way out here, just to end up playing, sit and wait. I mean, I don't even think there is air-conditioning in this hotel, and I just realized what the comforter smells like, cotton balls. I hate the smell of cotton balls."

"I'm sorry Love. I know this assignment is really important to you. So what do you want to do? Do you want to try to hire someone to take us out there?"

"Heck no, I'm not, the risking my life type. So we will just have to wait for a while and make the best of it, I guess. Since neither one of us have ever been to Ethiopia before, let's figure out what there is to do here, that's still safe. Just call and give everyone our International cell phone numbers to contact us if there is any news. Basically we might as well enjoy being tourist."

"That's fine with me, looks like we can finally start having a little fun on this trip." So John explained to the hotel concierge their predicament and that they decided while they were waiting they would enjoy the town. The concierge set Love and John up with a driver from the hotel, and gave him strict orders to take them wherever they wanted to go, as long as it was deemed a safe traveling destination by the government. Love said hello to their driver and got into the back of the little red Cherokee jeep with John. For the first time since they started this assignment she felt a hint of her old carefree attitude. She was happy she had made amends with her friend John. She thought, "today may be uneventful and unproductive but at least I'll have John to hang out with; I'm glad Mr. Swanson sent him on this assignment after all."

Chapter 15
The Advocates

"I will send you the advocate, the spirit of truth. He will come to you from the Father and will testify all about me. And you must also testify about me…" John 15:26
And When You Testify About Jesus Let The Whole World Know That…
The spirit of the Lord speaks through me; his words are upon my tongue. 2 Samuel 23:2

The Prince and his Hope

Hope felt a new purpose in life. She was use to feeling responsible for the lives of the men and women she commanded, but for the first time in her life, she felt a responsibility for not just the physical life, but the spiritual and eternal life of another person. Hope even started to wonder if her true purpose in life was just now being revealed. She wondered if her purpose in life was actually just to bring her to this one moment in time. This one moment, where she would meet this young man, this boy with the name of a Prince. Maybe she would be the only person he would meet in his life that would testify to him about the love of Jesus Christ. Hope remembered how Nana used to always tell her to listen carefully in church, because one day she would have to be a witness to God's Words. Now that very moment that Nana foretold was here. She was patiently waiting for Amir, and she knew he was coming to her to hear the Word. Hope started praying to God for the right words to say. Then Hope heard someone whisper. "Who are you talking to now, yourself again?"

It was Amir. Hope was so engulfed in her conversation with God she didn't even hear Amir's footsteps. "I was talking to God. I'm glad you came back Amir."

"Well, you have me to talk to now, about God."

Hope felt a huge wave of happiness fill her, from the sound of Amir's voice and his obvious desire to learn more about God. "So you still want to hear more about God and Jesus today?"

"Of course I do, do you think I'm really here, just to talk to you?"

"Well I'm glad you have a reason to keep visiting me."

Amir opened the slot in the door and passed Hope her food. "So go ahead, tell me all about Jesus, or if you want I can wait until you finish eating. I put extra portions in there for you today."

Hope wasn't thinking about food. She felt confident now that this was God's purpose for her at this moment, to testify to Amir. Hope wasn't sure where to start. This was all new to her, she had never tried to witness to anyone before. She started to feel a little bit overwhelmed. She was wishing she had a bible. So many random thoughts were simultaneously running through her head, and then she heard a soft voice in her head say, "the words you need are already hidden away in your heart." Something in Hope's heart told her to just "start at the beginning", and as if the words she had needed to say to Amir had always been tucked away, written in her heart, she started to speak, without anymore doubts or hesitation.

"In the beginning was the Word, and the Word was with God, and the Word was God. The same was in the beginning with God. All things were made by him; and without him was not any thing made that was made. In him was life; and the life was the light of men. And the light shineth in darkness; and the darkness comprehended it not...[13]

Amir interrupted her. "What are you talking about, this "Word"? I thought you said you were going to tell me about your Jesus. What is the "Word", do you mean the words in your bible?"

"Amir, close your eyes and try to listen with your heart not your head. *....And the Word was made flesh, and dwelt among us, ..., full of grace and truth.*[14]*He is the Word of life.*[15] *His title is the Word of God.*[16] And his name is "Jesus".

---

[13] John 1:1-5 (KJV)
[14] John 1:14 (KJV)
[15] 1 John 1:1 (NLT)
[16] Revelations 19:13 (NLT)

Then Hope was quiet; and Amir understood, without more explanation, because the spirit of the Lord had opened his ears, and had given him an understanding heart. From that point on Hope spoke life into Amir's heart until there was no more darkness left inside of him, until he was filled with an ever-shining light.

Amir continued to visit Hope every opportunity he could, sometimes three times a day. And every time he came to her, Hope was able to speak to him about the Lord as easily as speaking about her own self or her own life, because the spirit of the Lord was speaking through her and God's words were constantly on her tongue.

Hope told Amir about the many prophesies foretold in the bible about Jesus, about the reason for Jesus' birth into the world. She told him about how Jesus had become God in man's form, and about the many, many miracles Jesus had performed. Then she told Amir about how Jesus voluntarily laid his life down for mankind's redemption. She said, "one day Jesus will return to the world and fulfill revelations and that day is the believer's hope." She also told him about all the other great people in the bible. How all of them were so ordinary, yet they did extraordinary things through God's spirit. She told him about people like Abraham, Noah, Jacob, Joseph, Moses, Issac, David, Solomon, Esther, Ruth, and Mary and many, many more. Hope explained how she understood Amir's fears of breaking God's laws. She spoke about the Ten Commandments. She knew she had broken so many of God's commandments, as Amir had, and then they discussed the consequences they both had worried about that awaited them, for breaking them. But then Hope told Amir how she was sure she would not be punished for the commandments she had previously broken, because she believed Jesus was her savior, and she believed in *his* message. Amir wanted to know what Jesus' message was. Hope explained.

"Jesus' message is about love, and how love is more important than any of the other spiritual gifts. Love is the greatest of all the commandments. Jesus said, *"Thou shalt love the lord thy God with all thy heart, and with all thy soul, and with all thy mind. This is the first and great commandment. And*

second is like unto it, Thou shalt love thy neighbor as thyself."[17]
And our neighbor is all of mankind. Jesus loves us so much he
will forgive all our sins if we only ask him for forgiveness.
Amir, if you ask God for forgiveness of your sins, and accept
Jesus into your heart as your Lord and your savior, and as the
only way to the Almighty Father, our God, he will forgive you
and love you always. Then if you walk the remainder of your
days **in love**, you will receive Eternal Life."

Amir knew he wanted, and he needed to be saved. This
was the very thing he had been seeking. He got down on his
knees, bowed his head, and prayed for forgiveness, and he
accepted Jesus that day, into his heart, quietly, right outside of
Hope's jail cell. It was so calm and peaceful at that moment.
But then a sound broke through the silence. The two of them
heard what sounded like an enormous thunderstorm erupting
outside.

"I better go".

All of a sudden, Hope felt a quick panic run through her
body and she yelled to him as she heard his footsteps running
away from her, "Amir, wait!"

Amir turned back around. "Yes?"

Hope's voice was very soft now. "Emmanuel".

"Yes I've heard that before. It means *"God is with us"*,
with me and with you. I believe that now, because of you, so
don't worry."

"Yes, but that's not what I meant. What I meant is that
Emmanuel *is* my name. You've asked me several times what my
name is, and my name is Hope, Hope Emmanuel."

"Hope Emmanuel, that is a beautiful, perfect name for
you. Thank you for trusting me, *Hope.*" Then he ran off to see
what all the commotion outside was about.

Hope knew she shouldn't have told Amir what her name
was. She wasn't sure why she did it. Amir didn't "need" to
know her true name, for them to continue their conversations.
She wasn't planning on ever divulging that information to him.
It just came out of her mouth, but she had no idea where it came
from. One thing she couldn't deny, although she had just met
Amir, he did not feel like a stranger to her, and he did not feel

---

[17] Matthew 22:37-40. (KJV)

like her enemy. Then she resigned herself, "what's done is done. It's in God's hands now, and I will put my trust in the Lord. For some reason I feel he wants me to trust young Amir Ishmael Abdul." Then she started to pray. She prayed for Amir's safety. She prayed for her troops' safety, and she prayed for her own safety, and she prayed that God would deliver them all out of the enemies' hands.

When Faith is Lacking

Faith thought, it seemed as if they had been on the road for hours, and in fact they had. So far there was no sign of anyone. Faith and Darryl's escorts decided it was time to set up camp for the night. It was starting to get dark. They found an agreeable spot and started setting up. Faith heard the escorts talking about the fire-watch schedule while they were setting up tents. Darryl was helping the men set up and Faith was starting a fire. The men had brought meal rations for all of them to eat. But Faith thought that even pre-packaged meal rations taste better when they're warm. While Faith worked on getting a fire started, she watched Darryl and the other men set up, and her thoughts started to drift back about the first time she was in Africa.

When she was just a child her parents took her with them to Africa. Faith and her adopted parents had been in Africa, for over a year, before her grandmother died. Faith had made many friends with the other children in the village. Those friends had become like brothers and sisters to Faith, and they had helped her through the pain of coping with the lost of her Nana and sisters.

Years later when Faith was back home in the states she found out about the destruction of her mother's village. She wondered how her little friends died. If they screamed out for their own mothers before they were murdered. Rationally, she knew there was nothing she could have done to save them. She was only ten when the village was destroyed, and she was home in America with her family when they heard the news. However, rationale thinking did not pierce through the aching pain in her heart. Faith always thought, "if only they could have got on that plane with us. If only we didn't leave them behind. If only we didn't abandon them to come back home and be safe in America, while they faced death."

For a long time Faith blamed her parents for not doing more and she blamed herself. This guilt, however misplaced, developed into something more. Faith began to make it her mission in life to save the ones she could, to make up for the ones she couldn't save in her past.

Throughout her travels around the world, Faith had seen many horrible sights. She had seen young babies dying from malnutrition and young girls raped and mutilated. She had come upon whole villages destroyed. She had seen young mother's breast cut off by rebels to keep them from nursing, and babies delivered out of mothers stomachs by butchers. All of these things Faith had witnessed and all these things she kept to herself, never telling her parents, and never telling Darryl. She chose to focus on the ones that she was able to rescue, instead of the ones she had lost.

But in reality Faith was carrying all those lost children in her heart, and the burden was becoming almost too great for her to carry alone anymore. She could hardly sleep anymore. The nightmares and the nameless faces she had come across in her travels kept her up at night. All of that should have made her want to quit her job at SACAA. Even now she couldn't stop thinking about what her and Darryl might find when they finally found the orphans. She couldn't bear to think about what they might find. The memories of her murdered friends, back when they were happy and alive, kept her doing her job. She felt she owed it to them; they didn't have anyone trying to save them back then, so now she would save as many as she could in their memory.

Darryl came over and sat next to Faith, by then she was staring intently into the fire. He wondered what was on her mind.

"A penny for your thoughts?"

"Darryl there's something I have to tell you. There are many terrible things I've seen these rebels do, all over the world. I just want to warn you that you might see things that will haunt you for the rest of your life. That is if we even find any of the children, or the other SACAA workers."

"Don't worry about me I've seen a lot as a doctor, and don't worry about the children, we will find them Nene. I believe we will find them alive and well."

"I'm glad you're optimistic. I wish I could be. We have been driving around for hours and we haven't seen or heard anything yet. What makes you think we will find them, and if we do, what makes you think we will find them alive?"

"I know we will find them, because I have faith, faith in God. He has never let me down before. He will come through for us, you'll see."

"What makes you think God will come through for us? What about all the times and all the other people in the world he hasn't come through for, Darryl? What makes our predicament, our problems, anymore significant or important than anyone else's problems in the world? I tell you what Darryl, I learned a long time ago to put my faith in two things, that what can go wrong, probably will go wrong, and if you want to fix what's wrong in this world, you've got to get out there and fix it yourself. So that's what I put my faith in, myself. What I'm afraid of is this may be one of those situations where I just can't fix it." Faith paused while she processed her thoughts. Debating questions like this was something her and Darryl often did. But this time the debate was more real for both of them, no longer hypothetical. "Darryl really, what is "faith", besides a word, oh and besides "my name", what is it really?"

"Faith, is the substance of things hoped for, and the evidence of things not seen."[18]

"And exactly what is that suppose to mean Darryl?"

"I can't explain it to you Nene. You either have it, or you don't, but you need it if you are going to trust in God, and believe that God loves you and will help you out in situations that are out of your own control. I believe in God's goodness as much as I believe we are meant to be together. It's easy for me, somehow I just don't have doubts."

Faith wished she could be more like Darryl. She repeated what he said to herself. "hmm, *Faith, is the substance*

---

[18] Hebrews 11:1

of things hoped for, and the evidence of things not seen. Well, I'm glad one of us has it, and maybe I'll get some credit for it too, since it is my namesake after all."

Darryl smiled at her, and he gave her a gentle kiss on her cheek. He always prayed that one day she would come to have the same faith that he had in God, but he knew, ultimately, it was up to her to make the decision that she would believe.

Then something startled them. It sounded like gun shots coming from the west. The military escorts that were with them hurried over. They told them to put out the camp fire. Then they moved the two military jeeps into the rear of some foliage where they would hopefully go undetected. They quickly set up a perimeter, with Faith and Darryl in the rear. Everything was happening so suddenly. Faith felt like her head was spinning. It seemed like they had gotten themselves hidden within seconds before the caravan of rebels appeared. They saw several vehicles speed by, with rebels contained in all of the vehicles. Darryl thought to himself, that some of the rebels looked younger than junior high students, and they were all toting rifles bigger than themselves. It seemed as if the caravan was passing by without even noticing they were hiding. Not one vehicle paused. There were four vehicles in the caravan. In the second vehicle, it was clearly visible that there were children, little girls and boys without any rebel uniforms on, but they did have on identical white shirts and blue pants.

Faith's heart jumped when she saw the children. She recognized the SACAA uniforms they were wearing. They were alive. The only problem was, "how were they going to get them back when they were being held by the rebels?" Darryl, Faith and the military officers stayed hidden for what seemed like forever to Faith. All Faith wanted to do was to get up and just start running after those vehicles and towards the children. Thoughts raced through her head. She thought the soldiers that were escorting them were waiting too long to pursue the rebels. They would lose the rebels and the children if they didn't follow after them soon. She thought the rebels would end up killing the children before they got to them. One fear after another fear, one panicked thought after another panicked thought, cluttered and compounded in her head. Finally the scout that the Commander sent out returned. He was the fastest runner in the group and had followed the caravan as far as he could. He reported that the rebels did not expect they were hiding and were not heading back to their location. He said he never saw a vehicle leave the caravan, and the direction they were heading in was to the north. The scout said it would be very easy to track the vehicles if they started now, but the Commander disagreed.

The Commander felt they should go back to the base camp for reinforcements. He said, "it's too risky to pursue them because we have no idea how many men the rebel force had back at their camp, or how much firepower they possessed."

Faith was frantic. "Commander, we can't go back now! Didn't you see, they have the children with them?"

"I saw the children, but we are only on a scouting mission. If we found the children wandering lost then we would bring them in, but this is an entirely different situation. The children are hostages, and we are not equipped to raid a rebel camp with the small group we have here."

Faith knew what the commander said was true. She was an intelligent woman, but her passion made her act and think irrationally at times. "You said they didn't detect us. So, why can't we send radio communication about the rebels' location, and still continue to follow the tracks before we lose them?"

"The rebels have most likely compromised the airways and they would pick up on any message we sent out by radio. I'm sorry, Ms. Faith, but, the best thing to do is to go back for reinforcements. Now that we are positive the children are hostages, we also know that most likely the SACAA and UN forces are being held as hostages also."

Faith wanted to cry she could not see how it would be possible for them to get the children out safely if they turned back now, not when they were in the hands of ruthless rebels. She had seen the handiwork of similar rebels who killed their own people for what seemed like sport and all in the name of some political or religious cause.

Darryl could see how distress Faith was and he wanted more than anything to help her, so he came up with an idea. "How about you send one vehicle back for the reinforcements, and the other vehicle can continue to follow the rebels tracks. Maybe if you try during night fall you could free the children without being detected. If not you could just wait for reinforcements to return. What do you think?"

The Commander was becoming frustrated. "I don't like the idea of leaving anyone out here without being able to communicate with them. Like I already explained we can't risk radio communications because the airways have been compromised."

"Faith and I have two international cell phones. I believe they also have text capability. So even if we can't call each other we can still text each other messages between the two phones. One vehicle can take one phone, and the vehicle that stays back can keep the other."

The Commander reluctantly agreed because he also had the same fears as Faith; that the children would soon be dead if they didn't act soon. "I guess we could try that, but it will be dangerous. Therefore, I will stay back with my sharpshooter. The rest of you, I'm sending back to base camp. I hope, good doctor that these phones work as you say they do."

Faith was relieved the Commander was sending a convoy after the children, but she didn't want to go back without them. "I'd rather stay back with you Commander. I want to follow the children. They are my responsibility, since they are considered under the care of SACAA."

The Commander objected without any hesitation to Faith staying behind. "What good can a woman do us now but maybe a doctor could be of good use to us."

Darryl knew by the looks of things that medical care may be needed. "You're right, I'll stay back with you Sir. If you think you and the children might need my help."

Now Faith was furious. "Darryl, you can't stay back! You're not in the military!"

"Neither are you Faith, but you risk your life all the time doing this job, for the children. Look, I didn't understand before Faith, but after seeing their little faces pass by in those trucks, and seeing them all chained together like cattle, well now I understand how you must feel. Who knows maybe God has brought me on this trip with you for just this purpose."

Faith felt overwhelmed with dread. She thought to herself, "what have I gotten Darryl into. He is a peaceful man. He doesn't have a combative bone in his body, and now because of me he is out here in the middle of nowhere, without any combative training getting ready to possibly face some of the most ruthless men in the world. What have I done?" She knew at that moment if anything happened to Darryl she would never forgive herself. She also knew that there was no changing his mind once he had made it up, but she still had to try.

The Commander was anxious to get on with things and follow the rebels' caravan. He motioned to his men and to Darryl. "So it's decided, we better get going."

"Can I have just one private moment with my fiancée Commander?", pleaded Faith.

"Of course, but it has to be just a moment. If we're going to do this we need to do it now."

Faith grabbed her knapsack and walked off a little ways with Darryl. She turned to Darryl. "I'm so sorry I got you involved in all this...."

"Faith it's not your..."

Faith interrupted him right away and said, "please Darryl, let me finish. We don't have much time. You know how much I love you, and I honestly can't understand why I've put off marrying you for this long, but Darryl I couldn't go on without you, if, if....", then she fell to her knees, and she started crying and pleading with him not to go.

Faith rarely cried and Darryl couldn't take it when she did. He had known her for so long that whenever she did cry he still saw that little five year old girl he met years ago and, it broke his heart. "Faith, Nene, my little Nene, please don't cry Nene. Please don't cry. I promise you, I will come back. I have to go, I have to..., I feel as if God wants me to, but I promise you I'm coming back."

Faith knew her attempts to change his mind would fail, but she had to try anyway. "I knew you wouldn't change your mind. Darryl please keep your promise and come back to me, and when you come back I'm asking you now, will you marry me?" She waited for her answer on bend and knee. Never had she imagined, she would be the one doing the formal proposing.

She didn't care about her pride, or the fact that she probably had an audience of amused men watching her from behind. All she knew was she had a revelation, and the revelation was life without Darryl just wasn't worth living. She knew without anymore doubts she wanted him, till death do them part. "Darryl, you are my one true and only love, and I've been a selfish fool. Please forgive me and marry me." And as she was talking she reached in her knapsack and gave him a gold metal case. The case was as large as a wallet.

Darryl was a little stunned and his heart was filled with so much love for Faith. "Yes, of course, I will. You know marrying you is what I've wanted more than anything for so long." Then he pulled her up to him and he kissed her. When their lips parted he told her that he would marry her right then if he could. Darryl noticed something familiar about the case she was holding in her hand. He realized it was his deceased mother's travel jewelry box that she carried with her whenever they went on vacations. The gold box had been handed down to his mother from her mother, and her mother's mother, and so on. Darryl had always assumed that his father held on to his mother's jewelry and her little box as well. He never imagined Faith had it.

"Faith when did she give that to you?"

"The day before she died. I was waiting for the right time to show it to you. I think now is the right time. Darryl your mother gave me her wedding ring. She said she knew that I was destined to be your wife one day, and she wanted me to wear her band when we married. She said she always thought she would live to see the two of us married and giving her grandchildren, but since it didn't look like she would live that long, she wanted a piece of her to be with us, and be a part of our marriage."

Darryl remembered that at his mother's funeral he thought something was missing, something that he couldn't put his finger on when he held her hands for the last time as she laid lifeless in that casket. Now he knew what was missing was her wedding ring. When Faith opened the box, Darryl saw there were two rings, not just his mother's ring, but his father's ring was also in the box.

Faith looked at him and already knew what he was thinking, "Your father told me that in your mother's Will she wanted her ring to be left to me. He knew she had given it to me already, before she died. So he told me he figured what was the point of holding on to his ring till death. After the funeral he gave me his ring, and told me whenever we got married to give it to you. It was like they had no doubts that we would end up together. I use to find it overwhelming, that both your parents were so positive we would be together, but now I know they had something I didn't have, faith. What did you say it was, *the substance of things hoped for, the evidence of things not seen.*"[19] Darryl maybe I don't have the kind of faith you have, in humanity, in God, but I do have faith in you. So I want you to hold on to this box and our rings. Keep your promise to me, and come back to me with those rings, because I don't want to just hold on to them anymore. I'm ready for us to put them on our fingers."

The Commander was motioning to Darryl to wrap things up so that they could be on their way. Darryl didn't want to leave Faith, but in his heart he knew it was what he had to do.

"I'll be back, with the rings and the children Nene. I promise."

Then the two of them parted. As their jeeps drove away in opposite directions and the distance between them grew, both of them felt their love and their souls and their spirits grow closer together than ever before. After a while Faith thought she couldn't tell anymore where he began and where she ended. He was a part of her, and her a part of him. She knew for sure that if she lost him she would fall apart.

The Commander looked back at Darryl with compassion and he said, "rest assure you will see her soon, and honestly I can't wait to see her again myself."

Darryl looked at him with curiosity and asked, 'why can't you wait to see her, Sir?"

The Commander answered, "just to make fun of her. I mean only an American woman would get on her knees and beg a man to marry her. I've never seen anything like it, so desperate. You must have really put some *mojo* on her man.

---

[19] Hebrews 11:1

But she'll probably deny doing it once she sees you've come back to her safe and sound."

As Faith rode back to the military base in the second vehicle she was thinking out loud to herself. "There is nothing I can do to help Darryl or the children now. Those children are my responsibility not Darryl's and now I'm also responsible for putting him in danger."

Denzel, Faith's military escort, had known Faith for many years through her work with SACAA. Faith had traveled back and forth to his country several times, and each time he had been assigned as her escort. She always talked very openly about her life in America, and about her man, Darryl. He knew how much she loved Darryl, and the children that she came here for, year after year. "I know I am but a mere man of war and not an expert on religion, but even so at times like this I look to the bible when I'm discouraged and I think of David, because he was also a man of war, much like me."

Faith looked up happy to have Denzel there to talk to. "David who?"

"David, is the man that God described as, *"a man after his own heart "*[20]. David was a shepherd boy, a courageous warrior, a King, a poet and of course a man who feared God. The one thing David always did, whether he was sinning or being a righteous man, was he prayed. Whether he was mourning or joyful, fighting or losing a battle, he prayed. When David could not fight, when he felt lost, when he felt defeated, when he felt ashamed, he still prayed. So there is always something you can do in those times when you feel as if you can't do anything. You can always pray, Ms. Faith."

"Denzel, I didn't know you were a religious man."

"I wouldn't call myself religious, but I do believe in God and his Word. Although, I don't read as much of the bible as I should and I haven't been to church in a very long time. Still God is inside of me, don't be so surprise Ms. Faith, yep, God is everywhere even in the places you least expect."

"But Denzel, I'm not like you, I'm one of those people who are not sure what they believe in."

---

[20] Acts 13:22

"Maybe so, but I'm sure God believes in you, he knows how good your heart is and of the good work you do. I believe He listens to his children with good hearts."

Finally, they arrived at the base camp. Denzel reported in to his superiors, and explained what they had observed, and what the Commander had ordered them to do. The base General was alerted and he immediately made plans and preparations to send out reinforcements. Denzel said he would ride back out with them since he could show them the last location that they saw the rebels. Faith gave her cell phone to the General so that they could await any text messages that may come in from the Commander. Denzel also offered to escort Faith back to her hotel room. Faith said, no. She wanted to make sure she was right there as soon as any word came back. Denzel told Faith she was welcomed to wait in his barracks room if she wanted, and that she should try to get some rest. He escorted Faith back to his room, which he shared with his brother, Sidney. Sidney was the Commander's Sharpshooter who stayed behind with the Commander and Darryl. Denzel wanted to get back to being by Sidney's side. While he walked Faith to his room and thought about his brother he whispered to himself, "Emmanuel".

Faith overheard him and asked, "what did you just say Denzel?"

"I said, Emmanuel, "God is with us. It's something my brother Sidney would say whenever we went out on a mission together."

"Funny that was my name, before I was adopted that is. It is my middle name now, but not many people know that."

"That's a good name to have, Faith Emmanuel, how could you not believe in God with a name like that?"

"I didn't know Sidney was your brother." It made sense to Faith now, their mother named them both after famous black actors Sidney for the older brother and Denzel for the younger one. Faith felt a little embarrassed about how little she knew about these men she had spent time with over the years, compared to how much they knew about her. For the first time she realized that these men that seemed so rough and sometimes uncaring to her, were real people, with real feelings and family.

All this time she had taken their courage and kindness towards her for granted.

When they got inside Denzel's room, he said, "it's not much, but the bed is soft and clean, and there's a soft rug in front of that cross if you decide you want to take my advice and kneel down and pray."

"Denzel, the last time I prayed I was so little I barely remember. I remember I was with my big sisters the last time I prayed. They really did all the talking. I was too young to recite by memory the prayers our Nana taught us. I don't even know how to pray or what to say to God anymore."

"Christians believe it's really simple you just have to ask Jesus to help you and speak from your heart. He will help you to know what you need to pray for most of all, and then just ask God." As Denzel was getting ready to leave, Faith touched his hand. "Thank you and you take care of yourself Denzel."

When he closed the door behind him, Faith looked around the small room. There were two beds, two small writing tables, and the little worn rug Denzel had mentioned. Next to the rug there was a small table with a bible on it and a cross with the depiction of Jesus on it that hung above the rug. Faith got up off the bed and walked over to the rug. She looked at the cross and then she fell to her knees, and started sobbing again. She was so worried about Darryl, about the children, even about Sidney and Denzel. It seemed like she had lost almost everyone she loved one way or another in her past. She didn't want to think the worse but she was use to the worse happening. For a long time Faith just stayed there on her knees crying with her face in her hands. And then she finally looked up. She looked up at the cross, and she said, "Please save them God, even me, save me.... I want to know you like Darryl does, and have faith in you like he does. I do still remember you. I mean I remember what Nana told me about you. What I need most from you God, what I ask you to give me is... Darryl and the Children back safe, and I need faith, it's what I'm most lacking in, and I need it more than anything right now. I need faith in you, faith that you will make everything alright." She felt exhausted from worrying. She thought to herself that she could not remember crying so much since she was a little child. Then she laid her head down on the rug, and tucked in her knees. Before she knew it she dosed off, laying right there on Denzel's little prayer rug in the fetal position.

When she awoken she didn't have any idea how long she had been asleep. She quickly threw some water on her face and went running out the room to see if there had been any word yet from Darryl and the Commander. Faith realized the sun was now up. She couldn't believe she had slept for so long that it was now day time. She asked one of the officers she saw, what time it was? He said that it was almost 6:30am. Then Faith realized she had been asleep over eight hours. She thought to herself, of all times for her body to finally decide to get a good night's sleep. Then she thought to herself, if it was daylight, then Darryl and the other men no longer had the cover of the night to help hide them. Faith asked the officer, had they heard anything from the men that stayed back yet. He told her he thought they had and then he escorted her to the General's office. Once they were in the General's office he left Faith in the reception room, and he informed the General that the American woman was waiting to speak to him. Faith was waiting impatiently. She felt disgusted in herself for falling asleep, when so much was at stake for Darryl, how could she fall asleep like that. Then the General walked in and touched Faith on the shoulder. "I hope you were able to get some rest Ma'am. We did not want to disturb you, until we had better news."

Faith felt her heart drop. "Better news? What have you found out Sir?"

Then the General proceeded to update Faith on the situation. "Your fiancé and our Commander texted us with the rebels location, hours ago. I sent out my troops to the location and had them leave your cell phone back here with me. They just text me and stated that they arrived at the location the Commander gave us just moments ago. They came upon the other cell phone that the Commander had, in the woods while doing recon. They have observed the rebel's camp site, and it was abandoned. Unfortunately, they did not see any children or women left behind." Then the Commander took a deliberate and deep breath and paused for a moment before he continued briefing Faith. "They also observed that our Commander is hanging from a tree, and he is dead."

Faith only had one thought, and she blurted her thoughts out loud. "What about Darryl, did they see Darryl?"

"No, I'm sorry there was no one else there. As soon as we know anything further I assure you I will tell you right away. Until then feel free to get some coffee from the command room. You can wait there or go back to the barracks room, or we can even have a driver take you back to your hotel. If you rather go back to your hotel we will send you updates as soon as we hear anything."

It was obvious to Faith that the General was trying to be as polite as possible but that he really didn't want her hanging around. But she didn't care. She told the General that she would rather wait right there. The General didn't object. He may not have wanted Faith around but he was not a man without compassion. He asked Faith to follow him to his command room where they kept the coffee. When the two of them entered the command room the men inside got quiet and they quickly looked away and tried not to make eye contact with Faith. She felt as if they all pitied her, as if they all considered her a widow, before she was even a bride.

She knew in her heart that Darryl was not dead, if he was she would "feel" it. Then she whispered to herself, and this time with conviction, "*Faith, is the substance of things hoped for, the evidence of things not seen.* I believe they are alright, even if it appears to be impossible, I believe it." By saying it out loud, she decided she was making a commitment that she would choose to believe, choose to hold on to hope, and to keep the faith. Now all she could do was wait and pray, there was nothing else she could do. She had to accept that this was out of her control. So she sat down and she did not shed anymore tears. She told herself she would believe. She would have faith. She wouldn't listen to the doubts that tried to fill her mind anymore. She would pray them away. As she sat and waited she started talking to God quietly in her head.

"God I do believe you will answer my prayers. I know you must be thinking, who does she think she is to ask me for so much when she hasn't even given me a second thought in years.

I know I am not worthy, but Darryl is, and the children are worthy God. While Faith had her eyes closed in silent prayer, one of the General's men brought her a cup of coffee and he whispered to her, *"his yoke is easy and his burden is light.[21] So cast all your cares upon him, for he cares about you.[22]*

Faith was a little startled by the sudden whisper in her ear that happened to answer her silent pleas. At that moment she no longer saw life as a series of random coincidences, but felt that God was sending messages to her from everywhere, and from everyone, all she had to do was just sit quietly and listen. That stranger's reassurances in that instance made her faith in God strengthen, tenfold. She opened her eyes and saw an old Gunny Sergeant. He had been standing in front of her with her cup of coffee and he winked at her, with a warm, reassuring smile. She thought if she didn't open up her eyes she would have swore it was God's voice speaking to her directly. She took the cup of coffee from the seasoned Sergeant, with the kind face. "Thank you for the coffee and the comforting words Sergeant."

"No problem, Miss."

Then Faith closed her eyes again and sipped her coffee, waiting with the confident expectation that she soon would hear some good news.

Love of the Law

The air felt great against Love's face as her and John road in the back of the jeep enjoying the sights of Ethiopia. Love had let down her defenses and she started to remember just why she loved being around John so much. Besides being intelligent, John had a great sense of humor, and he was just plain cheerful most of the time. Unlike herself, she knew she was always wound up pretty tight, usually and she concerned about her next deadline or case, and she rarely allowed herself to live in the moment. Her only outlet was the few hours at night where she went out drinking with her girlfriends or had sex with

---

[21] Matthews 11:30.

[22] 1 Peter 5:7

one of her many boyfriends in order to release stress. It was rare for her to just relax and enjoy herself without sex or alcohol involved.

John knew this about Love, but what he didn't know was that he was the only person she could enjoy being around without sex, work or alcohol involved. John had a way of always being able to help lighten Love's mood. She was beginning to realize just how much she missed him. They were enjoying the city. They enjoyed the local food and brought some souvenirs from the local shops. They went to the local museum and then they went to a café where Love enjoyed the best cup of coffee she had ever had. She realized while they drove in the back of the jeep that she was actually smiling for no reason at all, and what she enjoyed most of all was just talking and being around John. Just being in his presence, made her feel happy, and happy was a rare emotion for her to experience so easily. After enjoying some of the sites in the city, they asked their driver to take them to some more scenic sites. Their driver drove them outside the city, to the Falls. Love thought to herself that it was the most awesome, yet tranquil scenery she had ever seen, and she loved the fact that she was seeing it with John. They walked through an ancient castle and stopped at a place where they enjoyed another local dish. It was unlike anything either of them had ever tasted before.

A part of Love wanted this carefree day with John to never end. However, she reminded herself that this was in fact a business trip. So even though she was enjoying the time they spent together she said to John, "we should really be getting back to see if there is any word for us back at the hotel. It is close to four pm now. Before we know it, it will start getting dark. I want to get back to the hotel and call the embassy before it's five o'clock, and the officials might be gone for the day."

John was excited about spending time with Love, but he also wanted to see some of the religious sites in Ethiopia. He was hesitant to mention he wanted to see these places to Love because he knew how much she hated any talk about religion. Plus the two of them had not had this much fun together in a long time. It seemed as if it had been years since they had spent time talking to each other like this, and he didn't want it to end.

They had been out since early this morning, almost for about eight hours now and he had not mentioned anything about Christianity or God the whole day. But he knew he would not forgive himself if he left this place without even attempting to see the places he was most interested in just to appease Love's dislike of anything religious. So he decided to bring the subject up. "You know Love there are two more places I would like to see before we head back to the hotel."

"Oh, what are they?" Love already suspected John was talking about some religious spots.

"Do you remember how I told you about the Ark of the Covenant story, back when we were still in New York. Well there are rumors that the sacred ark is right here in a temple in Ethiopia. I would like to just swing by there and take a picture of the temple. I'm pretty sure we would never gain access inside. They say they only let the holy men who guard the temple go inside. So I will probably only get a picture of the outside of the temple, but then there is a little Christian Church I would like to stop by that they say is pretty close to the temple.

The Church was founded by descendants of the Ethiopian man, in the bible, that was witnessed to by Phillip, one of Jesus' apostles. The bible says that during a great revival, Philip, had an angel of the Lord speak to him. The angel told him to leave where he was at and travel into the desert. In the desert, Phillip came across an Ethiopian man, who had great authority under Queen Candace. The Ethiopian man was trying to understand the scriptures that talked about the "Lamb of God". Phillip asked the man if he had understood what he read, and the man answered that "he did not". Then Phillip, witnessed to him about "Jesus". He explained to him that Jesus was, "the Lamb of God". Later, Phillip baptized that man in the water and when they came out of the water the spirit of the Lord caught away Phillip, and the Ethiopian man saw him no more. But the Ethiopian man did not forget Phillip, and what he had taught him about Jesus. So the bible says the man went on his way rejoicing and praising the Lord, and believing that Jesus "was" the Lamb of God, the Son of God and his Savior. Isn't it a remarkable story Love? Picture it, God led Phillip away from hundreds of people he was preaching to just to witness to this one Ethiopian man. I wonder why?"

When John had finished his story, Love knew he was probably expecting her to object, but she didn't have the heart to say no to him, because they had been having such a wonderful day. So Love asked the driver how long it would take to get to the two locations that John wanted to see. The driver explained it would take about three hours because they would have to drive to the outskirts of town.

Love wanted to know if it was still safe to travel there then, and the driver said, "although the location of the temple and church was somewhat remote the government still had it listed as a safe tourist location to visit. That location is considered holy ground, untouchable, and it has always been respected."

Love was not convinced. "I don't know John, even though the driver says it's safe, it's still a three hour drive. If we go there we won't be able to make any phone calls before the end of business and it will be dark soon, and...."

"But Love, even if the Doctor's son is back and the orphans are found, we still will not be able to get anything done today. The courts will be closed by the time we get back to town even if we don't go to these locations, and I'm sure the Doctor's son isn't going to fly out as soon as he gets back into town. In fact, I already know the flight schedule and the next flight is in two days."

"Okay, but it will be dark by the time we get there and I'm not sure if I feel safe traveling out here in the dark with everything that is supposed to be going on. It will be a three hour ride there and another three hours back, John."

John was quiet he did want to see the temple and the little church, but not at the expense of making Love feel unsafe. But then their driver interrupted them. "It doesn't get dark around this time of year until about 8:30, sometimes 9:00pm, Ma'am. If you want, there is an inn, midway there. We could check in and stay there on the way back for the night, instead of driving the whole three hours back after dark."

Love could see how important this was to John so she agreed to go reluctantly. During the three hour ride there, John decided he would use this time alone with Love to talk. Love, was such an important person in his life. He had known her now for years and he couldn't deny that if he had to describe his feelings for her he would have to use the word, love. But he also couldn't deny that he really knew very little about her past. So John decided to ask her some questions about her past. After all there was nothing to do on the ride except talk. "So Love, did you grow up going to church when you were younger, or was your family just not religious at all?"

"What does it matter to you John?"

"I just wanted to understand why it is you are so opposed to talking about religion, but you seem to have no problems talking about the other taboo topics, like sex, race and politics."

"I have my reasons. I really just don't like talking about religion, or my childhood, John. Can't we talk about something else?"

Then John thought carefully about if it was worth pushing the subject when things had been going so well between them. He wanted more than anything to gain a better understanding of this woman he had grown to care for so much over the years. "Love, what will it take for you to trust me, to open up to me and really let me in? We've known each other for ten years now and you know everything about me, the good and the bad. I've held nothing back from you, except for maybe one thing."

This peaked Love's curiosity. She was surprised that John had any secrets, because he was always an open book. From the very first day she met John he had always been so straightforward about himself and his opinions. Love started speculating, "what could be the one thing John could be holding back on? I knew he was too good to be true. Maybe, he secretly had some kids he never mentioned. Maybe he even has a wife he abandoned, or maybe he's on the down low, maybe that's why he is able to abstain from having sex for so long, you never know. Or maybe it really took him something like five times to pass the bar, instead of how he is always bragging about how he passed the bar the first time without even studying and still got the highest score in the State's history." Love thought she would really love it if this was John's little secret, because she was so sick of hearing him brag about that over the years. She had to know what it was that John was hiding.

"So you've been holding back on me after all. Okay so what's this one terrible secret you've got? If you tell me, then "maybe" I will tell you some of my secrets."

John gave her a serious look, and she knew then that this was a *real* secret to him, not just something for her to take lightly, and that made her nervous.

Then John took in a deep breath and he said, "If I tell you Love, will you promise to really open up to me and tell me something about your past, something you haven't shared with anyone else?"

Love was silent for a long time. She knew if she didn't answer John's questions afterwards he would be hurt. She couldn't promise him something she wasn't sure she deliver. "I'm sorry John. I take it back. I just can't promise you that I will answer all your questions. Opening up about my past is very hard for me. So it's up to you, if you want to tell me your deepest, darkest secret or not, and I totally understand if you don't." She wanted to open up to John. She wanted to share her true self with somebody, finally, after all these years, but she feared how he would look at her afterwards. She feared that he would end up rejecting her if he knew, the true person she was, and the things that she had done. Especially now, now that he was so into the church.

John stared at Love and he could see how troubled she was just thinking about her past. He felt such compassion for her at that moment because there was nothing in his own past that caused him such pain. Then he knew what he had to do. He had to offer her his unconditional love, without expecting anything in return. "I love you. That's what I've been holding back from you, I'm "in love" with you."

"What?"

"I said, I'm in love with you, Love. I haven't told you this because, I've always knew if I told you, it would scare you. I didn't want to lose you as a friend. So that's the one thing I've never told you, all these years. I know you don't feel that way about me, but still you should know how I really feel about you.

I hope it want make things too weird between us. I know you are not looking for that right now in your life."

Love was thinking. She wasn't sure what to say. She knew how she thought she felt for John, and it did feel like love, but she wasn't ready for a real relationship. John's confession was just something she didn't want to confront. She decided she would rather tell him about her past, than get into how she really felt about him. She thought, that in some ways once she told him about her past, what he thought he felt for her would soon go away.

"So you want to know more about me, Okay. John I will tell you everything, but once I tell you, you may not feel the same way about me as you do now. I was raised by my Nana, and she was a good. She also was a Christian and she taught me from the time I was a child to fear God, to love God, and to obey His Laws. I was baptized in her little church when I was only eight years old. I believed in and accepted Jesus Christ as the Son of God and my savior. Then after Nana passed away and I was older I went my own way. I was sixteen when she died and I was separated from ..., well I was alone. They put me in foster care. I was also sixteen the first time I slept with a man for money. I quickly learned how to lie, cheat and steal. I saw that everything Nana taught me just was not real, or at least not real for me. It didn't seem like God loved me, or cared about what was happening to me or anyone else I loved. I had two sisters, and after my Nana died one of them was adopted and left the country, the other was killed in a fire. I don't have any idea what happened to my own parents. For as long as I could remember they were both drug addicts. So I did what I wanted once I was on my own, and I did what I felt I needed to do to take care of myself. Like I said, I lied, I prostituted myself for money and clothes and jewelry. I committed adultery, and I even killed my unborn child for my own selfish reasons. I did everything my Nana taught me not to do and all the things that I know that you are also against. But you know what? Once I started living for myself, instead of living for some unseen force like my Nana did and like you do now, I realized something. I realized that I couldn't change the bad things that had happened to me in the past, but I could make myself happy in the present, by becoming rich, successful, and independent. Now I am the master of my own destiny and my own happiness. God didn't help me when I asked him for help, and he didn't strike me dead for all the sins I committed either. So I don't think God really cares about what us humans do on this Earth one way or another. What I do is up to me. I have no regrets for what I did in the past. I don't talk about my past because it isn't anyone's business. I've made my life better, by following my own ways. Look at me now. I'm one of the most successful, youngest, richest partners at any law firm in America. I mean I can't complain much about my past because it has driven me to get where I am now. But I'm sure your feelings about me will change now that you know these things about me. Everyone thinks I am this born rich kid, who went to all Ivory league schools, without a care in the world. Actually this person you know today is someone I created back when I was sixteen years old, even my name is a lie. King isn't my real last name. Don't get me wrong, I'm not making any apologies for anything I've done or for any of the lies that I've told. I'm just telling you because you wanted to know so badly. No matter what you might think of me now, I do trust you, and I trust you would never tell anyone what I've just told you. So now you know all about my past for better or worse."

The feeling of happiness that Love was feeling earlier that day had passed and now she was feeling her usual emptiness inside again. She turned and stared out the window as she put up that comfortable wall of stone around her heart again.

John had become very quiet. John was a man that never was at a loss for words, but he wanted to choose his words carefully. He could tell that Love was hurting inside even more than he had ever imagined. He didn't want to say anything that would make her feel even worse than she obviously already felt. He just wanted to say something that would convince her that none of what she said mattered to him, and that he still and always would love her. So even though John wasn't sure of the right words to say, he knew exactly what the right thing was to do. He gently touched Love's hand, then he moved closer to her, and he put his arm around her and just hugged her tightly.

At first Love tensed up. She tried her best not to turn around in her seat, and not to look into John's eyes. She feared she might break down and cry.

John felt her tense up, but he held her even tighter. Then he whispered in her ear. "God can forgive you Love, but you need to forgive yourself. As for me I still and always will love you; none of what you said matters to me. I don't care about what you did or who you were in your past. I just wanted to feel closer to you and that is the only reason I asked you about your past."

Love still had her back turned to John, but he wouldn't stop holding her. She tried to hold the tears back, but she felt them falling from her eyes and down her cheeks. Then finally she slowly turned around and looked into his eyes.

John took her hand and gently held it in his hands. "You are so beautiful inside and out. I love you. Even if you can't love me, nothing could stop me from loving you." Then he gently kissed her on her forehead, he kissed her tears away, and then he kissed her softly on the lips.

For the rest of the ride there were no more words exchanged between the two of them, only the warm embrace of John's arms around her, as she felt for the first time in a long time, safe, secure and loved. For the moment she surrendered to his unconditional love, and just listened to the strong, soft sound of his beating heart.

Chapter 16
To Faint, Fear, Tremble or Fight

The commotion outside Hope's prison cell kept getting louder. Hope hated to have Amir leave her. She worried as much about his safety now, as she did about the safety of her troops.

Amir ran outside to see what all the commotion was about. His father was back earlier than he had expected. Amir saw that his father and his men had returned with more children, but these children were not the young male recruits they usually brought back from the surrounding villages. These children were the ones Amir had heard about that were cared for by the orphanage. They all had on school uniforms. There were also UN workers tied up with the children in the caravan.

Amir's father walked over to him. "Son, have you been watching over the camp well while I was gone?"

"Yes father."

"Good, help the men confine these children. I will decide later which of the boys are worthy."

"Father, what about their caregivers?"

"I've already told my men to confine the foreign ones in the stone cells with the other foreign prisoners. They may be valuable to us later. The native women and girls, they are of no value. I've given the men permission to have them tonight. We can dispose of them later. My men have served me well they deserve their reward. You too son, it is time that you have a woman. The men who stayed back here in camp and yourself can watch over the camp tonight. The rest of my men will take a well deserved break tonight and enjoy their drink and their women. Come and see me when you are done assigning posts and confining the hostages. We have much to talk about."

Amir felt like he was drowning in a dark pool of deep water, now that his father was back. He could not go on living this life and following in his father's footsteps. He knew if he didn't obey his father, that he would kill him. It was time for him to choose between his father's life; a life of darkness, or to choose to live his own life filled with light. In his mind Amir asked God for guidance. Until God's guidance was revealed to him he would pretend the best he could that his time spent with Hope while his father was away had not changed him inside.

Hope was anxiously wondering what all the noise was that she heard outside. She was concerned about Amir, and she kept listening at the door hoping he would come back and tell her what was happening. It sounded as if a hundred men were in camp. She also heard women and children screaming, and gun shots. It had been dark for a few hours now. Amir had not come back to Hope's cell yet. Then finally Hope heard footsteps. But the footsteps sounded like there was more than one person approaching. The footsteps stopped abruptly at her cell door, and then the door opened. Hope didn't know what to expect. She thought they were coming for her finally, but then two women were thrown down on the floor inside her dark cell. The women's clothes were torn and dirty. They sat on the floor just sobbing. The younger woman seemed more distraught than the older one. Hope asked them if they spoke English. They were both White so it was obvious they were not natives from the villages.

The younger woman was in no condition to talk yet but the older lady spoke to Hope. "Yes, I speak English. We work for SACAA, it's a US based humanitarian agency. We take care of the orphans here. Who are you? I can tell from your accent you're not from here?"

"No I'm not, I'm American. I'm also with a UN agency. We were assigned by the UN to assist the locals here also. However, as you can see we were not very successful. I'm not really sure how much time has passed since I was taken hostage. You women are the first people I've seen or spoken to, besides the young man who brings the food to me once a day."

Hope noticed how the young woman, was still sobbing. "Is she okay?"

"No, she isn't. The rebels wasted no time raping her in the back of the truck on the ride to camp and right in front of the children. They also raped the Ethiopian women that assist us in caring for the children, and I overheard them saying they were going to kill them when they were finished."

Hope walked over to the young woman and smoothed her hair. "I know things seem hopeless, but I believe God will save us."

The older lady looked at Hope and said, "I believe it too. I may be an old lady, but I believe God still has plenty of work left for me to do."

Out in the rebel camp, Amir finished assisting the other rebels with confining the children and he observed in disgust as they molested the young girls. Then he did as his father ordered him to do, and he reported back to him. His father was sitting in his tent, drinking, and looking at his map. Amir walked into the tent and realized his father was so engrossed in thought that he did not even notice he was there, so he announced himself. "Father you told me to report back to you."

"Yes, son, come sit. I wanted to talk to you about how we are gaining support from the surrounding countries, and we even have a few secret supporters within our own government. Soon Amir, soon we will have the power we need to make this country a better place."

On the outside Amir listened obediently to his father, but inside he was thinking of all the awful things he had seen done because of his father. Amir's first memories were watching his father give the young boys in the village talks about politics and power. Back then Amir thought his father was a good man. But as he grew older he saw how his father used his quest for political power to rationalize all of his evil deeds. Amir remembered the first time he saw his father murder someone. His father had made him stay and watch as he shot two boys. When his father shot the boys he was standing so close that their blood sprayed onto his forehead. His father turned to him and wiped the boy's blood off of his face with the bottom of his shirt, as if it was merely sweat on his son's brow. While his father wiped the boy's blood off of his forehead he remembered how all along he talked about politics, and the greater good for their country.

Throughout the years Amir had come to learn many things from his father, but he could never kill like his father did without remorse. If not for his mother, Amir was sure he would have become a monster just like his father.

There was nothing that Amir feared more than his own father. He knew his father would be able to rationalize killing him if he was disobedient. Never once had Amir ever thought about betraying his father, until now. Now things had clearly changed. There was an internal struggle growing inside of him and he had to decide between obeying his father, or obeying God.

No longer could Amir ignore the voice coming from his mother's grave. No longer could he ignore the voice screaming at him from his own conscience. No longer could he ignore the new voice that his new friend Hope had brought into his life, the voice that spoke louder to him than all the others and cleared all the confusion in his head, the voice of God.

"Amir are you listening to me?!

"Yes father I was just thinking about mother. Today would have been her birthday, if she was still alive."

"Amir, the time for mourning your mother is done, and now it is time for you to take your rightful place as second in command. All of your brothers are dead and you are now my only living son. Still my men will not respect you until they can see you are willing to do whatever it takes for our cause to be victorious. So it is time for you to choose."

"Choose what, father?"

"Choose if you will go on to lead after me. To start with, you will be tested by choosing the new recruits. No longer will I choose which ones are worthy and which ones are not. You will choose. Just like when you first were brought into the camp, and you had to show your worthiness by pledging your allegiance to our cause. You did what I told you to do, and always have, but I knew you were "my son" and you were born to lead one day. Even so you know that being my son, will not help you escape the consequences if you could not complete the tasks that were given to you. So I'm giving you the important task of deciding, by tomorrow morning which boys you think are worthy enough to join us and which are not worthy. Those you deem worthy we will give the rifles to in the morning. Those you deem not worthy will meet their end in the morning. Yes, you my son will decide for me from this day on which ones you deem as worthy. So go in and get to know these boys. See which ones you think will be courageous and loyal enough to join us, and strong enough to fight for our cause. Do you understand Amir?"

"I understand father. I will choose by tomorrow, as you have commanded."

"Very good son. Now why don't you sit down and have a drink with me?"

"No thank you father, this is an important task you have given me and I want my head to be clear when I make my choices."

He was proud that his son Amir was already taking this assignment so seriously. "I believe you will be a strong and effective leader one day. I will see you in the morning then son."

Amir left out of his father's tent. He had decided he could no longer follow his father's way, but he had not figured out how he could escape, and how he could escape, with Hope. He couldn't leave Hope behind. Amir headed out to the confinement area where the young children were located. He did not want to make his father suspicious. He knew he needed to appear to be following his father's instructions. So he decided he would get to know the boys as his father had ordered. It was then when an idea to escape came to his mind.

The boys were fearful when Amir entered their cell. Some of the boys looked to be the same age as Amir, around 13 to 15 years old, but some of them looked much younger. Amir walked in and talked to the many boys with authority. He ordered the boys to tell him their names and what villages they were from before they came to live at the orphanage. Some of them wondered how a mere child like themselves could have so much authority in the camp. They saw how the other rebels allowed Amir to pass by and how they obeyed his orders without question. Amir told the boys that he would speak to them individually in order of age, oldest to youngest. Then he commanded the oldest boy to follow him. The boy immediately got up, and followed Amir out of the cell as ordered.

The boys prison was an iron pen that the men kept outside. It was meant for animals to be held that they planned on slaughtering eventually for food. Two of the soldiers were assigned to guard the boys' pen and they sat at a table close by playing cards. The guards kept their rifles close by as they enjoyed drinking gin and playing cards. There were also men assigned to the enclosed cells where the hostages they considered valuable were held. The men who were not assigned to different posts were the men who had just returned to camp that night after raiding with Amir's father. Those men were in their tents resting, drinking, doing drugs, and raping the native women and girls that they had captured. The rebels were all confident that they had not been followed back to camp, and therefore they were feeling very relaxed for the night.

Amir walked the oldest boy over to a sitting area. The area was still in sight but far enough by the edge of camp so that the guards could not overhear their conversation. Amir asked the boy his name and what village he came from.

"My name is Razeeq, and I do not know what village I came from, because I was left at the SACAA's orphanage when I was just a baby."

"My name is Amir and my father is the leader here. Do you understand that your life as you knew it is over now? You will have to make a choice between joining our cause, or death. If you join us you will have to pass some difficult trials. First, you will have to kill, whomever we command of you, without any question. Second, you will have to give your life to the cause, and forsake all that you knew and all that you were in the past. Then you will be ordered to swear in blood your loyalty to my father, our Commander and to us, for the remainder of your life; whether that be a short life or a long life. If you ever betray us you will be killed. Do you understand?"

"Yes I do."

"Do you have any questions for me?"

"No, I don't."

"What will you choose then?"

"I don't know, must I decide this moment? I don't want to die, but I don't want to kill anyone either."

Amir knew he was not the right one, not the boy God was guiding him to choose. So he escorted the boy back to the cell. And Amir ordered the next oldest boy to follow him out. This boy looked strong, just as the last one did. He was even older than Amir. Amir knew if his father was choosing he would want these two boys to join them. They were the oldest and the strongest ones in the bunch. Amir told the next boy to sit down and he told this boy the same things he had told the last boy. After Amir was finished the boy put his head in his hands and said, "I just don't want to die." Amir knew once again, this boy also was not the boy he needed to help him; this boy was full of fear. Then Amir walked the second boy back to the confinement pen. There were almost twenty boys in the pen. Amir had spoken to five boys. About two hours had passed by. He decided he was not getting anywhere with the method he had chosen. So when Amir returned to the confinement pen, this time, he decided to pick one of the less impressive boys.

He had noticed a young boy, who looked very unremarkable, but yet stood out. The boy appeared to be no older than nine years old. What made this very young, unremarkable boy stand out to Amir were his eyes. The boy's eyes were filled with hatred for him, and he never once looked away from Amir's glance like the other boys. Amir pointed with his rifle to the young boy.

"You, you get up and come with me."

The boy stood straight up as Amir had instructed him and he never did break the hateful stare he had on Amir. Amir was more cautious with this boy than he had been with the others. He kept his rifle pointed at the boy at all times. Once they were sitting, he told the young boy all the same things he had explained to the other older boys. After he was finished explaining what was required of anyone who joined the rebel force he asked the young boy, "what will you choose? Will you join us; will you do as we demand?" The boy just stared at Amir with disgust for what seemed to be a very long time; and then Amir impatiently shouted to the boy, "don't you know how to speak boy, or are you deaf and dumb. Just nod your head if you have nothing to say so we can be done here."

Then the boy began to talk, and his voice sounded steady, and mature for his age. "I can talk, and I have a question for you. Do you believe in God?"

Amir was surprised by the young boy's question. "Why, what does that matter to you boy?"

"I believe in God and it matters to me if you believe in Him or not. I can't tell you that I couldn't kill a man, but I have never killed a man before, but I can't say that I haven't wanted to. When I look at you in your uniform, I remember how someone like you, a rebel in a uniform just like your uniform killed my parents and my sister. If I had a rifle back then I would have killed those men and if I had one now I wouldn't hesitate to kill you. So my answer is "yes", I "could" kill a man if I needed to and if I hated him enough. But I will never kill for you!"

Amir was quiet. He listened to the young boy in amazement of how he could be so bold to say the things he was saying to him while he was pointing a rifle at him. Even more so Amir was amazed at how all the time the boy talked to him he still had not broke his stare. The boy's eyes were filled with fire and ice almost daring Amir to shoot him.

With boldness, the boy continued to talk and he said, "I asked you if you believed in God, because if I did have an opportunity to kill you, I would ask God to forgive me, and then I even would ask God to forgive you for the things that no doubt you have done. So as far as my pledge of loyalty to you and your cause, my answer to that is "no". I will forever be loyal to one, my Almighty Father above. You do not decide my fate, decide my life or my death, if you think that you have the power to, then it is only so, because He has made it so."

Amir knew right away that, God had chosen this boy. Then he quickly explained to the boy, that he too believed in God, and how he was trying to plan an escape. "Can you trust me? If you say you can trust me, then I will believe you because God is telling me to believe in you, then together we will try to escape and rescue the others."

"Why should I trust you? You are a rebel."

"I have no time to try to convince you to trust me. So you said you believe in God. If you trust God, if you have faith in him, then close your eyes, and ask God what you should do, because I cannot wait much longer for your answer."

So the boy closed his eyes and within seconds his eyes were wide open and he said, "I will trust in God, and I feel he is telling me to also trust you."

  "Good. This is my plan; I will tell the men that I am taking you in to see my father. I will tell them that I have found that you are from the next village on our map in which my father plans on raiding. They will understand then why I would bring you inside my father's tent, so that we could extract information from you. My father has been drinking and smoking since he has returned, like most of the other men that left out with him. The last time I saw him in his tent, his speech was already slurred and he did not even notice I had entered into his tent until I announced myself to him. That was over two hours ago. So I'm sure by now he is asleep. I will take you into his tent, and in the state he is in he will not be much of a match for the two of us. There stands one guard outside. I am the only one who is allowed to enter and leave my father's tent unannounced, and with a weapon on. No one else in camp is allowed to enter his tent with any weapon on their body. If he is not asleep then I will tell him that I think you are the best pick out of them all, although you are young. I will tell him that I have discovered you are a skilled scout and runner from your village. He will not question why I have brought you into the tent.

  Then Amir told the boy how he should answer his father's questions if this happened. Hopefully my father is asleep. If my father is asleep, then we can quietly take some rifles from the tent. I will leave you in the tent. I will tell the guard my father wishes to not be disturbed so that he may ask you some difficult questions. The men trust me they will not question any of my actions. Then you wait for me in the rear of the tent where a secret escape hole is located. When you hear me come behind the tent, pass me the rifles through the escape hole. Once we have secured the rifles out of the tent, you can slide under the crawl space and follow me. I hope you are fast. You will then need to follow me into the marsh. I will give you the key to the boys' confinement cell. When you see that the two guards have left the areas they have been assigned to, on my command, free all the other boys and give them the extra rifles. Then all of you run as fast as you can into the marsh. You have the advantage of the night to cover you. Do you understand all that I have told you?"

"I understand what you have said, but why are you doing this, when your father is the leader? Are you ready to betray your own father?"

"I don't believe in my father or his war. Just know that I believe it is God's will that I must go against my father."

"Fine, I will remember everything you have instructed me to do and I will do exactly as you say."

Amir escorted the boy to his father's tent and he told the men guarding the other boys where he was taking the young boy. No one questioned his intentions. Once Amir and the boy entered his father's tent Amir announced himself again to see if his father was awake.

"Father, it is me."

This time there wasn't an answer. He slowly approached his father's bedside, until he was close enough to see his eyes. As he suspected, his father was in a deep sleep from drinking and using drugs. Amir unlocked the rifles and ammunition that was in his father's case. There were twelve weapons at his disposal in his father's tent, and he gathered up all of the weapons. He also wanted to take the side arm that his father usually kept strapped to his hip. He walked over to his sleeping father, he was afraid he would awaken his father if he took the sidearm off of his body, but he didn't see it on him anyway. So he proceeded to leave out of the front of the tent as he had planned, leaving the young boy inside.

When he was leaving the tent he explained to the rebel that was guarding his father's tent that his father wanted to question the young boy and that he said he did not want to be disturbed.

Once Amir was out of the sight of his father's bodyguard, he sneaked behind his father's tent. Everything was going as he had planned. The boy followed Amir into the marsh after they had completed the transfer of all of the rifles, then they ran with the rifles to an undetected spot close to the boys' confinement pen. The two rebels who guarded the boys' pen were seated in front of the entrance. Amir told the young boy to wait in the spot he had taken him in the marsh until he gave him the signal. Then he started running back towards the rear of his father's tent, so that the two rebels guarding the boys' pen would not see him walking out of the marsh and wonder why he was in the marsh in the first place.

While he was heading back he thought he heard a noise in the marsh. Amir was raised in this terrain, and he had developed a keen sense to detect what was a natural sound of the surrounding habitat versus something unnatural. The sound Amir heard he could have sworn sounded like a snapped reed beneath someone's feet. It was too crisp, a little too loud to be from one of the small animals that lived in the marsh. He knew none of the other men were outside of the camp perimeter. Only the young boy he had left there should be in the marsh, but the sound did not come from that direction. He got down low. Then he did a low crawl over towards the direction he heard the sound. Something else surprised him even more so than the sound he had just heard. He smelled perfume. It was not the native scent of the oils the Ethiopian women wore that he was use to, but a scent somewhat like the perfumes his mother use to wear on special occasions. What Amir smelled was the faint scent of Faith, still lingering on Darryl from earlier that day. He thought maybe what he heard was the sound of one of the female workers from the orphanage, hiding in the marsh. He decided he would take a chance and announce himself, so he whispered,

"I am trying to help. I know you are out there. I will not hurt you, show yourself."

Darryl decided to trust him and he stood up. The Ethiopian Commander whispered to Darryl, "you fool get down, it's a trick." Darryl and the Ethiopian Commander and his Scout, Sidney had been scouting out the rebel camp for hours waiting for their reinforcements to show up. But so far no one had come. Darryl had a feeling that it was not a trick. Then Amir started walking towards Darryl's direction. The Ethiopian Commander kept a close eye on Amir, and a close grip on his gun. It did appear that Amir was alone and he had also observed how Amir and the young boy had snuck a bunch of rifles out of one of the tents.

When Amir approached them he asked them who they were and what were they doing hiding in the marsh. Darryl told him how they were waiting for reinforcements but they had a vehicle hidden a few miles away. Amir saw this as a sign from

God, that he had sent him more helpers. He explained to them that he was attempting to release the hostages and that there was no more time to waste, they had to act now.

"Follow me and I will show you where the boy I positioned in the marsh is waiting with the rifles. We can use your help in releasing the others. After we release the others we can ride away from here in your vehicle. We have no chance of trying to win a fight. There are hundreds of men here in the camp. All of them are skilled killers. We can only hope that most of them are too drunk and high to respond quickly enough to stop us once they realize we're gone. Don't do anything until I give you the signal."

Amir planned to find a way to release Hope. He didn't want to leave her behind. He started to worry that he had been gone for too long and someone might notice. After he explained things to the young boy helping him, he left Darryl, the Commander and Sidney with the boy and headed back towards the rear of his father's tent through the marsh. When he got back to the rear of his father's tent his father was still asleep. His father's bodyguard had not even noticed anything was out of the ordinary. Amir made sure to be very quiet so he would not awake his father.

The bodyguard sat outside with his back facing the entrance of the tent. He didn't hear Amir approaching him from behind. By the time he felt Amir grab hold of his mouth from behind, it was too late. He didn't even have time to scream when Amir plunged a knife into his neck. Amir was careful not to get the bodyguards blood on him. He dragged the guard's body into the corner of his father's tent and concealed it completely from sight. Amir didn't have any pleasure in killing the man, but his father's bodyguard had a perfect view of the rear of the cell Hope was confined in, he knew there was no way he could release Hope without him seeing and possibly reporting it to his father. Hope and her troops were the only hostages that were not allowed to leave there cells unless the rebel leader personally retrieved them. Any rebels that noticed the missing bodyguard would assume that he was inside talking to their leader. There were two guards posted in the front of Hope's cell and the cell her troops were confined in, but he already had a plan in place to deal with them. Now that he had eliminated one guard he proceeded to walk back towards the pen that held all the boys' from SACAA.

The two guards sitting outside the boys' confinement pen noticed Amir coming back, and one of them asked him if his father was in a good mood.

"He is in the same mood he is always in. Why do you ask?"

"He's assigned us to guard these boys all night, so that the men coming back from raiding can rest and drink. But we were thinking, maybe they could let us have one of the women they brought back if one of them were finished for the night? One of us is due to go on a break soon, and the other one can continue to stand watch."

Things were going better than what Amir had ever expected; he was just wondering what excuse he would use to get the two rebels to leave there post. "Well my father did say he does not want to be disturbed while him and his bodyguard question the young boy inside his tent. He also told me that I can have my pick of any women that they brought back. I've decided on the young, foreign girl with the long red hair. If you want I can share her with you men when I finish. Whichever one of you that is due for your break can come with me now, and I'll take the other one afterwards."

The outspoken rebel that had made the request got up and followed Amir.

"Since I was the one who spoke up, I get first dibs and you stay here and keep watch."

The other rebel begrudgingly agreed. Only Amir and his father's right hand man had the keys to where the important hostages that his father planned to ransom were held. His father's right hand man was drinking and relaxing also, like the rest of the men who had returned. So Amir escorted the ignorant outspoken rebel to Hope's cell and as they passed the two rebels that guarded the front entrances of the two hostage cells, one of them asked Amir where the they were headed.

"Just on our way to enjoy the reward my father has bestowed upon me. Don't worry you don't have to check with my father, I'm not going to take any of them out of the cell, what I'm here for we can do inside the cell."

The guard understood what Amir was implying, and he let them pass without any more questions or suspicion.

Hope and the other two women heard the footsteps coming. Their hearts stopped when they heard the key being used in the door. Then Hope felt relieved when she saw it was Amir, but the other two women were paralyzed with fear. The young woman had just recovered enough to talk again, and she said, "I'd rather die than have them touch me again." Hope understood how she felt. The three women just stood there staring at Amir and the other rebel who were standing at the door.

Amir held the door open for the other rebel who entered the cell first. After Amir closed the cell door behind him he shined a flashlight in the young red-head girl's face and said, "see isn't the young one very pretty".
Before the man could barely get a good look at the young woman, Amir slit his throat from behind with his K-bar. Then he quietly laid the rebel down on the floor. The man was three times Amir's weight, but Amir took him down swiftly and with ease.

The two women didn't know what was going on, and the young girl started screaming; but the screams of a woman in the camp would not concern any of the rebels in the camp. The young Ethiopian women in the camp had been screaming all throughout the night. Amir looked over at Hope and said, "it's now or never."

"Ladies, he's here to help us escape."

Then Hope stripped the clothes off of the rebel that Amir had just killed. She put on the rebel's uniform, and armed herself with his weapons. Then Hope and the two women followed Amir out of the cell. There were two guards outside the hostages cell that they had to get pass. Hope had to get her troops out of the other cell. She was not escaping without them. Before Amir and Hope left the cover of the cell they were in Amir gave the oldest women a rifle, and he said, "wait in here for us to come back. Do you know how to use this?"

The old lady calmly answered, "yes".

"Ma'am, you and the girl stay here. If you don't hear my voice saying, "it's okay", before this door opens, shoot whoever comes in and run for your lives. There are three men waiting in the marsh right next to the children's holding pen. They have a vehicle to get all of you out of here. Run into the marsh towards them, and don't look back. Do you understand?"

The old lady had been through worst situations during her lifetime of missionary work. "I understand, and God bless you child for risking your life to save us."

Then Amir gave Hope a knife and he didn't offer any advice, besides. "Just do it quietly." They walked out of the cell together, Amir walked towards the direction of the guard that stood watch to the east of the hostages' cells and Hope walked towards the direction of the guard that stood watch to the west.

When Amir reached his guard, the guard commented, "say that was quick, were the women no good?"

"I wouldn't know. The young red-head surprised me. She had something in her mouth and cut me, down there! If she wasn't an important hostage to my father I would have slit her throat! Look at what she has done to me!"

The guard put his rifle against the wall. He had no reasons at all to not trust Amir. Then he stood up to take a look at Amir's wound. Amir had rubbed the blood from the rebel he had just killed all over his pants, and the guard could clearly see it.

"God man, it looks like she really got you good."

Then while the guard was looking down and distracted without his rifle still in his hand, Amir grabbed him by his neck and he shoved the rebel's face deep into his chest. The guard was caught by surprise and he was totally confused about what Amir was doing. They both fell to the ground and the rebel fell on top of Amir. Amir kept a tight grip on the guard's head. He smothered the guard's face into his chest as he simultaneously shoved the K-bar he held in his right hand into the rebel's back. No one could hear the guard's screams because Amir made sure he never loosened the grip he had on the guard's head. He made sure no sound escaped out of the rebel's mouth. Once he felt the rebel's body go limp he released his grip.

While Amir was quietly killing the one guard, Hope was approaching the guard to the west. She was trained to recognize when her physical strength was not an advantage and she needed to use an alternative strategy. This was clearly the case. The guard was visibly much stronger and larger than she was. Also the uniform she was now wearing from the guard Amir had just killed was much too big to fit Hope properly. The rebel guarding the west side of the hostages cells looked up at Hope when he heard her approaching. He immediately noticed how the uniform she was wearing seemed to fit strangely. He remembered that the soldier he saw walk into the cell with Amir was much larger than this soldier that was now coming out of the cell. He felt that something was wrong and he stood up from his chair. He was getting ready to yell out "halt", but he hesitated just a few seconds too long.

Hope had been walking towards him very swiftly. She didn't want to alert him by running, but she realized it would not take him long to notice she was not the guard that he had previously saw. Her right hand was gripping the knife that she had concealed. Hope kept her head down while she walked towards the guard so that he wouldn't see her face. But she could still see his hands, his rifle and his chest from under the rebel's cap she wore. She knew she had no time to get close to him before he would make too much noise, and alert the other rebels in the camp. Hope also knew she had to be quick and precise, or he could just shoot her if she took too long to attack or missed her target. So as soon as Hope saw the guard stand up, and make a motion as if he was going to lift his rifle, she threw her knife. She threw it with all of her strength and accuracy. In one smooth, swift motion she aimed for his heart. The knife plunged into the exact spot she aimed for on her target. She was close enough to not miss him, but still not close enough to kill him with one throw. His hands moved towards the knife which was sticking out of his chest, and Hope ran towards him and leaped on top of him. With all her forced she made sure the rest of the knife plunged deeper into the rebel's chest. The guard let out a yelp, that Hope quieted with her hands. Then to her horror she heard someone approaching her from behind. Her heart was racing but when she turned around, she saw Amir.

Amir was already walking back towards the cell to retrieve the two women that had been placed in the cell with her earlier that night. Hope heard Amir whisper to them, "it's okay". It didn't appear that anyone else had heard the guard's brief yelp of pain. Hope got to her feet, and she saw Amir and the two women come out from behind the cell door. They all dragged the bodies of the rebels they had just killed into the cell, and unclothed them. Amir was busy giving the two women more instructions. He handed the rifle belonging to the second guard he had just killed to the young red-head this time.

"Do you know how to use this?"

"Olga just showed me while we were waiting for you two to return." She took the rifle from Amir. The four of them proceeded towards the cell where Hope's troops and her Major were being held. There were no rebels nearby for them to worry about for the time being. Hope could not wait to see her men's faces, but another part of her walked towards their cell in dread. She dreaded the idea that she may find that the rebels had killed some of them. When they reached the cell where Hope's men were being held, she asked Amir and the two women to wait outside. Amir agreed and handed the keys to the cell to Hope.

Hope took her cap off as soon as she walked through the cell door. She had her hair down from the bun she usually kept it up in at all times. She didn't know what her men's mental or physical condition was, but she thought they would try to attack anyone with a rebel uniform on entering their cell. So she wanted to make it obvious to them that she was a woman, even if they didn't recognize that it was her right away. This may have been the first time anyone had opened the men's cell doors since they had arrived. After all no one had ever actually opened her cell door until tonight when they placed the other two women in the cell with her.

As soon as the cell door opened Hope's Major who was the second in command of all of her men leaped towards her. All of the men were readied to attack. The Major paused in disbelief when he saw the person in their cell was Hope. After the initial shock he felt a flood of joy and relief.

"Colonel, you're alive!"

Hope saw that all of the men that had made the mission with her were still alive. She thanked God out loud. It was obvious to Hope that some of her men were in very poor physical condition, but at least they were alive.

"Major, are all the men able to move on their own without assistance?"

"Yes Colonel."

"Good, then take these rifles and I have some rebel uniforms, whoever is the healthiest, change into them. This boy, Amir, is helping us all to escape. He was forced to join. We have one guard left to get rid of, he is guarding the children. Amir has told me there are three men with the Ethiopian military waiting in the marsh with a vehicle to help us all escape. The rest of the rebels are in their tents drunk."

Hope left out the fact that Amir was also the rebel leader's son, that she had confided in him, and that she had told him her real name. She decided it was best to leave out any information that wasn't helpful in regards to them escaping. "Listen to what the boy says Major, I trust him."

The men followed Hope out of their cell. Once outside of the cell, the Major looked at Amir standing there in his rebel uniform with suspicion, but he trusted his Colonel. The Major thought to himself, "she has never led me astray or ever lied to me before. I trust her completely. The troops need to see me show him trust." So as soon as they approached Amir and the two other women the Major whispered, "Colonel, what do you and him, (motioning to Amir), need us to do?"

"Send our two men who put on the dead rebels' uniforms to act as if they are standing guard at those posts; this way if one of the other rebels comes out of their tent tonight it will look like the rebels are still at their post. We have to get out of here without any commotion, so we can't do anything to cause suspicion. The rest of you position yourselves in areas close by the stone cells for the time being, ensure you all maintain your cover."

Hope decided it would be best for her Major to put on the rebel uniform she was wearing. It was much too big on her anyway. She thought Amir may need assistance taking down the last rebel guard that was left on duty over at the boys' confinement pen. She knew her Major could pass at first glance for the rebel guard Amir had just killed; they were of the same body built and complexion. Hope positioned herself with the rest of her men, and they all maintained their cover. They were all able to observe Amir and their Major walking towards the boys' confinement pen with the SACAA women from a far off distance.

The Major told Amir to just keep the rebel guard distracted and that he would take care of the rest.
The rebel that was left guarding the children turned around when he heard the approaching footsteps.

"You guys are back. Why are you bringing those women out here? Amir did your father give you approval to take these women out of their cell, because you know how he is, I wouldn't want to upset him. Besides, I thought you were going to take me with you to them when you were finished?"

"Don't worry my father has given me permission to take them out of the cell. See these women asked to see the boys, and they swore they would do whatever we desired, if we would only show them all the boys were still alive. We've already explained to them the girls are alive but busy in the men's tents for now."

"Well I guess it is always better when they are willing participants, isn't it? You have blood on you Amir, what happened?"

Amir was trying to keep the guard distracted while he walked towards the boy's pen, so he made sure to answer all of his questions quickly and keep the guard engaged in their conversation.

"That red-head one did it. She has a lot of fight in her, but once I told her I would start killing the children if she didn't cooperate she calmed down. Then when I told her I would take her here to see the boys; that was when she promised she would do whatever I asked. She is worth the cut she inflicted on me. Look at her she is indeed as beautiful as my father told me she would be."

This really got the guard's attention. He had not had the opportunity to really look at the female hostages yet. The man rested his rifle against the card table to approach the young woman and take a good look at her. The rebel didn't even notice the man with Amir was not his friend who had left out with Amir earlier. When the rebel came within an arm's length of the young woman he reached out his hand to touch her, beautiful flowing red hair. It was at that moment that he felt a sudden, sharp pain in his back.

The Major had stabbed the rebel from behind. Once they had the last guard down, the Major turned around and waved his arm. He was giving Hope the signal that all was clear. Hope gave all of her troops the same signal, and they all moved out quickly and cautiously.

Amir had already given the young boy hiding in the marsh the signal that they were safe. Amir knew the young boy and the other men from the Ethiopian military were in the marsh observing everything from their position. Then the young boy, Darryl, the Ethiopian Commander and Sidney, the Scout came out of hiding. They all worked quickly to release the boys from their holding pen. Darryl, the Ethiopian Commander and Sidney were handing out weapons to Hope and her troops and the older boys they had released. The whole interaction took a matter of seconds. There was no time to waste. If a rebel came out of their tent now they would see that there were no guards left at their post and that all of the boys were missing from the pen. They all knew they needed to get to the truck they had hiding many miles from the rebel camp now to escape. They were all about to head out towards the vehicle when the older women, Olga whispered, "Just the boys are here. What about the other Ethiopian women and girls? Are they alive?"

Amir said, "they are alive but they are in the tents with all the rebels."

"But there alive, we can't just leave them behind."

Hope looked at her men and she said, "Olga's right we can't leave them. I can't leave them. Major get our men that are too weak to fight out of here. Myself, my Major, and my troops that are in good condition will try to get the other women and girls out. After all that's what we were originally sent here for before we were captured. Our mission isn't over yet. We were not sent here just to save ourselves."

The Major looked at his men and he asked them, "who is feeling too weak to stay and fight? If you know you are too weak and would only be a liability, leave now." But none of Hope's troops responded. None of them would leave her or the Major behind. They were more than a squad of military men, they were a family. Hope hated putting her troops in this position again. They had the chance to escape after months of being imprisoned, and she was asking them to stay and fight, and possibly to die, but this *was* their duty, their responsibility, and their sworn oath to protect and defend the innocent. But this was not Amir's duty. Hope thought, Amir is really still a child. He has a chance to escape this horrible way of life. He should not stay.

"Amir you go with the other boys."

Amir had formed a bond with Hope. He felt a motherly love from her and he wasn't about to let his father murder Hope the way he suspected his father had murdered his own mother. "I won't leave without you Hope. I will stay in fight with you."

The Major and the rest of Hope's men were shocked that this young boy addressed their Colonel by her first name. They all knew that no one in their unit was suppose to give out their true identity to anyone, outside of the unit, especially someone considered a possible enemy. But these men had been under Hope's command for many years and they trusted that if their Colonel gave out her name to this boy, she must have had a good reason. So they all put their momentary doubts aside. Since it had been established that neither the troops nor Amir were leaving they needed to now come up with a plan and listen carefully for their next instructions.

Hope said, "well it looks like we are staying back." Then she looked at Darryl, the Ethiopian Commander and his scout, and she said, "But you should all go now, with the two women and the boys, and send back reinforcements."

The Commander replied, "I will send the Doctor back with these two women and the boys, but me and my Scout, we will be staying back with you to try and rescue the others. You don't think I would leave a foreign woman and her foreign soldiers behind to fight my country's battle? We consider these women and girls our mothers and sisters, and we are sick of what is happening to them by the hands of these rebels."

Hope expected he would refuse to leave. She would have done the same thing if she was him. "Commander, I guess I didn't really think you would leave anyway, and I'm sorry if I insulted you by asking.."

The Ethiopian Commander cut Hope off, there wasn't time for apologies. "Apology accepted, but before we move out to rescue the other females, I want to make sure the Doctor, these two women and the boys are safely out of here. If things go wrong I want to make sure they have a decent head start on the rebels."

They escorted Darryl and the two SACAA women with the boys back to the vehicle they had hidden. The Ethiopian Commander made sure Darryl was sure of the way back to the military base camp.

"Don't worry doctor our reinforcements were already on their way and should be coming soon. You may even pass them on your way back to base."

Darryl suspected that what the Commander was saying wasn't true. He thought, "after all it took them over eight hours to get to where they were from town, so it would probably take reinforcement eight hours to get here." Darryl felt guilty leaving the Commander and Sidney. During their short time together he felt as if they had already developed a sort of kinship. All the help the Commander and Sidney had against hundreds of rebels were six men in poor physical condition, a young boy and a woman. Even if she was some kind of military Colonel, she was still a woman. The odds were definitely against them." But Darryl knew his first responsibility was to the children and to Faith. He promised Faith that he would return safely with the children, and he was going to keep that promise. Maybe he would be coming back with only the boys, but that was better than nothing. So Darryl got all the boys and the two women in the vehicle. He hugged the Commander and Sidney goodbye and then he gave them his cell phone so that they would still be in contact with the base camp. They were both surprised by Darryl's affection. Soldiers didn't hug.

The Commander said, "Americans... Look Doc, you will see us in less than 24 hours, I assure you."

"I know Commander, God be with you all."

"God has always been with me, and he will be with me in death too, my friend. That's why I am never afraid in a battle."

Darryl rode off slowly with the lights off at first, until he felt he was a safe distance away from the rebel camp. Once he thought he was a safe enough distance away, he put the lights on and he put his foot to the gas pedal and drove as fast as the vehicle would take him, back to safety and back to his Faith.

Meanwhile, Hope and her troops were ready to come up with a plan to rescue the remaining women and girls. They had to also figure out how to get one of the rebels' vehicles to escape with. They needed to escape without being detected and that meant no gun shots. They knew it all seemed like an impossible task, but they were all prepared to die trying.

Then the Major said to Hope and the Ethiopian Commander, "maybe we should wait it out until reinforcements get here? Commander didn't you tell the doctor they were already on their way and may be here soon?"

"I only told the doctor that to ease his worries. I could see the dread all over his face about leaving us, the women and the boys need to have hope, because they have a long ride ahead of them. But we did contact someone back at the base camp with this here cell phone by text message however it will take them at least eight hours to get here by land. Our General knows if they came by air the rebels would spot them miles away and kill everyone and abandon the camp immediately. So if we wait for them chances are all the men would have recovered from their drunken states and we also will no longer have the cover of the night to help us escape."

Hope agreed with the Ethiopian Commander. "Then we have to do this now. If we have any chance of succeeding we can't wait any longer." Everyone agreed. The Commander took charge and gave instructions, he said, "you and the boy, (pointing to Hope, and Amir), will wait here. You can be in charge of driving the vehicle we take. The rest of us men will go in and retrieve the women."

Hope was not offended by the Commander's orders. She was use to men wanting to protect her, simply because she was a woman. It didn't matter to most men that she was a military leader and officer herself. She always had to prove herself. She had proven herself to her Major and her troops many times in the past, but the Ethiopian Commander did not know of her or her abilities. So she simply responded without offense, "Commander, with all due respect, I can't let my men go into danger and sit back and wait. You have to understand. I am a woman, but I am also their leader and very well trained. I am trained well enough that my country has placed all these men's lives into my hands."

The Commander looked at Hope and reluctantly conceded. "Okay then what are your thoughts?"

"Commander, I think it would be safer for myself and Amir to retrieve the women versus sending all you men into the tents. Amir can move in and out of the tents without raising any suspicion at all. All of the rebels know him and trust him. And if you haven't noticed I already traded my ragged military clothing I had on for the young woman's SACAA t-shirt and khaki's. So the rebels will think I am one of the native women who cared for the children at SACAA if they see me in their tent. There are hundreds of rebels. If we have to fight, we will never win. We need to try to escape without a fight, if at all possible. If you go into those tents there is more likelihood of trouble. You don't have a rebel uniform on Sir, besides even if you put a uniform on the rebels won't recognize you as one of their own, or even worse they may recognize you as part of the Ethiopian military. If they've used intelligence to identify the military members here they may know what you and your Scout look like. Even my three men who have the rebel uniforms on won't be recognized by the other rebels up close as one of their own, but we can send them in as a last resort. But Amir is trusted, and I'm a woman, and women don't concern them. We should go."

So much was going on that none of them had even noticed that Hope had switch clothes with the young SACAA woman. Then Hope continued.

"So myself and Amir will quietly try to slip into the tents and retrieve as many of the women and girls as we can without using gun fire or causing any noise. Hopefully the rebels will think I am one of the native women roaming around if they see me. I'll take the Commander's small 9mm and my K-bar so I can hide my weapons in the cargo pockets of these khakis I have on. Amir can walk in plain view with a rifle because they already trust him and believe he is with them. The rest of you men, stay ready close to the outskirt of the camp keeping us in your eyes' view. You can cover us if there is any trouble. Two of the strongest men here need to retrieve a vehicle. The largest one you see, since we don't know how many women and girls we will be bringing out. Quietly push it to the road, hot wire the vehicle when it's out of ear shot. So does anyone have any questions or suggestions?"

The men all nodded that they did not. There was no time to come up with a perfect plan, and her plan seemed like a good enough one to them all.

"Just one more thing, try not to fire your weapons, unless there's absolutely no other option, because as soon as they hear shots it's going to alert the whole camp, and then…., well God help us if that happens." Hope didn't want to or need to go on. They all were aware that they were outnumbered and with less firepower. They all knew if they got out of their alive it would be a miracle. So they proceeded to put Hope's plan into action.

Amir was checking the tents to the east and Hope took the tents to the west. There were twenty tents in the camp all together. At least one hundred rebels altogether were in the camp not counting the ones that Amir, Hope and the Major had already killed. One by one they would have to go through each tent to check for women and girls being held in there. They didn't waste any time getting started.

Amir had already gone through five tents and brought out twelve young women and girls. It was simple for him. Many of the rebels were asleep, and the rebels that were still awake asked Amir no questions, they assumed Amir was bringing the women to his father's tent or to have for himself. All of the females were in poor physical and emotional condition. Some of them were still suffering from the shock of all that had happened the previous day and that night. They all had been raped. The one's that fought back were beaten the worse. Once Amir got the women out of one tent he would quickly escort them to the edge of camp. Amir would briefly explain to the women as they were walking that he was helping them escape, and that they needed to be quiet. He didn't want them to think he was taking them into the marsh to kill them. Then the Ethiopian Commander and Hope's men would take over and rush the women to the vehicle they had taken. So far retrieving the women and girls was going very smoothly for Amir.

On the other hand, Hope wasn't as successful. While Amir was close to finishing up on his tenth tent, Hope had only retrieved five women out of three of the tents so far. Hope would find that the women were too afraid to just follow another woman that they didn't even recognize. They didn't trust that Hope was there to rescue them, and they were too afraid to try and escape with her even if they did believe her. It did help that in most of the tents the rebels were already asleep. This gave Hope the time and opportunity to try to whisper to the women and explain who she was and what she was doing. But still some of the women were in shock, and too afraid to move for fear of being raped, beaten again, or even killed. So Hope had to plead with them to trust her, and follow her. Unlike Amir she couldn't just grab the women and muscle them out. They needed to voluntarily sneak out quietly with her to not wake up the rebels' and make them suspicious. She had only retrieved a handful of girls and she still had seven more tents to go.

Amir was finished retrieving all the women out of the tents to the east. He headed in the direction of the tent that he had last saw Hope go into. Then he heard a woman belt out a blood curling scream. He immediately feared that it was Hope and she had been discovered. When he got to the tent he saw that the scream came from a young girl. The girl looked to be no older than nine years old. The little girl was standing and pointing at Hope. Her scream had awoken all the men in that tent. She was in shock after being raped. She was screaming at Hope, "leave me alone, they'll kill us, they'll kill us."

Then one of the rebels that was awoken by the girl's screams walked over to Hope and sleepily said, "Who are you, I don't remember you being in here?"

Amir immediately stepped in. "She's with me now. I came because I saw her walk into this tent from the tent across from here."

The rebel looked at Hope curiously. "Oh, were the men in that tent not enough for you, you want real men now?" Then he grabbed Hope by her breasts.

Amir didn't know what to do. Hope was concerned that the rebel would feel the weapons she had hidden under her clothing, and that would immediately blow her cover and ruin all their chances of escaping. But then all of a sudden they all heard a loud commanding voice yelling from outside the tent.

"Amir, Amir where are you!"

All the rebels knew the sound of that voice. It was the sound of Amir's father, and their leader. The rebel in the tent holding on to Hope's arm said to Amir, "you better go see what your father wants."

"Yes, I know what he wants. It was him who sent me out to bring the prettiest women back to him, and he probably is growing impatient because I've taken too long. I've been to all the tents and I think she is the prettiest, motioning to Hope."

The rebel grabbed Hope's face and he was much too drunk to recognize where he saw her last. "I agree, she's the prettiest woman I've ever seen. I know I've seen her before, but for some reason I can't remember her traveling back with us after the raids. She must have tried her best to hide her beauty. Take her to your father Amir. We don't want to keep him waiting any longer. You know how he gets."

Amir grabbed Hope's arm and then he said, "And if you are finish with this young one, I'll take her too. So I can let my father take his pick."

The rebel had no objections to Amir taking the loud girl who had woken all of them up. They were indeed finished with her and now he just wanted to sleep.

Amir took Hope and the young girl who was still in shock out of the rebels' tent. Unfortunately his father was already standing in the doorway of his tent looking for Amir.

"Son where were you? Oh I see you've decided to take a woman or make that two, I see. I am sorry now that I interrupted you."

Amir's father was still so drunk he did not even recognize his most valuable hostage, Hope from afar. Amir threw Hope to the ground to conceal her face from his father's view, and then he said, "stay here you women, don't even think about moving or I will kill you both!"

The young girl was confused, she believed exactly what Amir said, and she still did not realize that he was actually working on helping her escape. Then Amir ran to his father's side.

"Father, what do you need me to do for you?"

"Amir, I woke up and yelled to my bodyguard to go get me some soup and coffee. The dog didn't answer me. So I looked outside my tent and he is not here either. Do you know where he has gone son?"

Amir became nervous. He had killed his father's bodyguard by stabbing him from behind before he had even released Hope and the other hostages. Unbeknowest to his father his bodyguard's dead body was hidden right inside his father's tent. Amir knew if his father woke, it would be a big risk leaving his tent unguarded, but it had to be done. Now all his father had to do was take a walk around the camp to notice that all the men he had assigned to guard the camp that night were no longer at their posts. If it wasn't for the fact that his father was drunk he would have already went walking around camp by now. He needed to get his father back into his tent as soon as possible.

"Father I know where your bodyguard is. Go back into your tent and I will bring you food."

"So where is he then?"

"Father I hope you don't mind, but you did tell me to take more of a leadership role in the camp. So I relieved him long enough for him to have himself a woman also."

This explanation made Amir's father furious. "You relieved him for him to have a woman and you left your father, the leader of this camp, vulnerable, with no protection? I do not understand this stupid thing you have done?"

"Father no, you misunderstand, I took his place at your tent myself. I only left for one moment because I saw this woman running out of the tent with the young girl. She was trying to escape, while the men inside her tent had fallen asleep. I left for one brief moment to retrieve them."

Amir's explanation calmed his father's anger towards him slightly, but he was still upset. "Son this was still a stupid decision you made. I am disappointed in your poor judgment. My protection is always of the upmost importance, much more important than some women trying to escape. She wouldn't have gotten far anyway. One of the other men would have caught her. Even if she did escape, she would not survive so far away from any civilization and if she did who really cares. Women are no threat to us. These women are expendable to us they are of little value. You know we will dispose of them eventually once we have no more use for them, son. So that was poor judgment to leave my guard even for a brief moment. Perhaps you are not ready to lead yet, as I had hoped."

"Yes father, I see now, and you are right. I'm sorry. I am not ready to lead yet. I am not as smart as you or as experienced with making the right decisions."

"Son, don't be discouraged in the beginning you may make bad decisions. At one time I showed mercy, but then I learned that the weak don't deserve mercy. But you will see you will become a great leader. It is in your blood, you are my son."

"Thank you, father, I will do better. Please, go rest now. I will go get your food and your bodyguard."

"No, I've changed my mind. I am wide awake now, and I've had no woman tonight. You stand guard outside my tent until he returns and bring that one who tried to escape to me. I like my woman with a bit of spirit. From here she looks very pretty, and still in good condition. The other one you can do what you want with her she is a bit too tiny for my taste."

Amir stood there still not knowing what to do or say next. He felt paralyzed as his listened to his father yell his demands to Hope.

"You, long hair women, come here."

Hope didn't dare move. She stayed on the ground with young girl. She couldn't risk blowing her cover and risking everything. Amir's father would surely recognize her up close. He was the one who had initially interrogated her.

"I said come here girl! You, the older one!" Hope still refused to move and obey his commands. He was drunk and he didn't want to have to walk over to her so he yelled again, and this time his tone was much more irritated. He was a man not use to anyone not immediately responding to his commands.

Amir knew he had to do something. "Father she is a stubborn one. Are you sure you want this one? If you go back into your tent, I will bring you a tamer one, that's just as pretty."

His father was so focused on Hope not responding to him that he didn't even acknowledge his comments.

"Woman are you dumb and death! If I have to go down there and get you myself, it will not go well for you later, do you understand?"

Hope still did not move. Hope knew that Amir had plenty of opportunity to stab his father from behind, quietly. But he had not done it. Then it dawned on her. This was not just another obstacle to Amir, not just another rebel, this was indeed his flesh and blood, his father. How could she expect Amir to kill his own father so easily. Amir may have wanted to escape his father's way of life, but that didn't mean that he wanted to kill his father.

The furious rebel leader started to take a step forward to go retrieve Hope, when he felt dizzy. He turned around and started to vomit. All of the alcohol he had consumed that night had gotten the best of him. When he recovered he yelled to Amir, "bring me that insolent woman now!"

Amir ran to Hope. As he grabbed her he whispered, "I don't know what to do?"

Hope said, "punch me in the face."

"What?"

Hope pretended to struggle from Amir's grip on her, and she started swinging at him, while she was swinging, she whispered again, "punch me in the face, it's the only way, so your father won't recognize who I am. You have to hit me hard enough so that he can't recognize me."

Amir understood. He punched Hope several times in the face. He made sure he punctured her skin so that blood was covering her once pretty face. Amir's blows were even more forceful than she had expected. She was stunned. Her eye swelled up fast, and there was blood running from her lip and her left eyelid, she made sure she also used her hands to cover her face with more blood and dirt. Then Amir took a good look at Hope's face. He felt disgusted over what he had just done to her; he couldn't recognize her at all, so he knew his father wouldn't either. He dragged Hope over to his father and threw her to the ground. His father stood there with his breath reeking of vomit. He was amused by watching his son beat on this insolent woman who had disobeyed him.

Hope's Major, her troops, the Ethiopian Commander and his Scout Sidney were quietly observing and prepared to attack when there seemed like there was no other option. They understood that Hope and Amir were simply trying to maintain their cover.

After Amir had dragged Hope to his father, his father grabbed the back of her hair and said to his son, "good work, even though I do like to look upon a pretty face. But even so, good work son. Stand guard here for me until my bodyguard returns, then you can go get me my food. I should be finished with her soon."

Then the rebel leader dragged Hope into his tent. Amir watched in silent horror, he was not sure what to do. Hope motioned to Amir secretly to leave. She knew he had to get the rest of the women out. She also knew she could kill this man easily with her knife in his drunken state. After all even though he was a huge man, Amir said there were no weapons left in his tent and he was drunk and sluggish. It was only a matter of waiting for the right moment then she would attack him and make sure she did it quietly.

So Amir reluctantly left Hope alone with his father. He knew at the moment he had no other choice. He had to finish getting the rest of the women and girls out of the rebels' tents. Amir quickly ran towards the Major and handed him the one young girl.

"What's going on with the Colonel Amir?", asked the Major.

"She told me to hit her in the face so that he wouldn't recognize her, and then she motioned to me to leave her alone. I know she has a 9mm and K-bar in her cargo pockets. He doesn't have any weapons in the tent, and he's still drunk."

"She will be fine then, she knows what she is doing."

"I hope you are right Major. If not it will be all my fault, I should have…"

"The Colonel can take care of herself Amir. You just get the rest of the women out."

Then Amir started to run towards the last of the tents that Hope didn't get to. Despite the near disaster he still was able to retrieve the rest of the women and girls out of the remaining tents quickly and without suspicion. He couldn't stop thinking about what was happening between Hope and his father. He kept reminding himself that Hope was not a normal woman she was a woman of war. After all, he had actually observed her kill with ease earlier that night. Surely she could kill his father with no problem in the drunken state he was in with her K-bar. She seemed to be very good with a knife. He didn't even think about how he had betrayed his father, and how he was now also going to be the cause of his father's death. His father was a monster, this Amir was sure of, but he didn't have it in him to kill his father. As far as Amir was concerned, Hope was his father's angel, his angel of death. But if anything happened to Hope because he could not bring himself to kill his father, he knew he would never forgive himself.

After Amir had retrieved the last of the women and girls out of the tents, he was walking back towards the Major and his men in the marsh. It was then that he noticed something shiny in the dirt. It was Hope's K-bar, and gun! They must have fallen out of her cargo pants during the struggle the two of them had staged for his father's benefit. A huge wave of guilt came over him, he should have ensured she had her weapons on her before he dragged her over to his father. "How could I have been so stupid? I will be the death of her." Amir knew that if he left Hope alone with his father much longer she would have to fight him off with her own body strength or give in to him raping her. Either picture was torture for him to imagine. He was only comforted by the fact that he had previously taken all of his father's knifes and weapons out of his tent earlier that night with the young boy's assistance. He looked back at his father's tent and knew he couldn't leave Hope in there alone with his father any longer. So he turned around and headed inside his father's tent.

The Major and the rest of the men were watching Amir from their positions in the marsh. They saw him pick up Hope's fallen weapons from the ground. The Major told his troops he wasn't going to leave without the Colonel.

"Hopefully, Amir will be able to get her out without any commotion. If they don't come out after a reasonable period of time, I'm going in after the Colonel. But I'm ordering all of you to leave out now since we have all the women and girls."

Inside the tent Amir's father had already pushed Hope unto his bed. He was kissing and groping her. At first she just pretended to put up a fight because she knew it would be what he would expect, but she was secretly reaching into her cargo pockets to retrieve her k-bar. It was then that she realized her weapons were no longer in her pockets. She looked around sporadically to see if there were any sharp objects or knifes or anything that could be used against him close by. He was an extremely big man, at least five times Hope's size, but even in his drunken state Hope was realizing he was incredibly strong and she was no match for him.

She didn't want to do anything further to arouse the rest of the camp, but at the same time there was no way she was going to let any other man rape her ever again. She had made that promise to herself a long time ago. She would rather die than be raped ever again. So Hope knew that someone in this tent was going to die tonight. The question was would it be him, or would it be her. All she knew was she wasn't going down without a fight. So she bit down with all her force on his ear, tearing a piece of it off.

He was indeed a hard man. He didn't even scream when she bit his ear off, and he never once loosened his grip on her. Instead he responded by punching her in the face again. His punch was so hard it almost knocked her out cold, but it didn't and she continued biting him and fighting for her life. Her teeth were now the only weapon she had. He had arms and legs pinned underneath him. She was able to finally free one arm. Her nails had grown while she was in captivity; she dug them into his eyes. That got a reaction out of him and he let out a painful scream.

Two of the rebel men in the tent closest to them overheard the scream and they grabbed their weapons to respond. They saw Amir going into his father's tent and they assumed he was also responding out of concern for his father.

The Major also saw the two rebels heading towards their leader's tent. He ran after them holding a knife in each hand. By the time the two rebels heard the Major's steps from behind, it was too late. The Major was already straight behind them and he drove his k-bars into both of their backs. The Major dragged each one of the rebel's bodies into the marsh and then he waited outside the tent, pretending to be the rebel leader's bodyguard that Amir had previously killed earlier that night. The Major was ready to take out anyone else who tried to enter the tent before Amir came out with his Colonel.

Meanwhile, Amir was standing inside the doorway of his father's tent, and he saw Hope struggling for her life underneath of his father. His father was also busy struggling to keep Hope from biting and gauging out his eyes. Neither of them noticed he had entered the tent. Then Amir realized his father was reaching under his cot, with his right hand, while he fought off Hope with his left. Amir remembered his father kept his side arm either on his person, or hidden close to him beneath his cot. When he didn't see his father's sidearm on him earlier that night he had forgot then to check for it under his cot. Before he could react and come to Hope's aid his father had retrieved his sidearm and already had it shoved into Hope's chest. Then he heard his father say to Hope in a raspy, pain filled voice. "You're not worth this!"

Hope froze instantly. She was not aware Amir had just entered the tent. She thought she was alone, and that this would be her end.

It was clear to Amir that if he didn't do something now his father would kill Hope. So he yelled out, "Father stop!"

This surprised his father and kept him from pulling the trigger. "Son, this demon possessed woman tried to kill me. She has bit off my ear, and gauged out my eye. Go get me the first aid kit, and when you come back you can dispose of her body.

She is not worth all of this." Amir had saved Hope's life for the moment. His father was now up on his knees kneeling over Hope. "Amir Why are you still standing there?! Bring me the first aid kit. Didn't you hear me? She just bit my ear off and dug her nails into my eyes. Better yet, just wait there until after I shoot her so you can take this trash out on your way to getting the first aid kit."

"Father please don't shoot her here. You will get blood all over yourself and your bed. Give her to me and I will kill her for you, outside of your tent."

His father stared at him with fury. He had no patience for his son's ridiculous suggestions right now. "I'm bleeding already all over my cot you idiot! Just get me the first aid kit. Where the hell is my bodyguard already, and where the hell is my food I asked you to get me?! You don't even have that with you. What have you all been doing tonight?!" While he continued to yell at Amir, he held the gun he had shoved into Hope's side in place, and he stared at Amir in anger wondering why he was standing there and doing nothing.

Amir knew he had no other choice he was going to have to stand up to his own father. He pulled out his rifle and pointed it at his father. "Son, what are you doing?"

"Father I said, do not shoot her. Put down your gun." Amir's voice was filled with desperation. He hoped it would not come to this.

The rebel leader only had a few people in the world that he had trust in, his bodyguard, his second in command and his son. His son is the one person he trusted the most. Now his son was standing there, holding a rifle at him. "What is this Amir?! What does this woman mean to you?"

Hope was still too afraid to move with a gun shoved in her chest ready to go off at any moment. Amir was now her only chance of living.

"Just know you can't kill her father."

"Answer me! Who is this woman to you, that you would defy your own father, and threaten to kill me?"

"I just can't let you kill her."

His father continued to stare at his son confused by what he was saying and doing. He did not put down his gun. He didn't feel any fear, only irritation and anger towards Amir. As usual he had underestimated his son. Amir was determined to keep Hope alive, by any means necessary.

"Son, I don't know what is going on in your head, but I'm going to kill her and if you are still standing here when I am finished with her, I will kill you too. So you are going to put that rifle down, turn around and leave my tent now, or I swear by Mohammad and Allah, you are my own flesh and blood but I will kill you, when I finish with her."

Then the rebel leader turned his focus once more towards Hope. She closed her eyes as she prepared herself for the end. When the shot went off, it alarmed the entire rebel camp. Hope's heart stopped when she heard the gun shot pierce through the air. Then she felt the full weight of his heavy, sweaty, bloody body fall down on top of her. After a few seconds of shock she realized he was dead. She pushed his body off of her, and she looked up at Amir. Amir stood there with his rifle still smoking and pointed in the ready position. He had a blank, empty expression on his childlike face. Hope realized this was the second time in her life that someone she barely knew had saved her life. Ms. Armstrong was dead she promised herself she would keep Amir alive.

From the very first time Amir talked to Hope he knew if it ever came down to it he would choose her life over his own father's life. He had prayed it would never come to that. He prayed that he would not have to add his father's murder to the many other faces he had murdered that haunted him in his dreams. When Amir shot that one shot that went straight from his rifle into his father's right temple, he whispered "father forgive me." He really wasn't sure who he was asking forgiveness from when he whispered it, whether he was talking to his earthly father, or his heavenly one. A part of him was seeking forgiveness from them both.

Hope wanted to grab Amir and hold him tight. To her he looked like a lost little man child. He was technically an orphan now, just like she was when Nana died. Hope knew this would haunt him possibly for the rest of his life. It would also haunt her, knowing that he had killed his own father to save her, but there was no time to tell Amir how sorry and grateful she was for what he had just done. Right now she had to think about how the two of them were going to get out of there alive, now that all the rebels in the camp had heard a gun going off and out of their leader's tent, of all places.

Amir snapped out of his momentary shock and motioned to Hope to follow him to the hidden exit in the rear of his father's tent. "Quickly Hope, we have to get out of here." The Major came inside the tent when he heard the gun shot. He saw what had happened, and there was no time for any conversation. So Hope and the Major followed Amir out of the hidden exit behind his father's tent. The Major had told his troops if they heard any shots to immediately run towards the vehicle and leave out with the women and girls.

The rebel men just as Hope had expected were alerted by the shot which came from their leader's tent and they were already running out of their tents armed and ready. When the other rebel men came out of their tents they saw their leader's tent was not guarded.

Hope, Amir and the Major had already left out of the rear of the tent by the time the other rebels got there. The rebels saw their leader's dead body on his cot, with his brains splattered across the tent wall. By then Hope's troops had all of the women and girls boarded on to the vehicle. The Ethiopian Commander and his sharpshooter had stayed back in the marsh waiting for Hope, Amir and the Major to make it out, or if not to go and rescue them. They did not believe in leaving fellow soldiers behind, even if they were foreign soldiers, they all fought for a common cause. They were just about to move in after hearing all the commotion when they saw Hope, Amir and the Major running towards them. Unfortunately, the Commander and his sharpshooter weren't the only ones that saw them running from the rear of the rebel leader's tent. Some of the rebels had also spotted Hope and the two men running towards the marsh, and they started shooting at them. They were all hit. The Commander and his Scout were expert shots, and they returned the rebels' fire with accuracy. Hope, Amir and the Major kept running for their lives, and the rebels wasted no time pursuing. They wanted vengeance and the blood of the people who had murdered their leader.

The Ethiopian Commander made sure to head off any shots as he fell back to return gun fire in hopes of giving the others a chance to get away alive. The rebels were coming at them from all directions now. The situation seemed hopeless. So the Commander yelled out to them to just keep running and to not look back. He had been saving two grenades in his cargo pockets for just this type of occasion. Sidney fell back also, assuming his Commander would want him by his side. But the Ethiopian Commander ordered his trusted and loyal Scout to run with the rest of them to the vehicle. When Sidney paused the Commander yelled, "that's an order, Go!" Then Sidney ran and caught up with the others.

The Commander stayed hidden and allowed the rebels to approach. When he felt like enough of them were close enough he stood up and threw both grenades one towards the east and one towards the west, then he turned and ran away from the blast. The blast killed many of the rebels heading towards him, but the force from the blast lifted the Commander several feet off of the ground. After he landed he tried to get back up and run again, but then he realized the fall had broken his leg. The others now had a slim chance of escape, but escape was no longer an option for the Commander. The blast from the grenades didn't kill all of the rebels and he was out of grenades. More rebels were already in pursuit. He couldn't run anymore with a broken leg so he dragged himself to the cover of a nearby tree. He accepted his fate and thought to himself, "at least the woman Colonel and the other's are out of sight." Then he felt the first bullet hit him. He propped himself up with his back to the tree and decided he would shoot and kill as many as he could, before he died. With his last breaths he would try his best to take out as many of the rebels as possible to give the young women, and his new foreign friends a chance to escape and live. With his last breaths he squeezed out perfect, precise rounds that were shot with the intention to kill each target he aimed at with only one shot. He knew he didn't have any time or bullets to waste.

On that night the Ethiopian Commander killed twenty five rebels that were running towards him, and towards the road where the vehicle holding the women and young girls waited.

He died knowing that he did what he declared he would do with his last breaths, he gave his sisters and his friends a chance to escape and live.

Hope's troops refused to abandon their Colonel and Major. They were all waiting until the last possible moment to drive off with the women. Finally they saw Hope, Amir, the Major and Sidney appear. They had reached the vehicle in just enough time. All of the women and girls were staying down low on the floor of the vehicle for cover. The troops had positioned themselves in the vehicle to cover the gun fire if it reached them. The Major and Hope had given their troops orders to leave them if it meant staying would put the women and girls they were trying to rescue in jeopardy, but their troops for the first time ever had disobeyed their orders. Sidney, the Commander's Scout took the driving seat, he knew the terrain and the route back better than anyone else. As the vehicle drove off some of the rebels continued shooting and pursuing their vehicle on foot. Hope had gotten hit again while getting into the vehicle. That last hit made her fall into the truck. The women tended to Hope and the others that were wounded as Sidney drove the vehicle away.

There was no way the rebels could continue to pursue the vehicle on foot, so they headed back towards camp, but once the rebels returned to camp they realized Hope's troops had immobilized all of the other vehicles in the camp. The rebels were furious over their leader's murder and they were not ready to give up so easily, but every minute that went by they knew the men who had killed their fearless leader were gaining distance away from them. They realized then there was no way they were going to be able to repair the vehicles in time to stop Hope and her troops before they reached the military base. The rebels started debating amongst themselves about whether following behind the ones who had escaped was the best thing to do.

Then the rebel leader's Second in Command spoke up. He had an undying loyalty to his now dead leader. He had been a follower of Amir's father since he was a young boy himself. For twenty years now, he had served his leader without question. He took his leader's murder very personally. Above all he realized that Amir was missing and that he must have betrayed the entire camp, and his own father. He wanted to kill Amir for his betrayal and treachery. He made killing Amir his new mission in life. It was then when he was cursing and mourning over his leader's dead body, that the thought occurred to him to try his murdered Commander's personal jeep. The jeep was small and only fit about four or five men. Amir's father kept it parked right outside of his tent, unlike the other vehicles in camp. The Second in Command feverishly searched his dead leader's tent for the jeep keys and he found them inside a pair of boots sitting under the cot. He ran to the jeep and it automatically started when he turned the key. He swore to his dead leader, "I will not let those dogs or that traitor who called himself your son get away with this." He took four rebels with him, as many as he could fit into the small jeep. Then he yelled out orders to the remaining rebels in the camp before he drove off, "I am your leader now, since I was Second in Command to murdered leader. Once the other vehicles are repaired follow fast behind. We will avenge our leader's death!"

While the remaining rebels waited for the vehicles to be repaired they hung the Ethiopian Commander's body upon a tree. They celebrated his death and showed his body no honor or respect. These rebels were not honorable men and being in the rebel army had made them survivors with no code of honor. The rebels main thoughts were on their own survival. So they decided they would not follow the orders of their new leader, the Second in Command. Instead, they made plans to abandon the camp as soon as they had the vehicles running again. Within two hours they had repaired all the vehicles. They abandoned camp and traveled North towards the neighboring country that sympathized with the rebels' cause. They knew it was only a matter of time before the Ethiopian military would be there to try to attack and eradicate the rest of them that were left in the camp. To follow behind the Second in Command was suicide, this they all knew.

Meanwhile, Sidney, the Commander's Scout was driving the truck as fast as it could possibly go. Sidney knew the terrain well. He grew up in the villages. He drove the vehicle off road to make it harder for the rebels to detect them in case they were still in pursuit. Hope was still alert. She looked at her troops,

her Major and Amir, and she realized it was only by God's grace
that they were able to get out alive. It was a miracle. Hope sat
back and began to feel the adrenaline keeping her conscious
fading away. As the adrenaline subsided she unfortunately was
also able to feel the pain from the bullets that had hit her. She
was losing a lot of blood. Her troops all looked near exhaustion
and they were also wounded. She thought to herself, "it could be
hours before we can stop driving and get somewhere safe." She
wondered if she would make it, because she was in so much pain
and she could feel herself slipping away. She was feeling light
headed and weak. Then the young girl, who had screamed in the
last tent and caused Hope to be discovered by the rebels, crawled
up to Hope. She was no longer in shock, and she realized now
what Hope had done for her, she had saved her life. She brushed
Hope's hair back and wiped the blood off of her face. Then she
took off her dirty, torn school dress and tore it in half. The little
girl started wrapping it around Hope's waist to try and slow the
bleeding. She had been beaten and raped and wounded herself,
but she no longer thought about her own pain, she only wanted
to heal Hope. The other women started doing the same for Amir,
the Major and all the other troops who needed medical attention.
For the rest of their journey, the women and girls put aside their
own trauma and thought only of caring for their rescuers.

Sidney looked back briefly at the road behind. Hope
saw Sidney's look and she knew he was thinking the same thing
as her, "what if the rebels were pursuing them, would they make
it?"

She yelled to Sidney, "continue to stay off road, and
whatever happens don't stop driving, don't stop this vehicle until
you're positive we are somewhere safe!" That was the last thing
Hope said before she passed out from the pain that was now
piercing through her entire body.

The rebel who was Second in Command knew Amir and
the others had a huge head start on him and his men, but he was
an expert tracker and he knew the terrain very well. He was
determined to catch up with them. He now was driven by his
hatred of Amir, and he was blinded by his revenge; so much so
that his own survival no longer mattered to him. He only wanted

to kill the boy who had betrayed them all and had forsaken his own father.

Chapter 17
Waiting for the right time, and Waiting On God

Faith had been waiting in the Ethiopian's General's Command room now for what seemed like forever. The General's reinforcements reported back to him that they arrived at the rebel camp and found the Ethiopian Commander dead, and hanging from a tree. They reported that it appeared as if the rebels had abandoned camp and fled north to their neighboring country. The General inquired on the whereabouts of the others. His reinforcement troops informed him that they had not seen any children or anyone else at the rebel camp site, but that they did find the cell phone left behind on the ground.

The General was enraged about the murder of his most loyal Commander. He ordered his reinforcements to follow the rebels north before they made it to the border and to shoot and kill any who fought them, and bring back those who surrendered for questioning. The General knew if they allowed the rebels to reach their neighboring country that were synthesizers, it would be too late to ever capture the murderous rebels. The country that bordered them was known to supply the rebels with firearms in hopes of overthrowing the current Ethiopian government. The General was a man of his word, and he kept his promise to Faith and updated her about everything. He told her that he assumed the rebels still had the hostages and were attempting to escape with them.

Faith thought, "if Darryl and the other's were nowhere to be found then they must be in the rebel's custody, but at least they may still be alive." The General's assumptions all made sense to Faith, and it was a better alternative than thinking they were all dead. Faith had accepted that there was nothing she could do but wait, and pray. Whenever the phone in the command room rung the whole room became quiet. The phone was now ringing and everyone held their breath as the General picked it up. Strangely, it was the operator, wanting to patch through an urgent call from Saint Phillip's Church. The General told the operator to patch it through. Within a few seconds Faith and the General's men heard the General say to whoever was on the other end of the phone, "we're on our way, right now."

Faith boldly walked over to the General and said, "if that has got anything to do with Darryl and the children, I'm going with you!"

Love And John Go To Church

Love and John had finally made it to Saint Phillips Church, the little Ethiopian Christian Church that John made them travel for three hours to reach. John thought Love had fallen asleep in his arms, because she was so quiet and still, but she hadn't. Love hadn't felt so safe and secure in a man's arms in a very long time. She couldn't believe how she had opened up to John, and yet he still wanted her despite her past. She wondered, "how could he love someone like me?" Finally the driver stopped the vehicle and Love whispered to John, "so I guess where here."

"Oh, I thought you were sleeping. Yeah, we're here. Come on, let's check it out." John grabbed his camera and started taking pictures right away. He wanted to get as many as possible. He was so happy he had a good flash since it was dark.

Love just stood by the jeep, stretching her legs, and watching John. To Love the church looked unimpressive. She didn't really see what the big deal was, but she knew it was a big deal to John. Then she followed John inside. They walked into the church and they saw no one else in the building. Their driver said he would wait outside.

It was very small and modest looking on the outside and inside. The first thing that caught John's eyes was a huge, ancient looking book sitting on a pedestal. John went over to the pedestal to take a look. John told Love how the book contained names of all the people throughout the years that had come and visited the church and signed the book. The book seemed to date back over a hundred years. Then they were startled by a voice.

"I thought I heard footsteps in here. We don't usually get visitors so late. You kids do know that the nearest hotel is an hour and a half away?" It was the caretaker for the church, coming up from the basement.

Love said, "we know Sir, but he, (motioning to John), still insisted we make the ride up here."

The caretaker smiled and said, "Well would you like me to tell you a little about the history of this church?"

John was excited. The long ride had not dampened his curiosity. "Sure, I want to know everything."

The caretaker began telling John and Love all the things that John actually already knew about the church, and had already told Love. But the two of them still sat and listened, after all they had driven up there, and it would have been very rude not to show appreciation to the elderly caretaker.

When the caretaker was finished giving them his history lesson that he enjoyed telling people over and over again he said, "I still have some things to attend to downstairs, but you kids can take your time and explore the different artifacts and books in the church. Just yell down to me when you are ready to leave so I can lock up behind you." Then the old caretaker went back to his room downstairs to finish watching TV and eating his supper. Love just remained seated in one of the pulpits, while she watched John take pictures and look around. John was busy trying to take in as much of the church as he could, and he also was taking plenty of pictures of Love.

"Love come look at this, these scrolls are over two hundred years old, and look at this picture, it says it is an actual picture of the Ark of the Covenant during the time it was supposedly being kept in the basement of this very church for safekeeping." Then John noticed another old large book open on a pedestal beneath an ancient looking cross. There was writing in a glass under the cross and he read it to himself. He was getting ready to tell Love to come look at it when he noticed she had her eyes closed.

"Love, I'm sorry, I'm just going on and on, are you okay?

"Oh yeah, I'm fine. I was just thinking that maybe this whole assignment is just a lost cause. It doesn't seem like we are going to find the Doctor's son or get an adoption done, with all that is going on out here with these rebels. We've been here two days now and haven't been able to get anything done. I guess this will just have to be the first time I didn't come through for Mr. Swanson. I guess he'll understand. I just really hate disappointing him. I've never failed to come through for him before."

John looked at Love and realized that she wasn't just interested in succeeding at her first assignment as partner in the firm. He realized that this assignment meant something personal to her. He could tell that Love just really wanted to please Mr. Swanson. He wasn't sure why, but he knew her reasons were platonic and unselfish. "You know Love, we can always put a little prayer about it in this book here."

"What are you talking about John?"

"It says here that for over a hundred years people have felt this church sat on holy ground, and that this cross that hangs here was crafted by the Apostle Phillip's hands himself. It says that legend tells how he gave this cross to the Ethiopian man who founded this church and that if you write your prayer request down in this holy prayer book, and of course as long as your prayer request is not against the will of God it will come true."

"Oh really? I don't think some magical book is going to help us here John."

Then John walked over to Love with the book and the pen and said, "Well it can't hurt things either, right? So what the heck, why not try it? You know sometimes it doesn't hurt to ask for help when you need it Love."

Love didn't respond, and she wasn't planning on changing her mind and writing anything down in the hocus pocus book John was holding.

But John believed in the power of anything that had to do with God. "Well, I'm going to try it, because I do believe that with some things you really need or want in life you just have to ask God to bring it to you." Then John started to write down his prayer request in the book.

Love had to admit that she was a little curious about what John was writing in the book. She wondered and even wanted his prayer request to be about her, even if she would never admit it. When John was finished writing he looked over at Love. He noticed her sneaking a peak over at him while he was writing. "So do you want to read my prayer request?"

"I guess so, if you want me to." Then Love took the book from John. She read what he had written in it, "God, please bring Love everything that she needs in her life, even if she is too stubborn to ask you herself, and, God, help her to love herself as much as You and I love her. – John."

Love looked at John and smiled. "Very clever."

"You know have I ever told you how much I love your smile?"

Then the two of them started to silently read some of the other prayer requests that were in the book. They flipped through the pages, skimming what was on them. All the prayer requests seemed so sad, and so desperate. Then Love gave the book back to John. "I just can't read anymore it's so depressing."

John found it all very interesting and he had faith that God *did* answer all of the prayers that were written in the book. "Hey, just look at this one Love."

"I told you John I don't want to read anymore. It's depressing."

John ignored Love's protests. "Love I believe that God did answer all of these prayers, just like he's going to answer all of mine's, eventually. Now I wanted you to look at this one because it is really interesting. It's written by a little girl from America it says,

"God I hope you will answer an American girl's prayer in Africa too. Please help bring me and my sisters back together. I love my new Mommy and Daddy, but I miss my big sisters all the time, and God tell Nana I love her. Faith, age 9."

Love, didn't you say you use to call you're grandmother, Nana too?"

Love couldn't believe what John had just read. Someone named Faith had written a request about her two sisters and her Nana. This was really eerie.

 John noticed the strange look on Love's face. She looked like she had just seen a ghost. "Love what's wrong?"

"John I had, well I *have* a little sister named Faith out there somewhere." The guilt of never trying to find Faith after she found out Hope was killed in the fire started to rush through Love. Love had to stop talking for a moment to swallow the nausea she suddenly felt before she could continue telling John. Then she continued, "Actually I had two sisters, Faith and Hope. But like I said in the jeep, my one sister, Hope died a long time ago in a fire. Faith was adopted when she was only five years old, and I have not seen her in over twenty years. I could have tried to find her, but I don't know…. I guess I thought that she was probably better off without me. She was adopted into a good family, and everyone else in "our" family was dead, but me. Honestly, I don't think I would have made much of a big sister for her anyway." Love had never told anyone about her sisters before.

John was stunned. He realized there was so much about Love that he didn't know. But everything he found out, just made him want to know her better, and made him love her even more.

"What if your little sister was the one who wrote this? That would be a miracle that you happened to be here to read it. It's a sign that it is time for you to try and find her Love."

"It's probably a coincidence, like you said there are thousands of prayer requests in there, some are bound to be similar to someone else's life. Plus if I find her now, she probably hates me for abandoning her, or she probably doesn't even remember me anymore."

"That would be a pretty big coincidence Love. To tell you the truth I don't believe in coincidences I believe in God's will. I believe in fate and miracles. I think it was fate that brought us here just for you to read this. Obviously four years after she was adopted she still was missing her sisters. She hasn't forgotten you."

"Well John if God knows everything that's going to happen to us, if life is all about fate, why ask him for anything? He's already decided what's he's going to give us and what he's not going to give us, right?"

Before John could answer Love' hypothetical question, a noise outside startled the two of them. It sounded like the sound of gun shots going off outside of the church. John and Love looked at each other nervously.

The caretaker of the church came running upstairs because he heard the shots also. The old man ran upstairs from the basement with a rifle in his hand. He looked over at John. "Did you two hear that? What was that?"

"We don't know, we just heard it too, but it sounded like someone shooting to me."

The three of them went to the front windows of the church to see what was going on, and when they looked outside they could hardly believe their eyes. They saw a truck load of children, all little boy's, some looked as young as four, some looked as old as sixteen, and they all had on matching school uniforms. Love and John instantly knew that these were the orphans that were missing, all standing there right before their eyes. Love and John's driving escort ran up the church stairs to let them know everything was okay and that he had shot his gun into the air, to alert them of possible danger when he saw a vehicle approaching. Their driver explained to them that he didn't know if the vehicle approaching contained rebel soldiers inside it or not until it came closer.

Then Darryl got out of the vehicle. "We're all civilians, we've been on the road for over five hours and our vehicle has run out of gas. Can you help us? I've just escaped with these children from the rebel's camp. I don't know if the rebels are following behind us or not. Some from our rescue party stayed behind to try and rescue the female hostages that the rebels had taken into their tents."

Then Love and John's driver let Darryl know that he carried extra tanks of gas in his vehicle, whenever he went out. The driver apologized for shooting his gun and for possibly scaring him and the boys. He then started filling Darryl's truck up with his extra tanks of gas. Darryl was checking all the boys and the two women who worked with SACAA over to make sure they were all still in good physical condition. Love, John and the caretaker offered their assistance to Darryl. While Darryl was checking the boys over, and tending to all their bumps and bruises, he was also telling Love and John, the most incredible story the two of them had ever heard. Then Darryl ended his story by explaining that he swore he had heard grenade blasts going off from far away in the rebel camp as he drove away.

After listening to Darryl's story they were all frightened that rebels may be coming. The church's caretaker decided to go down to the basement and call the military base to inform them of what was going on, and when he came back up from the basement he told them that he had spoken to the General of the Military Base directly, and that the General told him he was going to send troops out to the church right away.

"But still I wouldn't wait for the Military if I were you, as soon as your driver has that truck filled with gas you guys need to get on the road with those kids. I won't leave here. I'm an old man and it's my duty to watch over this old church at all times. I've been the caretaker of this church most of my adult life and I've seen many, many things happen, but through it all this church was respected as holy ground, and I don't think even the rebels would be bold enough to defile it."

Love and John tried to convince the old caretaker to leave with them, but he was stubborn and could not be swayed.

Darryl knew Faith would kill him if she knew he volunteered to stay back once more, but something in his heart told him he was still needed to stay behind. "I'll wait with you then. If the other's made it out with the women and the girls they may need immediate medical attention, so I'll wait and see if they come. Now that I know the boys will leave out safely in the truck with you two and your driver I feel better. Plus the caretaker and I can leave out in the little jeep you guys rode in, if we need to."

John looked at the two brave men before him and before he even knew what he was even saying he spoke. "I'll stay too. You men will need as much help as possible regardless of who shows up here first the rebels or the other children. Plus like you said we will have the jeep if we need to leave quickly."

Love looked at John like he was crazy, "John! You're a lawyer, not a soldier! You need to leave in that truck with me and these boys right now!"

Darryl thought that if Faith was here she would be saying exactly the same thing. "Listen to your wife, she's right. I know if my fiancée knew I was voluntarily staying back, for the second time, we'll she would kill me herself, if the rebels didn't kill me first."

John laughed. "But she's not my wife. She's my boss and my friend depending on what time of the day it is. Believe me, she will be just fine without me." John was sort of hoping as he answered Darryl that he would get some type of reaction out of Love. Like maybe she would suddenly proclaim her undying love for him. But he knew she was right about one thing, he had just made the most spontaneous stupid decision of his life, but at the same time he had his pride and he wasn't going back on what he said.

Love glared at John. She felt so angry at him right now for voluntarily putting himself at risk. "You know you are acting incredibly stupid right now, right? But if you are staying, I'm staying too. The jeep is made to fit four, so there's room in it for me too if we need to make a quick get-away."

"Love, what can you do to help if anything happens? You know you complain when you break a fingernail."

"John, I can help out about as much as you can! Unless you have some special military or medical skills you're not telling me about." Love didn't want to stay, but she thought her bluff would make John change his mind and get in the vehicle heading back to base with her and the boys, but it was obvious he wasn't going to change his mind. They were both equally stubborn people.

Their driving escort had finished filling the truck with gas, and he was listening to their conversation about staying back in disbelief. "I think you four are fools for even thinking about staying back. I don't think you all realize just how ruthless those rebels are. The doctor here said he heard grenades. What makes you all think the others made it out of there at all? But I'm telling you one thing, this truck with all these boys and these two women here is leaving out now. I'm driving it and you don't have to worry about us making it back safely, because once I start that truck I'm not stopping until I get to the military base. So I'm giving you all one last chance to do the sane thing and leave out with us."

Darryl, Love, John and the caretaker stood there staring at the driver in silent stubbornness.

The driver shook his head in disapproval. "Well good luck guys. I'm out of here."

The four of them watched the truck speed away. The caretaker looked at Darryl and said, "I see you already have a rifle, and I have one." He turned and looked at Love and John and said, "I have more rifles in the basement for you two also. I'll run down to the basement and get them so we can make sure everyone knows how to use a rifle, just in case. Let's pull the jeep in the rear of the church, right outside of the back door, so it's ready to go if we need to jump in it. I will turn all the lights in the church off also so it appears no one is in here. Other than that, I guess we can post ourselves at the windows, and just wait. God help us. Hopefully *He* will bring the other children to our doorstep tonight and not the rebels." Then the caretaker ran downstairs to get his extra rifles.

Love wondered to herself, "what kind of place was this, that a church needed to have a basement full of rifles in it?" Love had never shot a gun in her life before. When the caretaker came back upstairs he gave Love and John a rifle and some instructions on how to use it. Then the three of them followed the caretaker's instructions and they turned off all the lights, and moved the jeep to the rear of the church right in front of the back door. The four of them posted themselves at the four corner windows of the church and then they just waited. They were waiting for a while and intently staring out the window. About an hour had passed by and they hadn't heard or seen anything.

The caretaker was the first to break the silence. "So what made you kids come to our little church anyway?" John explained how he was a Christian and had heard about the church and wanted to see it, and that he believed the church was very special and protected by God. The caretaker saw Love roll her eyes at John, and he asked Love, "I take it that you don't have the same beliefs as your friend, John here, huh?"

"Not quite, but I do believe one thing, if I see the rebels driving up that road instead of a truck load of little girls; well I believe I'll be the first one in this room out that back door and in the jeep."

Then all four of them started laughing, even Darryl, who had been so quiet and serious the whole time. He had been through too much to carry on a casual conversation. In fact, after everything Darryl had seen in the past two days he couldn't allow himself to relax or even join in the conversation with the others. Darryl had always been a very peaceful soul. He was in the business of saving lives, and now he was toting a rifle. For the first time in his life Darryl had seen people killed, and he knew in his heart if he had to he would kill too, to save himself or someone who was innocent. He had never before coming here to this country, even imagined the possibility of him ever having to kill another person.

John looked over at Darryl and was curious about him. "We never even asked you what your name is and how did you get mixed up in all of this. It's obvious you're not a soldier, but your accent is American and you're a doctor, are you with a UN medical group out here? Or do you also work with the children at the orphanage?"

"I don't work out here, but my fiancée works for SACAA, the people who sponsor the orphanage located here. I was just out here with her on sort of a vacation I guess. I'm actually a doctor at a hospital in New York. My name's Darryl."

Love and John stared at each other. There was no doubt that this had to be the man they were looking for, he had to be the doctor's son, and Mr. Swanson's fiancé's long lost son. Then Love gave John a discreet look and quietly shook her head. John knew right away that her look meant she didn't want him to say anything to Darryl, at least not right now.

Love didn't think that this was the best time to explain to Darryl who they were and tell him about the mother he never knew who was searching for him. She thought to herself, "this is just too much for anyone to take in at this moment. And these are just too many coincidences occurring all at the same time." Love decided to wait to explain it all to Darryl after things were a little calmer; that is if they all made it out of this mess alive to explain it to him.

"Well I guess all three of us are a long way away from home", said Love. Then before she could introduce herself to everyone, the four of them heard and saw a huge truck coming up the small dirt road towards the church. Darryl and John had posted themselves at the two windows in the front of the church, while Love, and the caretaker sat by the two windows in the rear. The caretaker did not have as good a vantage point as Darryl and

John did from their windows. He was almost too afraid to talk, even though there was no possible way anyone in a vehicle could hear him talking inside the church, so he whispered "can you tell? Are there rebels in the truck or girls?"

Darryl replied, "I can't tell just yet. I see rifles poking out, but they may be the rifles belonging to the others who stayed behind to help rescue the girls. Just in case, get to the back door, have the keys for the jeep ready to go."

Love and the caretaker ran to the back door. Love had her hand on the doorknob and the caretaker had the keys in his hand ready to go as soon as Darryl or John said so. They all waited and seconds later, Darryl said with joy in his voice, "it's them! It's the children, the little girls and the women, and the soldiers. It's all of them! They made it!" They all breathed out a sigh of relief, and they went outside to meet the vehicle. Darryl went running up to Sidney who was driving the vehicle.

When Sidney saw Darryl running out he was also happy to see him and he yelled, "Doc, thank God you are here, we have a bunch of wounded that need your attention. I've been driving non-stop for hours. I was afraid to stop. The women say the soldiers are wounded but still alive."

Darryl immediately got on the truck and started checking all the wounded. Amongst the wounded were Amir, Hope and her Major and three of her troops. All of them had sustained gun wounds and other injuries. Hope was still unconscious, and she had lost too much blood, her skin was very pale. Her face was also severely swollen. Darryl could see he needed to get Hope medical attention immediately, or she wasn't going to make it. "She looks to be the worse off, and she has lost a considerable amount of blood."

Amir and the Major were weak, but conscious and stable. The Major said, "She's our Colonel. You have to save her Doctor, tend to her first. The women have stopped the bleeding and given the rest of us enough first aid until we get to a hospital. We will all be fine. Just tend to her."

"You're right Major. It does look like the rest of you have suffered flesh wounds, but the women did a good job fixing you all up. But she is still bleeding, because the bullet has penetrated too deep. It may even be puncturing her lung, her breathing is very shallow. I have to get the bullet out of her now. I don't think we can wait, and I don't think she will make it if we travel with her any longer in her condition. If I don't get that bullet out and close her up, her lung might collapse, she might drown in her own blood, or if she loses too much blood she might go into shock."

"Doc, just do whatever you have to do to save her." The Major and Hope had been through so many things together throughout the years and he couldn't imagine losing her.

"The Ethiopian military has been contacted by the caretaker over an hour ago. They're on their way now. By the way Sidney, where is the Commander?" Darryl had just realized the Ethiopian Commander wasn't with them.

Sidney looked down. "Doc, I'm sorry, my Commander didn't make it."

Darryl felt his heart drop, but he knew he couldn't think about losing the Commander right now. He was needed and he had to stay focus. "Help me carry her into the church so I can get to work on her." Once they were all into the church, Darryl instructed the caretaker on what he needed in order to do a field surgery on the female Colonel. Sidney pulled the truck to the rear of the church, alongside the jeep. The truck was out of gas, and there was no way they could fit everyone in the little jeep. They would have to wait for the military to show up. They kept the lights in the church out, just in case some rebels showed up. The caretaker said they could take the wounded lady downstairs to work on her in the lighted basement. The light in the basement would not be seen by anyone outside.

Darryl placed Hope on the caretaker's bed in the basement. Once Love and the caretaker came down to the basement with everything Darryl said he needed they asked him if there was anything else they should do. "One of you can stay to assist me with this, and the other one can go back upstairs with everyone else."

The caretaker had no desire to assist in a surgery, and he didn't like blood. "I'll go upstairs." Love wasn't much for blood either, but it looked like she had been volunteered by the caretaker for the job of nurse. She went and crouched down next to the bed where this bloody, beaten woman laid, and she tried not to look at her for too long, because the sight of the woman laying there close to death, terrified her. Love asked Darryl, "So what do you want me to do?"

"I'll need you to just pass me the tools I ask for as soon as I ask for them. Wipe the sweat from my forehead, if you see it getting into my eyes. Just like you've seen on Television. Pretend you're on "Grey's Anatomy". Love tried to smile at Darryl's attempts to put her at ease, but it really wasn't working. "I'll tell you when I need you to do something. For now you can hold her hand, talk to her, and try to comfort her. Even though it appears she is unconscious it may help her if you talk to her, you never know."

Love looked at Darryl nervously. "I've never been real good around blood and stuff."

"I understand, try not to focus on the blood, just try to focus on what I ask you to do, and other than that just try to focus on comforting her."

Love wasn't sure how to go about comforting someone who was unconscious, and someone that was a stranger to her, but she did what the doctor told her to do and she held the woman's hand. She whispered in her ear. "Hang in there, fight, don't give up, you can do it." Love thought to herself, "I sound like a cheerleader, what the heck am I saying." She tried not to look at what Darryl was doing to the woman whose hand she was holding, but she couldn't help but peak out of curiosity. Love saw Darryl poor a bottle of alcohol and clean all the blood from the woman's chest. Love saw him give her some type of needle he had in his bag. It was a localized anesthesia that Darryl was giving Hope so she wouldn't feel the cut he was about to make into the side of her chest. Then Love saw Darryl take the scalpel out of his bag, she saw the sweat beads getting ready to fall into his eyes, and she immediately grabbed the cloth and wiped the sweat off of his forehead. Darryl smiled at Love briefly and said, "See you make a great nurse. How's your patient doing? She's going to need you now, I'm about to make the incision."

Love looked back down at the woman on the bed, and looked away from the doctor that was about to cut into her. She whispered in the woman's ear, "be strong, I'm sure there's people out there that need you, that love you. I don't know you, but you've got to be the bravest woman I've ever known. How you saved all those girls, and taking a bullet for them it's amazing." Then Love swore she felt a slight squeeze of her hand by the woman. "Oh my God, doctor, I think I felt her squeeze my hand!"

Darryl didn't stop what he was doing and he didn't seem the least bit phased. "Don't worry, by now the shot I gave her should be working. If she comes to she won't feel what I'm doing at all. But you have to keep her focused on you, so she won't move and look down at what I'm doing, and go into shock. Keep talking her through it."

Love just hoped this woman would not wake up until after the doctor finished doing what he had to do.

Hope was dreaming.... She was dreaming she was twelve years old again. She was playing with her sisters. Back home all the kids just played out in the street. Drivers knew to drive slow, to beep, and to wait for the kids to move out of the way. Nana's block on Mathias Ave. in Queens was always filled with kids. In the summer most of the kids stayed home alone, and the street was their playground. Nana was the person that looked over the whole street and the kids that lived on it. They would play kick ball, flag football, tag, foot races, and scully, until lunch time, and Nana usually fed every kid who was home alone in her little house. On the really hot days the firemen would come by and open up the fire hydrant for the kids, and they would run through the water, pretending they were at the beach, while they sucked on lollipops from the corner candy store, and ate Italian ices all day long. It was the life of a city kid. When you are poor and growing up in the city you learn quick how to make the best out of what you've got.

But Hope never felt poor when she lived with Nana, she only felt happy. Hope was dreaming about the first time she realized she was stronger and faster than almost all the other boys on the block. They were all playing Scully. Love was her partner. Nana hated them playing Scully, it was a form of gambling to Nana, and she tried to stop them whenever she came outside and caught them playing. But they still played with all the other kids, all the time, especially when they knew Nana was busy cooking lunch for everyone. Nana told them next time she caught them playing Scully, they were gonna be on punishment for two weeks. But Hope and Love still took their chances. They were addicted to scully, just like every other kid in the neighborhood, and they were the neighborhood champs, so everyone was always challenging them. They were even starting to teach little Faith. Faith was only three so they just put her in charge of collecting and decorating the bottle caps."

Hope was up and it was her turn to knock Heathcliff's bottle cap out of the box. Faith was yelling, "go Hope go." But Hope missed the shot just by an inch. Then it was Love's turn, the girl's were playing teams against the boys, and it was their team left against Heathcliff and Anthony. Love made the shot, but that left them at a tie. They needed a tie breaker.

Heathcliff had an idea. "We should make the tie breaker a foot race. You girls may be winners at scully but that's just because it's not physical. You two could never beat a boy at a foot race, especially you Love."

Hope knew Heathcliff was talking about her sister Love being fat, and she wouldn't stand for anyone insulting her sisters. "Fine we'll have a relay race, you and Love run first and then me and Anthony race to the finish, I'm sure my sister is gonna stomp your fat, ugly butt, Heathcliff!"

"Only in her dreams Hope, only in her dreams. Fine, it's settled, winner takes all the candy and the other team's bottle caps, and the loser gets their sneakers thrown up on the telephone wires. I can't wait to see you explain that to your Nana, Hope. You two are going to end up on punishment for the rest of the summer and I hope she whoops you twos outside."

Hope didn't care about the consequences she loved a challenge. Love was a little more worried about what Nana would do to them if they loss. She whispered to Hope before Hope headed off to her end of the street to start the race, "you know Nana's gonna whoop us and put us on punishment if we get our sneakers thrown up on the wire!" Hope just grinned at Love. "Well then, I guess you better run fast and make sure that don't happen."

One of the neighborhood girls started the race, "get on your mark, get set, Go!"

Love took off first. She was ahead of Heathcliff, but midway through the race she started to fall behind him. By the time Love touched Hope's hand, Anthony already had a big lead on Hope. But Hope was fast, and that day she was phenomenally fast, she heard her sisters yelling, "Go Hope Go, You Can Do It", and she did, she caught up with Anthony in no time and then she passed him before he even saw her coming. Hope won the race hands down. As Hope was standing there catching her breath, and brushing her unraveled pony tail away from her face she looked over at Anthony, and she was feeling full of herself, when she said, "we'll I guess me and my sister are the best at scully, and foot races too, huh?"

Anthony was embarrassed that his friend had put him up to running against a girl in a foot race and he was even more embarrassed about actually losing to a girl. "Oh shut up Hope! The only reason you beat me is because I wasn't going as fast as I would have because you're a girl, even if you are a tomboy, butch girl, and your fat sister couldn't out run old Larry the drunk on the corner if she had to, so she can't take no credit for you winning anyways!"

Hope wasn't much for keeping her temper under control, so she just walked up to Anthony and punched him in the stomach. The punch knocked Anthony down hard. Heathcliff came running over, and he jumped on Hope's back. But, Love was right behind him and started punching on him until he fell off of her sister's back. Then Love started shoving Heathcliff's face into the pavement, while she sat on him, and she yelled, "I guess my fat ass is good for something, huh Heathcliff?"

Next thing you knew everyone in the neighborhood was fighting, boys against girls. These type of fist fights broke out at least once every other week. Lil Faith knew her sisters could take care of themselves, and her sisters always told her, "your job is to make sure you get all the candy and bottle tops", and that's just what Faith did as everyone else fought. It wasn't long before Nana had ran outside and yelled, "what you dag on kids doing, get your butts in here and come clean up and eat lunch."

All the kids stopped fighting at the sound of Nana's voice. They all brushed themselves off, and started heading into Nana's house to get lunch. Nana asked the kids, "now what was all that about?" But no one said anything. "Well I don't even want to know this time. You all just go wash your hands then come sit at the table."

Hope had a big grin on her face when she nudged Love. Then she stuck her tongue out at Heathcliff and Anthony......

Hope was waking up from her dream. Darryl had finished getting the bullets out and had already closed her back up. The surgery, no matter how crude was a success. Darryl was now busy dressing Hope's wound. She started to open her eyes. She could smell blood and alcohol in the air. When she looked around she could see she was laying down in an unfamiliar room and when she looked up she saw Love staring back at her. Hope was still a little disoriented and Love looked so beautiful and so familiar to her. "Are you an angel? Where am I?"

Love smiled and felt a wave of relief that the woman seemed to be okay and actually talking already. "No I'm definitely no angel. I guess you can say I'm your nurse. Be still and rest you are going to be okay and you're safe now. You're in a church, the doctor just finished operating."

Then Hope remembered all that had just happened to her. "Where are the girls and my men, and Amir?"

"Everyone is okay. They are all waiting on you. Do you want to see anyone?"

"Amir, can I see Amir, and my Major."

"I'll go get them." Love ran upstairs and when she opened the door, she said, "she's awoke, and the doctor says she's going to be okay, whose Amir, she is asking for you and....?" But before Love could finish, something startled them all.

Someone or something had just busted into the back door. Love was so shocked she didn't move she just looked towards the back door, paralyzed. At the door stood the rebel leader's Second in Command and his small group of men. The place was total chaos. The women and girls started screaming. The rebel commander and his small group of men had left their jeep in the brush and in the darkness of the night they snuck up to the back side of the church on foot. Now they all stood there at a standstill with their rifles ready.

The Second in Command stared at Amir with hate in his eyes and he said, "look we want the dog that is responsible for our leaders death, we want that traitor Amir! If you give him to us, we will leave and there will be no more bloodshed."

"Let them take me then; I don't want to see anyone die because of me." The Major was next to Amir, and he said, "this boy risked his life and saved us all. You can't have him." Sidney agreed, "it's decided, you can't have the boy and if that's all the men you've come here with, you better leave! Just so you know, I'm a perfect shot. I never miss my target."

The rebels knew, they were facing off against skilled military men. The Second in Command didn't care he was prepared to die to get his revenge. All was quiet as the men held their positions and kept their rifles at the ready. They were prepared to push back on the triggers at a moment's notice. They waited to see what the new rebel leader's response would be. Then he finally said, "so be it", and he shot his weapon in the direction of Love who was the closest person to him, and she happened to be standing in the way of his main target, Amir.

Darryl had heard the commotion and had left Hope's side down in the basement. He had just made it up the stairs and was standing next to the basement door when he saw the rebel point his gun at Love. Darryl was able to push Love out of the way. The bullet missed her, but it hit Darryl square in the chest, and he fell to the floor.

Through all of the chaos John's mind was only on Love. John immediately leaped towards Love to cover her from any gunfire when he saw the rebel point his weapon at her, but he was too far away and Darryl got to Love first. Everyone else was trying to cover themselves from the gunfire by hiding behind the church pulpit chairs. Sidney, Amir and Hope's soldier's returned fire against the rebels. John was now right by Love's side. He thought she had been hit but before he could even ask her if she was hurt they heard a booming sound come from outside.

It was the Ethiopian General and his platoon. They had finally arrived at the church and at just the right moment. The shooting momentarily stopped inside the church as they all paused to listen to the General's voice coming over the loudspeaker.

"We have the church surrounded. If you rebels come out of the church without your weapons and surrender, you will live, but if you continue to hold these hostages, one thing is for sure, you rebel's, you traitors to your country, will all die."

All was silent inside the church, except for the small sounds of the young girls weeping from behind the pulpit chairs. The rebels one by one put down their weapons and decided to surrender. But the Second in Command stood his ground. He watched as the other rebels abandoned him until he was the last rebel left behind in the church.

"What are you going to do? All of the other rebels have abandoned you. Is your revenge really worth dying for?", asked Sidney.

He didn't answer Sidney. He just stood there with his rifle still at the ready in his hands. Then with full knowledge that what he was about to do was futile, he raised his weapon and pointed it at Amir. Before a bullet could even enter into the chamber of the rebel's rifle, they returned fire. Then the last rebel left was dead.

Sidney handed his weapon to the Major and he ran outside with his arms up. He yelled to his General, "all is clear, all is clear." The General instantly recognized his young soldier, and he motioned to Faith, who was in the vehicle in the far rear, to get out of the vehicle and follow him. Faith ran over to the General and she was practically holding her breath the whole time he spoke to her.

"Ms. Faith, I don't know what we are going to find in there. Do you want to wait out here or do you want to come in with me?"

"I can't wait out here, I want to go in. I can handle whatever we see."

So the General entered the church with Faith by his side and his medics behind them. The medics immediately started attending to the wounded, and they bagged up the rebel, who was clearly dead. They went downstairs to also attend to the young lady Sidney told them was the American Colonel that was wounded and operated on.

Faith looked around with her wide eyes dodging from one person to the next, she was searching for Darryl. All around Faith were these scared little girls, hiding behind the pulpits, but for the first time in her career the children were not her priority. This time she was searching for Darryl. "Where is Darryl?", Faith asked herself. Then she saw him, lying unconscious on the floor. His shirt was soaked with blood and two of the medics were attending to him. The medics and a young woman and man were hovering over Darryl.

Faith ran over to Darryl, she recognized the woman and man. She remembered briefly seeing the couple checking into the hotel days ago, right before her and Darryl first left out to find the children. She kneeled down low at Darryl's side and whispered in his ear, "Darryl, can you hear me?"

He didn't answer. The medics were tearing through his shirt to find the wound which was causing his bleeding. They told Faith, Love and John to please stand back and give them some room.

Love looked over at Faith and she said, "He saved my life, are you his fiancé?"

"Yes I am."

"He's a good doctor. He also saved the woman's life downstairs. He just finished operating on her, before he was shot. He was amazing."

"I know, he's a really good man, and it's all my fault he is here, and it's my fault that he's hurt."

Then Faith broke down and started crying. She felt as if she was dying inside. The regrets were already filling her mind. She couldn't help but think about all the things she should have said to Darryl, all the times she should have been with him, instead of running off working and putting everyone and everything else in her life before him. While Faith was crying she started saying out loud all the things that were in her head.

"God if I could just have one more chance, one more chance to get it right, to treat him the way he deserves to be treated by a woman, just one more chance, God. I would marry him at this very moment and give him a house full of little babies to love."

Love looked over at the poor girl. She could feel the hurt and pain the girl was feeling and Love thought to herself, "what if that was John on the floor bleeding to death?" Love couldn't even bare to think of it. So she reached out, and she held the young woman in her arms. She didn't know what else to do or what to say to her, but it looked like the girl needed a hug, even if she wasn't really the hugging type.

As Faith sobbed into the stranger's shoulder she heard Darryl's soft voice. He had regained consciousness. Everyone stared down at Darryl.

"I heard that." Darryl whispered with his eyes still shut. Then he opened his eyes. "I heard that, you said you will marry me right now? And something about a house full of little babies. Come here Nene."

The medics let Faith through. She leaned down at Darryl's side. Then Darryl reached into the inner pocket on his vest and he pulled out the gold case. It was the case Faith had given him yesterday that contained his parent's rings. Faith looked down at the case, and her tears of despair started to turn into tears of joy. Lodged inside the golden case was a bullet. It was the bullet that could have killed Darryl, but instead it had gotten lodged into the case. Only the very tip of the bullet had punctured Darryl's chest, and it left behind only a small little flesh wound which the medics had already cleaned and stitched up.

"He's very lucky, if not for that case being in his vest pocket, the bullet would have went straight through his heart I'm sure of it.", said one of the medics.

Love and John stood there amazed of all the things they had observed that day. John whispered praises, "thank you God."

Love just stood there silently. She was still in a state of shock. She had to admit if she didn't believe in miracles before, tonight was definitely the night to make her a believer.

Darryl was a little sore in his chest area, but he had gotten his breath back and was recovering quickly. He was holding the golden case in his hands.

"You said to give you this when I came back. Didn't I tell you I would come back to you and with the children?"

"You did say that."

Then Darryl positioned himself onto one knee and in front of everyone he opened up the golden case with the bullet that had almost killed him, and he said, "My Nene, Faith Emmanuel Carpenter, will you marry me?"

Faith was still crying tears of joy. She could barely get the words out to answer him and finally she found her voice. "Yes, yes..."

John was looking over at Love and he knew exactly what she must have been thinking. The two of them had just heard Darryl, call his fiancé, "Faith". Could this be the same Faith that wrote that prayer in the prayer book years ago? Could this be Love's little sister, Faith? It was just all too coincidental to just be a mere coincidence.

Love took a good, long look at Faith, and she thought to herself, "how did I not notice? She looks just like I remember our mama looking when I was a young girl. She's so beautiful, so grown up, could this be Faith, my Faith? But this is crazy, no, it couldn't be her."

While Love continued staring at Faith and Darryl hugging each other, John continued staring at Love as he waited for her to say something. John was just about to say something himself when the medics carried Hope up from the basement on a gurney, and everyone directed their attentions to Hope.

Darryl, looked over at Hope and said to Faith, "that lady is an American Colonel. She helped save all these girls. I had to do surgery on her and it's really a miracle she survived."

"Today seems to be a day full of miracles", said Faith.

Darryl got up and walked over to Hope, and Faith followed him. Hope could barely see them clearly out of her swollen eyes. Love eyes followed the two of them, but her body didn't move.

Hope was fully alert and conscious now.

"How are you feeling Colonel? I'm the doctor you met back at the rebel camp. I had to operate on you."

Hope's voice sounded hoarse and it was obvious she was still in pain. "I've felt better. But I'm alive right, that's all that matters. Thank you so much doctor, and where is your nurse?

Her voice really helped me hang in there. Where is she? I want to thank her also."

Darryl motioned to Love to come near. She walked over to Darryl and the women she had comforted through her surgery. She still couldn't stop staring at Faith, who was standing right behind Darryl, and all the time Love was thinking, "could this woman really be my little sister Faith?"

Love walked over to them and once she reached them the women laying on the gurney grabbed hold of her hand.

"Thank you, nurse."

"You have nothing to thank me for, really I didn't do anything. The doctor here did everything."

Hope could hardly see out of her swollen eyes, but she didn't need to, she could still recognize Love's voice. It was the voice of the caring nurse that had talked her through her surgery.

"No that's not true you did a lot. If not for your encouraging words I don't know if I would still be here. At first I thought you was an angel, you sounded so familiar to me, I felt like I was safe at home, like when I was a little girl. I realize now why I felt like that, you sound just like my older sister, Love. I haven't seen her in years. Well, I just wanted to say thank you to you also. I know the doctor here did the surgery, but your presence helped me pull through it. Doctor, how are my men, and the children, and the boy Amir?"

The medics helped escort the wounded Major and Amir over to Hope. Love stepped back and she just stood there dumbfounded by what she had just heard Hope say.

The Major realized after almost losing his Colonel just how much she had come to mean to him. Losing her he realized would have devastated them all. It would have devastated him more than he could bare to think of.

"Colonel, the troops are well and so are myself and Amir. You don't worry about us, just focus on getting yourself better, okay."

"Okay."

Amir was overwhelmed by the events of the day. He just gave Hope a very careful hug and then he started to follow the Major and the medic escorts out of the church and into the medic vehicle. But before the medics escorted them outside of the church Amir looked back and ran to Hope's side. "I want you to know, in case I never see you again. You saved me by bringing me God, and your love. I will always think of you like a mother, like a sister, and a friend. Hope, thank you for all that you have done for me, and I really pray I will see you again one day."

Hope felt the same strong bond and motherly love for Amir. Now the church was empty, and all except for the three sisters and John and Darryl were left. They were all standing over Hope while they waited for the medics to come back and carry her into the last medic transport vehicle.

Love almost felt like she was out of her body just looking down at everything and everyone. She felt like she was caught up in some weird, whirlwind, twilight zone episode. She wondered, if she had gone crazy and was hearing things. Could this really be happening? Were these two women actually her little sisters?

Faith was still oblivious her thoughts were only on Darryl. She wasn't paying attention or listening to anyone's conversation.

Then suddenly Love passed out and she fell to the ground. John caught her, and he held her in his arms.

Darryl left Hope's side and went over to attend to Love, and of course Faith followed. Darryl was afraid Love may have been wounded during the gun fire and not have even realized it due to shock. Sometimes during times of extreme shock people did not even feel pain, until the adrenaline rush wore off. So Darryl checked Love over. "You seem to be okay. You probably, just passed out from the rush of adrenaline leaving your body. You should be alright. Do you want some water?"

Love couldn't talk, she felt light-headed. She just kept staring at Faith and at Hope. She was still wondering if they could be who she thought they were, but it all seemed so impossible. Then she saw the medics began to carry Hope's gurney out and she knew she had to say something now, she had to know now. She finally got the courage to speak out.

Love stood up still unsteady and she yelled out all wild, like a crazy woman, "stop! My name is Love Emmanuel."

Everyone in the room stared at her.

Faith looked at Love, but this time she looked at her with her heart and not her eyes, and she saw now so clearly, that this was her sister, this was her sister Love. Faith whispered, "Love is it really you?"

Then Love rushed into Faith's arms. They were both crying and hugging each other when they heard Hope, crying behind them. They walked over to Hope. As they stood over Hope's broken, beaten and bloody body, Love said softly, "Hope?"

"Love, Faith, my God...."

While the three sisters talked, John and Darryl watched in amazement. Then John whispered to Darryl.

"Well it looks like your fiancée and my um, friend Love have a lot to catch up on. So I guess this is a better time than any other to have a little talk with you about something."

Darryl was curious. "About what?"

John was exhausted from being on this truly emotional rollercoaster ride, and he decided to be as direct with Darryl as possible. "Look the reason myself and Love were in Ethiopia in the first place was to find you. You do know you're adopted right?"

"Yes, I've always known that. But what does that...."

"Let me finish. We were hired by someone who knows your biological mother, to find you and bring you to her to meet her. There's a lot more to this, and I know this is a lot to take in, in a short period of time, but hey, look at everything we've just been through. When you think about it after everything that has happened to us, this unexpected news shouldn't phase you at all."

Like John, Darryl was also exhausted. "How about you just tell me everything on the way to the hospital?"

The medics carried Hope into the medical van and Love, Faith, Darryl and John sat on her sides, Love and Faith held their sister Hope's hands while John and Darryl kept a close watch over all of them. God had given them all second chances that day. Now it was up to them what they would do with it.

Chapter 18
The effectual prayer of a righteous man availeth much.[23]

Over a month had passed by since the day when the Emmanuel sisters had been reunited. Since then a lot had changed in a very short period of time. Hope's injuries, and wounds had healed, and she had decided to end her military career by taking an Honorable Discharge from the Marine Corps. She received a sizeable retirement and several decorations and honors, and a very sizeable financial package attached to a confidentiality agreement she had to sign to never mention the government agency and missions she had been sent on. Now Hope was trying to figure out what to make of her life as a civilian. She thought about going back to school, maybe becoming a teacher, but her main priorities right now were her family. She knew whatever she ended up doing her priority was going to be to her sisters and of course her first priority had to be to her new adopted son.

Hope thought, being a single mom to a teenage boy may be harder than being a Colonel. Especially since, her new son, Amir Emmanuel, was definitely not your ordinary teenage boy.

Love had taken an extended vacation. The first vacation she had actually taken in years. The associates at the firm thought it was very strange for a newly appointed partner to immediately take a vacation. But Love wasn't worried about what anyone thought, after all, she knew her boss was very, very pleased with her work.

Mr. Swanson had already announced that he would be changing his status to *of counsel;* and only giving the firm advice on clients' cases and affairs. Mr. Swanson was now ready to devote his life to his new wife, Mary and their adopted children. He had just gained a wife and a very large family which included fifteen Ethiopian boys and girls, not to mention his wife's adult son, Darryl. Mr. Swanson was enjoying bragging about his new son, "the doctor." He thought back about the joy on his wife Mary's face weeks ago when he had proposed. The day he

---

[23] James 5:16

proposed to Mary is a day he would never forget. Every detail was engraved in his mind.

After he popped the question, Mary said he was the first man she had ever loved in her life. She said she didn't care if she had to live out the rest of her days with him in a cardboard box, she just wanted to be with him. Then she said "yes", to his proposal of marriage.

After Mary had agreed to marry him, Mr. Swanson told her he had a few more surprises up his sleeve. First he told her he was wealthy and she never needed to worry about them ever living in a cardboard box, and then he told her he had someone very important waiting to speak to her and Darryl walked into the room.

Mary looked up, and said, "Doctor Darryl! How sweet you got my favorite doctor to be here to celebrate with us. You know Doctor Darryl is like the son I've never had." Mary still had no idea what was going on.

Then Darryl said, "Mary, I just found out that I really am your son. I'm the son you gave up so many years ago."

Darryl explained things to Mary and she had tears of joy streaming from her eyes. She was still in shock over Darryl being her real son, but she barely had a chance to recover, when in walked a bunch of little children who were calling her, mother. Mr. Swanson looked over at her and said, "well honey you said you wanted to take care of as many children, orphans like you were as you could. So here they are. Are you happy?"

"Happy, I don't think I could ever be happier than this!"

But just then Mary saw three beautiful women walk into her room.

"I'm sorry to barge in, but we have been waiting out there for a while", teased Love. "Ma'am it's nice to meet you my name is Love and Mr. Swanson is my boss, and your son is my sister Faith's fiancé...."

Mary took one look at Love, and there was no mistaking who she was, she screamed out, "Love, Love Emmanuel!?" Then she looked over at Mr. Swanson and she said, "but how did you know to find the Emmanuel sisters, I never even told you about them?"

Mr. Swanson just stood there and shook his head. "I don't understand…"

Faith and Hope were standing behind Love. The three sisters had been stuck together like glue ever since they found each other in Ethiopia. They were confused about why Mary was so excited, at first.

"Love, I would know you anywhere, you look just like your Nana, you do, you always looked more like her than any of her girls. Don't you girls recognize me? I'm Mary, your Nana's best friend, Mary."

Then Love looked at Mary, she had changed much over the years. She remembered Mary and how she looked when she was much younger, but now she looked like someone's grandmother. Mary's youth was gone. But when Love took a closer look at her she could see that it was Mary, her eyes, those dark, haunting eyes, and her sweet smile, she hadn't changed that much.

"Mary! Mary's such a common name, I never imagined Mr. Swanson's Mary, was "our" Nana's Mary. Mary, this is Hope and little, baby Faith, all grown up."

Mary was crying and she said through her tears to her son, Darryl and the Emmanuel sisters, "I'm so sorry, I'm so sorry, I thought I would never see any of you ever again. Can you all ever forgive me?"

Darryl said, "of course I forgive you. I had great parents Mary, and I already fell in love with you even before I found out you were my birth mother."

Faith felt so sorry for Mary. She had no bitterness for her at all, she could barely remember her. "Mary, I was only a little child when Nana died, but I do remember how much Nana loved you. I remember how you always made her laugh and how you made us laugh when you came around. In my mind there's nothing to forgive. You have to forgive yourself, because I think I speak for the three of us when I say, we are just happy to see you alive, and happy to have another piece of Nana with us again." Love and Hope, shook their heads in agreement with Faith, and Faith continued speaking. "Besides I really want my new mother-in-law to like me."

Mary looked over at Mr. Swanson. "This is the happiest day of my life. Somehow you have given me everything I've ever wanted. You're amazing."

Mr. Swanson just kissed her on the forehead and smile. Then he said, "well that was the impression I was going for, amazing."

The two of them got married by the justice of peace a few days later and then they moved into their new house with their fifteen children. Then three weeks later, Mr. Swanson, Mary and their fifteen newly adopted children from Ethiopia were all sitting down in church attending another wedding.

Darryl's father was his best man. His father held the golden case with the bullet hole in his hands. He anxiously waited for the little girl next door that he had grown to love to come walking down the aisle, and marry his son. Darryl's father's only wish was that his wife was there to see their son getting married today. Then he thought, "I know she's up there watching it all and smiling to herself, because she always knew this day would come."

The music started playing and the bridesmaids and their groomsmen came walking down the aisle. First one to come down the aisle was Love, the oldest Emmanuel sister with her groomsman, John by her side. Then Hope walked down the aisle with her groomsman and newly adopted son, Amir Emmanuel. Now it was time for the bride to come down the aisle. Faith was waiting outside the hallway of the little church. She had decided to have her wedding in Nana's little church. One day when Faith was trying to decide where to have the wedding Love told her a story that she had almost forgotten.

"When we were all little girls and went to Nana's church we attended many weddings there. We would always pretend we were brides, after church services, and we all agreed that if any of us ever got married it would be in Nana's little church on Mathias Avenue."

Faith did remember then how when they were girls they would giggle and pretend they were all brides walking down the aisle as they played in the church after Sunday school. She decided then that if the church on Mathias Avenue was still standing and available that she would get married there.

Standing there in that little church she felt closer to Nana than she had ever felt since the day Nana had died. Faith's mother was getting ready to walk to her seat and watch her daughter come down the aisle, but she was concerned about the far off look on Faith's face.

"Are you okay baby, are you nervous?"

"I'm just fine Mom, I'm not nervous at all, I'm positive that he is the one for me. In fact I'm better than fine, I am so unbelievably happy. All the people I've ever loved in my life are here today in person, or in spirit. I can feel Nana's spirit as if she was here watching over me. Everything I've ever wanted in my life, everything I've ever needed is right here in this little church today. When I open this door, and walk down the aisle, the man God has blessed me with will be waiting at the end of that aisle, waiting to spend the rest of his life with me. I just can't believe how God has blessed me with so much, with all that I've ever asked for and even with the things I never thought about asking for. Mom, is this how you felt when you married Dad?"

"Well not exactly, honestly I was pretty nervous when I married your Dad. Your Dad and I were so different, me being African and him being Caucasion. I was so young and I wasn't sure if I was doing the right thing in getting married so young, but one thing I did know for sure was that I loved him. It wasn't until years later that I realized how lucky I was to have married such a wonderful man. But, I do remember one time in my life, a time when I instantaneously knew something was right and I had absolutely no doubts or nervousness that I was making the right choice."

"When was that mom?"

"It was when this little girl with two pigtails and two missing teeth in the front came running into that little room at the old Social Services building, and the social worker said, "Faith meet your new foster parents." I took one look at you and I fell in love right there and I knew then you were the one. Then I asked, "how do we go about adopting this little girl?" I didn't need any time to think about it. I wasn't nervous at all. I knew right away I loved you and that I was meant to be your mother."

"Mom you are going to make me cry."

Faith's father walked over to his wife and his daughter. "It is time for you two, to break it up now. Go take your seat honey. I have to walk our little girl down the aisle. Boy I was starting to think that this day would never come."

The music was playing, the guest stood up, and then they opened the church doors. Faith looked like an angel. She looked magnificent. She saw Darryl waiting at the end of the aisle and they looked into each other's eyes. They were already one, and neither one of them had any doubts their love would be forever.

Later that day at the reception, everyone was dancing and eating and having a wonderful time. Love looked around at her sisters. She thought to herself "they look so happy." They were all sitting and eating at the wedding party table. Darryl was talking about how he couldn't wait to get to the honeymoon and finally see Hawaii for the first time. Love also overheard Darryl say to Faith that there was something else he couldn't wait to do with her for the first time. Love thought to herself, "she must have heard wrong. There was no way the two of them hadn't done it yet." Love made a mental note to herself to ask Faith about that, right away, when she got back from her honeymoon.

Then Love looked over at Hope and Amir and how the two of them were engrossed in a conversation at the table about Amir getting up the nerve to ask a girl sitting across the room to dance. The girl looked to be close to Amir's age. But Love doubted that there were many people Amir's age who had seen as much in life as he had. Hope was busy giving Amir advice on how to be a gentlemen. Love heard Hope telling Amir to say, "you look very lovely tonight, may I have a dance with you?" Love found it all very amusing considering all that they had been through just a few weeks ago. She thought maybe Amir needed a little bit of a push.

"Amir if you don't ask that girl to dance with you already, I'm going to get up and ask for you myself. I'm going to say, my nephew would like to dance with you, but he's too chicken to ask you himself."

"You wouldn't!"

Love looked at him with a very serious look. "Oh yes I would."

That was the push Amir needed. He stood up and asked the girl for a dance, but she didn't waste any time turning him down. But as he walked back to his table with his head hanging down, another very beautiful young girl stopped him and she asked him to dance.

Hope was sitting back observing it all. She was amazed at how it seemed as if her heart was connected to Amir's. She felt her heart sink when Amir was rejected by the first girl, and then she felt her heart suddenly leap in her chest when the other young girl asked him to dance. Hope thought to herself, "motherhood is going to be like a rollercoaster ride. I've never even been this nervous about going on a mission."

Watching Hope and Amir made Love think about how she almost had a child herself, and how that child would have probably been around Amir's age right now, if she would have had it. Love wondered if she would have been like Hope with her own child, giving him advice about girls, and holding her breath as she watched him ask a girl to dance.

John was watching Love like always. He noticed she had finished eating and was just quietly looking around at everyone and everything. He leaned over and asked her to dance. The two of them got up to dance and while they were on the dance floor the music changed into a slow love song. John pulled Love closer. He could feel Love's tension over him holding her so close. She hadn't ever brought up what he had said to her back in Ethiopia. She acted as if he had never said, "I love you." But John didn't want to push the subject if she wasn't ready for it, even though he suspected she felt the same way about him. No matter what happened he knew they would always be friends, but he hoped for much more one day.

Ever since they had returned from Ethiopia she was avoiding him. He was back in California at work, and she had been staying in New York on vacation with her sisters. He had tried to call her everyday while they were apart, but she always made some excuse to get off the phone. Every time he called she was never alone, her sisters were always around. He understood they had been separated for twenty something years, but he desperately needed to talk to her. He had been in New York for three days for Faith's and Darryl's wedding, but still he had not been able to get any time alone with Love. So this was actually going to be the first time John had a moment alone with Love, since he had arrived in New York for her sister's wedding. While he held her in his arms he decided then to have the conversation he needed to have with her. He whispered, "Love, why are you avoiding me?"

"Um, I've just been so busy helping Faith plan all this last minute wedding stuff, you know. I'm sorry."

John knew Love had a lot going on. He thought maybe he was just overreacting. "That's alright. It's just that I really need to talk to you about something."

Love thought John wanted to talk about his feelings for her, and she was trying to avoid that, so she tried to change the subject. "John it is so good to see you. How are things back at the firm? When are you flying back out? My vacation is coming to an end maybe we can catch the same flight back to California."

"That's sort of what I wanted to talk to you about, in person, and why I kept calling you."

Love felt a lump form in her throat, she was trying her best to put this conversation off for as long as possible, but it looked like John was set on declaring his love for her once again. "Okay then, what is it you want to tell me?"

"I'm not going back to the firm. I'm not coming back to LA either, Love. That's what I've been trying to tell you. I left the firm. You know how I've been the co-pastor at my church for some time now. Well my church has sister churches, all across the country, and one of the pastors retired earlier than expected. My pastor has been grooming me to take over his church one day, but he called me into his office and told me that one of their sister churches needed a pastor and that he had recommended me. I prayed over it and I decided God was calling me and I needed to answer the call. So I agreed to pastor the church. I wanted to tell you earlier but whenever I got you on the phone you rushed off within seconds. I just want you to know I'm leaving the firm, but not you. I'm always here for you whenever you need me. I'm just a call away."

Love was stunned. She always assumed she could put whatever was happening between her and John on the back burner. She always assumed since they were co-workers and they were good friends; that he was always going to be around. Suddenly, the thought of returning to California, without knowing he would be there waiting for her, was unbearable. John was the one good thing about returning to California. Knowing he would be there, just for her to talk to, was what gave her the strength to leave her sisters and go back to work. For the first time she realized how much she really loved John and needed him. She also realized that now it was probably too late for her to tell him that. Half of her wanted to tell him right now, but still, the fear of telling him how she really felt about him overwhelmed her. She just couldn't find the courage to tell him so instead she said,

"Well that's great John. You are going to be a great pastor. But you know I'll miss you. You will keep in touch still, right?"

"Of course I'll keep in touch. We can still talk on the phone all the time. And the church is right here, right in New York. So when you are in town visiting your sisters, you can also see me. Maybe even come by for a Sunday sermon."

"I don't know about all of that, I was surprised the church my sister had her wedding in didn't burn down when I stepped foot back in it."

John laughed. "Well, I'm really going to miss seeing you every day Love. You know I always knew you would be partner one day too. You're the type of woman who can do or be whatever she wants to be, once you put your mind to it. But what I want to know is, are you happy? Are you really happy?"

"Why do people keep asking me that, of course I'm happy. I mean besides finally being partner, I've also found my two sisters. I have everything I've ever wanted in life. I can use the company jet to come out here and see my sisters every single weekend if I want. Mr. Swanson has already promised it to me and made it clear to the rest of the partners that it's for my personal use. I mean really when you think of it what possible reason would I have, not to be happy?"

John didn't know if Love was trying to convince him or herself. But he decided not to push the topic. There was silence between the two of them for a while as they just swayed to the music and then Love said, "but you know, I am really going to miss seeing you at work every day too, I really am."

"I know you will. And one more thing Love, I have to tell you this now before, well before I lose my courage to say it again. I meant what I said to you back in Ethiopia, I'm still in love with you. I know you may not want to hear it, but my feelings for you will never change. So if you ever decide you are not really happy I just want you to know I'm always here as a friend or more if you are ready for it."

Love didn't know what to say, so she didn't say anything. The two of them finished dancing and after the reception John asked Love if she wanted to hang out some more, just the two of them. Love told him she was tired and needed to get back to Faith's apartment and help her pack for her honeymoon. So John gave Love the address to his new church, she already had his cell phone number, and he told her which hotel he was staying at until he found an apartment in town to rent. Love promised him she would call, and visit him, but even when the words came out of her mouth, she knew she didn't intend on keeping them. Love knew it was only a matter of time before her friendship, or romance or whatever her and John had together, would end. She felt as if John was too good for her. That she would never be able to live up to the standards a woman he would be with should possess. And now that he was going to officially be a pastor, and head of a church of his own, responsible for maybe hundreds of people, how could she ever be with him now. Love knew the type of life she had lived and was still living, and she knew how church people thought of people like her. She thought to herself, "even if I changed my lifestyle and tried to settle down with John or anyone else, I can't run from my past. As they say, what's done in the dark always comes to light." So she kissed John gently on the cheek after their last dance and said, "I'm happy for you, and I'll call you, after things settle down and I see Faith off to her honeymoon."

John had no reason to question what Love said to him. He thought that even though she may not be ready, or may not even care for him the way he cared for her, that they were friends. He felt like their friendship would always remain, regardless of long distance.

After the reception the Emmanuel sisters and Amir went back to Faith's apartment. Amir had asked the young lady he danced with at the reception for her phone number. On the ride back to Faith's apartment, Amir and Hope had been strategizing over how he should go about asking the girl out on a date.

Love looked at how excited Hope was about Amir's possible first date and thought to herself, "this is what they mean when they talk about parents living out their lives through their children. She needs to be worrying about getting a date for herself. When is she going to do something with that hair?" Love made another mental note to herself, that when she came up next weekend to visit she was going to take Hope out on a girls' beauty day. Hope was a natural beauty, but she seemed like she tried her best to hide her beauty.

Faith was still glowing. Ever since she had said her vows, her face was full of radiance and joy. When they arrived at Faith's apartment, Amir grabbed the phone and ran into the guest room that Faith had set up for him to stay in. Hope was going to rent the condo from Faith. The newlyweds had already closed on a two story single family home in Long Island, before their wedding. Their new home had enough room for three frequent guests and for a little addition to their little family one day. Their new home would be somewhat close to their parents houses also, but not too close. The three sisters had been sleeping in Faith's bedroom on her king size bed. It was as if they were little girls again. Every night they would stay up and talk, eat junk food, and reminisce.

So everything in life seemed to be perfect for the three sisters. Faith was married to Darryl and now getting ready to go off on her honeymoon in Hawaii. Hope would be living with her new son, Amir, and Love was a partner and due back at her firm; first thing Monday morning after her vacation was over. This was going to be the first time the three of them would be apart, since they were reunited in Ethiopia. While the three sisters were trying to get Faith's wedding gown off, Love started to feel sadness come over her.

"You know I'm really going to miss you guys."

They all stopped for a moment and they hugged each other tightly. Faith wiped her tears away. "Well I already told

Darryl that I know it's our honeymoon, but I'm still going to call my sisters every night while we're gone."

"I know, we should synchronize our phones to alarm us all at the same time so that we remember to call each other every day on three-way while you are away Faith. What do you think about that Love?"

Love laughed. "I think that's very military of you Hope. Synchronized calls…"

"I know Love, I can't help myself. It's going to take me some getting use to being a civilian again. So I guess you are going to have to tell Darryl to wrap everything up in time for our daily phone calls Faith, if you know what I mean."

Faith just giggled like a school girl. Then Love remembered the question she wanted to ask Faith before she left on her honeymoon. "That reminds me Faith, I've been meaning to ask you, what exactly was Darryl referring to when he said, "he was looking forward to doing something else with you for the first time in Hawaii?" Tell me he was talking about sky diving, because I know there is no way that you two haven't done *it* yet. I mean the two of you have known each other forever right? And you two are old as I don't know what, I mean in terms of doing *it*, that's all I'm saying."

Hope was curious now too. She, like Love had just assumed Faith and Darryl had already been intimate. Hope always felt uncomfortable talking about sex and she tried to avoid it. She had no idea her little joke was going to lead to this uncomfortable conversation.

Faith smiled at them. "I know it must be hard to believe being how old I am, but I'm still a virgin. I mean Darryl and I have come really, really close over the years but I would stop myself, and sometimes he would even stop me. See I always had this thing since I was a little girl that I wanted to save myself. I've always wanted my first time to be with my husband. My mother, my adopted mother that is, always told me how her first time was with my dad, and how it was the most beautiful gift she had ever given him. It just seemed so romantic to me, and I decided then I wanted my wedding night to be like that."

The idea of any woman abstaining for so long was so incredible to Love. "But didn't your mother get married when she was like sixteen or something? I mean Faith you are almost thirty, for real, how can you go for so long without doing it. Worse of all, what if it's no good with him. Then you're stuck with it."

"Love! How can you say that!"

"I'm sorry, of course it won't be bad. It will be perfect because you guys are in love. But you know Faith all mothers' tell their daughters they never had sex until they met their husbands?"

"That's not true Love, I don't remember our mother ever telling us that", interjected Hope.

"Oh come on Hope, she probably couldn't remember when she had sex for the first time cause she was always doped up." replied Love.

"Well Faith, I think that's beautiful that you're still a virgin. What a wonderful gift to give your husband on your wedding day. Don't you agree Love?"

"Yeah, sure."

Faith's sisters were beginning to make her feel a little nervous about her first time with Darryl. "Well I'm sure since we are in love it will be wonderful. But, since we are talking about this now I do have a question. How will "I know" if it's good or if I need to work on it?"

Love started laughing. "Oh you'll know. Believe me I'm an expert on the subject. You will just know, don't you agree Hope?"

Hope still had not told her sisters about Mr. Smith's abuse of her when she was a little girl, and how what had happened to her had scarred her for life.

"Oh yeah Faith, Love's right, I definitely agree with her, besides she says she's and expert on this subject so I guess you better listen up to her. In fact I'm going to make sure I take notes myself since she says she is an expert on it and all."

The three of them were laughing and Faith had gotten pass feeling embarrassed. "So Love how many men have you been with?"

Love looked at Faith all indignant. "Don't you know you never ask a woman that question?"

Faith laughed at Love's hypocrisy. "Now Love didn't you just interrogate me about my love-life?"

"That's different because I'm the big sister. Okay, I'm not giving you a number because I probably can't remember the exact number even if I try, but I've been with enough men and even a few women to know what I'm doing when it comes to this particular subject."

"So do you always reach that climax every time you do it?" Faith was very curious now.

"Well yeah, I mean that's the only reason I even have sex." The three of them started laughing uncontrollably. Once they recovered Love continued. "I've never been much on faking it. I mean I guess I've never cared enough about a man to try to spare his feelings. If he wasn't doing it right, I just say, "look you are just not doing it right, and then I will show him how I want it done."

"Okay......", Faith's eyes were very wide now.

Love could see that she was just making Faith get nervous about her first time, and she felt bad about that. "All joking aside, don't worry. With you and Darryl, it will be perfect, because he loves you and you love him. Plus he is a doctor after all, I'm sure he knows plenty about the female anatomy. But if it doesn't seem right the first time, don't worry. I don't know any women who have had the perfect "first" time. But just in case, after the third go around if it still isn't right don't be afraid to tell him, because remember he loves you and he is going to want to do whatever it takes to make you happy."

Faith knew Love was right. Darryl's number one priority had always been making her happy. "Yeah you're right Love, but do you have any tips for me? You know tips where I can make sure he's happy too?"

"He's a man it really doesn't take much to make them happy, but I could give you a few pointers to make him deliriously happy."

Hope just laughed and pretended she was comfortable with the conversation they were having, so she chimed in. "Hey, can I have a copy of that list of tips too; just for rainy days if I'm bored and need something to read."

"No problem lil sisters. In fact, now that I think about it I should probably make sure I copyright this, you never know."

Finally, Faith was all packed up and ready to go. The limousine was ready and waiting to take her to the airport with Darryl inside of it, and she could hardly wait. Love and Hope walked Faith to the front door.

Hope yelled to Amir, "your Aunt's leaving, come on out and say goodbye."

Amir came running out his room with the phone still in his hand.

"So did you make the call, what did she say, is my son going to be going on his first date?"

"Well I haven't actually made the call yet. I've dialed the numbers a few times, but then I hung up." Then he ran up to Faith and gave her a hug and a kiss goodbye. "Travel well and God be with you Aunt Faith."

They all had a group hug, and Faith, couldn't hold back the tears in her eyes. She was really going to miss all of them. "Remember the phone calls, and I love you guys."

Darryl assured them he would take good care of her, and they knew he would. Before she got into the limousine, Faith whispered one last question to Love, "is having sex with someone you are "in love" with, well is it like the romance novels, is it like being in heaven?"

Love looked at her little sister and said, "Faith you are really blessed to be truly in love. Honestly, little sister that's the one question I don't have the answer for. I guess you are going to have to tell me the answer to that."

As Faith watched her sisters from the rear window while the limousine drove away she realized at that moment just how truly blessed she was to have Darryl; and she said a quiet prayer in her head that one day her sisters would be with someone they were in love with, the way that Darryl and her loved each other.

Darryl turned Faith's face towards him and away from the rearview window and he said, "not having second thoughts are you? A bride shouldn't be crying about leaving to go on her honeymoon. Seriously, I know you hate to leave your sisters after just reuniting with them, but we will be back before you know it."

"I know. But don't ever, ever think I have any doubts about you ever again. I love you forever."

Once they couldn't see the limousine anymore Love, Hope and Amir went back inside the apartment. Amir was heading back into his room, to get up the nerve to make that phone call.

"Amir, I need the phone so I can confirm my flight plans back to Cali tomorrow."

He gave the phone to Love, but what he didn't know was that she had pressed redial once she had the phone in her hand. Love knew Amir had called the girl's number several times but hung up. Once the phone started to ring on the other end she asked Amir to hold it for her while she took care of something and to listen out for the airline reservationist to come on line. Amir took the phone and listened as it ringed without suspicion, but then, a familiar voice answered the phone. "Hello, Hello." He realized his aunt had just tricked him and it was the girl he had danced with from the wedding reception on the phone with him. Love was secretly peeking from behind the refrigerator door at him. Hope came out of the bathroom and saw Love spying on Amir.

"Love, what's going on?"

"Shhh, Amir's on the phone with that girl from the reception."

"Finally he's brave enough to make the call and not hang up."

"Uh, not exactly Hope, I'll tell you later."

They both tried to pretend that they were not eavesdropping on Amir's phone call, but they were carefully listening to every word that came out of his mouth. After he hung up the phone, he knew his mother and aunt were eavesdropping and waiting with their questions.

"So, tell us what did she say?"

"I'm not telling you anything Aunt Love cause that was a real dirty trick you played on me."

"That's alright you don't have to tell me, that big grin on your face is saying it all, so she said yes, am I right?"

Hope was so excited for Amir. "She said yes, that's great. I can't believe it's your first official date."

"Well I don't know if you can consider it a date, because she said her father will not let her go out with any boy that he hasn't had a chance to talk to. So, she said if I wanted to, I could come to church with them tomorrow and then to Sunday brunch to talk to her parents. Then, if they approve of me we can go out on a date alone."

Love started laughing. "Oh boy, good luck with that one Amir, you sure you want to date this girl. She sounds like a whole lot of trouble, high maintenance."

"Don't listen to your aunt Amir. I think it's a good thing she has a strict father, she must be a good girl then."

"You ever think her father is so strict because she is a bad girl. Just because she goes to church does not make her a nice girl Hope. Heck, remember all those loose girls we went to church with growing up at Nana's."

"Let me repeat myself. Amir, don't listen to your aunt. You should go. Where's the church, I'll drop you off, you don't know your way around New York yet."

"It's the church Auntie Faith got married in, that's why she was at the wedding reception, she's a member and one of the church greeters. Her father is the pastor of the church."

"Oh boy, the pastor's kids are always the worse ones, everyone knows that." Love was finding this very humorous, but Hope was serious, after all this was going to be her son's first date, it was a big deal.

"Now just be quiet, Love, you're going to make him nervous. Don't worry, everything will be fine Amir."

"Hope, I mean mother…" Then he flashed Hope the most adorable smile, "can you come with me to the church?"

Hope thought her heart had just melted right in her chest when he called her mother, and she thought to herself, "I would go to the ends of the Earth for you." "Amir, of course I'll go, and we should come up with some kind of sign. In case you want to be alone with her, okay."

"How about the flanking position sign?"

"Oh yeah that could work, just make sure you are covert about it when you give it to me. Like you can just make a small V in front of your face and then just put your head in your hands, no one will notice that. Let's test it out."

Love shook her head at them as she walked off into the den. She was thinking, "they are perfect together, two military geeks." She decided to watch a repeat of Law and Order on TV, then she thought, "I don't want to see anything serious, maybe Faith has Tivo'd some Ellen shows. Now she's hilarious. I love her."

After Amir went back in his room to listen to his music, Hope joined Love in the living room. She was already missing Love and she hadn't even left yet. Love was sitting on the sofa laughing at the *Ellen* show.

"You know I met Ellen once, Hope."

"For real? You and her, didn't ...."

"No get your mind out the gutter Hope. I've met a lot of entertainment people working in LA. I've even met Oprah, and before you ask, no to that question too."

"I'm just saying you're the one who said all that stuff about being an expert and everything on men and women. So anyways Love, when is your flight leaving?"

"First thing in the morning. This will give me a little time to readjust before starting work on Monday."

"I was thinking maybe you could come to church tomorrow with me and Amir and then we could drop you off at the airport. You know, this is so important to him, and he's so nervous meeting the girl's parents, he really wants me to come and I don't want to miss it."

"I understand. You're a mother now, your son comes first. Don't worry I'll just catch a cab to the airport. I really don't want to go to church twice in one weekend. I'll call you as soon as I get back home and settled in and you can tell me all about how Amir's first, semi-date with the girl and all the parents there went."

"Well, were you able to get on the same flight back as John?"

"No, that's the thing. John told me earlier today at the wedding reception that he's not coming back to California. Apparently, he's accepted a position as pastor out here in New York. I don't know if that is how they refer to it, as a position, or a calling, whatever, but anyway, he's resigned from the firm and he's not coming back, end of story."

"Oh no. What are you going to do without him?"

Love was surprised about the comment Hope had just made. She had never acted like she depended on John. At least she didn't think she did. "What do you mean, what am I going to do without him? I'm not going to do anything. I mean John and I are just friends Hope."

"Yeah, I know you said that before, but it seemed to me that there was something more going on between the two of you; something much deeper."

"Well maybe there was, but there's sure no chance of it now."

"Not necessarily, I mean, the two of you could try a long distance romance."

"Come on Hope, he's going to be pastor of some church right in New York, but he might as well be over in Tim Buk Tu, as far as I'm concerned. I'm not exactly pastor's girlfriend material."

"Why do you say that? I mean you are going to be coming out here all the time to visit us anyway, right? So you can see him too, and you should start going to church again, that is what Nana would have wanted for us. You can go to his church. I think you would make a great pastor's wife one day."

"I'm definitely going to be out here all the time, at least every other weekend, I promise. It's just that I'm not going to go back to church just because of a man, or even for Nana. That's my decision to make and I won't be pressured into it. I don't believe in all of that religious stuff. I do care for John, but he's a pastor now. He doesn't need someone like me. He needs a woman, well a woman, more like Faith, than like me, you know what I mean."

"Why don't you let John decide what he needs for himself, because it seems to me that he loves you, and he's not interested in any other women. The question is do you love him?"

Love was quiet for a long time, and for the first time she finally was honest to herself about what she felt for John. "I've known him forever, and he has been my best friend for so many years. I think I do, I do love him, Hope."

"So why don't you tell him, and just see what happens?"

"I can't Hope, I'm just not ready."

"What do you mean by ready, ready for what, what's holding you back if you know you want him?"

"I'm not exactly sure. But I need to know that when I tell him I love him that I can be the type of woman he deserves me to be, or that I'm at least working on it. And I know I'm not that woman, not yet, maybe not ever."

Hope didn't know what else to say to Love. After all she was probably the last person who needed to be giving other people love advice. So Hope just hugged her sister, and said, "okay then I'll just say a prayer over it for you. Oh, by the way earlier at the reception, Mary and her new husband asked me if we could all come over for dinner tonight at their house. What do you say?"

"I guess so, we got to eat right, and neither one of us know how to cook. Besides I'll be able to see if there are any last minute tips Mr. Swanson wants to tell me about being the newest partner at the firm."

"Good then, I'll go call Mary and tell her we will be there. Just one more thing I have to ask you Love."

"What's that?"

"How could you say you don't *believe* after everything we've been through within the past month? Can't you see that God has blessed us?"

"If anything He's blessed you and Faith and He let me slip through the cracks. I don't deserve His blessings."

Hope tried to stay and talk to Love some more about it, but Love didn't want to listen. "Seriously Hope I just want to relax and watch television right now."

Hope went into the bedroom and after she got off the phone with Mary she got on her knees and prayed for her sister Love.

So, later that night they went to dinner at the Swanson's home. They were greeted at the door, by fifteen very energetic kids. Even for a house like the Swanson's, which was the size of a mansion, all those kids made it pretty noisy in there. But it didn't seem to bother Mary at all, or Mr. Swanson. The two of them seemed to be completely at peace and content with their surroundings. Mary gave Love, Hope and Amir a huge bear hug.

"We have a meal like a thanksgiving feast ready for tonight."

Amir's stomach was already growling. He had eaten enough for an army at the wedding reception earlier that afternoon, but he already felt like he was starving again. "It sure smells good, Ma'am."

"Don't call me Ma'am Amir, we are family now."

"What would you like me to call you?"

Mary was quiet. She wasn't sure herself what Amir should call her, maybe Miss Mary or Aunt Mary would be good. Then Hope blurted out a suggestion, "Just call her Nana, Amir."

Mary smiled at Hope and her eyes began to swell up. But then Mary looked over at Love with a worried sort of look. Mary wasn't sure about how Love felt about the newly appointed title, and she also wasn't sure if she was worthy of being called her friend Jennie's old title.

Love knew exactly what Mary was thinking when she saw Mary look over at her anxiously. "Yeah I think that is the perfect name for Amir to call Mary, "Nana", it's perfect. Nana use to watch over all the kids and now you are doing the same thing Mary, watching over everyone else's kids."

Mary smiled at her new family and announced in a booming voice that everyone was there and it was time to eat. The dining room table was decked out with food. Amir thought he had never seen so much food in one place in his entire life. One thing was clear already about Hope, she was a great soldier but she could not cook anything, she even messed up boiled eggs. Amir had already figured out he would probably be doing most of the cooking for them both. Then Love noticed John sitting at a corner seat at the table, and John said, "About time you guys got here, cause I'm ready to eat."

Hope smiled at John and then she looked over at Love, and whispered, "you can't fight fate." "Good to see you again John, I haven't really had a chance to talk to you during the wedding."

"Hi Hope, Amir, Love. Well I have to warn you guys, I don't do much talking when I'm hungry and eating, but we will have plenty of time to talk after dinner. So Love I guess I'll get to spend a little more time with you before you fly out after all?"

"I guess so. Mary, you sure did go through a lot of trouble tonight. This is so extravagant. Thank you for inviting us."

"Oh, I didn't do this all on my own. With all these children I would have to cook enough for an army, every day. My husband, got us not one, but two world renowned chefs for tonight. But the kids and I did prepare some special dishes on our own. It was a lot of fun. I'm just having so much fun, having my own family. Everyday is better than the next day."

"That's good Mary, I'm so happy for you, and I know Nana would have been so happy for you too."

Mary went to gather up her husband and all of her children, and then they all sat down to eat. John motioned to Love to take a seat right next to him, but Amir inadvertently grabbed Hope and Love's hands and rushed over to sit across the table from John with his mother and aunt on both sides of him.

John smiled, he wanted to be close to Love, but he couldn't be upset at Amir; he was happy to see the boy so at peace after everything he had been through. Children are so resilient, he thought. "So Amir, are you starving like Marvin, like I am?"

"Who's Marvin, John?"

All the older people started laughing. "Oh he's no one Amir, it's just an old folks saying. Finally, everyone's here and seated. Can we eat now Mary?"

"John since you are a pastor now and I still can't believe one of my best attorneys just up and left the firm. Well anyway like I was saying since you are a pastor now how about you do the honors of saying grace for your old boss?"

"No problem Mr. Swanson. God bless this food and the hands that prepared it. Amen."

"Wow you weren't joking about being hungry John. I hope your sermon on Sunday isn't as short, or I might see you back at the firm Monday morning", said Love.

"This goes without saying John, but you know you are always welcome to come back to the firm, just in case." Mr. Swanson was also now having his doubts about John's sudden career change after hearing his unimpressive grace.

John tried not to laugh at what Love said because his mouth was already full of food, but everyone else at the table started laughing, and it felt like a real family dinner. Everyone felt it. Once John had chewed and swallowed his food he said, "Thank you Mr. Swanson but this is where I need to be, I'm sure of it."

The food was delicious, but Love really wasn't that hungry, plus she was very distracted. She tried not to stare at John the entire night but she couldn't help looking over at him every chance she got. Love was also really enjoying the new family she now belonged to. She saw how comfortable John was in his conversations with everyone else in the room and she thought to herself, it seemed like with or without her, John now belonged to this family also.

When the night was over and they were all about to head home, Mary, said to Love and Hope, "do you think you girls could come to church with me tomorrow? I'm going to be baptized and become a member of your Nana's old church in Queens, where Faith got married?"

"What a coincidence. Amir and I were already planning on going there tomorrow for service. Love's not coming she says she's leaving out first thing in the morning. Amir was invited by his new girlfriend, and I'm just coming to keep an eye on him."

Amir overheard Hope and yelled, "She's not my girlfriend, not yet."

"Well I really wish you could be there too Love. You see at the wedding I was thinking, thinking about Nana and thinking about God. I want to dedicate the rest of my life to God. I want to call Jesus my savior, just like your Nana always prayed I would. I wish Faith could be there too, but I don't want to wait until she gets back from her honeymoon. I want to do it now in front of the whole church."

Love was feeling pressured, she really didn't want to go back to church again, especially two times in one weekend. "Well I would like to be there Mary, I really would, but my flight leaves before the morning service."

Mr. Swanson was eavesdropping on their conversation and interrupted. "Love aren't you taking the company jet. I know it's last minute but I will call the pilot now and tell him to change your flight plans because you will be leaving out later. It will be fine. You are a partner and I told you the jet is at your disposal whenever you need to use it. Remember you are in charge, the pilot is only your very trained and expensive chauffeur."

"Um, thank you Mr. Swanson, well Mary I guess I will be there after all." Love knew there was no way she was going to contradict what Mr. Swanson said, that would probably be career suicide, plus she really didn't want to hurt Mary's feelings anyway."

Then John walked up to them and he whispered to Love, "wish I had clout with you like old Mr. Swanson does. Somehow I seriously doubt I will be able to get you to agree to come visit my new church so easily."

"That's right John. Oh, and I meant to tell you good luck on your first day tomorrow and your sermon." Love wanted to say so much more to John but she could never find the right words. Her feelings for him were always so confusing to her. She wanted to be with him so badly, but then she was also scared of being with him at the same time. Everyone had went back into the dining room to say their goodbyes and collect their doggy bags from the chefs.

John pulled Love aside to a quiet part of the house, and Love felt her heart quicken.

"Love can I drive you back to your sister's house so we can have just a little time alone? Maybe we can stop off and get some coffee at a café and just talk for a while. I have so much I'd like to say to you."

Love fought back her desire to say yes, and her desire to just kiss him. He was standing so close to her that she could practically taste him as he whispered his questions to her. "I'm sorry John I have so much to get done back at Faith's place before I leave tomorrow, and I haven't even started packing."

John was disappointed, and he didn't try to hide it. "Well I guess I will have to settle with a phone call to you tomorrow night then, that's if you pick up."

"I'm sorry John."

"No, that's alright Love. You have a lot to do, I understand."

Everyone had returned to the front room to end the night. They all gave each other hugs and kisses, and said their goodbyes for the night at the door. John hugged Love at the door and she felt her body go weak in his arms. She wanted so much to stay in his arms. It was as if the chemistry between them was growing by leaps and bounds ever since their first kiss in Africa. Back at Faith's house Love dreamed about John all that night.

At church the next morning, Love sat through the service, uncomfortable, feeling as if she didn't belong there. There were the pristine ladies sitting in their big hats. The choir sounded better than any band she'd seen in LA. They had the whole congregation jumping and after every pause someone would yell out, "Amen". There were people talking in tongues during the service, and screaming out praises. The pastor was talking about the sins of the world, and how to be a saint in a sinners' world.

Love imagined if all the women and elders there knew all she had done in her life that they would all stand up and just quietly usher her out the side door. It was obvious Hope did not feel the same way. Hope and Amir were both all into the sermon. Hope was crying sometimes and praising God and yelling out, thank you Jesus. Hope was all into it and so was Amir. And from the looks of it Amir wasn't even preoccupied with looking over at the pastor's daughter, who he was sitting next to being that he was her guest. Love was surprised about that most of all. She assumed Amir would spend the whole sermon staring at his new love interest. After all wasn't that the whole reason he was there.

It was then that Love realized she seemed to be the only one in the church who wasn't lost in the pastor's sermon. It seemed like she was the only one who wasn't moved in an extraordinary, spiritual way. Love couldn't help wondering, "what's wrong with me?" Then finally the pastor was finished with his sermon. Love was thinking, "thank God, I thought he was never going to wrap it up." Love looked at her watch, noticing they had been there for almost three hours already and now the pastor was making an altar call. She thought, "I should have known." He wanted the new members to come up. He introduced them to the church. He explained that not only had they all decided to join the church as members, but that they also had decided to declare to the church that Jesus was their savior and to be baptized that day. Then one by one each member was dunked in the water. When the last member was baptized the pastor asked for the elders of the church and family members to come up and pray over them.

Mary looked so proud to be standing up there. Mary was crying tears of joy and her husband was too. Mr. Swanson, Hope and Amir went to stand and pray next to her. Love stayed in her seat, she felt uncomfortable enough. There was no way she was going to get up and pretend she was praying in front of everyone.

Mary had her eyes closed as she listened to the elders praying over her, and she could have swore she heard Jennie's voice whispering, "see Mary, God does answer our prayers, he does."

After service was over, the church had a reception with food in the basement for its' new members and their guest. Love stayed and helped the others clean and put away the dishes. She saw how happy everyone seemed around her, and how connected they all seemed to be, but somehow even though she was surrounded by people, she still felt all alone. She had already called a cab with her cell phone to take her to the airport, and she had placed her one suitcase in the front lobby closet. The pastor's daughter came in the kitchen and told Love her cab was waiting for her outside. Love told everyone she had to head out, that she had a big day ahead of her tomorrow. Hope said, "wait Love, Amir and I will come with you and see you off."

"No Hope, you and Amir stay and enjoy your selves." It was obvious to Love, that Amir wasn't ready to leave. He was looking very comfortable around the pastor's daughter, and also around her parents. Hope wanted to spend what little time she had left that day with her sister. Then the pastor's wife offered to give Amir a ride home later on that day, if it was okay with Hope.

Amir was in the back, secretly mouthing, "please", to Hope. Hope said thank you to the pastor and his wife for volunteering to drive her son home, and then she left out to take Love to the airport.

On the cab ride to the airport, Hope talked about how nice the pastor and his family seemed and how down to earth they were. She mentioned how the pastor talked about all the different outreach programs and members groups they have at the church and how she thought she would find out more and join some of them. Love noticed how Hope's face seemed shining with the expectation of a new and joyful life ahead of her. Love was happy for her sister. She was so happy for both of her sisters. But she couldn't help but think how it seemed like after all she had been through she was just going back to the same life she had before and she didn't understand why going back didn't make her happy. After all, her life back in LA was everything she thought she had ever wanted, success, power, she had friends, and riches. Now she also had her sisters, and she knew she would see them every single weekend. Mr. Swanson had already promised the company jet was hers to use anytime she wanted. Besides, even if she did work in New York, her work would keep her so busy during the week that she doubted she would be able to see her sisters during the weekdays if she lived in New York anyway. She knew she would talk to them every day on the phone also. So why was she so sad? She had everything now. Yet she still felt so unfulfilled. She thought about John, but she wasn't sure being with him would make her happy either.

Hope noticed Love seemed as if she was in another world, not really listening to what she was saying to her, but thinking about something entirely different. "Is something wrong Love?"

"No, nothing's wrong, I'm fine."

"Are you sure because you don't seem fine?"

"I guess I'm a little sad about leaving, that's all."

"I know, I'm sad to see you and Faith gone too, but it's only temporary. I mean Faith will be back in two weeks and I'll be seeing you on Friday night, right?"

"Definitely Hope, I'll be back Friday night I promise. I was thinking, on Saturday we can have a girls' day at the spa, and then on Saturday night let's have a ladies night out."

"Um sure that sounds great." But Hope was really wondering what Amir would do all alone while she spent a whole day and night out with Love. Love seemed excited so she didn't want to mention her misgivings, so instead she said, "you just promise to call me as soon as you get in, alright?"

"Yes Ma'am, as soon as I land I will call you."

"So is it John? Is that's what has you looking so down? Why don't you just stop by and see him before you fly out, Love?"

"Okay maybe it is John, a little, I admit it. But it's also more than that, I just haven't really put my finger on it Hope. But I don't want you to worry about it, okay."

"I won't worry, if you don't forget to call every day."

"Deal."

Once they arrived at the airport Hope hugged Love and she knew then she couldn't let her go without finally being honest. Then she abruptly blurted it out,

"Love I never met you that day long ago, at the bus stop, because...., Mr. Smith, my foster dad, had found out about our plans and had threatened to kill you if I ever told you that, ... he raped me. He used to rape me, all the time, Love, all the time. I should have told you. I'm sorry I didn't. I often thought about it and maybe if I would have told you, you would have known I was staying with Ms. Armstrong and you would have spent your last night at Ms. Armstrong's apartment with me and her, and maybe you would have been at her apartment waiting for me the night of the fire and who knows maybe you would have stayed in New York if you knew I wasn't dead and we would have never been separated all these years..... I'm sorry, sorry that I wasn't honest with you and I'm sorry I didn't try to find you. "

Love looked at Hope in shock. A part of her had suspected that bad things probably happened to Hope, but she didn't know what. But Love never once thought it was that bad, and now she just felt a deep sense of guilt for not protecting her little sister. "That's a lot of maybes Hope. It's not your fault, if anything it's my fault we were separated, I'm the oldest. I was suppose to protect you. I'm so sorry Hope, I'm so sorry, I wasn't there for you."

"No it's not your fault either Love. He was a sick man and I'm okay now. There was nothing you could have done, you didn't know. I've even forgiven him for what he did, he was a sick, sick man, but I wanted to tell you just because I didn't want to keep any more secrets from you. And I needed to tell you, that what happened to me is what kept me from God for so many years. For so many years I was angry at God, for allowing it to happen to me. I was angry at God for everything, losing Nana, you and Faith and then for letting Mr. Smith hurt me. I noticed you didn't come to the altar, and I knew I had to tell you then what had happened. I wanted you to know, if there is ever anything you want or need to tell me..., well I just don't want anything that's burdening you, to keep you from God, like it did me for so many years."

"Hope I promise that if I ever need to talk, you know, you will be the first person I call. But really I'm okay. It sounds like my life has been a bed of roses compared to your life Hope, and I feel so bad and guilty about that."

"Don't feel bad for me, I'm happy and at peace now, and that is all that matters."

On the plane ride back to LA, Love had a lot to think about, like imagining all the horrible things that had happened to Hope. She wondered how Hope survived all she had gone through and how she could seem so happy and grounded. She wished she was as strong and as good as Hope.

Love thought to herself, "I don't feel like crying, but I also don't feel all joyful and happy like my sisters are feeling, I just sort of feel, empty inside, just empty."

She wondered why she just couldn't feel excited about coming back to her home in La, back to her firm and her new title as partner. When Love reached the airport in LA, and got off the jet, there was no one waiting for her because she hadn't called anyone to meet her; she wasn't in the mood to see her friends. She grabbed the cab to her luxurious home in the Hills. She found her mailbox filled with mail, and her answering machine so filled with messages from her friends and male acquaintances that no more messages could be left. She knew she had some great girlfriends in LA. She had girlfriends who loved her no matter who she was or what she did, but she still never opened up to them either. She saw on the kitchen table all the pictures her real estate agent left of the beach houses she was considering purchasing. Her agent was also one of her close friends. But she didn't feel like looking at the pictures, or going through the mail, or returning phone calls, she didn't even feel like going through her emails to see what her schedule looked like back at the firm for tomorrow.

She sat back in her sofa and she picked up the photo album on the coffee table. Then she looked at the pictures of herself and her friends in California. There was a picture of her and John at one of the office barbeques that she paused and stared at for a long time. She felt something pierce through the emptiness she felt inside when she thought about John. Looking at John's picture filled her heart up. She thought briefly, "I should call him", but as soon as she thought it, she changed her mind.

Then she looked at the pictures that she kept in the back of the photo album. The ones that she kept in the cuff of the book, and never displayed, because it was always too painful to explain to people when they asked who the girls in the picture were. Love looked at the few pictures she had of her and her sisters, back when they were little girls, sitting on Nana's stoop, with Nana.

In a feverish rush, she opened one of her suitcases and threw the clothes out on the floor. She was searching for the wedding pictures they had taken with the instant camera at Faith's wedding. Love had went and gotten those pictures developed right after the wedding reception. Then she ran to her hallway closet where she had extra picture frames sitting there collecting dust. She wiped the frames off and she put the old pictures of her and her sisters in frames as well as the new pictures. Then she placed the pictures on the coffee table.

The whole time Love had lived at her house she only had expensive art on the wall, and expensive statutes on her coffee tables, never any pictures of friends or family. The one photo album is all she had. Mostly because she didn't want to seem strange when her friends came by to visit, and not have any personal pictures at all. Love sat back and looked at the pictures of herself, and her sisters in the frames. She realized for the first time ever, this house she lived in felt almost like a home with those pictures up. Then Love remembered, she was suppose to have called Hope as soon as she had landed. So she got her cell phone out of her purse and called Hope. The first thing Love said when Hope picked up the phone was, "I know I should have called you an hour ago. I was thinking, do you think it's too early to call Faith up?"

"Naah." And they called Faith up on three way. Faith answered her cell right away. "Hey guys what's up?"

"I just got back to LA, and Amir has a girlfriend."

"Amir has a girlfriend?! Boy, he doesn't waste any time. Hope, you've got your hands filled with him Sis. Well I gotta say Hawaii is even more beautiful than what I imagined. I'm glad to hear from you twos, I miss you guys already."

Hope and Love heard Darryl in the background yell, "I know that's your sisters, tell them I said hi, and I'm going to go get in the shower now babe. Tell them that you better be off the phone by the time I'm out."

Faith giggled, "okay hubby. Hey he's in the shower now, I can talk. I just wanted to tell you guys, *it is*."

"*It is* what?" Love and Hope both asked.

"When you are in love, *it* is just like the movies, just like the romance novels, just like you always dreamed it would be when you was a girl."

"Well Hope I guess our little sister, is really, all grown up now, after almost thirty years, you're a *real* woman now." Then the three of them laughed together.

When Love was off the phone she looked around her home and she started to feel empty and lonely again. She thought about John and wanted to call him, but she felt like she shouldn't. The two of them lived such different lives she thought, maybe it was better to just let her friendship and whatever else she felt for him slowly drift away. Instead she looked at her journal book, sitting in her open suitcase and she decided to write, write what she was thinking about John versus telling him what she was thinking. Love's journal was still the only time she was totally honest about all her secret fears, desires, and feelings. She knew it was messed up that she had not one person in her life she had felt she could be totally open and honest with, but it was what it was, and it had worked for her for years, she didn't know how to open up anymore.

Now that she had her sisters in her life again, she felt like maybe one day she could get to the point where she could be open with them about everything. But she had to admit she wasn't there yet, and a part of her wondered if she ever would be. She was just so use to being alone, being disconnected from others. So once again, like so many times in her past, she resorted to writing what ailed her down in the pages of her journal.

She wrote love letters and poems that she knew she would never send to John, but somehow writing her feelings down made her feel less burdened by them, even if only for a moment. After she finished writing she decided to get herself ready and prepared for her first day at the firm as partner. She knew this was the day she had lived her whole life in California for to walk into her firm not as an associate, but as a partner. But she wasn't excited about it, she knew she should be more excited about it, but for some reason, she just wasn't. She had always pictured John being there at the firm on the day she became partner and sharing it with her best buddy. Now she felt like preparing for work tomorrow, and going through the tons of emails her co-workers and the partners no doubt had sent her while she was away was nothing less than a chore. She fixed herself some coffee and she got through her work.

Hours later she was finished with her work and laying in bed still tense and wound up, but exhausted all at the same time. She hated nights like this where she felt so exhausted, but insomnia kept her up. In the past when she had insomnia she would call up one of her male friends to help her get a good night's sleep. Sleep aids, really any drugs wasn't Love's thing, not after seeing what it did to her mom and dad. If wine couldn't do the trick then a man always did.

She just stared up at the ceiling and she started thinking about John. She thought about how close he was to her the other night, when he was whispering to her at Mary's house after dinner. She wanted so bad to kiss him then, to go off somewhere and be alone with him. She wished she would have now. She thought about how good he smelled, like coconut and spices. How whenever he was close to her it made her heart speed up and her body heat up like she had a fever. She thought about how long it had been since that kiss they shared in Africa. Then she thought about that kiss, and how his lips were so soft, and so full. Love knew she had never felt so lost before in a kiss, and she couldn't help but remember how his kiss left her feeling. The next thing she knew she had found another way to relax herself in the quietness and darkness, alone in her bedroom while she thought about John. Before she knew it she was falling fast asleep, after whispering John's name out loud, several times....

The next day Love arrived at work bright and early. Love was the first person to arrive at the firm for work besides Wendy, the early morning receptionist. Wendy was excited to see Love. Most of the female staff admired and respected Love for being competitive, but also down to earth. There were only a handful of female attorneys that worked at the firm and it was amazing to most of the employees there, that the next partner after twenty two years of no associate being selected as partner, was going to be a woman, and a black woman at that.

"Good morning Love, did you enjoy your vacation? We really missed you around here."

"Thank you Wendy. I had a great vacation, thanks for asking." Then Love started walking down the hallway to her office; when Wendy yelled to her, "Love, you're going the wrong way."

"What do you mean Wendy?"

"Your office is now located on the fifteenth floor, *you know* where all the partners offices are located. So you need to take the elevator to the right, up there, and the early morning receptionist up there, his name is Kevin, he will be there to give you your keys to your new office."

"Oh. I knew they would be moving me, but I didn't think they would do it before I got back. Thanks Wendy, well I guess I'll be seeing you later." Love walked back towards the elevator to go up a few more floors. Before the elevator doors opened, Wendy whispered, "you go get them." Love smiled at Wendy, and she couldn't help teasing her by humming the theme song from *"The Jeffersons"*, "where a moving on up…" Wendy was an older black woman in her late fifties and Love knew she would really get a kick out of hearing her sing that song.

She could hear Wendy laughing to herself even after the elevator doors shut behind her.

Love had been on the partner's floor several times, but like most of the other associates, usually she was there for firm meetings in the conference room. However, because Love had a special relationship with Mr. Swanson, he had invited her up to his office to share a brandy on the balcony every once in a blue moon. The other attorneys were always envious and had a million questions to ask her about what the inside of the senior partner's office looked like. Love had fun telling them how incredible it was, and how the offices looked like penthouse apartments. But today Love was on the fifteenth floor, the prestigious partner's floor, to go sit behind her own desk, in her own office. For the first time Love started to feel excited about being back to work and in LA. When the elevator stopped and Love got off she saw Kevin. Kevin was a third year law student and the partner's part-time receptionist and law clerk.

"Good morning, Ms. King. My name is Kevin. Wendy already informed me that you were here. Here are your office keys. They already transferred all your belongings from your old office to your new office. Your office is the third one to the left."

"Thank you Kevin."

"No problem, you just let me know if there is anything at all you need. Wendy already told me how you take your coffee, so I took the liberty to leave a hot cup and the newspaper on your desk Ma'am."

Love smiled. Kevin was very pleasant to look at and very young. "Please Kevin just call me Love, all the staff did on my old floor. Ma'am is for old ladies and you don't think I'm old do you?"

"Oh no Ms. King, no not at all, I mean Love."

"That's good because did you know I'm the youngest partner at any law firm on the West Coast. At least that's what I read in the California Lawyer's weekly yesterday."

"Wow Ms. King, I mean Love, sorry."

"I know that's what I thought when I read it, Wow. You know Kevin I think I'm really going to like it up here, especially with you as the receptionist."

Kevin started to blush. Kevin was not use to anyone flirting with him, especially someone so beautiful, and his superior at work. He was a young law student, with brown reddish curly hair, pale milky skin and huge dimples in his cheeks. Love thought he was just adorable. Being that Love was a natural flirt, she really couldn't help herself but to flirt a little with Kevin.

"I'm sorry Kevin I didn't mean to embarrass you. So are any of the other partners in yet?"

Kevin stumbled over his words for a quick second before he regained his bearings and was able to answer Love. "No, Ms. K…, Love you're the first one in. In fact, none of the other partners come in this early unless they have an early morning appointment. If you want I can ring you as soon as the others show up, but most likely, they will all be going straight to your office to greet you anyway. I know most of the staff is intimidated by the other partners, but they are really a bunch of laid back, friendly guys. I mean they have no reason not to be when you think about it, they are all filthy rich."

"I guess you're right about that. I hope one day you will be referring to me as "filthy" too Kevin." Love gave Kevin a quick, very charming smile and then she continued down the hall to her office.

As Kevin watched her walking away he could tell his cheeks were hot from blushing again. He thought, "I am really going to have to control this now that I will be seeing her regularly." Kevin had went to observe one of Love's murder trial's his first year in law school, and he'd had a crush on her ever since. He couldn't believe he would now be working in such close proximity to her.

Once Love got to her office the first thing she noticed was the name plaque that was on her door. *Love E. King, Esquire,* and underneath that was, *Partner.* When Love opened the door to her new office she was happily surprised. She expected her office as a partner would be bigger, and fancier, but she never expected this. Her office was and exact duplicate of

Mr. Swanson's office. Love always assumed that Mr.
Swanson's office was the best office in the building because he
was the founding partner of the firm. He started off as a solo-
practice attorney, almost fifty years ago right out of law school,
back then the firm was called Swanson's Law Office. So she
just assumed Mr. Swanson's office was just special, she had
never imagined that all the partners had the exact same office
design. Love quietly closed the door to her office behind her,
and then she quietly, jumped up and down. She felt like a kid in
a candy store for the first time. She locked the door so no one
could walk in on her acting so juvenile. The office was covered
with balloons and flowers from all the partners, associates and
staff members that Love worked with. First thing Love did was
to take the time to read all the cards that were attached to the
different bundles of balloons, flowers and bottles of wine. There
were also various gifts from old clients among the other gifts.
And there was a bouquet of flowers from John, his card was
simple, "Congratulations Love, and I miss you." Love felt a
sudden pain in her heart, but she quickly told herself to dismiss it
and to stay focus on the here and now.

She shook it off and moved on to the three other large
rooms inside her office. Besides the actual office area, where
her desk, files, books, guest chairs and computer were located
there was also a conference room, a relaxation room and a very
spacious bathroom. The conference room included a flat screen
TV, swivel chairs, podium and an overhead for presentations.
The relaxation room in the rear of the office was what Love was
really excited about, it was equipped with another flat screen TV,
a stereo system with an outlet for her IPOD, a pull out sofa that
turned into a bed, love seats, a kitchen with all the amenities, a
wet bar, free and fully stocked with all types of spirits, a
treadmill and free weights, because the partners all knew Love
was an exercise fanatic. The private full bathroom had a huge
Jacuzzi tub, and another balcony, overlooking the beautiful,
foggy City of Angels, and a walk in closet. Love thought to
herself, "I could live here in this office, and never need to go
home again." She knew that was exactly what the senior
partners were thinking when they first designed these partner
suites for themselves.

As an attorney, you were expected to work constantly, and after a while your office became a second home. Becoming partner really didn't change any of that, except that no one kept tabs on how you put your 80 hours in. Partners were considered to always be working. If they were playing golf, they were actually making a deal. If they were out eating dinner, they probably were handling a client between bites. There was no doubt that they still worked just as hard. But now Love could see that the benefit of becoming partner was not just the money, the power, the prestige. It was obvious the biggest benefit was going to be the extra perks. Before Love could really take it all in, she heard her phone ringing and people knocking at her door. She took a deep breath in, and said to herself, "this is my life, everything I've worked for and always wanted, now it's time to get back to living it, and stop acting like a crazy woman, depressed for no good reason at all." She turned around, whipped back her hair, and walked over to her office door to greet her co-workers and to start her work day. She was determined to stop acting like the pathetic, love sick girl she had become within the last month and to start acting like the confident, independent, strong woman on the title of her new office door again, "Love E. King, Esquire, Partner."

Chapter 19
Then the Lord God said, "it is not good for man to be alone. I will make an helper who is just right for him."[24]

    Six months had passed by and John's church was growing and striving. John had improved on so many things in the church. He had initiated ten different ministries that the church did not have. Now with John as their pastor, the church had become well known in the community as a place to go for food, for shelter, for spiritual help, and for guidance. This was the original mission of the small church when it was first founded, but as the founders got older, the spirit of the mission died away. But now the once small church was growing by leaps and bounds. John's congregation now loved and respected their new pastor; even though his first day did start off sort of rocky.

    On John's first day as pastor his sermon was on the Christian concept of "church". He preached about how he did not want to have one member in his church go home that day worrying about how they were going to pay their rent or put food on the table for their children, while some members were going home worried about how they were going to buy a bigger home they didn't really need, or afford both the BMW and the new boat, or take a vacation in one of the tropical islands versus the Poconos. He wanted the members in his church to look at each other and care for one another just like family. John ended his sermon with some very stirring words about the true Christian meaning of church.

    "Today is a new day for our church. I stood outside the front doors of our church building, *and that is all it is, a building.* I want you all to remember that a building is not the church. *We* are the church. It's pouring down raining today and I saw some people drive up in their cars and get out all nice and dry, but I looked down the street and I saw some young mothers walking the four blocks from the city bus stops with their children to make it to the building; and I wondered didn't they know anyone from church who could give them a ride this

---

[24] Genesis 2:18

morning? I looked across the streets and saw young boys
hanging out at the corner grocery store smoking cigarettes and
drinking booze on a Sunday morning, and then I saw our
parishioners pass by those young boys, and I did not see anyone
stop an invite one of those lost children to come to church with
them this morning. I'm here today to say, today is a new day,
my brothers and sisters. Today *we* will stop just coming to the
church building and *we* will start *being* the church. And I call
you my brother's and sister's, not because we share the same
ancestry, but because we have the same father, Our Almighty
Father God and our big brother is, Jesus Christ, and we all
belong to *His* family. And when I stood outside at the front
doors of this, building, I heard my Father, and my Big Brother
speaking as one to me, and He said, "John, do you love me?"
And I answered, "you know I love you God." And He said then,
"feed my sheep." So today, won't be church as usual, and I
pray, that those of you that don't like that it won't be church as
usual will not leave, but my Father God is telling me, "John, if
you love me, feed my sheep", and that's what we are going to do
for now on, starting today….

      Now don't get me wrong, there is absolutely nothing
wrong with having a big house, or even two or three houses.
And there's nothing wrong with having the BMW, the boats and
the vacations in Hawaii. But if you say you are a Christian, if
you tell me you are one of God's children then there is
something wrong with it, if we don't try to help out our brothers
and sisters that have no home to go to, no car to drive, no food to
eat, and no job to take a vacation from. There is something
wrong with that because church is not a building, church is a
family, church is the family of God. And I don't think God
wanted us to get together every Sunday only to worship him, I
mean yes that is the main reason we come here, but think about it
we can worship God on our own all day long, everyday. I think
God wanted His church, His family to get together to also get to
know each other, help each other and love one another.
Remember *church* Jesus said, *"The most important
commandment is this, …., the Lord our God is the one and only
Lord. And you must love the Lord our God with all your heart,
all your soul, all your mind, and all your strength. The second is*

equally as important: Love your neighbor as yourself. No other commandment is greater than these. [25] "

Then there was silence, you've could have heard a pin drop at that moment. The church was quiet after hearing the shortest sermon they had ever heard. A portion of them wasn't sure whether or not to be offended, and a portion of them knew that what John had said was the truth and they felt convicted. But there were still no Hallelujahs, no Amen's coming out of the aisles. There was just quietness in the building. John had told the choir to take a break that morning, so there wasn't even any praise music playing, but the quietness didn't seem to worry John at all. John gave the congregation a few moments to let what he had just said sink in and then he started giving everyone instructions.

"Okay now everyone get out a pen and a piece of paper. Please if you don't have one ask your neighbor for one, and ushers, please go into the offices and find some extra pens and some paper for our family. Once everyone has a piece of paper and a pen, and I'm talking about children too, if they can write. When you have what you need please say, Amen."

John waited quietly for his congregation to say Amen. He heard a few snickers, a few comments, "is this church or is this school?" "What's he giving us homework?" Then finally John saw the nods of his ushers and heard a few more Amens from the congregation, and he asked, "does everyone have a pen and paper now?" And his new congregation responded with a very monotone "Amen."

"Thank you good people, now rip that piece of paper in your hand in half." And they all did as John instructed them. "Now on one piece of paper I want you to write down something you desperately think you need right now in your life more than anything else, something you don't have, and on the other piece of paper I want you to write down something you have, but you really don't need, and don't use. Take your time and think about it before you write it down. Then my ushers are going to come around with the baskets. The baskets with the scarlet ribbons around them are to put the *don't have* notes in, and the baskets

---

[25] Mark 12:29

with the blue ribbons around it are to put the *don't need* notes in."

Eventually the ushers collected everyone's notes, and brought it up to John. John started reading from the scarlet *don't have* baskets first.

John picked up the first note and read it out loud.

"My wife is about to leave me, and I can't get a job since I got out of jail. She's been working her butt off, and providing everything for my kids. I feel like I can't win. I can't get a real job to provide for my family, but if I go back to making money like I use to I know I'll end up back in jail and away from my family, again. So I desperately need a job, a job that pays more than minimum wage, so I can support my whole family. I need someone to give this felon a second chance. I'm not asking for a hand-out just a good job."

Then John read another note out loud from the same basket. "I need a car. My car broke down, it's beyond repair. Even if it could be repaired, I can't afford it. I've been getting up at 4:00am in the morning to make it across town to my job. I've been late five times already. The boss done fussed me out, and threatened to fire me if I'm late again. I can't afford to lose this job. My eight year old girl has to get my four year old twins ready for daycare and drop them off on her way to school. Then she picks them up when she gets off from school, because I get home so late now. I still don't trust her to cook dinner, so the kids have been eating tuna-fish, peanut butter and jelly sandwiches and cold cereal for dinner for the past three months. My four year old twins I've noticed are starting to call my eight year old, "mommy" on mistake. I know they don't know no better, but it hurts me bad when I hear them call her that. And her eyes look so tired, her eyes look more like she is forty eight instead of only eight years old. I'm a single mom, both of the fathers of my children bailed out on me a long time ago. I'm just feeling so tired, and I guess I should be asking for a good man, but unless he come with a car that ain't gonna help none. What I really need right now is a reliable car."

John went on reading note after note. While he read he looked out at the faces of his congregation. Each note revealed that there was a member sitting right there in that church, who was in desperate need of some help. No one knew who those members were, the notes were anonymous. John started to notice that some of the members in his church were crying. He noticed how they were hugging each other, how some of them had automatically started praying, praying for the people who had written the notes.

Then John said, "I'm going to start reading from the blue *don't need* baskets now church, but I notice these baskets are nearly empty. So family if any of you have thought about something that you don't really need, that maybe you just didn't think of before, well why don't you write it down now. The ushers will come around one more time and pick up any extra *don't need* notes to fill up these blue ribbon baskets."

John looked out at his congregation, he saw people fervently writing down things on their papers. He heard them calling out to the ushers, "over here", and waving their papers in the air for the ushers to collect. Then the ushers brought back the blue ribbon baskets to John, they were now filled with *don't need* notes inside of them.

The first note John read out loud said, "I don't have any money to give away, but I do have a car and I can cook. My eye sight is too bad to drive anymore, so I need a driver. I always have plenty of food in my pantry, and I'm lonely, now that all my children are grown and my husband has passed away. So if anyone needs a cook or a nanny, I love children. I'd be happy to do it for free and provide the food for free too."

John shouted with joy. "God bless you sister whoever wrote this note. You just confirmed what God was saying to me, "Feed my sheep." Now that single mom with the three girls. The one who needed the car, if you can put away your pride, please come up here, and meet your sister has a car, who love's kids and can cook. Now that's a true blessing. Can I get an Amen?" Then the congregation shouted, "Amen".

The older lady who had offered her cooking and nanny services stood up and walked up to the altar with John, but no one else got up. John called out to his congregation again, "remember young mother, this is your family, no need to be ashamed to have pride with your own family. That goes for all of us. We are here to help each other, not to look down on one another, not to condemn each other, but to love each other. God wants to answer our prayers, but sometimes his answers just got to come through other people."

Then the congregation looked up, and John saw the young lady he had observed getting off the bus with her three girls that morning get up with her children and come up to the front of the church. Her eyes were filled with tears. It was obvious she was only in her twenties. But she looked so worn out, and so tired for her tender years. The young woman looked at the older lady next to John, and she wasn't sure what to do or what to say to her, but thank you. The older lady grabbed her, and held her in her arms, and said, "baby you sure are a skinny little thing. I need to fatten you up and your children's too. Oooh I'm gonna cook you some good meals, you and your babies. My name is Ms. Gloria."

All the young mother could do was cry. "Thank you Ma'am. I never had a mama myself, so I don't really know how to cook that good, I never learned."

John wasn't a man who even tried to hold back his feelings when the Holy Spirit came upon him. He let his tears flow, tears of joy, and tears of thanks to God. He could feel the Holy Spirit moving throughout the church. His congregation was praising God, and yelling Hallelujah to the highest. He also noticed people in the church were looking at each other, and without him even reading the notes anymore they were asking each other, "is there anything I can do to help you? Is there anything you need? John had to raise his voice a little to get the congregations attention again.

"You know I don't want to interrupt this praising, I really don't, but we've still got work to do." John looked over at the older man sitting in the front row of seats and he asked, "Brother do you think you can finish reading the rest of these notes to the congregation?"

"Why sure I can pastor, whatever you need me to do, just let me know."

Then John made his last announcement inside of the church. "To all my Saints out there, I'm going to give my sermon now. Now you all didn't think my sermon was going to be that short did you?"

And everyone started laughing. Then John continued talking, "but this sermon is going to be given outside. This sermon is for all the non-believers, for all the lost children who are hanging outside at the corner store. My Saints in here are welcome to come outside with me. But you may be better use to your family inside this Sunday, listening and answering each others' needs. But all the young men and teenage boys I see out there in my congregation; you young mighty men of God. If you are here today not just because your Mama made you come here or your wife made you come, but because "you" believe in God's love. Then if you are brave enough and love God, like David the shepherd boy did, grab your bibles and come outside with me. Your bible is your weapon to fight the evil outside. Join me and help save your lost
brothers outside. Today's sermon outside will be about Jesus' salvation and his death on the cross. I'm going to give it outside at the corner store, and I'm going to need some of God's warriors out there with me. I'm going to need you all for a spiritual fight, to help God fight the devil that wants some of those young boy's souls who are standing out there. Are you with me young mighty men of God?"

Then there was a rustling and a multitude of young men jumped up out of their seats with a holy fever in them, and they left their mothers behind and followed their pastor outside. Their mothers' faces all shined with motherly pride and concern, but they couldn't stop their sons from going, after all this was the day they had raised their boys for. The day they could all say, "my son is a mighty man of God."

Later that day, after the congregation had all went home John and some of the teenage boys from the church, and even some of the teenage boys that earlier that day had been standing outside at the corner store, all helped him post a sign on the church billboard outside. The sign read, **"HELP WANTED. NEEDED SAINTS, AND WANTED SINNERS. ALL MAY COME APPLY INSIDE. EVERYTHING YOU NEED YOU CAN FIND IN HERE."**

John sat in his office inside of the church at the end of his first day and he was praying at his desk for God to protect his flock and protect the boys he had preached to outside. He prayed that those boys would return to church, because John knew how the enemy comes quickly to try and snatch the Word of God from your heart. John's new secretary, Ms. Lilly, an older, kind lady, who had been a member of the church all her life, interrupted John to bring him a cup of tea.

"Thank you Miss Lilly."

As she handed the tea to John she couldn't help but to be curious about her new, young pastor. "Pastor, I thank God, so much that he brought you to us, but I noticed you're the only person in church who didn't fill out any notes."

"Being pastor here is exactly what I want and have to give the people, and I know it's what God wants me to give. I promise you Miss Lilly that I will give this congregation all I can, all that God will require of me I will give."

"But pastor, what about *your* needs, what is it that you need and don't have, pastor? Our church is really full of good people and we all care about our pastor and want to make sure you are happy too."

"I'm so blessed Miss Lilly, thank you so much for wanting to take care of me, but God has either already answered my prayers, or I have faith he is working on answering them. So don't worry about me, I don't need anything, God has given me everything already. I'm just so grateful to have the honor of serving God."

Miss Lilly smiled but before she left for the night she said, "Well I just want you to know if you ever need a home cook meal or just some good company, I don't cook anymore because my young niece cooks everything for me. She's a graduate student at NYU and her parents sent her to come live with me after she graduated college back South. She cooks like she could be a chef."

"Thank you Miss Lilly and I will definitely have to take a rain-check on that. Wait, let me walk you out to your car." John knew it wouldn't be long before people would try to set him up on dates, they did the same thing at his old church, but he just wasn't interested.

When John came back from the parking lot he sat back down at his desk and he couldn't help but to start thinking about Love. He figured she should be settled in and back at home in

LA by now. He wondered if she was nervous about starting her first day back at work tomorrow as partner. Even though he had just saw her at dinner last night at Mr. Swanson's he already missed her so much. He tried calling her cell phone. He got her voice mail and left her a short message. Then he called up the florist he use to use back in LA and placed an order for them to send flowers to Love's office the next morning. He hoped she would give him a call back before the end of the night. She never did return John's phone calls that night or any night after that.

Now six months had passed by since John had became pastor and had given his first sermon at his new church. Within those six months John had started a homeless ministry, gang ministry, youth ministry, senior ministry, jail ministry, singles ministry, mothers in need ministry, and many more. His church was known in the community to have a compassionate and giving congregation, with a pastor who was a mighty man of God. But at the end of every day, at the end of every night, John's thoughts always went back to Love. He wondered how she was doing, what she was doing, and he started to wonder if she was really the woman God wanted him to be with after all. It had been over six months since he had spoken to her. She had never returned any of his phone calls, emails or letters as she had promised. She had not tried to visit him once in New York, even though he knew she flew out to New York every weekend to visit her sisters.

John had become good friends with Darryl and they would meet for lunch or golf once a week. Darryl would let John know how Love was doing, or at least what Faith had told Darryl about how Love was doing. Other than that, Love had totally avoided John.

John knew that he wanted, that he needed a help mate, but his heart only wanted Love. During the six months that he'd been pastor, several mothers, grandmothers and single sisters had expressed their concerns over their pastor not having someone to take care of him, while he looked after his flock. He always told them the same thing, "don't worry God is taking perfect care of me." However, he knew he was growing weary of being alone and he wondered if God was trying to tell him, that it was time to open his heart up, to another woman besides Love.

Chapter 20
Though we are overwhelmed by our sins, you God forgive them all. [26]

Love had been very busy during the past six months, since she had returned to California. Her life was totally back to the norm, except for her weekend visits with her sisters. She could hardly believe just seven short months ago she was in Africa reuniting with her sisters after twenty years. After twenty years the three of them were so close you would have never thought they were ever apart.

Being partner was even more demanding than she imagined. As a partner, she had much more responsibilities, but still her case load had not diminished any. The firm still assigned her all the high profile cases because her name alone as head attorney on a case meant a higher retainer. So Love had been working non-stop and the new office that was designed to function as a second home had definitely proved to be useful. Love was spending much more time in her office now than ever before. The firm made it easy. At lunch time the firm's chef took orders for any partner who was going to take lunch in their office, and they did the same for dinner. Kevin, the partner's law clerk, usually had Love's breakfast and coffee waiting on her desk for her with the morning paper. She found herself eating all her meals in the office, whenever she was not in court. Also the firm had put a treadmill in her office because they knew she liked to exercise, she had a walk in closet to keep her work out gear and suits, and every partner's office also had a personal bathroom with an enclosed glass shower, and a Jacuzzi bathtub included. There was really no reason to go home. That is if you were like Love and had no one home waiting for you.

But despite her new demanding schedule, she kept her promise to her sisters and returned home to New York to visit them every weekend. The company jet flew her free of charge, every Friday night and returned her back to LA safely every Sunday morning while her sisters were attending church. She lived for the weekends and being reunited with her sisters once

---

[26] Psalms 65:3

again. It was rare for her to hang out with any of her friends in LA anymore, because every weekend she was home with her sisters.

She used her Friday nights to wrap up all her paperwork at the office, and then when she was finished she flew the jet to New York and caught a cab to Faith's old apartment that Hope and Amir lived in now. The three of them usually met up with Faith on Saturdays.

Back in LA, she had no time left for partying or sleeping around, instead she wrote in her journal every night before she fell asleep. She worked all the time and hardly ever saw her girlfriends. She had even stopped seeing her *boy* friends. She only thought about John now, and when she did get an itch late at night that needed to be scratched, well she had gotten into the habit of fantasizing about John and then scratching it on her own.

She had intentionally stop answering John's phone calls and emails, and she never once tried to contact John when she went to New York for the weekends. In fact the topic of John was so sensitive, that Faith and Hope, stopped bringing his name up around her. Love would get so defensive when they questioned her. They didn't understand why she was so set on ending her friendship and any hope of a relationship with John. Especially after all she had told them about him and after all they had all been through in Africa. It was obvious by the look in Love's eyes when John's name was mentioned how much she cared for him.

It was midnight on a Friday night, and Love was still in her office in LA. She had been working on a high profile case that was set for a jury trial on Monday morning. The case was in all the papers, and a lot was riding on it for the firm. Love had contemplated not visiting her sisters this weekend, so that she could use the whole weekend to prepare for trial, and to take care of any last minute complications that may come up. But she didn't want to disappoint her sisters. She had not missed one weekend seeing them yet.

The case she was working on was a murder in the first degree case. It involved a young woman who was accused of murdering her child, and trying to cover it up. The autopsy showed the child was given an apparent overdose of Tylenol PM.

Love's client was twenty three years old, a single mom, and the father of her baby was a married man who she was having an affair with. He abandoned her once she informed him that she was pregnant. Cases where young, single, overwhelmed women have abused or neglected their newborn unfortunately were really nothing new under the sun. However, this case had become a high profile case, because of who the mother and father were. The mother was a young inspiring actress. She was new on the scene, but she was considered "hot" and "the next big thing" in Hollywood. The father was later found out to be a very famous movie star after the child's death became news and the media did their digging. The father was considered to be one of those rare things in Hollywood, an actor in a stable marriage. To make matters worse his wife was a three time Academy award winner.

Love's young client had quickly confessed under pressure to giving the child Tylenol PM and she also told authorities who the father was after they questioned her. DNA testing was done on the deceased child and the father and it confirmed paternity. The parties' entertainment agents and managers, tried to keep the information out of the news, but news this juicy can never stay secret. Now the father's publicist was trying her best to portray the prominent male actor as someone who did not know anything about the girl's pregnancy, and as a wonderful family man who made a terrible mistake. As penitence for his one-time mistake the tabloids all said, he was now spending everything he could to pay for the defense of the young lady he got into trouble. The prominent male actor had even started a charity up for "Single Mom's in Need."

But Love knew the truth. The truth was that he had knocked this naïve girl up, he tried to pay her off and convince her to get an abortion, and then he abandoned her when she wouldn't terminate the pregnancy, and he refused to answer any of her calls after the child was born. However terrible all the choices were the young woman had made, and however terrible the situation was she had gotten herself into, Love thought, "she still had one thing going for her. She had the best legal defense anyone in the world could afford. She had her." So despite the fact that the father of her child was a real jerk, he was a real jerk with lots and lots of money, and now Love's firm had full access to his money.

First thing Love did after she was assigned the case was get the girl a bond. Now her client stayed in a condo that her former lover was paying for. Love went to visit her client daily, to discuss the case, because the girl didn't want to leave her condominium. Her picture was in all the papers. She had come from a Southern Baptist family, and her predicament was a real disgrace to them and to her. No one in her family had contacted her ever since the news of her legal troubles had hit the stands. It was sad, but the woman actually considered Love to be her only friend now. Her ex-lover was still not taking her calls, even though he was flipping the bill for all of her expenses.

Love felt sorry for the girl. She had no record of any kind, not even a traffic ticket. What she had one in Love's opinion was not premeditated murder. It was clear by all reports the girl was suffering from depression, sleep deprivation and exhaustion. She had confessed that she gave the baby a half of a pill crushed up in it's milk because she had not slept for three days straight. Then she called 911 immediately when the child did not respond. She said she only wanted her baby and her to get a little sleep, because the child constantly cried. There was also medical evidence that the pill didn't cause the baby's death, but it was actually caused by Sudden Infant Death Syndrome, SIDS.

So Love tried to plea with the prosecutor to give her a deal in the case, other than life in jail for her young client. Love tried to persuade the prosecutor by arguing that the girl just wasn't in her right frame of mind. But because her client was considered a star; politics came into play, and the prosecutor was trying to make a name for himself with this case. So there were no deals offered to Love, and the State demanded a jury trial.

However, Love was still confident that she could win the case. Although she had done plenty of guilty pleas with agreed recommendations over the years, and she never felt any qualms about getting someone a guilty plea that kept them out of jail. Most times her clients "were" guilty. They just wanted to do as little jail time as possible, and whether they went to trial or not, she still got paid the same. But whenever she did have to take a case to trial, every time she had won. In fact she had won more trial cases than any other attorney in LA, and that was what had made her a celebrity in her own right. To date she had never yet lost a case. So she had absolutely no plans of losing this girl's case. She didn't even consider she could "lose" it. Winning was the norm for Love she didn't know how to not win, and failure wasn't even in her vocabulary.

Love had already went over her winning strategy several times. The first day in court, the judge would hear her motion to suppress, she planned on attacking the confession as involuntary and coerced. She knew she would succeed, even though the motion really wasn't necessary. She wasn't planning on attacking her client's actions only her motives. Then she planned on calling a team of experts on infant mortality and experts to show evidence of SIDS, to prove that most healthy two months old babies would not die from the exact same dose of Tylenol PM the girl had given her baby. One of the girl's older friends had admitted that she had previously told the girl she had given her baby a half of a crushed pill to get some sleep, years and years ago, and that her child was now healthy and just fine. This woman had agreed to be Love's first character witness. She felt overwhelmingly guilty that she was the one who had inadvertently given the girl the idea. She also had a team of psychological experts to attack the girl's alleged intent to murder, and to prove that murder was never in her client's mind. She was going to have them testify to Post Pardum Depression and every other psychological syndrome known that could have affected her client's state of mind, and her judgment. Plus she had a sympathetic client. She was young, although she was technically an adult, Love knew in the eyes of most people when she put this young girl on the stand, without any makeup on, she would look like a child herself. After all she had become famous by playing a teenager of only fifteen on television. Before Love's client got pregnant she had previously played a teenage girl in the high school drama, Danny's Lake, every Wednesday night on television. Every young girl and boy knew about the show, so no doubt their parents would know about it too.

Love also planned on blasting the religious lobby groups she knew would be picketing the hearing, and emphasizing that the girl's religious convictions and her upbringing as a Christian kept her from legally terminating the pregnancy in the first place. She was going to show how the girl valued human life and how although she had committed adultery with an older man, she had still attended church every Sunday, right in LA.

Love had carefully thought out every aspect of the prosecution's case and had prepared a rebuttal and a defense against it. She felt fully prepared, and because she felt fully prepared she planned on keeping her promise to her sisters and going to visit them the following day in New York. Tonight it was just too late, and she was too tired to fly, so she decided to leave very early the following morning. That would give her at least one full Saturday with her loved ones this week.

Once Love had wrapped up her work for the night she started to think about John. She missed the days when John was still working at the firm and she would give him midnight calls to discuss the latest case she had, and bounce ideas off of him. Love put her files down and she picked up her journal. She had filled up a new journal, with almost one hundred and twenty pages filled of letters never sent, poems never recited and thoughts never said out loud, about John, and strangely in a way about God too. Love found that whenever she thought about one she ended up thinking about the other. Love had figured out months ago why she was afraid of being with John. To Love being with John was the equivalent to coming back to God, now that John was a pastor. She had been hiding from God for so many, many years now. She knew there was no way she could be with John until she was ready to submit herself unto God again. The fact was her and John were so unequally yoked. She would not dare insert herself into John's Godly life, and she wasn't in any way ready to accept his life either. So Love continued to make her journal the only source of emotional release in her life.

Once she was finished writing her thoughts down she opened up the pull out sofa in her office to finally get some sleep. She made sure the door to her office was locked, and she called the night security guard to let him know she would be spending the night in her office, and that she would need a 5:00 am wake-up call and a car to take her to the company jet to leave for New York the next morning. While she lay in the sofa bed her eyes were still open and she couldn't stop thinking about John. She closed her eyes as she turned over and fluffed her pillow and then tried her best to make a conscious effort to make herself think about something else besides John. So instead she started going over her case set for trial on Monday morning in her head, but thinking about work always made her lay awake in bed. So she started counting sheep. That mundane task eventually put her to sleep most nights, but it wasn't working tonight. She was extra wound up. Then her thoughts drifted back to John. She thought about his lips, his skin, and his smell again. And she figured even if I can't be with him in reality, no harm in being with him in my fantasies. So she imagined John was laying there next to her and then she imagined him laying there inside of her, and when she was finished imagining she finally fell asleep. As soon as her eyes closed and she began to dream, and of course she dreamed of John. He seemed to be the last thing she thought about before she fell asleep, and the first thought on her mind whenever she woke up. No matter how hard she tried it was no escaping the feelings she had for him. As each day passed by she only loved him and wanted him more.

The next morning Love woke to the sound of her office phone ringing. It was the 5 am wake-up call she requested. Love jumped right up eager to get in the shower and be on her way to see her sisters. She shook off the aching feeling in her heart she always felt after a night of dreaming about John, and she told herself, "all I need is my sisters, for now that's enough." During her weekend plane rides she always used her time on the plane to work on her cases, and this weekend would be no different.

Once the plane landed Love caught a cab to Darryl and Faith's new house in Long Island. Usually Love stayed with Hope when she was in town, because she didn't want to impose on Faith and Darryl's weekends when she knew they were still newlyweds. But this weekend was Darryl's birthday, and Faith had planned a big surprise birthday party for Darryl at their new house.

Faith had been very busy being the perfect, little wife since her and Darryl had gotten married. She had not been on any out of the country assignments since they were last in Ethiopia. Faith worked at the main SACAA office in New York and she had not gone on an out of country assignment for nearly six months, ever since she had returned from her honeymoon. She was also given a huge promotion upon returning from Ethiopia. She was now in charge of supervising and training the new hires, and assisting in placement and review of new adoptees. She seemed to be extremely satisfied and content with her new life as a wife. Still Love sensed a mysterious longing in Faith that she didn't think anyone else seemed to notice and she had been meaning to mention it to her, but not today. Even though Love thought something was not quite right with her little sister, she knew Faith was completely and utterly in love, with Darryl. So it definitely wasn't Faith's marriage that was bothering her. So Loved decided she would save her questions for Faith for another visit.

The cab dropped Love off in front of Faith's house. Faith, Hope and Amir ran out to greet her. Love was greeted with huge bear hugs, as usual, every single weekend. When Love was with her sisters and Amir, it actually was one of the few times she felt a relief from the emptiness inside her.

"I missed you guys as usual. Has Darryl showed up yet?"

"No, not yet, he's playing golf with John, and they won't be here for at least another hour, but all the other guest are already here. Come, let's get your bags into the guest room, and let me get you a glass of lemonade, Love. Have you had anything to eat yet?" Faith figured if she talked real fast maybe Love would miss the fact that she mentioned John was coming to the party, but it didn't work.

"John?!, you guys know I don't won't to see him! How come you didn't warn me?"

Hope interceded for Faith. "Love it is Darryl's birthday, and Darryl and John have become good friends. How could we not invite his good friend to his surprise birthday party? So Love, you are going to have to suck it up, and remember, today isn't about you. It's about your little sister throwing her first big party, in her first home, for her husband on his birthday!"

Love instantly felt bad for being so self-absorbed. Hope was always straight forward, and she loved that about her. "You're right Hope, I'm sorry, Faith. I'm so selfish. You don't ever have to choose between me and John. I don't want you guys to feel that way. You forgive me lil sis?"

"That's okay Love. But, I really don't understand this whole thing you've got against not wanting to see John, anyway. I mean what's the deal with anyway?"

Love avoided the question as usual. "Like Hope said, today is about you and Darryl. You've went all out for him. Don't you worry I'm not going to do anything to spoil this day for you, or embarrass you. But if I'm going to see John, I think I want to have a drink, and I'm not talking about lemonade."

"Love it's not even noon yet?"

"Faith, I'll take care of Love, you tend to your guest." Hope grabbed Love's hand and left Faith to finish being a hostess to her guest. They put Love's bags away in the guest room and then they started to mingle with the other guest, after they spiked Love's orange juice with a little something Faith had stored away in the basement.

Mary, Mr. Swanson, and their kids were there too, along with several people from Faith and Darryl's neighborhood, jobs, and church. Love figured she was the only guest there who was drinking an alcoholic drink, but to everyone else it looked like Love was just drinking orange juice anyway. She forgot that since Faith and Darryl had gotten hitched, the two of them had went ahead and been baptized together also. Although Darryl said he was already a Christian, he was drinking as much as Love did on the return trip home from Africa. Love figured, "he probably doesn't drink anymore either." It seemed like everyone at the party was a devout, born-again Christian, even Hope was. Then it suddenly dawned on Love that Hope *did* have to go down into the basement and look in one of the old moving boxes just to find a bottle of booze for Love to make some type of drink out of. Love started to feel very out of place. So she swallowed down her drink and made another one. She was working on her third drink when she had to admit she was starting to finally feel relaxed. Then Love heard someone yell, "here comes Darryl", and she felt so nervous all of a sudden, because she knew John was with him. She downed the drink she was holding in her hand, and then she made another one, and downed that one down too. She had just had five drinks in less than an hour's time, and that was even too much alcohol for her, but she felt like she needed to have the drinks just to relax her nerves about seeing John again for the first time in over six months.

Amir yelled out to everyone, "Uncle Darryl and Pastor John are in the driveway now, everyone hide!"

Love felt her stomach flip flop, she wasn't sure if it was the alcohol in her stomach she had drunk down too fast or just fear from seeing John.

Faith was whispering, "everyone take your places and remember as soon as the door opens yell, surprise."

Love went to stand behind Hope in the hallway and she had almost lost her balance walking towards her. Hope grabbed her arm, and asked her, "are you okay?"

"I'm fine Hope, it's just these damn heals." Hope replied with a frown on her face, "yeah sure, you're breath smells like a brewery."

"Dag, quick give me some gum."

"I don't have any, shhsh, they're at the door."

Then the door opened and everyone yelled, "Surprise!"

Love didn't even notice Darryl. All Love could focus on was John walking in behind him. He was standing right behind Darryl, looking so fine! He hadn't changed a bit. He was still tall, dark, and handsome, with a clean shaven face, wait and a clean shaven head now! Love thought, "Oh my God he done shaved his head for the summer! It was so sexy!"

Love thought back to the first time John had showed up to work with his hair shaven off. It was right after she had mentioned seeing some gray in it. She wanted to do him right then, that moment she saw him get off the elevator at work that day. Since then he alternated between shaving it and letting it grow out. He was already sexy, but with no hair on his head he was superstar sexy. She just couldn't stop thinking about rubbing her hands on his smooth head. And then all she could think about was licking, those soft full, voluptuous, juicy lips when she watched John smile at Darryl when Darryl asked him if he knew about the surprise party? Love looked at those two big dimples John had on each cheek when he smiled, she loved those dimples and those dazzling white teeth against his dark brown skin.

She had admired her receptionist Kevin's dimples every day back at the office, and she was amused at how Kevin blushed every time she complimented him on his dimples and his smile. But she had never wanted to take her tongue and lick the dips in Kevin's dimples, like she wanted right now to lick John's. Suddenly, Love realized it had been a really long time since she got any, the longest she had ever gone that she could remember. Love felt her heart racing. All the alcohol she had drunk wasn't making matters any better. She was sure the drinks she had were adding to this crazy, immediate, physical reaction she was suddenly having from seeing John. Usually, arousal didn't sneak up and surprise her like this; she was usually always under control. That was the thing about John, he made her feel out of control and she didn't like that. She definitely didn't want to feel this for him, not now surrounded by a room full of Christian people. She rather feel this way about him in the privacy of her dark, secluded bedroom, without his or anyone else's knowledge.

Hope was already eyeing Love with suspicion. To Hope it looked like Love might end up puking. She was all flushed and looked off balance. She wasn't about to let Love mess up Faith's first party.

"You sure you alright because it looks like you are sweating and Faith's got the air conditioning up so high I'm freezing, so you can't be hot."

"I told you Hope, I'm fine. I'm just a little jet lagged, and I admit maybe I shouldn't have had those drinks, but I'm okay. I'm going to the bathroom to throw a little cold water on my face now."

Then Love tried to ease pass everyone and quietly make her way to the restroom to throw some cold water on her face and get herself together, when she heard a booming voice from across the room call her name. It was Darryl.

"Love, sister-in-law hold up there. Where are you going so fast? Good to see you sister-in-law, how was your flight? I just spoke to you yesterday on the phone and you didn't even let on that Faith was planning all this." Darryl had a sly grin on his face. "Oh, and you remember my friend John. Don't you, Love?"

Love thought to herself, "Darryl was just like the annoying little brother she had never had. Guess I'm not going to get a chance to get myself together. Okay Love, pull it together, you can do this."

"I think I vaguely remember him. Hi John."

John walked over to Love and gave her a hug that lasted slightly too long and was slightly inappropriate and uncomfortable at what seemed to be practically a church social gathering. Love couldn't help but take in a deep breath of John's aroma as he hugged her. Love thought, "My God he smells even more intoxicating than what I remembered."

John looked into her eyes, she felt like he could see right into her soul. "I've missed you so much Love. How have you been?"

And just when Love was getting ready to give him an answer, she started to hiccup, she tried to say something after the hiccup, and just another hiccup came out. Love was sure John smelled the alcohol on her breath and she thought to herself, "why did I have all those drinks? Now he probably thinks I'm an alcoholic and that I'm all torn up about him being gone."

Darryl was still standing next to John and he couldn't help but laugh out loud, and before you knew it John and Love were laughing too. Faith walked up and asked what was so funny. Darryl said, "I'll tell you later baby, let's leave these two alone for a little bit and let me greet all my guests."

John looked at Love seriously now. "How about we go into the kitchen and get you some water for those hiccups?"

"That sounds good." Love answered, through her hiccups. The party was happily churning and Faith and Darryl looked blissfully in love. Now Love found herself in the position she had been dreading for six months, alone with John. John poured her some water and while she was drinking her water, he just stared at her intensely. It was obvious he had a lot he wanted to say to her, but he didn't know where to start. He decided to just speak what was in his heart and before Love could finish her glass of water he had already started talking.

"Love I'm through with playing games with you. We've been through too much for that. So I'm going to just get to the point. Why have you not answered any of my phone calls or returned any of my emails or letters? What have I done to you for you to cut me off like this?"

Love stared at John looking dumbfounded. She was not able to give him an honest answer, the answer he deserved, so she took the cowards way out. "I've just been so busy with the new job as partner and all the new responsibilities, you know. But I've thought about you. I'm sorry if I've upset you."

John wasn't going to stand for that sugar coated, shallow lie. He finally had Love in front of him, and he needed some type of closure with her, some real answers, even if this encounter with her was not going to end well.

"Love, that's an unacceptable answer. Come on, you must know that I know you've been coming here every weekend to see your sisters. You must know that I know that much. Now I didn't want to act like a stalker and just pop up on you at Hope's place or here at Faith's unannounced, even though I thought about it. But I was invited here today, so I haven't come here just because of you. And now that I have you in front of me, I need you to just tell me the truth. Why have you been avoiding me for the last six months?"

Love still kept pretending. "Honestly, I've just been busy, I am telling you the truth. What do you want from me? I know we were good friends and all, but lets' face it, our lives have turned down two very, very, different paths. I just don't feel like you and I have anything in common to share with each other anymore. You're a pastor and I'm, I'm a partner. I will always consider you my friend John, you know that. But when I say I've been busy, I mean it, I've been very busy."

"I don't believe that Love, how can you say that? I know you feel more than just friendship for me. I felt it in that kiss in Africa. I still feel it now, just looking in your eyes. How can you stand there and just lie and say that to me. You know we have an incredible connection, no matter what paths our lives take, you have to admit that Love. At least be honest with yourself and admit that our connection is unexplainable. When I'm in bed at night, it's as if I can feel your presence there with me. The truth is you are "always" with me. Yes we're friends, but we've always really been much more than that, even if we didn't admit it to ourselves. Even before the kiss we shared in Africa, we were really always more than just friends."

"I'm not saying I don't still care about you John, I do. I mean you are right we have or had a connection. But sometimes friends, people grow apart, because their lives just become so different. In this case, I think that's what has happened to us. I mean you can't really say we were ever more than just friends technically speaking, John. I mean we never even had sex with each other, just a kiss, under some very strange and stressful circumstances, that's all."

"Not everything is about sex Love. What I feel for you is much more than just sexual. You should know that by now. What I feel for you is deeper than anything I have ever felt for any other woman in my life, and it has nothing to do with sex. I can't explain it Love, but I feel like you are the woman that God wants me to be with. I strongly feel that."

"John, how can you say that, I mean have you really asked God, consulted with him, because if you really ask him, I think He's not going to give you the answer you want. I know that I am definitely not the woman for you. You need a virtuous woman. That's not me. You need a righteous woman. That's definitely not me. I'm not the woman you need John. I know that. You need to ask yourself, why you don't know that too? Why would you want to be with a woman who clearly loves all the things God hates, money, pre-marital sex, power, drinking in excess, shall I go on. I've told you several times I don't believe in the same things you believe in. You need to ask yourself that question, why do you want me if God wouldn't want me?" Then Love said something she knew she would regret and hate herself for the moment it came out of her mouth because it was the biggest lie she had ever told, she said, "But John all of that is besides the point. The truth is, I just don't have the same feelings about you, that you have for me. I'm sorry, but I hope we can remain friends, especially since it seems like our lives have somehow become entangled through in-lawship and friendship."

There was a brief moment of silence between the two of them. John wasn't sure how to respond.

Love was already starting to make her escape and walk away. "Well, I guess I better get back to the party. It looks like my hiccups have gone away."

But John grabbed her arm and stopped her. "I don't believe you. And Love, you're wrong about one thing, God wants you, God wants all his children to come to him, the only thing keeping you away from God is yourself." Then he let go of her. He accepted that if it was meant to be she would come back to him one day, and hopefully he would still be there waiting on her.

Love didn't respond to John's last comment, and she kept walking away from him until she was outside in the backyard with her sisters. John stayed in the kitchen. He was deep in his own thoughts. He thought about what Love had said, but mostly, he thought about the question she had asked him, "have you really asked God?" He knew he hadn't really done that, because he was afraid of the answer God might give him. He thought about Love all the time. He prayed for Love's safety and happiness all the time. But he never really asked God, prayed to God, to let him know if Love was truly the woman for him. He wondered it sometimes, but he never really got on his knees and seriously asked God if He wanted him to be with Love. John realized he was really afraid of God's answer, because he knew that God always gave you what you needed, but not always what you wanted. He always assumed Love was the one for him, because of the deep, strong desire he had within him to be with her. But John knew that sometimes sinful desires also had an amazingly deep and strong pull on a person, so much so, that if you didn't consult God about what you felt you could possibly rationalize anything you wanted and desired to be a good thing, even if it wasn't good in the eyes of God. John knew exactly what he needed to do. He needed to fast and to pray. Pray specifically to God about revealing to him if Love was really the woman for him or if it was time for him to finally move on. John felt like he had to start praying and fasting now, right now.

When John looked up from his deep thoughts, he realized Darryl was standing there in front of him. Darryl was spying on John and Love from afar. John's entire conversation over golf was about his feelings for Love, and Darryl was deeply concerned about his friend and his sister-in-law.

"Is everything okay man?"

"Not really. I'm sorry Darryl, but I've got to go. I'll give you a call tomorrow. Hey, Happy Birthday."

Darryl knew that whatever was the matter with John had to do with his sister-in-law, Love. So he didn't ask John any more questions.

When the party was over Love, Hope and Faith, were in the kitchen, putting the left-over food away, and straightening up. Darryl and Amir sat at the table and ate some more birthday cake. Hope asked the question that was already on everyone's mind. "Love, how's John doing? He really left out of here in a rush today. I didn't even get to say hello to him."

Love didn't look up from her dishes, and she replied, "he sounds like he's doing fine."

Faith rolled her eyes. She thought, "Love was such a bad liar." "Well, Darryl told me he didn't look so fine when he left out of here, after only being here for about twenty minutes. Isn't that right Darryl?"

Darryl's mouth was full of birthday cake, and he swallowed quick and looked over at Amir and said, "let's go watch the game man."

After the men folk were gone from the kitchen, Love looked up at her sisters and put her hand on her hip. "You know I just don't want to talk about John you guys."

"Fine, we won't talk about it, but he's a good guy Love. I hope you know what you are giving up, and I hope you are not giving it up for the wrong reasons?" Hope was really concerned for Love.

"Noted, guys, I'm really out of it, and jet lagged. Can we just enjoy the rest of the day and drop it. I'll be leaving out of here when you all leave out for church tomorrow. I've got a

big jury trial Monday morning and I want to make sure I'm well
rested for it and go to bed early tonight and tomorrow."

The topic of John was carefully avoided the rest of the
day and the next day on the flight home Love thought about what
Hope said. She thought about John and what a good man he
really was, and what she was giving up. But by the following
morning her mind was focused on the trial.

[Monday morning]

"Counsel for the State, are you ready to proceed with
trial?"

"Yes Judge."

"Counsel for the defense, are you and your client ready
to proceed with trial today?"

Love answered, "Yes, You're Honor."

The courtroom was packed. The media had gotten
permission to be in the courtroom. The matter was being
televised on all the court TV stations. Outside of the courthouse
stood reporters and bystanders, Right to Life advocates, and Pro-
Choicers. It never stopped amazing Love just how many people
in LA had nothing better to do than spend the day waiting
outside a courthouse. She wondered, "was she the only one in
LA that had a job?" Meanwhile, the judge told his court clerk to
swear the witnesses in, and the trial of the moment proceeded.

Love's young client, looked behind her, she did not see
in the seats anyone from her family or any of her friends that she
had met while living in Hollywood. Her hands started to shake.
A cold shiver went down her spine. Love looked over at her, she
placed her hand on the young ladies hand and she said, "don't
worry you are in good hands."

The young lady, being the Christian raised girl she was,
assumed Love was talking about, "in God's hands", so she said
to Love, "after what I did, I don't think God has room for me
anymore in his hands, Ms. King."

Love gave her a very serious look of authority. "I
wasn't talking about God's hands. I was talking about my
hands. If there is only one attorney in this whole country that
can get these charges dismissed against you, that attorney is me.
You are in the best legal hands available." This was Love's
patented, "calm them down speech" that she gave all her

criminal defense clients before trial. It was the perfect thing to
say, it was confident and reassuring, but at the same time not
promising or guaranteeing anything, except if I can't get you off,
no other attorney in the country could have gotten you off. It
was all in the way you took it. Love's young client seemed to
take her words in the same way all her other clients had in the
past. She started to calm down after Love's quick speech to her.

The young woman gave Love a blank look with no
emotion, but her small, fragile hands did stop shaking. Then she
whispered to Love, "I'm just ready to get on with this trial, Ms.
King. I'm just ready for it all to be over."

[6:00pm, Friday evening]
The past week was grueling. Love felt like she hadn't
slept, eaten or thought about anything else but the trial all week.
She was so relieved that it was finally going to be over. Love
never allowed herself to have doubts about her case during a
trial. One slip up that showed a lack of confidence in her case
could be fatal for her client, if the other side or the jury spotted
it. But after the closing arguments were over, after the jury was
sent away to deliberate, and Love knew her job was done, she
couldn't hold back all those doubts in her head she had blocked
out any longer. She couldn't help but to allow all those doubts,
and fears, about her abilities as an attorney, about the strength of
her client's case, about just how reliable the jury would be in
weighing all the evidence, enter her head. Although she still
managed to keep her concerns hidden from her client, inside her
mind was racing with worries about the jury's decision.

She wondered, "would the jury believe the case I
presented? That it was just a terrible judgment call, but not
premeditated murder." Finally, Love's worse fears of all would
take hold of her, right before the jury took their seats, she would
wonder, "will this be the first time I lose a trial, or will my
winning record stay intact?" Because no matter how wrong she
knew it was, winning was and had always been the most
important thing to Love when it came to the practice of law.

The jury came out to announce their verdict. The
courtroom became quiet. It was always hard to read the juries

faces after a trial. They always tried their best to keep poker faces on. The head juror read the verdict.

"We the people find the defendant...."

Love thought, "always that unnecessary, annoying pause! Please just get on with it already!"

"NOT GUILTY".

The courtroom was buzzing. Lights were flashing from the media taking pictures. There was chaos all around. But a rush of relaxation ran through Love's tense body and she exhaled. The partners from her firm who had come to observe and hear the verdict, and of course make any media statements that needed to be made came up to Love to congratulate her on another win. The prosecutor being the gentleman he was came over and shook Love's hand. In the middle of all the commotion Love heard a small voice beside her ask, "What happens now, Ms. King?"

Love looked at her fragile client. "Well, you are free to leave now, it's over. They've found you not guilty, and innocent of the charge against you. You can move on with your life now and start fresh. Do whatever you want to do and put this whole mess behind you forever. Did you want to drive with me back to the firm, or I can take you to your condo in the firm's car?"

The young lady grabbed her purse; then she turned around and reluctantly faced the crowd that was waiting for her. "No thank you Ms. King. I think I will just take a cab by myself back to my place and spend some time alone."

"You seem down, cheer up. I know you have been through a lot, but it's over now. Just think you were facing serious jail time, being locked up for the remainder of your life. But you are a free woman, you are innocent of these charges and you are free to start a whole new life. Come on, come with me we can go get dinner somewhere."

"Thanks, but I don't want to be out in public. I'm going home. Ms. King, I know the jury found me "not guilty", but no one ever said I was "innocent"."

Then Love watched her client walk off quietly as she avoided making eye contact with anyone and she refused to answer any questions. Love watched her walk away, and a part of her thought, "I should run after her, and take the cab ride with her to her home and see if she wants to just talk. Clearly she is in pain and she's all alone. She shouldn't be alone now." But just when Love had grabbed her briefcase and planned on catching up with her client some of the partners from the firm came up to her and told her that the media wanted her to make a statement; and that afterwards all the partners and associates were going to Razzi's to celebrate her newest win with some drinks.

Before Love knew it she had put her concerns for her young client out of her head. She was making statements to the media which lasted for another hour, and then she was celebrating, eating and drinking with the partners and the people she referred to as her friends. She had to admit, she did love winning, and she did really love the limelight.

Eight hours later, and many, many drinks later, the restaurant bar was clearing out. Love was one of the last ones left. Two partners and Love were sitting at the table together finishing up their last drinks. Then the last two partners decided to call it a night. They finished what was in their glasses, and they said their goodbyes to Love. One of the partner's asked Love if she wanted to share his cab ride home since she seemed to be the last person left from their firm. Then Love's cell phone ringed. Before she answered she told the partners she was okay, and they could leave without her, because when she finished up her last drink she planned on taking her own cab home. Love waved goodbye to them as she answered her phone.

"Hello. Yes, this is Ms. Love E. King? May I help you?"

"Ma'am, this is California Medical, Emergency Services. We're calling because a young lady was checked in tonight, and we didn't know who to contact. The 911 response team found your name and number on her nightstand. We were wondering if you are her next of kin, or a close friend, or if you knew the number for a relative for this young lady so we can contact them?"

Love instantly thought about her young client. She already knew it had to be her client that they were referring to, because everyone else she knew was at the bar celebrating with her that night. The hospital representative confirmed the young lady that she was calling her about was indeed Love's young client. Then the hospital representative explained what had happened to the girl.

"Ms. King, her neighbors called 911 when they heard a gunshot coming from her apartment. When the paramedics and police arrived they found her slumped over on her bed, with the gun still in her hand, and a bullet in her head. She is in critical condition, and they are not sure she will make it. So I am trying to contact any family members as soon as possible."

Love gave the lady on the phone the names of her client's parents and the city and state they lived in. Love told the lady on the phone that she knew the girl's parents' phone number was listed, because she had called it before and gotten the number through the operator. Then Love hung up the phone.

Love sat alone in the bar. She felt too stunned to cry. She picked up her full glass of red wine that she had been sipping on and she guzzled the whole glass of wine down until it was all gone. The barmaid was trying to close the place up, but Love was a well known patron that she was willing to accommodate.

"Are you finished for the night Ms. King, or would you like me to bring you another drink or call you a cab?"

Love pretended she was happy and smiled. "Thank- you Sally. I know you're ready to get out of here, but would you mind bringing me just one more for the road? It's on the firm's tab so bring something a little stronger. Plus I don't have to work tomorrow, since its Saturday. Let's see can you bring me a rum and coke, heavy on the rum please, and how about a shot of tequila too. After all this is a celebration."

"Coming right up Ms. King, and congratulations on your win again."

"Thanks Sally."

Once alone again, Love whispered to herself, "why would she do that?! She had a not guilty verdict, why?!" Then Love thought about her client's last words to her, "she said something about..., "they said I was not guilty, no one ever said I was innocent." Then Love knew the answer to her own question. "The jury may have forgiven what her client did, but her client couldn't forgive herself because she thought God could never forgive her."

Then the barmaid brought Love her drinks, and Love drunk each one down, one after another, without hesitation. Before the barmaid could even make it back over to the bar, Love pleaded with her to just bring her just one more round of the same thing.

Love started thinking to herself, "I should have went after her. I should have taken the cab home with her. Instead, I was busy taking in the limelight, giving stupid statements, like I'm some kind of celebrity." After Love completely finished blaming herself, she decided to place blame on someone else. She blamed the girl's lover, her fake California friends, her hypocritical parent's, Conservative Christians, and then finally Love whispered to herself, "God, if she wasn't one of those people who believed in God maybe she would have terminated the pregnancy as soon as she found out about it and avoided all of this, or maybe she would have found a way to forgive herself and not have taken her own life."

Love recalled all the protest signs people held outside stating "burn baby killer burn", and she recalled what the girl's mother said when she had called her up to see if she would come out to support her daughter for the trial. Her mother said, "she shouldn't have been out there committing adultery in the first place. That's not the daughter I raised, that's not my daughter."

Love thought to herself that her, and her client were really not that different from each other. She had committed adultery just like her client had, she had killed…" She didn't want to think of it anymore, so she guzzled her drink down to try and drown her thoughts away. She knew she was no better than her client, but unlike her client she was just too much of a coward to punish herself for her own sins. At that moment Love wished she was also dead. She felt like she hated herself, and her whole life…

Then Love noticed out of the corner of her blurry eye a very handsome man walking towards her. He had the most piercing blue eyes and blond locks that brightened up the whole room. Watching him was almost hypnotic. For a moment she completely forgot what she was thinking about, and all she could think about was how long it had been since she had gotten some.

The strange, handsome man stood right before her now and he was staring at Love intensely. "Looks like we are the last two left in here. Do you mind if I share your company for a little bit, until my cab gets here?"

Love tried her best to answer without slurring her speech. She was very aware at that moment that she had drunk way too much. "No problem, I think I would like a little company anyway. My name is Love King. What's your name?"

"I already know who you are Ms. King. You have become sort of famous around here this past week. I heard about your big win, and I figured now that all your entourage has gone I would come up and congratulate you myself. I watched the trial on TV like most people in town did, I suppose. I thought you did an amazing job, Ms. King. You must feel like you are on top of the world."

"Thank you, and please call me Love."

"Okay, Love. I bet your client is thrilled with the outcome of her case, isn't she?"

"Yep she was thrilled, thrilled enough to put a bullet in her head."

"I'm sorry is that some type of lawyer expression, like actor's say, "break a leg? I am a little out of touch with the slang phrases people use now-a-days."

"No, sadly it's not an expression. I just got a phone call from the hospital. She actually shot herself in the head tonight."

"Really, why do you think she would do such a thing?"

Love waited a long time to answer him, she had a lot of opinions about why her client did what she did, but only one came out of her mouth and her words were filled with bitterness. "God, she was one of those people that believed in all that bible stuff and she hated herself for it."

"Oh well that's unfortunate. Personally, I believe that every man answers only to himself, and that life is too short to waste it trying to obey and follow some rules from an invisible man who lives somewhere in a fairytale land up in the sky."

Love felt like, "finally, here is someone who I can relate to." "You know, I agree with your opinion, entirely."

"So is this why you are looking so down on what should be one of the greatest days of your life. You just won the case of the century, you know. You shouldn't be sitting here alone in a bar sulking about the stupid decision some poor lost girl made that had nothing to do with you. I mean it's sad but it's not your fault that girl was so brainwashed by her religious beliefs that she took her own life. It's very unfortunate, but it's not your fault, Love. You gave the best, magnificent, legal defense ever. What else could you have done for her, what else could you have said to her, what else could you have given her? Right?"

"Right.", agreed Love as she slammed her glass down on the table.

"Well Ms. Love King it has been a pleasure talking to you but it looks like my cab is here and it also looks like they are ready to close up this place. Hey I have an idea, how would you like to share the cab with me?"

Love was actually use to sharing cabs with strange men, and her body wanted to share much more than a cab ride with this strange sexy man. So she accepted his invitation and without much hesitation she replied. "I might as well."

Five hours later, Love awoken finding herself in a King size bed naked beside two other extremely gorgeous naked females. She had followed the handsome stranger back to his mansion in the middle of nowhere. They followed the night up with some more drinks, a few hits of cocaine, a little bit of ecstasy to go with it, and of course an all night party. This wasn't the first time Love had drunk too much and participated in these particular type of parties, but it was the first time she had ever tried any drugs.

All these years, using drugs was something she stayed away from, except for the occasional marijuana, that she had conveniently had a prescription for from her doctor friends. Love really didn't consider a little joint here and there as using drugs and she had never ever tried anything harder. But there was something about this strange, beautiful man she had met tonight. He was so seductive and so persuasive. He had her sniffing cocaine off his fingertips on one hand as he was fingering her with the other.

There was also nothing but beautiful, sexy, successful, powerful, rich people at his mansion that night. Some of these people Love had seen before, some of them she had never seen before, but one thing they all had in common, they were people with everything in life, everything except a moral compass. Love thought to herself, "she really fit right in."

She rolled the young ladies leg off of her and walked around the room. She was looking for the strange, beautiful, ageless man who had made her reach climax so many times that night that she had lost track, but she didn't see him anywhere. So she started looking for her clothes. Before she could find them, she heard and almost angelic, yet commanding voice from behind and she knew it was the voice of the man who had brought her there that night.

"You trying to leave so soon Love?"

She groggily turned around and smiled at him. "Yes, I have a flight to catch tomorrow morning. I mean later today I guess, to New York, to see my family." Then she suddenly thought about John. She wasn't planning on seeing John of course, she had clearly established the last time she saw him that nothing would ever happen between them, but a pain still shot through her heart when she thought about John and she thought about where she was at, and what she had just done with this man and these other strangers.

"Oh, you have family in New York. But for someone in such a rush to get going, you just had a tortured, painful look come across your face. I think you don't really want to go." Then he walked over to Love slowly.

Love thought to herself, "he is truly a perfectly, striking man, a perfect body, a perfect face, it was impossible to tell just how old or how young he really was, he was as perfect, as a Greek god or something. His skin was pearly white, his eyes piercing blue, his blonde hair shined like the sun, and his voice was hypnotic. Never before have I seen anyone that looked so perfect. Like what you imagine an angel looking like, if I believed in angels that is."

Then the man took Love into his arms, and Love felt perfectly comfortable in them. His skin was so cool, but it felt so good on her hot and sticky body. Then he whispered to her,

"I'm sure your sisters would understand if you are a little late seeing them. I mean you look like you need a break, you need to rest, take some time to just do something for yourself, enjoy yourself, think about yourself, you know. So stay here in my arms for the night, and just forget about everyone and everything else for a moment."

Love thought, "I don't remember telling him I had sisters, but then again I can barely remember what I did tonight, it's all so fuzzy. But it does sound so good, so tempting to just escape from the whole world and just stay here in his cool, comfortable arms. After all I have allowed him to do things to me tonight that no man had ever done before, and every moment of this night, sexually has been amazing. I can't deny it, his offer is tempting, very tempting, and I am so tired, maybe I will stay, just a little while longer. My sisters won't be too upset at me if I didn't show, just this one weekend." It was as if his love making gave her amnesia, made her forget her burdens and the guilt she was feeling earlier that night. She just felt numb and that was exactly what she wanted to feel anyway. Lately ever since Africa she seemed to be feeling too much. She wanted to stay numb.

He then held Love even tighter and he walked her over to the chaise lounge in the corner of the huge master bedroom. He sat down and turned her around so she wasn't facing him. There naked bodies complimented each other. Then he sat her down carefully on his lap, making sure he fit himself comfortably inside of her. As he was guiding her slowly, he reached with one hand and grabbed a needle that was sitting on the end table next to the chaise lounge. He asked Love, as casually as if he was asking her if she wanted a glass of water, "you want to try a little heroine while having sex?"

"No thanks."

"Why not? What's your reasons?"

Love felt numb and happily hypnotized again and she really couldn't think of a reason not to try it. "I've just never done it before."

"But there are a lot of things you've never done before tonight, right?"

"You're right, what the hell. I'll try it."

He shot it in her thigh, and Love felt it's effect immediately. She was feeling like she was floating. It felt like nothingness, no more turmoil, no more burdens weighing her down, just blissful nothingness, but then she heard a phone ringing, and she recognized the ring tone, it was her cell phone.

"That's my cell phone", and she attempted to get up to go get it, but he held her in place.

"Let it ring."

"It will just take me a sec, it could be important, it could be..." (Love thought about her sisters, John, the hospital where her client was, might be calling again, but she didn't say their names out loud). She just attempted to get up again. He grabbed her long locks of hair, and held on to it, as she tried to get up. Despite Love's drug induced state she was persistent about answering her phone. So he allowed her to get up, and she slowly staggered across the room and found her cell phone inside her purse, next to where her clothes were on the floor.

"Hello." The person on the other end of the phone responded, "Is this Ms. King?" Love answered, "yes".

"Ms. King, this is your client's mother. I'm calling you because the hospital informed us of what happened but our plane is delayed. My husband and I are sitting here in the airport. We're afraid, we're not going to make it to the hospital in time.... in time." Then she started sobbing.

Love responded, with no sign of compassion in her voice. "In time for what ma'am? Didn't they tell you, your daughter shot herself in the head? I think it really doesn't matter how fast you get to the hospital."

The lady was taken a little a-back by Love's lack of compassion and sensitivity, but then she thought to herself, "I deserve her contempt." She was remembering how Love had called her weeks ago, pleading with her to come out to LA to be there for the trial and support her daughter. Love had offered for the firm to pay for their hotel and plane tickets, but still the lady and her husband said no. They abandoned their child, when she needed them the most, and they wouldn't come. They were ashamed of her, and now she was ashamed, of herself. Yes, she deserved this ladies unkindness. But she was desperate and she put her pride aside and stopped sobbing and found the words she needed to say.

"Ms. King, I deserve that, and I'm sorry to have to bother you. I know how you must feel about me, but my daughter has no one out there, and the hospital said she was close to death, just barely hanging on. We don't want her to die, all alone. Can you please, please, go to her, be with her, until she goes? If we don't make it there in time, I don't want to think she died all alone. Please, I'm begging you, Ms. King, please? You are the only person I could think of to contact who would go be with her out there."

Love tried to sober up. She was trying to regain control of her senses and it was incredibly difficult. "So you are telling me she's still alive? I didn't know, I mean I didn't think... I just assumed she was dead, when they said she shot herself in the head, I just assumed by now she would be gone."

Then the girl's mother desperately asked Love again, "so you will go be with her, till we get there, will you?"

"Of course I will, at least I promise you I will try my best. I'm leaving now." Love hung up the phone and tried with all her might to stand up straight and get her clothes on. She heard the strange man's voice summoning her from across the room.

"Love, I know you feel it's your duty to go, your obligation, but really what good will it serve. Think about yourself and come back to me. Let me take care of you, like no one else can. It's just one night, one day. Everyone will understand, and in the morning your sisters, you can call them, they will understand too. But you know that girl is as good as dead, leaving now is a waste of your time."

Love looked over at the handsome man, and realized for the first time how dark his eyes suddenly look. How his once hypnotic, seductive eyes stared at her now, like a starved, cold, desperate person. He didn't look as beautiful, as perfect as he did just a few moments ago. Then she thought about what he had just said and what he had said before, "your sisters won't mind." She didn't remember telling him she had "sisters", only "family" in New York, and that really bugged her. Something about him mentioning her sisters turned her stomach and made her nervous. Then she realized she felt suddenly very uneasy and aware of his strange gaze, and that made her miraculously sober up. She just started putting on her clothes and she ignored his statements, but she did ask him if he could call her a cab.

"Look Love you're in no condition to go anywhere, stay here. You leaving now, in your condition is just ridiculous."

Love didn't respond, and she continued getting dressed.

"Why are you trying to go in such a rush anyway, Love?"

So she explained to him about the phone call, and how she needed to go to the hospital.

"Yes you don't have to explain, I know where you are trying to go already. But why, are you trying to go? What's the point, the girl will probably be dead by the time you get there. After all, you've already done all you can do for her. Even if you make it there before she dies, she probably is too out of it, after a bullet to the head, to hear anything you would have to say to her or even to realize you are there with her."

"That might all be true." Then Love thought about how Hope said she heard her talking to her during her surgery in Africa, when Love thought she was unconscious. "I can't explain why, but I just have to try to be there for her, I made a promise. Will you please just call me a cab?"

"I have no intentions of helping you go out there in your condition. Besides what cab would come out here in the middle of nowhere, at this time of night?"

Love started to feel furious with him. She had no idea where she was, let alone the address to call herself a cab. She needed his help. He didn't look so attractive to her anymore, his blonde hair wasn't as bright, and his eyes were not as baby blue. Everything that was good about him seemed as if it was just an illusion. It was as if he was just a fantasy fading away like the night with the rising of the sun. Then Love looked at the cell phone in her hand, and she mumbled to herself, "I'm an idiot", and she just dialed 911. 911 would be able to track her call, even quicker after she would tell them her name was Love King and they realized she'd been on the news all day. So Love gave the 911 dispatcher the info, she explained she wasn't sure where she was at but she desperately needed to get to the hospital. The 911 dispatcher said that wasn't a problem to just stay on the phone and they could track down where she was located. Love kept her phone on while she slowly made her way down the hallway towards the winding staircase.

She looked behind her, at all the people she had just shared her body with and she was wondering, "what was I thinking?" She was still carrying some of her clothes in her hands as she walked towards the stairs, when the man who had brought her there followed her out of the room. He grabbed her and said,

"I'm not ready to let you go Love."

Love muttered, "I'm sure we will see each other again.", as she tried to put on her bra. He kept groping and kissing her all over, and he refused to let her go, even though it was clear she was making her way towards the staircase to leave. She had, had enough of him. He was holding her from behind with his mouth sucking on the nape of her neck, but it no longer felt pleasurable to Love she just wanted him off of her, and she yanked herself free from him so suddenly and forcibly that her charm on her necklace caught his lip and cut it. He stopped kissing her neck and he touched the cut on his lip.

"Ouch. You cut me Love."

Love turned around and saw the blood dripping from his lip. "I'm sorry. It was an accident. I just really need to go now. Are you alright?"

Then he looked at her curiously wondering how she had cut him, while he wiped the blood from his lip. "I really don't know how you are able to still stand up after all the drugs and alcohol you had tonight. But don't worry, I'll be fine. I never really noticed that little silver necklace before. Your name is Love King, so what does the "*E*", on your necklace stand for?"

Love was steadily proceeding towards the stairs. She answered him nonchalantly as she headed down the stairs. "Oh, it's such an old necklace. I usually wear it under my dress shirts. I've had it since I was a kid so I hardly think about having it on anymore. It stands for Emmanuel."

He looked at her very strangely then, and said in a very irritated tone, "I thought you said you didn't believe in God and all that stuff?"

"Emmanuel is my family name it has nothing to do with my beliefs in God. I changed my last name when I became old enough to do so to, King."

The man's stare intensified and his eyes became colder and darker. "But you do *know* what Emmanuel means, and what it stands for, don't you?"

"Yes of course I do." And for no reason that she could fully understand she felt the need to say it out loud even though she had avoided saying those words since Nana had died, "it means, *God is with me.*"

Love could have sworn his eyes turned red like fire and for the first time she felt fear. She felt the need to say something to de-intensify the atmosphere. By then she had made it down to the bottom of the stairs and she was almost at the front door. "Well maybe we can go get some coffee or something this weekend. I will be back in town, Sunday morning. My office's answering service is in the book and on call 24 hours if you decide you want to see me again."

"No thank you. I'm a night owl, and I'll be blunt with you anyway. For your sake, it would be best that you don't see me again. And I won't try to stop you from leaving anymore. I release you."

Love thought to herself, "What an ego, I release you? What's that suppose to mean?"

"Well okay then, maybe I'll see you around."

"You really have no idea how close you came tonight."

Love felt strange and she moved quickly towards the front door and opened it, but she looked back and said out of curiosity, "how close I came to what?"

He answered with a sly almost sinister smile, "I wanted you for myself at first sight, and I had planned on making you spend eternity with me."

"That's romantic, but I'm not ready to spend eternity with anyone yet? I mean even as extremely sexy as you are, I'm not one for long commitments." Then she flashed him a superficial smile.

"Love if I had persisted on it I don't think you would have been able to resist. But go now, it was truly a pleasure meeting you Ms. Love Emmanuel. Who knows maybe the opportunity will arise for me to see you again one day. Maybe next time I'm in New York I will look your sisters up. I do travel a lot and I'm sure the two of them are as exceptionally beautiful and unique as you are."

Love wanted to scream, "stay away from my sisters!" But instead she walked out the front door and closed it behind her. She was questioning exactly what she had told him and what she hadn't told him that night. She couldn't remember, did she tell him she had family in New York, or did she say she had sisters in New York. She swore she never told him she had younger sisters. As she stood on top of the staircase leading to the mansion behind her, she felt a shiver run up her spine. She knew then that she never wanted to see him again. Yet somehow she wasn't fearful of him because she knew he wasn't coming after her, at least not tonight.

Love had just spent the past few hours with total strangers sharing her body, and her soul. She was so stoned, she felt numb. She didn't even feel the cold air, even though she stood on the stairs half dressed, in the middle of a very windy night, and she was still unable to get her blouse over her bra. She wondered, how did the best day of her life, the greatest win of her career, end up with her standing here. She was half naked on a stranger's staircase, waiting outside, in the middle of the night, for either the police or an ambulance to show up. She also hoped the police didn't show up because there were enough drugs back in that mansion to get a small country high. She wondered, "maybe I stumbled into some type of cult for the wealthy and bored." But despite the craziness of the night she still felt no real fear. In fact, she felt no pain, no sadness, not even disgust. She just felt empty and numb. If it wasn't for that phone call she had just received she would probably still be back in that room upstairs with those beautiful, sad strangers. But that call changed everything. Now the only thing she could think of was fulfilling a fruitless promise she made to a girl she barely knew, and a girl that she suspected was probably already dead. This she was accustomed to, doing her duty, while feeling nothing inside, remaining emotionally detached. That was what had always made her so good at what she did. Most times she felt nothing. She felt nothing intentionally. Numbness is what she had strived to feel emotionally most of her life. The only difference was that tonight, after all the drugs, alcohol and sex, she was also feeling physically numb. Now that she thought about it, she had felt numb on the inside, ever since, ever since, well ever since.... Nana died, almost twenty years ago. Love's mind was racing with one thought after another, non-stop. Her last thought was, "what was the name of the strange man she had spent the last five hours making love to. She realized she never did get his name."

Then suddenly she felt something. She felt a sharp pain run through her entire body. In that moment her body felt alive again, no longer numb. She felt like she had just been electrocuted. But then the pain she felt became even sharper and stronger and it just wouldn't stop. It was then that Love knew; she knew she was going to die.

She knew at that moment it was too late to change all that she had done, too late to finish everything she had left undone, and it was too late to keep the promise she made to the mother of the young lady who was her client. The strangest thing was at that moment she felt as if not being able to keep that one promise was what she was regretting the most.

Then the pain that pierced through the numbness continued. She couldn't take it anymore, she couldn't think anymore and then she couldn't breathe anymore. Love felt her frantically beating heart that she thought was going to burst, slow down. There was no time left for regrets, apologies, or goodbyes. She grabbed her chest as she felt her last heart beat, and she thought to herself, "so that's the kind of stuff one thinks about the moment before they die. Then Love felt herself fall into the darkness....

Her body hit the ground, but she didn't feel the impact, she didn't even feel her body anymore.

The paramedics found Love passed out, laying on the front steps of the mansion, with no blouse on and no shoes. They responded immediately and they rushed her to the hospital. They were giving her emergency treatment in the ambulance. Her heart had stopped from a drug overdose. They called her situation into the dispatch at the hospital, and they gave her emergency treatment at the same time. They had no idea how long her heart had been stopped before they had arrived.

When Love opened her eyes she realized she was someplace else. Love felt cold, and it was dark, but she saw a light a far ways off. Love wondered, "where am I?" Then she heard a small voice. It was her client. She saw her, she saw her client. She was in the hospital now standing next to her client's bed. She wondered, "when and how did I get here?" Love looked down at the young woman and said, "Your mother called me. Their plane is delayed, but they are on their way here."

"It doesn't matter Ms. King if they make it here. It's too late for me anyway."

Love thought this was her second chance to say the *right* things to this girl, to put aside her own self-absorbed anger towards God, and remember the things Nana taught her. To say the words she knew this girl needed to hear. It's never too late. Love heard the faint echoes of screams coming from somewhere, even though the screams were faint, the sound sent chills through her body. She assumed the sounds were from people in pain, waiting in the emergency room. Love thought, "I hate hospitals." Her client looked horrible. Her face was disfigured with blood still all over it. Love wondered how she was able to even talk in her condition, and talk so well.

"Why are you here anyway Ms. King? There's nothing else you can do for me. The trial is over, you won."

"I'm here because I promised your mother I would come, and I also wanted to say something to you."

"What is it you want to say?"

"Remember when you said to me before the trial started, that God has no more room in his hands for someone like you, well I should have told you something. I should have told you....."

Love noticed, the girls wound had started to ooze out more blood. She heard the faint echo of screams getting closer and getting louder. She felt a sudden urgency to say the right things to her as if the words she spoke would save the young girl's life. Then Love closed her eyes searching her soul, searching past her bitterness, past her shame and her fears, for the right words to say to her client, and then she found the right words somewhere deep down in her heart.

"I should have told you, *"nothing can separate you from the love of God...."*, then Love heard her Nana's voice in her head as she spoke the Word out loud to her client. *"Nothing can separate you from the love of God, neither death, nor life, nor angels, nor principalities, nor powers, nor things present, nor things to come, nor height, nor depth, nor any other creature, shall be able to separate us from the love of God."* [27]

Love's client listened to her yet Love's words still had not penetrated her heart. "But Ms. King, my parents taught me since I was just a little girl that, *These six things the Lord hates, and seven are an abomination unto him, A proud look, a lying tongue, and hands that shed innocent blood, ... A heart that deviseth wicked things, feet that are swift in running to mischief. A false witness that speaketh lies, and he that soweth discord among brothers."* [28] These things Ms. King I've been taught since I was a little girl that the Lord hates..." Then the girl held her head in her hands in despair, and in shame, and she looked down at her hands and they were covered with blood from her head wounds, and she whispered in self-hatred and shame to herself, *"and hands that shed innocent blood...."*

Love knew she had to say something to her client, something that would keep her from dying with this burden so heavy on her heart. *"You're right, God does hate those things*, but he doesn't hate you, he loves you. *"He is a God of forgiveness, gracious and merciful, slow to become angry, and he is rich in unfailing love."* [29] He will never abandon us, he waits, waits for us to come to him, and ask him, *"Lord forgive my many, many sins"* [30] *He feels our pain and our troubles, and he forgives our sins."* [31]

"Ms. King, I thought you didn't believe in God?"

"I thought I didn't anymore, but I realize now, even if I stopped believing in him, he never stopped believing in me.

---

[27] Romans 8:3-9

[28] Proverbs 6:16-19

[29] Nehemiah 9:17

[30] Psalms 25:11

[31] Psalms 25:18

Love touched the charm that Nana had given her so long ago. "God was with me, even when I didn't know it. He never stopped believing in me."

"After what I did Ms. King, even if God can forgive me, I just can't forgive myself, what I did is unforgivable."

"Maybe it is unforgivable to you, but not to God. If you can't forgive yourself, go to him anyway, and ask him to help you, forgive yourself" Love watched as her client closed her eyes, and the tears fell down her tender, young cheeks, and she heard her whisper, "Lord please forgive me."

At that moment it was as if the room had been flooded with bright light. All the other sounds of pain Love heard throughout the hospital had gone away. Love swore she heard something else in the hospital room, a strange yet familiar sound. The sound was as sweet as honey, she couldn't see her, but she knew in her heart the voice she heard was Nana's voice. Love whispered, "Nana?" Now Love was sure. She was sure that she must be dead, because she heard Nana's voice as clear as a bell. As real as this scene seemed to Love at that moment, she knew her Nana was dead. After all, Love was right there standing by Nana's bedside on the day Nana died. Love couldn't see her but she heard Nana say, "come home Love."

"Nana, I'm so far away, I don't know how to get back home anymore."

"God will show you the way home, Love."

"I don't know if I can change, if I can be the person you wanted me to be, the person God wants me to be, even if he brings me back home to you."

"Love, *remember nothing can separate you from the love of God.* God is inside of you, God is your home. Your soul is the house He lives in, nothing can separate you from His Love, only "you", can separate yourself, from accepting His love. Don't hide from Him anymore, come on home, before it's too late, Love, come home."

Love got on her knees and just spoke from her heart. "I'm so sorry God, I'm so unworthy of your love, and I'm so sorry, but I miss you so much, and my heart is aching, and every day I'm dying a little bit more inside. I don't know how to make my way back home to you, it's been so long, please help me find my way to you again Lord. Bring me home again?"

Then Love realized she was home again, she was standing in Nana's room by her bedside with her sisters and Mary right next to her again. But this time Nana didn't look sick at all. Nana looked bright and sunny and happy and beautiful, everyone did and then she looked in the corner of Nana's bedroom and there was John. He was holding his arms opened wide and he said, "come to me"….and Love felt a burden lifted from her heart and for the first time in a long time she felt free.

Suddenly she felt a piercing jolt, and took in the deepest breath she had ever breathed, as if she had been under water drowning, and her chest was in so much pain it was aching. The wonderful dream started to fade and seem more like a memory than real. Love heard some unfamiliar sounds and she opened her eyes and saw she wasn't in Nana's old room anymore.

The paramedic's were opening the ambulance doors. One of them told the doctor, "she is that lady lawyer that was on TV this past week. We don't know how long her heart was stopped, but we've got her breathing again. It looks like she did a little too much partying last night."

The doctor on call said, "the senior partners of her firm are on the board of trustees, do not mention this to anyone, and hurry up and bring her in."

Love felt herself pass out again. The next time Love woke up she felt the warm sunlight shining in from her hospital room window on her face. The nurse came into her room to take her vitals.

"Good morning Ms. King."

"Good morning. Nurse, um, do you know what happened to me? How long have I been here?"

"You've only been here since last night or shall I say very early this morning, Ms. King. It looks like what got you here is that you used a lot of different drugs and also your alcohol level was very high. Your heart momentarily stopped, they're not sure for how long. They revived you and they also had to pump your stomach; if you are feeling chest aches and queasiness that is why. You are very lucky, you will be okay.

But you need to rest up today, and tomorrow you should be feeling better."

"Thank you Ma'am. I am very tired." It all started coming back to Love, last night at the mansion, passing out on the front stairs, and the dream she had about talking to her client and Nana. Then Love realized, she had failed her client after all. She had never really made it to her as she promised her mother she would. It was all just a dream, just like hearing her Nana's voice and seeing her again was just a dream. Then before the nurse left the room Love asked her, "Ma'am, can you tell me, do you know if a patient by the name of Mary Sue McGuire, is here, and is she alive or is she dead?"

"You mean your famous client. I'm sorry to have to tell you this, but she passed away last night, right before the ambulance got you here."

"So she did die alone?"

"Well her parents' plane was delayed, but her doctor was in the room with her before she died. He said he held the phone to her ear last night, so she could hear her mother's voice, before she died."

Love was comforted a little by the thought that Mary Sue and her mother had spoken to each other before she died, but she still felt like she had failed.

"Ms. King, do you need anything else, because I'm going to go now my shift is over. But if you need anything don't hesitate to push that button on your nightstand and the morning nurse will come. Are there any family members or friends that you want me to call for you before I leave?"

"No thank you, I'd rather not anyone know about this, and I just want to get some rest." Love figured she would make up some explanation to give to her sisters later on. Right now she was so tired she just wanted to sleep.

Before the nurse left Love's room she ensured Love that the hospital would keep what happened to her private. "All of the staff has been advised to keep this all very hush, hush. After all I've heard your firm has gotten this hospital out of many a sticky situations."

"Thank you again. I really appreciate everything the hospital is doing for me, thank you." Then the nurse left her room and Love closed her eyes and fell fast asleep.

The next day, which was very early Sunday morning, Love received a visitor at the hospital. It was an older lady, with soft gray hair, and a kind smile. Love had just woken up and she saw the lady sitting in the corner chair in her room. "Hello, um Ma'am do I know you?"

"Ms. King, I'm your client, Mary Sue's mother. Our plane got in very late last night. I spoke to Mary Sue's doctor this morning, and I also asked about you because I know you came here to be with Mary Sue. The doctor told me that you were also here admitted in the hospital. I was a little surprised. I didn't realize you were sick. I wanted to see you, and tell you, thank you."

"Thank you for what, I didn't do anything to help Mary Sue?"

"That's not true. Thank you for being her advocate during her trial, and most of all thank you for getting here in time to speak to her before she died." Then the lady started to cry.

"I'm sorry Ma'am, but you got it all wrong. When you called me I was all drugged up, and I passed out before I had a chance to even make it to this hospital, let alone talk to your daughter."

"Well that's not what Mary Sue told me. I spoke to her over the phone before she passed away, while I was at the airport. She was so weak and her voice was so soft, but she could still speak. I asked her to please forgive me and her father for abandoning her when she needed us most. And I asked her to forgive herself for what she had done, and I told her God would forgive her. Then Mary Sue told me in her small voice, and I'm positive about what she said, she said,

"Mama I forgive you and daddy, and Mama Ms. King was here, and she helped me know and believe that God does forgives me, and that he's gonna help me forgive myself. Ms. King, Love, she reminded me, *that nothing can separate me from the love of God.* Mama please tell Ms. King I said, thank you."

Mary Sue's mother had to fight past her tears to finish telling Love her story, "That's why I had to come see you. It was my daughter's last request that I come tell you that she said, "thank you". So you must have forgotten or something, but you did speak to her last night. You know I really do love my daughter so much, so much, but I know I wasn't acting like it. I let my religious beliefs keep me from showing her my love, from seeing pass her sins, and remembering she was still, my little baby. I realize now, how precious and fragile our lives are. How short the time on this Earth we have really is, and I'll never let another day go by, keeping any fear, any belief, any grudge, from letting the rest of the people I love in my life know how I feel about them and how much I love them. So thank you, thank you for being there for my daughter when I wasn't." Then Mary Sue's mother leaned over and gave Love a hug and a kiss, and she left Love's room, just as the doctor walked in.

"Doctor?"

"Good morning, Ms. King. I was the doctor on duty the night they brought you in. I hope you don't mind that I told your client's mother about you being here, but she was adamant about already knowing you had come to the hospital. She knows nothing about your, um, medical condition, that's confidential. So how are you feeling this morning?"

"I'm okay, been better of course, but I think I'll make it. Doctor don't worry about telling my client's mother that I was here. I do have a question for you though. The other night, when I arrived at the hospital, did I have a chance to speak to my client at all before she died?"

"No Ms. King, I'm sorry, but I thought you knew, your client was dead before you even entered the emergency room doors the other night. In fact, there was no way you could have spoken to anyone. Technically you were dead yourself there for a while. Your heart had stopped beating. I have no idea for how long. But honestly it's a miracle you are not brain dead right now, and if it sounds like I'm trying to scare you, I am. That's why I hope you take this incident very seriously Ms. King. You've been handed a second chance in life. Please don't take it for granted. You know you can stay longer in the hospital if you want to. Even though you do appear to be physically fine for discharge today, that's after Psych clears you, but you can still take your time and stay until you feel ready to leave."

"No thank you, I've got something I really need to do." Love knew that even if she didn't see Mary Sue in the flesh that somehow, last night their spirits had met. Although she had gotten dozens and dozens of clients out of charges that would have put them in jail for the remainder of their lives in the past; for the first time in her life Love felt like she actually played a part in saving someone and setting them free.

The doctor told Love that he would be sending the hospital Psychiatrist in to talk to her before she could be discharged, since she was ready to leave. The psychiatrist cleared Love for discharge, giving his opinion that her overdose was not suicidal but was due to a serious lack of judgment. He recommended drug and alcohol abuse counseling for Love. Then she was on her way. She took a cab straight to her house, took a shower, and changed her clothes. She called the firm's jet pilot and got a cab to take her to the airport. When she landed in New York, she didn't call anyone. She knew exactly where it was she had to go. She had been holding on to the address in her wallet for months and months, and she had the driver take her straight there.

By the time Love got to the church, service was already over. The last people were walking out, and the inside of the church was almost empty. But the pastor was still there. He was straightening things up. Picking up some stray bibles and putting them back in place. Love didn't know what to say to him. She just stood there watching him quietly. Funny thing, Love was never at a loss for words, never in the courtroom, never when negotiating, never when writing in her journals, but there was something about.... John...

Love never could figure out the right thing to say to him. Then as if he sensed her presence he looked up, and saw her standing there. They just stared at each other.

John was standing in front of the altar. For a moment he could hardly believe his eyes, he thought he was having a hallucination. So he just stood there staring, waiting to see if she was a dream or real.

Love took in a deep breath, and found the courage to walk towards him. Once she was in front of him she said, "I just happened to be in town. Umm, so would you like to get a cup of coffee with me, because I could really, really use a strong cup of coffee this morning, it's been a rough couple of days for me."

John grabbed hold of her and held her tightly in his arms. Tears started to roll down Love's cheeks. Then he stepped back and held her soft face in his hands. He wiped her tears away, and he whispered, "finally". He looked deeply into her eyes, and he knew, he knew she was his, and he kissed her. She felt herself, for the first time in her life, really let go, and finally surrender to His love and to John's love too.

The two of them stood there in front of the altar just holding each other, and they could have held each other for eternity. Neither one of them wanted to ever let go of each other again. Then John finally said something. "So how about we go get that cup of coffee. There's this little place that serves a good Puerto Rican blend, it's called my apartment. It's just a few short blocks away."

"That sounds good. So I'll get to see your place then."

"Well there's not much to it. It needs a woman's touch. Maybe you can do something about that. So you say you had a rough couple of days, huh? Want to tell me about it?"

"Yeah rough, like you wouldn't believe. So I won't even try to explain it to you. I'd rather talk about you and catch up on what's been going on in your life here at the church." Love thought to herself, "I love him, but some stories are just better left between yourself and God."

"What Love King wants me to talk about church! Now that's a real miracle."

Love smiled back at John.

"Yeah, I guess it is."

Chapter 21
New Beginnings

Love was sitting in Faith's backyard. The whole family was there. Love sat back and relaxed while she watched John grilling the steaks, and talking to Darryl. She had a smile on her face these days and a joy in her heart that just wouldn't go away. She was still coming home every weekend, but now, she stayed with John at his place. They got together with her sisters, Darryl and Amir every Friday and Saturday night. On Sunday Love would alternate; sometimes she would attend church with her sisters, and sometimes she would go to John's church and listen to her man give his sermon. It was getting harder every Sunday to get on that plane back to LA, and leave all her love ones behind. So Love had made a decision.

John walked over to Love, and said, "you want a steak?"

"Thanks, but I'm okay."

"I know that look, what's on your mind?"

"John, I've put in my two week resignation to the firm, yesterday."

"Really! Well what are your plans now, moving back home permanently, right?"

"Well yes that's my plan, among other things."

"Love I won't pretend that I'm not incredibly happy to hear this news. Let's tell your sisters, and why didn't you tell me about this last night?"

"I was just waiting for the right time. But I don't want to tell my sisters right now. I'll tell them later, for now I just want to sit back and relax with my man."

"Now that sounds good", and he squeezed into the huge lawn chair with her. He started dosing off, and Love kept looking out at the sky, feeling at peace, feeling loved, and feeling at home in her own skin for once in her life. She was surrounded by her sisters, sitting next to the man she loved, and as she looked up at the deep blue sky, she whispered, "thank you God".

John opened one eye, and teasingly said, "I heard that, some of my sermons finally getting to you, huh?"

Love figured it didn't hurt to stroke her man's ego, and let him take the credit for it. "Guess they are Pastor, guess they are." Then she pulled out her journal that she had in her purse and she started to write in it. Lately she was constantly writing non-stop. She loved writing. She just wrote whatever came into her mind, and into her heart...

"I see turquoise, and light pale blues
Puffy, pure white and yellow hues
And specks of deep, marble black
Passing by, passing by
With each sight I thank God for this time

I see dark, wonderous green
Sharp and still, bending only
For the wind, the silent wind
Passing by, passing by
I'll never forget how precious is time

I see softness
I see beauty
I'm holding it near
I pray it will forever be here
But nothing in *this* world is forever I fear

So, I don't ever want to close my eyes
I can't even imagine a more marvelous sight
I prefer to keep my eyes open now
Open wide, open wide
And never again will I hide
From God, from love, or from life

So I'll no longer focus on the familiar dark yonder; I'll focus in on what is close, what is fonder
Like the turquoise, the white, the yellow, greens and blue...
(And Love stared down at her peaceful, sleeping man)
...And I promise to stay focused on you, most of all my love, I see you

I'll never lose sight, I won't waste not one more night,
Cause I know it's always passing us by, it's passing us
by….
And with every sight, I thank you God for giving me this
precious time."

John drowsily opened his eyes. "So babe, have you
given thought about what firm you want to go work for here in
New York? You know anyone would jump at the chance of
having you join their firm. Or maybe you should think about
opening your own firm Love. You know, that way you would be
more in control of your time. In case you ever decided to settle
down, and start a family one day. Who knows maybe one day
you might actually want those things."
Love could barely keep herself from laughing from
John's obvious remarks. He was so cute. But she decided that
she was going to continue to pretend that things like marriage
did not interest her at all, and just change the subject. So she
simply replied, "I've also decided that I don't want to be a
lawyer anymore."
That really got John's attention and he sat up in the lawn
chair. "Really, but I thought you loved being a lawyer? What
are you going to do then?"
"John, I don't really love being a lawyer, I love writing
and I think I want to be a writer. No I mean, I know I want to be
a writer, an author, because I'm already a writer. So I am going
to be a famous author. That's what I'm going to do."
John knew one thing about Love, once she said she
wanted something, she usually got it. "Well I'll start introducing
you as my girlfriend, the author, now, instead of my girlfriend,
the lawyer."
"Or you could also introduce me as your fiancé, the
author."
John felt his heart skip a beat, but he knew how to play it
cool too, just like Love. "Well maybe one day I can say fiancé,
we don't want to rush into things. You know a man has to do
that right, can't rush it. We might want to go to the church's pre-
marital class, and of course I still have to get rings for that to be
official and everything. Get down on one knee, make sure I

make the proposal really special, and all that stuff, you know. But don't worry now that you brought it up, it won't be long before I make it happen, if that's what you really want."

"I don't like waiting, when I decide I want something, I want it now, and I want you John. But yeah I guess you're right. We do need rings to make it an official engagement. But you know one thing I never agreed with is that the woman wears an engagement ring screaming to everyone that she is taken, but the man doesn't wear one." Then Love reached into her pocketbook. "So here's your ring John. I don't believe it's fair for me to be tied down with an engagement ring before the wedding and not you, seems sexist to me, so I got a little something for you. I picked it up from Tiffany's, it's nothing really."

John's jaw dropped he was looking down at matching interlocking diamond engagement rings. He had never seen anything so shiny. He couldn't even count how many diamonds were in those two rings. Inscribed inside were the words, "We R 1", when the bands were joined together. Love's ring fit snugly inside John's ring. Before John could even say another word, Love had separated the two rings and she was already placing his ring on his finger.

"Now you can introduce me that second way. Can I hear you say it John?"

John placed the ring Love had brought for herself on her finger and he said, "this is my crazy, beautiful, wonderful fiancé, the famous author."

"Now that does sound good."

"So I guess it's too late for me to get on one knee and hear you say "Yes", as I deliver my very romantic proposal."

"No need for all that. I think the ring seals the deal, but if you just want to hear it." Then Love looked into his eyes and said with all her heart and soul put into each word, "Yes, yes John, my best friend, my true love, my soul mate, I want more than anything else in this world to be your wife and I promise I will love you with all my heart and forever."

John looked at Love and he had no doubts that she did truly love him. "I love you too." He sat back in the lawn chair and he closed his eyes again, wondering with complete happiness filling his heart, "God what have I gotten myself into?" He let out a chuckle. And Love asked him, "what is so funny?"

"I was just thinking, this is probably not going to be a traditional wedding either, is it?"

"Probably not John."

"Well you stolen my proposal moment, you have already gotten the rings. What are you going to let me do?"

"You can plan the honeymoon baby."

"Okay then, I know a place that is luxurious and exotic and romantic of course, that fits you. Maybe, Rio..."

"I'm sorry John how about you pick the place we get married at instead, and if you want something traditional I'm fine with that. But I've been to enough exotic locations to last a lifetime. I think I'd rather stay closer to home."

"Closer to home? Like where, the Poconos?"

"Well I heard Virginia is for lovers, and we can drive there. Maybe, Virginia Beach."

"Virginia? You never cease to surprise me." John settled back down into the lawn chair. Love felt John's breathing start to get heavy while he lied there next to her, and Love could tell he was dosing off again.

It was such a sunny, perfect day and Love was starting to feel sleepy herself. She watched her sister Faith give Darryl a kiss on the cheek, while he flipped the burgers on the grill over. Then she looked over at her sister Hope, twirling her long locks with one finger as she strategized on how to defeat her son Amir in a game of chess. They both looked so carefree and at peace. Love realized she felt completely surrounded by love on every side of her and from above. Before she closed her eyes, she brushed her finger against the little silver "E" necklace on her neck that Nana had given her so long ago, and she whispered softly to herself, *"Emmanuel, God Is With Us."*

To Contact the Publisher or Author for more information:
Averyanya Publishing, LLC
P.O. Box 6761
Virginia Beach, Virginia 23456-0761
757-718-4830
http://www.averyanyapublishing.com
Author: Nicole Elise Title: The Emmanuels; A Story About
Faith, Hope And Love.

Author's Bio

Nicole Elise is the author of The Emmanuels; A Story About Faith, Hope and Love. Nicole was born and raised in Queens, New York. She left New York at seventeen and enlisted in the United States Marine Corps. After the military she attended college and law school in Virginia. She now currently resides in Virginia Beach, Virginia with her husband and two children. She is an attorney in private practice focusing on criminal defense of adults and children and representing the rights of children in abuse and neglect cases. This is her first novel and she is currently working on her next one.